The WAR TRAIL

Charles A. McDonald

Copyright © 2008 Charles A. McDonald
All rights reserved.
ISBN: 1522989935
ISBN-13: 978-1522989936

In Memory Of

Anton F. and Christiane Wilhelmine (Keuerleber) Hodapp.
Mr. and Mrs. Ed Stone, who traveled the Oregon Trail through Beckwourth Pass to California with the McMurphy-Bailey wagon train in 1864.
Emil Friederich Hodapp.
Wilhelmina Marie Hodapp.
George Anton and Maggie Edna (Stone) Hodapp.

The War Trail Series

The War Trail

Dark Moon

The Trail North

Path of the Wolf

Also by Charles A. McDonald

In This Valley There Are Tigers

ACKNOWLEDGMENTS

This novel was made possible by the generous assistance of many individuals. I am deeply indebted to them all. I would like to express my sincerest gratitude to the Wyoming ranch families who offered me a place of solitude where this story was inspired, thought-out and finished: Don and Diana Anderson, Frank, Helen, George, Marlene, John and Julie Ridinger.

Additionally, I am very grateful to Tim Fritz, whose friendship and memories of shared hunting camps in Idaho, Wyoming, and Michigan helped provide the fodder for this story.

I would also like to thank Chelsea Kellner, a reporter for *The Sanford Herald*, and Amanda Galeotti, who each read the draft and offered helpful suggestions.

David Shifren, a novelist who teaches fiction writing, was wonderfully accommodating by sharing his wealth of wisdom and knowledge.

My special thanks go to professor Chuck Kinder, director of the Writing Program at the University of Pittsburgh, and the author of the novels *Snakehunter*, *Silver Ghost*, and *Honeymooners*. He read the entire manuscript and offered me inspirational comments.

I am greatly indebted to Robert Griffing, the foremost painter of the eighteenth-century Eastern Woodland Indian, and Paramount Press, Inc. for permitting me to use the image of his painting "Friend or Foe" for the book cover.

Finally, I owe a great debt of gratitude to my wife, Dr. Keiko McDonald, who has supported my relentless pursuit of adventure for many years.

Chapter 1

It was April. It was the time the Indians called the Pink Moon, a name that came from the widespread wild ground phlox, the flower of early spring. Leaf buds were swelling. The sap was flowing in the sugar trees. The air was warm, and the white flowers of the dogwood and the showy white, purple and red blossoms of trilliums were easily spotted in bloom in the forest. Small birds migrating north were everywhere, feeding on the fruits of hawthorns and viburnums. The sweet smell of ramps permeated the air, and the rich green of their smooth, flat, sword-shaped leaves dotted the forest floor.

A man stood still in the shadows of a large tree trunk. Standing well over six feet tall, he had pale blue eyes seasoned despite his youth and shaggy blond hair that hung loose to his shoulders. He wore buckskin clothing that did little to hide his powerful build. Wolfgang Steiner was nineteen years old and a picture of health and strength.

Four freshly killed deer lay at his feet. As the designated "long hunter" for the men building Fort Prince George across the Monongahela River, Wolfgang would transport them back, as he had done many times, for the English and the Americans who were just starting to build the fort. The work site was just above the marsh where the Allegheny and Monongahela rivers merge to form the Ohio River. The French called it La Belle Rivière, and to the Indians it was the Spaylaywitheepi, meaning

'Beautiful River.' He could see why.

Wolfgang had stopped to rest and appreciate the beautiful day when the distant, deep-throated sound of smoothbore rifles drew his attention back to the fort. *Indians!* He heard faint yelling and whooping. Looking across the river, he saw no sign of the British or Americans. Hundreds of French regulars and Indians now occupied the site. He recognized the distinctive brown-red canoes of the Iroquois, made from the resinous bark of the white birch. When the wind died momentarily, the trilling war cry of these roving, raiding warriors carried across the river. *A people of roving, raiding warriors, they call themselves the Haudenosaunee, or "people of the longhouse." They show an overweening pride in themselves and total scorn for everyone else*, he thought to himself.

Since February, Wolfgang had kept eyes and ears alert for danger, waiting for the first signs of the marauding warriors. Now, gazing across at the chaos, he knew he would not return to the Fort. But his hunting camp above the tall bluffs had all he needed: a good supply of Indian corn meal johnnycakes; coffee grounds made from honey locust pods; fire-starting glass for sunny days, a fire-starting kit and his flint and steel; powder and shot; awl with waxed, linen thread; fishing gear; and his prized bow-hunting case, with a dozen straight arrows. His one utensil was a metal, two-pronged fork with a bone handle. He would take what he needed and head west -- to Illinois, of which he had heard much. His untamed restlessness had planted a seed of discontent a while ago, and he had been planning this journey for some time to escape the shackles of colony and crown. He felt a great need to see what was beyond the Allegheny Mountains.

But he must leave now: Indians were already crossing the river.

* * *

Wolfgang had worked his way from the river into the forest. He had seen no sign of his pursuers, though he felt sure the hostiles were close. He had decided not to follow the Ohio, knowing that, to avoid the labyrinth of rugged woods, the Iroquois traveled by water whenever possible.

These past days all of Wolfgang's senses were sharply focused. Traveling deeper into the forest now where giant oak, maple, chestnut and walnut trees stood as thick as he was tall and provided a canopy sixty feet above his head, he allowed himself a moment's idle thought -- that under different circumstances he might have enjoyed this forest's solitude.

But not today -- not with pursuers, who want my blood, he reminded himself.

Keeping the morning sun directly behind him and proceeding into the forest, Wolfgang planned to follow the east side of the river, passing the Ohio flat country -- territory of the Shawnee -- until he reached the steep elevations and deep valleys on the river's west side further south. There he would head west again, traveling on the high ridges, and camping in caves, since rainfall this time of year was common.

What lies beyond the river? he wondered. Despite his fatigue, Wolfgang felt excited to think of it: *a new life -- and freedom.*

* * *

It seemed hard to believe that just four days earlier, April 17, 1754 had begun as a beautiful day, for Wolfgang had smelled spring and had been enjoying a perfect morning amid the steep hillsides and low valleys of southwestern Pennsylvania, he recalled.

After four days of constant moving and little rest, he stopped beside a small seep flowing down the ridge, as the sun's gilded shafts paled and finally disappeared amid the leafy giants.

He was now deep in the forest.

The shadows were growing long and he heard turkeys gobbling back the way he had come. Somewhere due west a pair of wolves howled in the distance. As twilight stole through the forest, an eerie silence prevailed, and then, in what seemed mere moments, darkness.

It was cool beneath the branches of the great trees. Wolfgang's hunter's instincts were aware of all that took place around him: the melodious trilling of tree frogs; the monotonous night song of insects; the rotting leaves that emitted phosphorescent light; and at intervals the soft, padded steps of some small creature nearby stealing into obscurity.

Feeling bone-weary, Wolfgang chewed jerky to keep his hunger at bay. He lay back on his pack, staring up at the sky through the trees' skeletal limbs. He knew that he would soon fall asleep. But even in his sleep, his ears would register every sound, and his nose would catch every scent. His time on the trail had taught him well, and if he were to wake, he would be instantly and fully alert. The moon shone less brightly, making the stars easier to see. He had carefully kept track of the days by the moon's phases, and it was the third day after the full moon, the waning, yellow orb moving into its last quarter. As he drifted off to sleep -- or the nearest to it he could hope for -- he saw his father in his dreams. *If only we had had more time together.*

* * *

Wolfgang awoke at the darkest hour in the morning, listening and remembering. He thought of the voyage to this land from his native Germany four years earlier, how before his father fell sick onboard and died, he had encouraged him to practice daily with the rifle -- loading, re-loading, and re-loading some more. The days at sea had turned to weeks, then two months, and the eager young man had practiced with the exquisite weapon.

Finally, Wolfgang could re-load, as quickly as any man. As finely crafted as any quality musical instrument, the rifle had been a gift from his father -- the very rifle his hunter-father had used-- his prized rifle!

Wolfgang recalled his father's somber words: *"The man who re-loads fastest, is most often the last left standing."* Wolfgang took the lesson to heart.

* * *

A southwest wind scattered clouds on the horizon. Wolfgang's bones and muscles told him that the air pressure was dropping, signaling a change in weather. The cold, gray morning light came slowly, low clouds veiling distant ridges, as he blinked his eyes open. He couldn't have said when exactly his dreams left off, only that now he was fully awake -- woken abruptly by a patter of water droplets striking dead leaves around him -- droplets that, he now saw, had been jostled from a slender limb bouncing high above him. A raindrop hit his shirt with a loud *plock*.

"Squirrel." As if on cue, a contented cacophony of gray squirrel-chatter began in the near and middle distance. He saw the small darting shapes scamper along the limbs, stopping often with tails twitching, as they watched for danger below.

Seeing them content, Wolfgang, too, felt content: The squirrels' behavior meant that the Indians, if they were still following at all, were not close.

Rising quietly to his feet, he stood beside the tree and scanned his surroundings. Nothing but the usual sights and sounds of a forest came awake. Satisfied, he turned his attention to the rifle in hand.

Lifting the rough-faced steel cover that protected the weapon's pan, Wolfgang was pleased to see that the loose grains of priming powder still looked dry. Next he checked his flint, which also looked fine. He prayed it wouldn't shatter when he needed it most.

Wolfgang shouldered his pack and began walking a wide fishhook loop that would bring him back parallel to his route of the day before. Approaching the earlier path cautiously, he waited offside in heavy brush the distance of an arrow shot. From this vantage point he could see and hear anyone who approached. It meant he might also be seen, but it was a chance he must take: It was critical to learn if he were still being followed.

For perhaps ten minutes all was peaceful. Then...*Kuk-kuk-kuk-kuk-kuk!* The chatter of a gray squirrel barking its rapid distress rhythm sounded nearby.

Wolfgang peered in that direction. The wood still seemed at peace. But then, sure enough, he discerned a vague sound -- a light, cautious tread as from a white-tailed deer moving in its typically slow, nearly silent start-and-stop of three or four steps. *If I hadn't heard the squirrel's alert, I might have wondered if this tiny rustling of dry, brittle leaves were my imagination.*

Wolfgang waited.

For some moments he heard only the distant sounds of birds, squirrels, the buzzing insects and the wind. Then came a slight, tenuous rustle of a branch bending... slowly, being tested...No question of it being imagination now!

The sound ceased. *Whatever creature was there had stopped and was no doubt looking and listening.* And now another small sound came -- the crunch of a dried twig, barely a stone's toss away.

Keeping his body still, Wolfgang shifted only his eyes. Half a dozen yards away stood an Iroquois tracker, watching and listening amid the brush.

Chapter 2

With his rifle at the ready, the Indian trailing him focused his attention on the trail ahead. He bent slowly into a half-squat and cleared leaves from the trail.

Wolfgang, barely a stone's toss away, all but held his breath.

And now activity farther back on the trail caught his attention: Distantly discernible, low voices sounded, the noise of men pushing through light brush and grass. He heard the light tread of moccasin-clad feet.

Coming this way.

Knowing the tracker would be alert to the slightest movement, Wolfgang had no choice but to hold his position.

Soon three other silent, staring figures had joined the first.

All roughly six feet tall, they had broad cheekbones and prominent noses. The warriors were broad-shouldered and clad from head to foot in elaborately decorated fringed buckskin war shirts. Their knee-high leggings, partially covering their moccasins, dragged on the ground and the men wore metal rings through their ears and noses. Bald-headed except for a single tuft of long, black hair that hung from the crown of each man's head over the back of his shoulders -- this scalplock hung unadorned but for a solitary feather or two that pointed over each man's shoulder - the warriors wore small, round red spots on their heads, derived from blood-root, that signified the number of scalps each man had taken.

Wolfgang had hunted countless times but never before had he seen Indians tracking him. Now he avoided looking into the men's eyes knowing that in the forest, ofttimes creatures could sense another being looking at their eyes.

The Indians exuded an aura of strength and speed, and Wolfgang felt his heart thudding against his ribs.

The tracker pointed at the ground, then kneeled where Wolfgang's footprints had pressed through the mat of last year's leaves. Extending his arm, the Iroquois traced the outline of Wolfgang's track with his hand.

His confederates stood watching until he turned to whisper to them. "Yengeese." Suddenly the brown-skinned warriors grew more alert, eyes sharp, ears listening to the forest.

Wolfgang remained still. He could smell the bear oil on the Indians' bodies, could see the stern-faced warriors' black-painted faces -- darkened to show their readiness to meet death -- which made them look truly fierce. These were men who would eat his heart to boost their strength spiritually but also savor his blood to quench their thirst.

Wolfgang parted his lips to breathe through his mouth; he knew that even the slightest sound, of breath passing through his nostrils, might alert his pursuers. He forced himself to breathe slowly and shallowly.

After an endless time, the Indians rose. Gripping their rifles at waist-level across their bodies in classic hunting posture, they continued on.

Before long they will reach where I hooked back. He also knew that in any confrontation against four warriors, his chances would be grim.

Somehow, I need to improve the odds.

* * *

Moving slowly down the seep so as not to disturb the vegetation, Wolfgang passed wildflowers, shrubs, ferns and mosses - the luxuriant growth of a mixed hardwood forest where wildflowers grew. Bloodroot, cut-leaved toothwort, trout lily and trilliums - he noted them but dimly, his mind filled with other concerns. Wolfgang stopped often to look back and be sure he had left no sign; once he paused to gather up soft mud in his hands and applied it to his face, neck, and hands to mask their shape and shine.

A soft rain began and Wolfgang felt heartened: The drizzle would help cover his trail. At the bottom of the ridge he felt further gladdened to find a hardpan bottom creek. Stepping in, he moved carefully so as not to disturb the bottom. The light undersides of any rocks he inadvertently overturned would show where he had passed.

Soon heading west again, Wolfgang smelled the damp earth in his nostrils. After climbing over or ducking beneath dozens of trees fallen across the creek, he came to a seep that entered the creek on his right. Again he changed direction, heading north this time, up the ridge across from the one he had just crossed. The new ridge provided good cover, and, near the top, Wolfgang stopped and hid, to listen.

Breathing hard, his body hot and damp with sweat, his heart pounding, Wolfgang realized he had no idea how he would behave if and when the time came to fight for his life. He prayed he could do what he must -- and knew also that if he failed to control his thoughts, he might slip into a mental panic.

To survive, he must think quickly, clearly and decisively.

He settled in to wait.

* * *

A mild breeze stirred the leafy branches overhead.

Nothing else moved.

Listening, watching, Wolfgang knew that when the forest fell suddenly quiet, it was a bad sign. He cocked his head to better catch any stealthy tread or other ominous sound.

Nothing. Only a lone turkey call in the distance, the loud, coarse, slow-cadenced, one-two-three note of a young gobbler traveling on the ridge Wolfgang had just crossed.

But then a second gobbler called forty yards to his left -- and a third twenty yards to his right....

Wolfgang felt the itch of each hair bristle on his nape.

Young gobblers flocked together and would never have separated.

A branch bounced overhead -- just a squirrel, but the creature stopped in its run along the limb and sat upright, chattering and jerking its tail in agitation. Wolfgang saw the small creature's body hair bristle and its puffed-out tail twitch, as it stomped its feet and flicked its tail chaotically.

Peering in the direction that held the squirrel's attention, Wolfgang saw nothing. For a long moment he heard only silence.

Then...

Thock!

Wolfgang knew the sound of an arrow springing from its bowstring, and instinctively he ducked -- the telltale *hisssss* slicing inches from his head. The next instant... a solid *thunk!* The next instant... a solid *thunk!* The arrowhead embedded itself deeply into a tree, the killing shaft vibrating, and its feathers quivering.

Scrambling to his feet, Wolfgang stared in the direction the arrow had come -- and saw a coal-eyed face beside a tree, watching him.

Cluck! Cluck! Cluck! Cluck!

Wolfgang heard the excited cackle at the bottom of the ridge near the creek.

I have to move fast. That call is often used by turkeys to rendezvous. The call of a bird crossing the creek was in fact another Iroquois moving in.

A good archer could aim and release five shafts a minute; Wolfgang knew he must act now. But since the booming report and flash of his rifle in the gloom would betray his position to the others, he thrust his weapon against a tree even as he saw his opponent's hand reach for another arrow.

Lowering his head, focusing all his strength on closing the gap between himself and his would-be killer, Wolfgang pumped his legs and arms as fast as he could -- closing the distance to twenty paces... fifteen... ten... and as he saw the warrior draw his bow, Wolfgang dived into a roll -- *hissss* -- the arrow grazed his shoulder, then *phtted* and quivered in a tree.

Wolfgang was quickly up on his feet again.

The warrior tried to dodge, but Wolfgang caught his shirt, head-butted his chest, and jerked him backward. The man tumbled, and the next instant Wolfgang was on him -- gouging his eye as Wolfgang's hand sought purchase on his enemy's head.

Wolfgang plunged his knife into the warrior's throat.

* * *

Gasping to catch his breath, Wolfgang bent low to a tree, the pounding in his ears preventing him from hearing. He willed himself to relax, and blinked at the sweat dripping into his eyes: His gaze must be clear so he could sweep the area, near and far, to assess the many dead falls that might provide hiding places.

Taking deep breaths, Wolfgang concentrated on watching and listening as he quickly removed the fallen man's bag of *psindamoakan*. Every warrior on the warpath carried one since even a mouthful of the roasted corn flour-and-sugar concoction supplied a day's nourishment. *These extra rations will serve me well – providing I survive the rest of the day.* He grimly thought.

Retrieving his rifle and gear, Wolfgang swiftly moved from tree to tree. He stopped often to watch and listen, leaving the area.

Again heading west, Wolfgang traveled slowly so as not to disturb the vegetation and ground humus. Moving and stopping, moving and stopping, he covered ground all day long. He had never felt so alone, and he thought his eyes must look frightened as he glanced again and again at his back trail.

* * *

On the fourth day, as Wolfgang arrived at the high ground overlooking the Ohio River, the sun came out in full force -- brilliantly illuminating the hills, the pastures, and the river itself, which shone below like some magnificent vision.

Seeking a resting place in a large thicket of shreddy-barked high-climbing grape vines, Wolfgang kept alert for grouse. The small, spunky birds wintered in such thickets, and if he inadvertently flushed one, its loud flapping, fluttering retreat would alert every creature within a hundred yards.

From his high point above the river, peering out past his cover of wild grape vines, Wolfgang saw thick forest due west. A luminous, wispy mist rose from the water and hung among the trees, the veil lifting slowly to reveal a glinting surface as yellow fingers of gold spread across the hills behind him and over the Ohio Valley ahead.

The sheer beauty of the aged forest enlivened Wolfgang's senses and gave him pause. In sharp contrast to his former homeland, this forest was untouched. If ever there were a face for a new world, a place where he might live out a long life, surely this was it.

Now, as the sun told Wolfgang it was the second hour of the day, he knew all at once that his pursuers would not give up -- not while they were so close. Which meant he must take matters into his own hands.

* * *

Wolfgang had fish-hooked his back-trail, doubling back to ambush the warriors from an elevated spot above his back trail. He had been waiting in the shadows, his senses sharp as he watched and listened -- head cocked, eyes forward.

The sun had moved three hands across the sky when Wolfgang spied them from his place of concealment: a small war party of four making its way through the wood. All carried rifles, and, as Wolfgang watched, the group proceeded some fifty yards below the top of the oak-studded ridge.

Now, watching, he wasn't surprised when he saw his pursuers pause to study his footprints. Wolfgang knew the Indians could read a wealth of information from even a single set.

Although most white men paddled when they walked, the absence of scuff marks at the edges of Wolfgang's prints would tell them he walked as an Indian did, toes pointed forward. The fact he walked with feet parallel would indicate he was well built, while the length of his pace and depth of his track would reveal he was tall and carrying a pack.

Wolfgang gripped his rifle and felt comforted by its solid, familiar weight.

To make a good shot meant holding the weapon steady for some moments -- first, as the cock that gripped the flint tripped forward, then as the flint produced sparks to ignite the priming powder in the pan, then as the main charge exploded, and finally until the charge cleared the barrel. It seemed like it took forever, but was actually mere moments.

All this to get an accurate shot.

But Wolfgang knew also that an experienced warrior -- hearing the concussive report, seeing the flame and smoke spread like a funnel from the weapon's barrel -- would pinpoint the rifleman's location almost exactly.

Which meant unless Wolfgang moved quickly after firing, he stood a good chance of being shot.

Wolfgang gently squeezed the trigger, while the other hand pulled the hammer back into its locking position to eliminate the loud click. The rifle silently cocked, he released the pressure on the trigger and slowly snuggled the stock against his shoulder. Peering now along the barrel at the foremost of his pursuers, he took aim.

He gently squeezed.

Klatch!

The flint snapped forward onto the steel frizzen. The resulting sparks ignited the fine grains of powder in the pan.

Poof!

Flame shot through the touchhole of the barrel, igniting the barrel charge.

Boom!

The .490 lead roundball -- just shy of a half-inch in diameter -- burst from the 50-caliber flintlock, and the briefest instant later Wolfgang heard the soapy smack of the ball hitting flesh, followed by the heavy thrashing of a body on the ground.

Rising from the ground quickly, Wolfgang raced a short distance down the hill, using large trees for cover. The three remaining warriors returned fire uphill, into the smoke, and Wolfgang stopped to quickly re-load, using the loud rattling sound of their slow reloading as cover.

Pouring more powder into the muzzle, Wolfgang placed a tallow-soaked deerskin patch over the open end and spit a ball onto it. Yanking out the ramming rod, he spun it around so the splayed head faced downward, then thrust the rod down the barrel. Pulling the rod out, he spun it again and slid it back into its holding rings. Now, without needing to look at his rifle, he tossed the weapon into the air and caught it expertly under the lock. Pouring a pinch of powder into the open pan, Wolfgang snapped the cover closed. His right hand tapped the gunlock to bank the priming powder away from the flash hole. The same hand brought the hammer to full cock.

Ready to fire.

Wolfgang moved in closer, using the large oaks for concealment. He heard his enemies' screaming war cries as his pursuers leaped from side to side and blew their eagle bone whistles, working themselves into a frenzy to frighten him.

Then they charged.

Wolfgang sighted on the first warrior at perhaps sixty yards. As the man raced up the hill, Wolfgang set the front blade into the rear "V" and rested it on the man's chest.

Klatch! Poof! Boom!

Before the smoke had cleared, Wolfgang had darted from position. The remaining Indians fired into the small, rising, white cloud, but Wolfgang was well clear. With practiced smoothness and minimal clatter of the ramrod against the gun barrel, he reloaded yet again from his new position.

Only two left, he thought -- and immediately chided himself. *Overconfidence could kill a man as surely as a lead ball or steel blade.*

Dispatching the first pursuer had been easy -- the others weren't yet aware of Wolfgang's proximity or marksmanship. The second man had constituted a closer call -- that warrior had actually seen Wolfgang and the next moment might have used his weapon with deadly results.

Wolfgang risked a glimpse at his remaining adversaries, both of them barely visible among the trees, hunting him with their eyes as they reloaded their rifles.

Wolfgang squeezed the trigger. Flint struck frizzen, sparks ignited the fine priming powder, and with a concussive report, another heavy lead ball flew down the barrel. Again, the April afternoon air filled with a billowing mushroom of white smoke. It obscured Wolfgang's view, but did nothing to cover his target's anguished death cry.

Racing toward the last man, Wolfgang drew his ax. He heard the loud, unpracticed rattle of the Indian's ramrod, but then the clatter stopped -- as the warrior raised his weapon.

Wolfgang was almost upon him when he saw his foe blink one eye closed, aim along the barrel -- and squeeze the trigger. Wolfgang's own eyes grew wide as he saw the hammer fall -- *klatch!* Silence. *Misfire!!*

Then Wolfgang was driving forward, rifle and ax still in hand, and never before so thankful that the cheaper flintlocks traded to the Indians were so much more apt to misfire.

The warrior dropped the rifle and turned to run. Wolfgang kicked his legs out from under him and the man went down; the next instant he found himself pinned to the ground, Wolfgang's ax raised. Wolfgang looked down at the younger man, and saw in his eyes and face the stoicism that showed he was prepared to die.

To these warriors, Wolfgang knew, the most important moment of their lives was their death. How they met and endured it was a matter of honor.

Wolfgang decided he would not kill the younger man. Instead he would send a message to those who had ordered the warriors to pursue him.

Returning the ax to his belt, Wolfgang signed to the other man. He clasped his hands together, left under right, meaning, "Peace." Pointing down at the warrior, Wolfgang raised his forearm. He then aimed his index finger upward, signing, "Stand!"

The young warrior looked warily at the man standing

above him.

He noted the long blond hair hanging nearly to the man's shoulders and his shaved face; he noticed the fringed buckskin hunting jacket with cape over the shoulders, and the small pack secured with broad straps to the man's back; he noticed the homespun linsey shirt and breeches.

These details held the warrior's attention only briefly. Others he found more intriguing: the soft-soled woodland moccasins the white man wore, whose flaps reached up his legs, held in place by strapped thongs to keep out dust and gravel; the fact that the skin clothing the white stranger wore imitated the medium browns-and-greens of the forest; and the fact that the powder horn hanging by a thick leather strap over the man's shoulder was slung high up on his right side, with the its tip turned into his side so it wouldn't catch on brush or bounce when the man ran. And the warrior noticed the large leather-sheathed bone-handled knife in his waistband. These details -- and the fact that as the white man held his rifle, its muzzle followed his eyes -- told the warrior this stranger was someone to reckon with.

But of course the warrior knew that already: The man's fighting skills had proved that.

Slowly, and with infinite care, the Indian rose with uncertainty.

Wolfgang backed off a step and watched the frightened face. He now gestured in the universal language, motioning more rapidly, signing, Pointing his thumb at his chest, then his index finger at the warrior, he curled his hand palm up, then gestured from his mouth to the warrior, meaning, "We talk." Continuing, Wolfgang's hands gestured his name: "Wolf." After a moment Wolfgang saw that the other man understood. The Iroquois signed back for clarification, and when Wolfgang had given it, the warrior spoke the Iroquois word "Okwaho," meaning wolf.

"I no fight," Wolfgang continued, his hands motioning rapidly now. "Me long time walk west. Escape Yengeese. Me slave. All my family dead. Avoid Yengeese and François."

Wolfgang waited patiently for the other man to answer.

Each hand sign could have several meanings, he recalled, and the precise meaning of any sign depends upon all those that precede and follow it.

The Iroquois began to sign in reply.

"French and Iroquois many tribes," he gestured. "Ottawa, Huron, Algonquian, Chippewa, and Abenaki tribes."

Wolfgang pointed his right thumb at his chest then held his hand near his heart. Sweeping his hand next outwards and slightly upwards, he turned hand by wrist action until the palm was half-way up; thumb and index finger extended, the other fingers closed, thumb and index horizontal, index pointing nearly to the left, thumb pointing to the front: "I understand."

Wolfgang picked up the warrior's rifle, glanced at its firing mechanism, handing it to him.

"You, rifle, go," Wolfgang signed.

The Iroquois regarded him a moment as if acknowledging that this white man was sparing his life.

Then he turned and left, moving quickly and quietly.

Watching him go, Wolfgang wondered how long the young warrior would live. *His rifle had misfired because the flint was seated too close to the frizzen -- so close that it had kept the frizzen from opening.* It was a lesson Wolfgang's father had taught him long ago -- a time that seemed now more than a lifetime past.

Before returning to the trail, Wolfgang collected the bags of psindamoakan from each warrior. He also collected their buckskin shirts, having special plans for them.

After cleaning the bore of his own weapon with the coiled wire worm from his stock, and after oiling the bore and cleaning the touch hole with his vent pick, Wolfgang re-loaded. He was ready to press on.

Chapter 3

Looking south along the river, Wolfgang saw where, not far ahead, it twisted then disappeared from sight. Traveling by water would be faster than on foot and would leave no trail. Wolfgang deliberated for just a moment before making his decision.

But first -- some rest.

Choosing a spot near a deadfall that afforded him both a good view and a goodly amount of cover, Wolfgang hunkered in.

For the first time since commencing his flight it struck him how truly alone he was. With no friend to share his tribulations, and no one to lean on, he felt utterly by himself. His worst fears -- of a future utterly unknown -- now loomed before him. He accepted death as a distinct possibility and for the first time in his life faced months, maybe years, of never knowing when someone or something would try to kill him. If captured, he knew his fate would depend upon the whims of the old women and mothers of the village. His dream of freedom and adventure found him totally alone.

But there was nothing to do about that this moment. Nothing but work toward his survival.

Having plans for the captured rifles, he got to work taking them apart.

Removing each weapon's tiny tool kit that was stored in the carved compartment of each weapon's stock, Wolfgang laid the tools out and those from his own kit carefully: a small, stiff brush; a screwdriver; an iron nail; an oil can; and a torque bar to clean the rifle's lock and draw any bullets that had misfired. His eyes sweeping the landscape about him even while his hands inspected and cleaned the weapons.

For proper ignition, the touchholes must be centered precisely. After inspecting each weapon and feeling satisfied, he took the locks of each rifle apart, noting that all the flint wrappers were made of good leather and that the flints were sharp and straight. He examined the strength of their mainspring. A weak spring might produce a few sparks but not the shower of sparks necessary. Finally satisfied, Wolfgang reassembled the rifle locks.

Next he checked the fit of the pan and barrel, and the frizzen cover over the pan for gaps. Gaps would allow the priming powder to leak out, leaving the rifle with no spark to fire. Next Wolfgang set the cock at half cock and made sure the frizzen closed all the way, checking for perfect contact between pan cover of the frizzen and pan, to protect the fine powder for ignition on rainy days. The flint's edge almost touched the face of the frizzen, and Wolfgang flipped the frizzen forward and gently lowered the cock all the way. The edge of the flint aimed directly into the lock's priming pan.

Perfect.

After cleaning the rifles' barrels, Wolfgang unrolled the shirts he had taken. Carefully wrapping each gun, he moved to the river and, finding a suitable spot, he cached the weapons beneath an overhang, then stacked rocks around them. Once more his old teacher Tamanend came to mind: *To remain unseen a man must use his head.* Wolfgang studied the hiding place as if with a stranger's eyes.

Was there anything to detect?

He saw nothing.

* * *

Carefully surveying the low ground before him, Wolfgang noted the brown scar of a gully, which wound down to the river from high ground. A creek. It meant he could get to the river unseen. A tracker would know he'd entered the creek, but couldn't know for sure where he'd come out. Wolfgang's pursuers would have to hunt the river on both sides, up and down, to be sure.

As he moved down the creek he saw where green shoots were pushing upward, saw yellow dandelions in bloom and observed willows along the river that had a bright look to their limbs. There was a gentle stretch of bog along the slow branch of the creek. A faint musty odor rose to his nostrils. The small flat was covered with the juvenile mottled raw-liver, red-hooded patches of giant lettuce-head skunk cabbages. Carefully Wolfgang made his way through the grass in the springy cold muck, among the heavy, beaked whorls of giant leaves. He tried hard not to bruise the leaves knowing that bruised leaves would emit a strong-odored scent, a clear-cut trail to an experienced tracker. When Wolfgang saw signs of fresh digging, he realized that a bear had recently passed this way; he wasn't surprised soon to pass droppings as wide around as his wrist.

The fresh, earthy fish-smell of mud filled his nostrils. Having reached the river, he took off his clothes and pressed them into his pack. Jamming a wooden plug into his rifle-muzzle, he slid a feather quill gently into the gun's touchhole, wrapped the lock, and finally seemed satisfied the firearm was ready for its watery voyage. Lashing his equipment to a portion of broken-up tree, then covering his make shift vessel with broken limbs to conceal and break up its outline,

Wolfgang pushed off into the stream.

His body submerged and his head concealed by well-placed branches, he directed his makeshift vessel downstream.

The water was cold. *I can endure for a while,* he thought. *All I have to do is keep a good watch along the shores—and hope I don't smash my legs on a hidden rock ledge or snag my ankle on a submerged tree limb and drown myself.*

It was early spring so the river was still fairly low, but it was still deep enough to hide sharp rocks and ledges; coupled with the water's force, Wolfgang knew the journey would be treacherous.

He managed to avoid most such unseen dangers by watching for surface swirls. His only problem was the choppy waters of large riffles, where the river became more shallow as the streambed tilted, so that the current moved at an accelerated pace. But he could see these spots at a distance, allowing him enough time to lift his legs. Travel in this manner seemed slow. The river was broad, and smooth in the pools, but watching the low terrain on both sides of the river told him that this appearance was deceptive.

Wolfgang had been in the water for some time. Coldness began to creep into his body warning him that it was time to get out. If he were to survive, he needed time to rest. The cumulative fatigue was wearing on him. The terrain was much higher now on both sides.

He began watching the banks for a suitable place.

Spotting a side channel on the east side of the river up ahead, he tried his best to steer his makeshift vessel toward it. Kicking with his feet, taking long, paddling strokes with his free arm, he soon realized his efforts were having little effect. The water was flowing faster than before.

That was when suddenly he became aware of it: a distant roaring sound. Which was growing louder. An increasing continuous roar.

Squinting ahead, Wolfgang saw dangerous, turbulent white water. He knew he had to get out quickly or risk losing everything.

Kicking and paddling with all his strength, Wolfgang tried his hardest to direct the floating length of tree toward the creek. Gradually, he saw the foremost branches angle toward the shore, but with the mouth of the creek fast approaching, would he make it in time? His arms and legs numb, he felt he was moving in slow-motion; it took all his will and determination to keep paddling as the cold, swirling water washed over his shoulders and face.

And every moment carried him closer to the dangerous white water. With his last ounce of strength, Wolfgang redoubled his efforts. And now his rough craft approached the mouth of the creek.

As he got closer, his feet touching bottom, he directed the tree toward the bank, where a small stream entered the river. Struggling, Wolfgang pushed the tree as hard and as far onto the pebbled shore as he could. He struggled from the water, and fell to his knees on the grass. But it was no time to rest yet. Wolfgang could scarcely afford for any unseen eyes to be tracking his progress.

Drying himself quickly as best he could, he saw to his rifle -- removing the wooden barrel-plug, plucking the feather quill from the touch-hole -- and finding the hardpan stream shallow, he decided he would exit by using it for cover -- walking up the stream a good distance, toward the bluff that overlooked the river, where he would find a place to camp.

* * *

It wasn't far above the river that Wolfgang found a well-concealed cave. Making and lighting a torch, he carefully entered the craggy cavern to check for signs of fire on the floor, soot on the roof, or anything else that might suggest periodic use.

He found nothing.

The cave had two branches. Exploring the first, he

noticed strange markings on the walls. There were formations hanging from above and coming up from the floor. There were also columns and bottomless pits. A few well-placed cane torches mounted into the walls revealed a place of the netherworld, the spirit world. Whenever he left the lighted portion of the cave, he could hear bats flying around him and water dripping. But there were other slight, unknown sounds. It seemed as if the cave were alive.

Backtracking to the second route, Wolfgang soon noticed that the deeper he went, the more his torch-flame flickered ahead of him; feeling hints of cool air on his face, he realized another opening lay ahead. Hoping it would be large enough to offer an escape route should he need one, Wolfgang proceeded until the slant of his torch-flame aimed straight upward; raising his eyes, Wolfgang saw a hole wide enough for him to escape even while wearing all his equipment.

Yes, it would indeed provide an emergency escape route if he needed one. He felt he would be safe in the cave.

Wolfgang planned to build his fire deep in the cave's recesses, where its glow would go undetected.

* * *

He cut firewood from dead blow downs of white oak. The wood proved ideal, being straight, with few knots, and with a grain that made it easy to split -- Wolfgang knew it's aroma was almost odorless when burned, and it glowed radiantly for hours, and burned hot and clean, with minimal smoke.

Hauling the wood to the furthest recess of the cave where it would stay dry, Wolfgang next stacked piles of twigs, dead grass, and pinecones for kindling. He spent hours more cutting thin shavings of softwood pine for tinder, he felt exhausted and hungry. Since he planned to use the rifle only in emergencies, he would have to hunt a deer with his bow.

Chapter 4

For many days there had been a bout of cold weather accompanied by occasional rain showers, but now leaf buds were blossoming on the trees, and ferns were rising through the forest floor. It was May -- "Flower Moon," to the Indians -- and the fields were abundant with early, radiant flowers. Indian Paintbrush flourished everywhere, along with pretty yellow, white and blue flowers, and white-tailed deer were birthing their fawns in the dense vegetation.

As Wolfgang made his way, he was struck by the beauty of the freshly washed countryside and the variety of colors in this rugged land. He knew that the dense, luscious, low land brush, so full of willows and chokecherries, offered a promise of both abundant game and places of concealment while hunting.

Pausing on the trail, Wolfgang felt a light breeze on his face as soft as a cat's paw; blowing from the east, the moving air would almost certainly bring rain, and invisible fingers already rustled the leaves and strummed the river's surface. With hunger gnawing at his stomach, Wolfgang knew he must bring meat back to the cave before the storm arrived.

He had just resumed his progress when muffled growls and snarls, sounding like several small dogs, filled his ears. The sounds changed to yips of fright and alarm, then to high-pitched yelps of terror and pain. A larger animal's growl followed -- that of a bear.

Black bears, Wolfgang knew, recently out of hibernation and shaking off the effects of a long winter, would be prowling a wide swath of the low-lying area in search of food. Though they would later hunt deer fawns born during late May and early June, the bears now concentrated in open areas, replenishing their fat stores with winter kill, skunk cabbage and succulent grasses. Even a whiff of carrion on the wind, however, would be an invitation no hungry bear could ignore.

Following the distressed yelps quickly and silently, Wolfgang came around a boulder to behold an immense black bear, on all fours with a dead wolf pup in its mouth and one paw on another struggling puppy. When the huge animal swung its broad head toward Wolfgang, without thinking he raised his bow, picked his spot, came to a full, smooth draw and released the arrow.

Phhhttt!

The wooden shaft sprang free, flew straight, and sank deeply, its barred turkey fletching sprouting from the bear's chest. The bear dropped the dead pup from its jaws and spun in several quick tight turns, biting at the shaft. It stopped and stood broadside to Wolfgang, its head held low. Another shaft flew and sank deeply, piercing both lungs. The bear bit at it, then stood on his hind legs and raised his nose, looking and smelling the air currents. A third arrow hit the bear square in the chest.

The bear focused on Wolfgang now and dropped to all fours to charge, but he hadn't covered half a dozen paces before he staggered then fell to the ground, pushing one arrow all the way into his body. He made several futile attempts to stand and Wolfgang watched the mortally wounded creature try to raise its head several times; but then the bear shuddered, let out its death bawl, dropped its head to the ground, and collapsed.

Its eyes were still open, though, and not knowing for sure whether the creature was in fact dead or just watching him, Wolfgang tossed some rocks then finally touched one eye with the point of an arrow. There was no involuntary blink, and Wolfgang, satisfied, walked to the timberwolf pup that was free from blood. It was alive but unconscious. Wolfgang picked it up, secured its muzzle with a long, strong cord of fishing line made from nettle fibers, and fashioned a halter. Putting the pup in his pack, which he suspended above the ground from a tree, he moved to the bear and got to work.

* * *

By the time Wolfgang was finished, the wind had picked up, setting leaves and small branches into constant motion. The wolf pup was awake and whining, and Wolfgang had his hands full carrying the pack and as much meat and bear-hide as he could manage in this first trip. At the cave, he slung the pack from a rock projection with the puppy still secured then made two more trips back for hide and meat. The wind was now blowing in savage gusts, tormenting even the trees' larger branches, and whistling among the thinner branches and saplings. The air seemed alive with gust-snapped branches and twigs, and the surface movement of the river looked dangerous.

Inside the cave, Wolfgang settled in to begin cutting meat and fleshing the hide. The puppy began to whine more loudly. Wolfgang walked to the pack, the pup watching him with large yellow eyes, carried the pack to within an arm's reach of where he was working, and returned to his labors. He noted that though the pup was still frightened -- no doubt by both he and the storm -- now the small creature grew quiet and watchful.

Wolfgang, meanwhile, devised a plan. Knowing of the Indians' superstitious nature, he got to work on the bear's hind legs. He knew he would have to beat his adversaries at their own game; if his new scheme proved successful, it could well save his life. *When the snows come, I can change into bear boots if I'm being trailed.*

As Wolfgang worked, every so often he cut a small piece of meat, which he set just in front of the puppy. The pup divided its attention between the meat and the man, and though the hungry wolf looked worried, its ears down and forehead smooth, it remained attentive and quiet. Normally, Wolfgang knew, after weaning, the parents returned from hunting to regurgitate for the pups. Wolfgang had no idea how long this small creature had been without a meal, and every now and then he reached over to scratch behind the pup's ears. Before he was done with his work, he noticed the wolf pup's expression had changed from worry to watchfulness: now its forehead was wrinkled and its ears erect. It was time to remove the muzzle and let the puppy eat.

Walking to the front of the cave, Wolfgang looked at the sky. The air was now calm, but saturated with humidity. Not a bird was to be seen or heard, and the leaves suddenly began to chatter. A fast-moving front was rocking and twisting the tops of the trees. Crooked, white-hot fingers of lightning veined the sky -- striking directly overhead, joining forces with the thunder to cause a terrific din. The wind howled and a driving rain fell.

Worried, Wolfgang returned to his work on the bear hide. After a bit, he looked at the wolf puppy. It was calm but alert, watching him. There had been wolves in the old country, he'd encountered them more than once here, but he'd never had the chance to look at one closely before. For the first time he noticed that its oval eyes had slightly oblique pupils; the effect was disturbing. He understood why in the settlements the wolf was viewed as terrifying, savage, and evil. He inched the meat a little closer to the pup's nose, and saw the young one eagerly eyeing the food. Wolfgang gently scratched its ears, and untied its muzzle. He loosened the pack so that the animal could get out on its own when it was ready. Wishing he had an iron cooking pot, Wolfgang went back to working on the hide.

The clouds and sky outside were black. A piercing blue-white, ragged streak of lightning flashed across the sky with a splitting report. Wolfgang heard the puppy give a low, single yelp. Wolfgang set another, larger piece of meat in front of the pup's nose. The little animal quickly scooted forward half way out of the pack and took it, gulping it down, then scooting back into the pack. The pup paid close attention to the storm and appeared comforted by the man beside him. Wolfgang fed his new charge more meat, and soon the pup was fully fed and had fallen asleep.

Wolfgang worked through the night's storm. When he had finished with the hide early in the morning, he finally laid down to sleep. When he awoke a short time later, he found the wolf pup laying beside him and looking him straight in the eye-- watching over him. Wolfgang closed his eyes again, put his hand on the wolf and slept.

* * *

Through the summer months that followed, man and wolf kept close to the cave. Wolfgang spied buffalo crossing due south, and felt thankful that the last weeks of July -- "Buck Moon" to the northern Indians, since it was when new antlers first appeared on the buck deer -- proved less hot than the weeks before.

The young wolf stayed close, smelling, feeling, and tasting everything that belonged to Wolfgang so that he had to store all his possessions out of the animal's reach. When the wolf pup wasn't eating, it was sleeping, pacing or amusing its master by racing through the cave after imaginary prey. Often if Wolfgang wasn't heedful, the wolf would suddenly bound from some hiding place and pounce -- slamming into Wolfgang, growling, yipping and softly biting his leg, though never puncturing skin. Wolfgang always tried to grab the wolf, and those times he was able, he pinned it, buried his face in its fur, and uttered mock growls as he wrestled with it.

Wherever Wolfgang went, the wolf followed. Wolfgang was astonished by the size of the puppy's paws and legs, which looked far too large for its body but which made clear that, if well fed, the pup would develop into a formidable beast. Coupled with its speed and ability to scent game, Wolfgang knew that their alliance would lend to both a survival advantage. At night, the wolf's keen senses could warn Wolfgang of approaching danger, while Wolfgang, in turn, would feed, protect and raise his four-legged charge. Though savage and fearless, the wolf would, Wolfgang felt sure, make a loyal companion to someone it trusted. Listening to the wolf, the woodsman learned how it used its short, harsh low bark as a form of close-range communication, and before long he was "speaking" to the wolf in turn. A brief series of low barks followed by a clipped one: *Let's go hunting.* A short howl kept the wolf informed on his location when he was out of sight.

Wolfgang taught the wolf to obey both spoken commands and silent hand signals and insisted that all commands be obeyed. He reviewed earlier lessons as well as reinforcing new ones to be sure the wolf heeded a full range of directives. During training Wolfgang was quick with praise, and when finally he felt sure the pup was controllable, he set out from the cave one morning to hunt as the rising sun's light erased the last of the morning stars.

For an animal so young, the pup had great powers of concentration and persistence. When the puppy sat and stared with its ears pointed, Wolfgang learned, it meant it was focused on a deer or elk at a distance; but when the staring young wolf lay down, it indicated that game was near.

Hunting was fruitful because of the wolf's sensitive hearing and keen sense of smell; when a deer was stunned from an arrow hitting high in its back but was still on the move and far from dead, the wolf needed little encouragement to follow even the faintest of blood trails. Mad with eagerness, he would stare at

The War Trail

Wolfgang, with a mesmerizing gaze the command to follow the trail. Wolfgang loved seeing the wolf's eyes light up when finally given the command. Whereas it might have taken Wolfgang hours to track a wounded deer, the wolf puzzled out the trail in minutes -- racing along exuding energy and speed, his nose slightly angled toward the ground as he followed the dissipating scent. Wolfgang kept the training sessions inside and outside the cave short, but found the wolf capable of trailing for up to eight hours. Wolfgang could always tell when the wolf was tired for it would begin to lope diagonally, though almost invariably it was limited by only Wolfgang's ability to keep up.

The wolf responded well and Wolfgang repeated verbal and hand signs over and over; Come, sit, down, heel, stay, and track. They learned to hunt as a team. Wolfgang also learned to watch his companion's eyes, ears, paws, stance and tail. Not only was the animal highly sociable, its ability to communicate became more finely honed with each day -- as did Wolfgang's. He realized the wolf had great value to him practically, and personally as well, having become a companion he now loved as a brother. He talked to the animal as if it were another human being.

Chapter 5

One dark night, Wolfgang had been dreaming of a spirit-like figure flickering like a flame when a single, short high-pitched bark roused him from his slumber to immediate alertness. The wolf was staring fixedly into the dark toward the mouth of the cave.

"What is it?" Wolfgang asked, running his fingers up and down its back, feeling the tension there.

Normally the wolf responded immediately to Wolfgang's touch, but tonight it only stared ahead, its long snout pointed at the entrance. When the wolf began to rise as if to go out, his master commanded, "Stay!" The wolf gave a small, low warning growl and obeyed. Wolfgang moved to the mouth of the cave and gazed out, but the darkness revealed nothing.

As he scrambled for his rifle, the pup, close beside him, emitted a series of frightened yelps. Wolfgang heard the plopping sound of shuffling paws. Snatching a handful of small sticks, he tossed them onto the coals; they flared up almost immediately, illuminating something large and blocky looming in the middle of the cave. It looked like an enormous black bear, staring at him with glittering eyes. As it came closer into the firelight, Wolfgang realized it was indeed a huge, big-headed, bear. The animal's tiny ears seemed to grow out of the side of his head. A large, thick crease ran down the middle of its head, followed by a long nose and square snout. His huge forearms were supported with front paws so big that they just plopped at each cautious step. Showing no sign of retreating, the intruder woofed. Wolfgang saw the wolf's hair bristle.

Then the bear growled and snapped its teeth and Wolfgang snapped the rifle to his shoulder, aimed just below the bear's jaw at its neck, and pulled the trigger. He knew he couldn't afford to miss.

A deafening boom rocked the cave as Wolfgang tried to maintain his sight picture and follow-through, even though his vision was obscured as the rifle belched its cloud of thick, gray sulfurous smoke. The thunder reverberated throughout the cave, scaring the wolf pup badly, though it remained close to its master. The bear fell backward. Wolfgang and the wolf watched as its legs moved, then finally relaxed in death. Wolfgang quickly reloaded, rested the rifle within arm's reach, and went to work.

* * *

Wolfgang decided it was time to scout further west. Accompanied by the wolf, he entered the shallow water of the broad, shallow riffle in the river, crossing easily. They moved west, following the well-worn buffalo trace. He kept track of the sun by the direction and length of the trees' shadows. The buffalo trail was the largest path he encountered.

Remembering both what an old Delaware Indian friend had told him and various information he'd heard around camp fires on his way to Fort Prince George, Wolfgang knew that the major Delaware village of Goschachgunk lay somewhere due west, a brisk two-and-a-half-day walk from the Ohio River. The village was supposed to be located on the downstream side of the Tuscarawas River, where it entered the Muskingum River. Wolfgang would keep an eye out for Indians -- to do his best to avoid any of them -- but he also had to keep an eye on the weather. Dark clouds in the distance could mean a change in the water level, making his and the pup's crossing on their way back difficult if not impossible.

As he made his way, Wolfgang reflected on how lonesome the land looked with so few landmarks. That the eastern settlers called the territory the "Shades of Death" made all too much sense. Stopping, he slowly and silently observed the area around him. A little below where he stood rose towering hemlocks and beech trees. His eyes caught the movement of a large porcupine waddling near the base of a tree.

Wolfgang and his companion traveled west for three days, taking their time. Many of the trees were mauled with multilayered incisions in the bark and young hemlocks stood with their tops snapped off, indicating, Wolfgang knew, a large bear population. His eyes cautiously searched the still and shaded areas, and at one point he spotted a bear's old nest -- a large bed of branches high in a distant tree. Coming out of hibernation, the bears would soon make use of it again.

* * *

Wolfgang and his companion had just arrived at a large meadow when they felt a great vibration of thudding hooves on the ground. *Elk!* A small herd of buffalo grazed nearby. They camped there, killed a deer and spent several days resting, eating, and caching the rifles. Wolfgang groomed the wolf's hair and examined him for ticks and burrs. Each day, from a high point, they spent time watching the elk and buffalo that grazed at all hours of the day in the meadow.

One day the wolf alerted Wolfgang to the tree line at the far end of the field. Wolfgang looked, expecting more elk -- and felt his breath catch when he spied Indians. Traveling east, they wore breechclouts and leggings, and packs strapped to their backs. Their heads were shaved. Roaches were fastened to their scalplocks. They wore red and black face paint. With the sun shining on them, Wolfgang could make out that they were tattooed and wore ear ornaments. *Miamis.* The western Ohio country is their shared territory. Piankashaw, Atchatchakangouen, Wea, Kilatika, Pepicokia and the Mengakonkia are their traditional bands.

They appeared to be traveling in a hurry, which he found odd, because Indians usually traveled slowly and steadily. Wolfgang and the wolf followed the Miami warriors' trail -- a narrow, winding path little more than 18-inches wide, which often required him to crawl over or under tree trunks -- long enough to decide they were just passing through. Wolfgang felt proud to see that the wolf, while trailing, proved it had understood all those commands he taught it during their long evenings in the cave.

Wolfgang backtracked the Indians' trail, and thanks to the wolf's ability to follow a scent, eventually he found their camp near a small creek. As the wolf sniffed out every item of interest, Wolfgang examined the objects as well. This was a semi-permanent stop over campsite, he realized, a well-established stopping place complete with a huge fallen tree that served as a "stone boiling" cooking kettle. The butt of the tree had been burned on one side and hollowed out with stone tools. The Indians cooked in the butt of a tree by filling it with water and meat and dropping in red hot rocks from a large fire; the rocks were carried from the fire with split limbs serving as tongs, and placed in a small basket with a handle, then set into the wooden pot until the meat and broth were cooked. Wolfgang saw the boiling stones nearby, along with stacked wood, the tongs, and long-handled baskets.

He picked up one of the round, fist-sized rocks and examined it. It appeared to be granite. Checking the area, he found similar stones on the higher ground near the creek. In their system of travel, the camp was where the Indians would stop near sundown, remaining in camp until the next morning when the sun was one hand-span above the horizon. By this time they had eaten heartily and would repeat the previous day's routine at their next stopover.

Finally Wolfgang and his companion returned to the river, moving slowly into the wind and watching ahead. Wolfgang stopped frequently, concentrating on the ground signs. He could see that moving through unfamiliar terrain kept the wolf stimulated and happy. Before long the river appeared through the trees. It had not risen in their absence. Its rough, cobbled bottom still reflected up to the riffles' surface, the white water easy to discern even from a distance, these signs a guarantee of safe passage to those who knew how to read them. As usual, they would wait until last light to re-cross the river to the cave.

Then, while watching the river and listening in the deep shadows, to his great surprise, Wolfgang saw, four men on a flat-bottomed bateau just upriver.

* * *

They were white men, and the boat, of lashed-together logs, was loaded with supplies. As Wolfgang watched, it put into the bank.

Slowly, carefully, using the sound of the river and the men's loud voices as cover, Wolfgang drew close, and finally lay down to watch and listen. The men were so close Wolfgang could feel the vibration of their every step.

The men's speech soon told him they were French. After it was fully dark, Wolfgang waited till the moon was high. Commanding the wolf to stay, he left the pack and rifle for him to guard. He then drifted from tree to tree as noiselessly as a phantom until he was just outside the ring of firelight where his eyes would not reflect. He watched and waited, having already decided to steal something he needed badly: an iron cooking pot. Wolfgang patiently waited, and finally the men periodically stood and, one by one, trekked into the dark to pass their water. Wolfgang felt amazed that here in the Indian country these men acted as if they owned the territory.

After the men had finished dinner, the figure nearest Wolfgang got up and ventured into the darkness. He had no sooner pulled his pants down and squatted, before Wolfgang stepped close behind him, clamped a hand over his mouth, and pressed his knife to the man's throat. Immediately the man's bowels released, the loud sputtering sound prompting his friends, a dozen yards away in the firelight, to hearty laughter.

"Mon dieu!" cried one.

One of Wolfgang's moccasins had become soiled. Leaning in close, Wolfgang looked the man in the eyes, pursed his lips -- *"Shhhhhhh"*-- and shook his head.

The man's eyes were wide but he had the presence of mind to nod.

"Speak English?" Wolfgang growled in a whisper.

The blade gently pricked his throat. The man nodded carefully.

"Good... now listen," Wolfgang began. "You can return to your friends, but must say nothing about me. If you do, I will kill you and the others. Leave an iron cooking pot on a large rock on the shoreline where I can see it in the morning. Do this, and you will not be harmed. Understand?" he whispered.

The man responded again by nodding.

"Who are you?" asked Wolfgang, carefully lifting his hand from the man's mouth but increasing the pressure of the knifepoint at his throat. The man gulped several times before he began to speak.

"I am Jacques, the son of Louis-Thomas Chabert de Joncaire, a licensed fur trader, a coureurs du bois, who lives with the Nundawaono -- the 'People of the Big Hill.'"

The Seneca Indians, the westernmost nation of the Iroquois, Wolfgang remembered.

"I have been sent to explore and trade in the uncharted western lands," said Joncaire. "Monsieur, I know who you are. All the tribes of the Haudenosaunee -- the Mohawks, Oneidas, Onondagas, Cayugas, Senecas and Tuscaroras have raised the o-sque'-sont, the tomahawk, against you. The great Mohawk Sachem at Otstungo, has declared a deadly war on you. They call you the wolf -- 'Okwaho.'"

Jacques went on. "To the north, in the Nun-da-wa-o-no-ga, the territory of the Senecas, many warriors have already ritually prepared for war with you. The shaman has given protective medicine to assure their safe return. Word has been sent to tribes farther west, north, and east as well -- to the Hurons, Ojibwa, Abenaki, Ottawa and Algonquins. These peaux rouges savages are seeking to avenge your killing of their relatives. Many warriors hope to gain status by lever le chevelure."

Wolfgang knew what he meant: "Lifting the hair" – scalping.

"My countrymen pay more for the British and the American scalps than even for beaver pelts," the Frenchman said, adding, "and for *you* the reward will be especially big. The British are offering up to two hundred dollars for French and Iroquois scalps. If the peaux rouges capture you, they will torture you horribly. They will eat your heart to give them your power and courage. Your death will bring great status. They believe your rifle has magical powers and all wish to own it."

Wolfgang already knew that the Iroquois code of honor required revenge for a life taken.

"Turn your head toward your friends sitting in the firelight," Wolfgang ordered.

The Frenchman obeyed. Immediately, he felt the knife-pressure ease beneath his jaw. Hearing and feeling nothing behind, he waited a few moments and cautiously turned toward where the German woodsman had been. He saw no sign of him. Convinced he was alone at last, only then did the man begin to shiver violently.

* * *

Wolfgang and the wolf pup made their way back to the riffled crossing and forged ahead once again through the river. Wolfgang felt relief as the water flowed over his soiled moccasins, washing clean. Moments ago, returning to where the wolf had been guarding his pack, Wolfgang had heard the animal utter a low-pitched growl -- the pup confused, no doubt, by the odor of the Frenchman's excrement on his master's moccasins. Wolfgang felt proud of the wolf's response: It showed that the animal understood this was no game. Wolfgang had called the animal to him, hugged it, and rubbed its back and head with affection.

Since his arrival in this new universe, Wolfgang had some serious and tragic lessons in vulnerability. Thinking of Tamanend, Wolfgang admitted that, of all the people he had met and worked with, the Delaware Indian had been his only real friend. The absence of this close friend had been painful, and Wolfgang now recognized how crucial and life-preserving a good friendship could be. Now the wolf helped fill the void: Wolfgang would take care of and guard him as a brother and comrade.

* * *

From the cover of trees near the shoreline the next morning, Wolfgang watched the Frenchmen prepare their small craft; keeping an especially watchful eye on the man he had talked with the night before, Wolfgang was heartened to see him set an iron cooking pot on a rock near an out-cropping that would shield it from view of the other Frenchmen. Then the man hurried his fellow travelers at the river, pushing away from the bank and drifting below the riffles. They were soon out of sight. Wolfgang crossed the river with his two bear hides and rifles. Picking up the cooking pot, he examined it. It was good-sized and, though somewhat dented, would do nicely.

He carried the load along a well-used elk trail far to the west, to another distant cave he had found while scouting for a future passage west. Just inside the cave's entrance, Wolfgang and the wolf relieved themselves. Their smell would last a while and would discourage other four-legged creatures from entering.

That done, he used the vent pick to clear the touchholes of the rifles. Then he ran an oily patch down their barrels. When Wolfgang had finished and rested, he and the wolf returned to the Ohio River cave without incident.

* * *

It was several days later, while hunting in the forest above the Ohio River cave, that Wolfgang caught sight of a deer behaving such that the hunter took strong notice. Its body was tense and its tail out horizontally, leaning forward with its head bobbing as it focused in the opposite direction. The creature had, Wolfgang knew, identified potential danger.

The next moment, Wolfgang spotted the wolf, moving slowly and precisely into a grape thicket at the edge of the woods just ahead. The animal's long, black, upper-body guard hairs and tail were raised, and its nose was high to catch any scent. Wolfgang froze, his eyes turning from the wolf to follow its gaze, seeking the cause of its tension.

Then the wolf froze in the shadows of the low-hanging foliage, its head pointed in a stiff-legged stance, its body leaning slightly forward. When it turned its head to look back at

Wolfgang with that familiar posture and look that said, *"I see someone."* Wolfgang approached slowly. Kneeling beside the animal, staring ahead through the large, coarse leaves even as a deep, barely audible rumble sounded from his companion, Wolfgang saw them too. *Indians!!*

Chapter 6

Wolfgang barely caught a glimpse of them as they disappeared into the forest along a well-used elk trail. Traveling south, the braves wore bags of *psindamoakan* around their necks, a high energy food that would keep the Indians going on only a mouthful a day, which told Wolfgang that they were planning to travel a long distance. Emitting a low-pitched rumble from his throat, he told the wolf that it was right: these were enemies.

Wolfgang decided to follow their trail to make sure they were only passing through. Heading south, the Iroquois were probably busy expanding their power over the land. They would be raiding not only settlers, but other Indian tribes -- the Cherokee in Virginia and the Catawbas in the Carolinas. They would likely visit the Tuscarora tribe along the way, their relatives who migrated south long ago to the same areas.

Wolfgang realized he didn't know if the Indians were even still looking for him, but by following, he hoped to learn more. Gliding from tree to tree, stopping to look and listen often, his head and eyes always moving, Wolfgang followed at a distance, scanning and assessing the light, the shadows, ground litter, and all other sights, sounds and smells of his surroundings.

* * *

It was as he stopped a moment beside the trunk of a

large tree at the edge of the dark timber to stare into a lighted draw before him that Wolfgang suddenly felt a prickling of his scalp and a chill of apprehension. It was the feeling of being not quite alone, and he turned at once toward his back trail. It bore no obvious signs of anyone following. He tried to identify some shadow fluttering into hiding, but saw nothing.

Then Wolfgang heard the low growl of the wolf again and, turning to the animal, saw it focused intently ahead. He moved immediately to his companion's side, his hands reassuringly rubbing the animal's neck, eyes searching, in the direction the wolf was watching, high across the draw.

Just below the ridge, a group of Indians sat gathered on a rock bluff. Although distant, their painted faces told Wolfgang they were not hunters, and the fact their faces were gazing directly at him meant trouble. If they were of the same tribe as the warriors he killed before, no doubt they recognized him as the man they were hunting -- his light skin and hair would make that clear. Wolfgang knew that his only chance was to run -- now, this instant, while there was still some distance between them. Without another moment's hesitation, he turned and took to his heels.

Wolfgang bent into the hill, concentrating on a short, steady stride to minimize arm movement. He ran a hard, fast pace, climbing the steep rise at his best speed. As he topped the crest, he glanced back and saw that the Iroquois had almost reached the bottom of the hill. Although Wolfgang's heaving, rasping breath forced him to cut back to a rapid walk, this would be for only a few moments -- to regulate his breathing so his body might endure the stress he would soon place upon it.

Minutes later he was running again -- head tilted up, mouth slightly open, his eyes scanning the horizon. He had always been a good, solid runner, and knew the importance of allowing his body to breath in rhythm with his stride. Soon his muscles stretched into a long, easy, powerful rhythm. He forced himself to relax. He would need to hold some energy in reserve, though the surge of adrenaline made him feel he could keep this up for an hour.

Running north, Wolfgang decided to take advantage of the rough ground, and leapt onto the trunk of a downed tree to change to an easterly direction. Moments later he changed again, once more heading north, hoping the direction changes would slow his pursuers. He kept to the shadows of the great trees at all times so that no chance beam of light might give him away.

After traveling for some time, Wolfgang reached a creek with chest-high banks. The current looked fast enough to obliterate any footprints or discoloration he might leave. He quickly found a stiff, storm-broken tree branch and entered the creek on the rocks. Changing direction before long, he backtracked upstream toward higher, harder ground, dragging the limb behind him to eliminate any sign of his passing; the current would do the rest. Bent over, careful not to lift his feet, he gently shuffled forward, moccasins below the surface at all times, to preclude sounds of splashing. He stopped periodically to listen for the trailing Iroquois, heard no sign of them, and continued onward.

When he reached a place where the creek narrowed, Wolfgang sat on a rock amid lichen-splotched tree trunks and dried himself, then forked away from the creek, leaving no sign of disturbance. He was sure this would give him ample time to reach the cave ahead of the Indians, especially if he traveled straight west until he was again close to the great river, then turned north. Stopping to rest, he checked his rifle, all the while watching and listening. The sound of birds flitting through the trees and undergrowth were normal, as was the chatter of squirrels and chipmunks, but Wolfgang knew that all his tricks in changing direction would confuse and slow the Iroquois trackers for only a short time. Rising, he resumed his flight, at a slow run due northeast now, away from the cave.

He was looking for an ambush site.

* * *

The first bare-chested warrior emerged from the shadows carrying a coveted Pennsylvania-made Lancaster rifle. His head shaved but for a scalplock at the back and a turkey feather that rotated with his movement. His face was painted with a black rectangle covering both eyes and nose. He wore soft-soled moccasins, which, with squared, moose-hair-embroidered flaps, were only slightly covered by his leggings. He was the leader and tracker, and he squatted to study where he had last seen the white man and wolf. Noting the flattening of the leaves caused by his quarry's weight, the warrior determined that he was good-sized; the fact that the width from the heel to the instep didn't change -- that the spread at the ball of the foot then swept uniformly to the toe point -- told him the white man was wearing moccasins. The tracker also noted scuffmarks, made by the wolf.

The tracker's eyes traveled up the slope following the disturbance of the leaves, and he looked behind him to see if his two flankers were ready. Both were armed with lightweight, 28-caliber *Fusil de Chasse*. One flanker's face was painted with three black stripes on each cheek, the other with red-and-black stripes extending from eyes to forehead, black stripes radiating from his mouth down to his chin.

The flankers waited patiently ready to follow the tracker at a distance to watch for an ambush, as well as to detect whether the white man changed direction. Looking ahead, they saw the tracker's glistening eyes and slightly flared nostrils, as they had so many times before on the war trail. They followed alertly as he turned again to take to the trail.

The tracker felt sure that the lone man must be panicked. The man's wide-spaced stride, leaving deep impressions and scrape-marks where his toes left the ground, showed he was running -- a big, strong young man moving fast. The tracker matched the man's rapid stride as he followed the trail. Scanning ahead as far as possible, his eyes swept back and forth, using his peripheral vision as he ran. He wanted to race up to his prey and kill him before he had time to think or react.

But suddenly the tracker stopped running. The tracks had vanished! Looking back at his flankers, he pointed one eastward, one west. No longer sure of their quarry's route, he began to move slowly. Systematically he scanned the area, his eyes sweeping from side to side in a figure-eight pattern. *Nothing.* But then he spotted pieces of dislodged bark where the white man had come off a downed tree trunk. The leader set his big foot next to the white man's track and motioned for his flankers to come forward and note the difference. The man had a much larger foot and walked like an Indian, his toes pointed straight ahead and slightly inward. While the hurried, heavy-footed and toeing-out tracks of most white men were easy to follow, this man left little sign of his movement.

This man, the Iroquois knew, was different.

Now enjoying the chase even more, the tracker broke into a trot, following the tracks. He wanted to eat this man, his heart and his brain, so that he might capture his cunning and strength.

The flattened impressions visible in the brittle, dry leaves were easy to follow. Again the tracker found where the white man had changed direction to move north. He knew that all these changes in direction, intended to confuse him, would also slow the man down. He followed another one, the trail leading east again and merging with a creek. He followed it along the top of the creek at a run, until suddenly it disappeared. He waited for his flankers to catch up.

While he checked the stream, the flankers examined the near and far side of the creek, while the others behind them waited. There was no trail. He had entered the water, but which way was he going? The flankers split up, and when one spotted a wolf track on the far side of the creek, the leader joined him -- bending low to smell the track. Feeling confident that the lingering scent was fresh, he directed one flanker to follow the wolf uphill while he and the other flanker followed the creek to higher ground.

After moving along slowly for some time, the tracker's eyes noticed some lingering discoloration in the creek and disturbed sediment covering the stones. He knew he was on the right track when he next found impressions of footprints, then saw a rock newly splashed with water. The flattened moss on the rocks revealed where the white man had stopped to check his back-trail. Then the tracker saw a broken cobweb at head height: this was where the man had hurriedly exited the creek. A partial footprint showed on the embankment, and leaf disturbances beyond that. The tracker continued along the narrowed creek until he saw flattened imprints in the leaves moving due west.

Nothing the white man had done escaped the tracker's attention, but the direction-changes had taken time to trace, allowing the white man to get far ahead. The tracker looked to his right and saw his flanker following the wolf track. Their prey was skilled -- he thought like an Indian. The Iroquois set out at a fast pace, hoping to catch sight of the fleeing runner ahead.

* * *

Wolfgang let his instincts guide his feet, avoiding all obstacles that might cause noise. He paused frequently, remaining motionless as he hugged the shadows. At times the fear caught up with him and he convulsed in a shiver, but then he pushed on, alert to every shadow around him. Wolfgang knew what he must do. He checked his priming. He had to make each shot count, because he would only be able to make a few before the black powder residue fouled the barrel, making it impossible to ram a ball down, and rendering the rifle useless. He stopped. Standing motionless, waiting with infinite patience. Wolfgang closed his eyes to bring his hearing into focus. He felt a chill run up his spine, the hair rise on the back of his neck and forearms. In the thick silence, amid a mixture of fear and anticipation, he attempted to relax his mind. Still, he heard nothing.

Wolfgang removed his moccasins: his bare feet would allow him to feel even the slightest vibration of the hard ground while his pursuers were still distant. Very soon he felt a tiny tremor move up his leg bones, and continue to grow stronger. Wolfgang envisioned the runner's progress along the trail; peering around the trunk of the tree, he dropped to one knee both to reduce his size as a target and for greater stability, and brought the rifle halfway to his shoulder.

Suddenly he glimpsed movement through the trees: the first warrior came into sight, running quickly. Wolfgang held steady on his target, squeezed the trigger and...

Klatch! Poof! Boom! -- as the weapon punched back against his shoulder, there sounded a mighty cracking roar, the musket flamed, and its sound reverberated through the forest.

Momentarily blinded by the enveloping smoke, Wolfgang could not see the warrior fling up his arms as the ball passed through his chest, knocking him backward. Knowing all too well he had just revealed his location, Wolfgang ducked behind a broad tree even as another more deep-throated sound of an Indian smoothbore rifle answered.

Booooom!

One of the flankers fired into the hovering smoke of Wolfgang's weapon. Wolfgang heard a yell of victory from the shooter, but didn't stay to see the look of angry disappointment when he discovered that he had missed his target.

* * *

Moving at a slow, steady pace, Wolfgang reloaded his weapon on the run. With practiced skill he first drew back the cock, then spun the rifle around so that its muzzle pointed backwards under his right arm. He cradled the lock at his chest, being careful to hold the stock level and not knock it against any tree trunk, and used his left hand to bring the small powder horn to his mouth, gripped the plug, and pulled it free. Although he had practiced this numerous times, he still worried about spilling or wasting some of the precious gunpowder.

Behind Wolfgang came the whooping and hideous screeching of warriors who had found their dead brother. The sounds goaded him to move even faster.

Shaking some of the fine powder into the pan, Wolfgang thumbed the frizzen closed. Bringing the horn up to his mouth, he inserted the plug and let the horn drop back to his side. He slipped the butt of his rifle between the straps of his pouch and cupped the end of the barrel, while his left hand brought the powder horn to his mouth. Then he gripped the plug with his teeth and pulled it free.

In the midst of this, Wolfgang glanced around to make sure that the wolf wasn't nearby to give him away. He was also worried that it might get shot in the confusion, and so was relieved when he couldn't locate it in the nearby brush. He heard no more sound from the Indians now, which was a worse sign than the yelling.

After managing to center his horn into the bore of his rifle, Wolfgang tipped it, spilling a guessed measure down the rifle barrel. Bringing it back to his mouth, he inserted the plug and let it fall back to his side. Eliminating the patch, he slowed his pace a little and spit a ball, well covered in saliva, down the barrel and tapped the stock on the ground to hold the charge until he fired. He increased his stride and allowed his arms to make a

The War Trail

higher swing to run faster. He tried to regulate his breathing so as not to be breathing too hard when he stopped running.

Wolfgang ran until the trail made a blind turn. When he knew he was out of sight, he stopped behind a large tree and waited. He worked at regulating his breathing.

Peeking from behind the tree, he saw the nearest warrior twenty yards away. He raised his rifle to his shoulder, aimed for the chest and fired. The weapon thundered and belched smoke. As another warrior staggered and collapsed, those oncoming screamed out in anger and frustration. Wolfgang once more took to his heels, reloading the rifle while on the run through the thickest part of the forest on a well-used game trail.

Too much running dulled the senses. Wolfgang stopped and went back along the trail to where his tracks would reveal to the Indians that he was still running. Stepping behind a large tree, he waited for the next pursuing warrior. He used finer priming powder to increase the ignition speed of the lock, and moments later the rifle was again loaded and cocked. Wolfgang heard only his own labored breathing. His heart hammered, his hands sweaty and his throat dry as he prepared for the fast-approaching threat. Under the great trees it was dark and smelled damp.

* * *

The warrior felt secure, because the distinct, deep imprints of toe marks told him that the white man was still running fast. The Iroquois would follow quickly.

As the warrior reached a spot that screened Wolfgang from view, the hunted man stepped out from behind a tree trunk, the knife in his hand making a wide, backward arc. The stroke sliced deeply across the side of the warrior's neck, and blood sprayed through the air. The warrior dropped without uttering a sound.

Knowing a trailing brave wasn't far behind, Wolfgang listened as he raised the rifle to his shoulder and watched along its barrel. As soon as the running warrior came into view, Wolfgang saw his enemy tense, but the man had sensed his presence too late. Wolfgang had already squeezed the trigger, felt the rifle kick, and the next instant a lead ball tore away chunks of skin and bone as it passed through the Indian's chest amid thin veils of bloody spray.

The man flopped to the ground in a spasm. Wolfgang, rushing forward, found him still alive. The thrashing victim's face contorted in pain and his eyes shone with terror; quickly, mercifully, Wolfgang struck him with the butt end of the knife, targeting the side of the head where the skull was thin. Wolfgang grabbed the unconscious form in an embrace, stabbed him several times, and twisted the knife, creating larger wounds in the victim. The twisting knife ended the warrior's life as he sagged to the forest floor.

Wolfgang came upright and turned to face the trail behind him. His unbound hair was streaked with blood, his eyes had a feverish, widening glow. His face was manic. Wolfgang knew that he had only done what he had to do, but even after all of the killing he had done already, they hadn't stopped. A sense of dread filled him, as well as anger that they were forcing him to do this.

He turned and ran as silently as possible deep into the forest in the shadows beneath the great trees, reloading as he went. Before returning to the cave, Wolfgang would wait until there was no more sign of the Indians.

He retraced his back-trail, collecting shot-bags, powder horns, flints and the German-made rifle from his first victim. The lightweight, 32-caliber weapon had a tiger stripe maple stock with brass patchbox and crescent shaped butt plate. It was beautiful.

He continued in a new direction. That night, he would

sleep on a steep slope with a tree between his legs to keep from sliding downhill. Early in the morning, he would already be in position to observe his back trail. As he traveled, the natural sounds of the forest enfolded him; he pondered how completely he depended upon them.

Chapter 7

It was August, the season of the Red Moon. The three warmest months of the year now gone, it was a time of ripening. The thunderstorms and rains had not yet come, though they usually began at the end of the Buck Moon, a time of thunder. As Wolfgang left the cave early that morning, the wisp of mare's tails sweeping across the sky told him that the rains would come soon.

He worried. Once the rains start, the flooding river will make passage impossible. He prayed that the Iroquois had abandoned their pursuit.

This early morning the man and the wolf explored their way upriver, checking for signs of the Iroquois. Finding none, they made their way back down river to the bluffs. Wolfgang took a break on the far western side of a brushy clearing upriver from the cave so that he could watch his back trail.

It was while gazing down that he realized the woods had become quiet. No birds sang. A frightened flock of sparrows fluttering and skittering through the brush soared upward, startled. Following them with his gaze, he saw it: a distant, shadowy form moving amid the gray-trunked trees.

An Iroquois tracker! Wolfgang felt his pulse jump even as another shadow appeared behind the first, and then two more. The war party gazed up, as one man, to stare directly across the clearing at Wolfgang. Raising their clubs, they put their heads back and let out a series of long, loud, chilling war cries.

Before the braves had finished, Wolfgang and the wolf were on the run. Racing blindly through the dark forest, not looking back, Wolfgang sprinted over the rough terrain, branches whipping his face as the sound of fevered, exultant cries followed close behind. High above, the branches of gigantic trees met and mingled, permitting little sunlight to reach the forest floor. Amid the forest's gloom, Wolfgang made his way higher into the hills.

As soon as he was sure he was out of his pursuers' sight, he thought to himself, strategizing. *I'll change direction, turning at a right angle run a ways, and then resume my original direction. I'll repeat it over and over again, zigzagging my way higher into the hills. It will slow their tracking time down, and allow me to gain more time and distance on them.*

Wolfgang pushed himself harder.

Finally, at a switchback that afforded him a view of the way he'd just come, Wolfgang risked a look back.

He saw the five shaven-headed Indians below confidently following his trail. Four were a distance behind, which made clear who the tracker was. Wolfgang knew that if he couldn't elude them all he would have to fight, and with the odds so badly against him, Wolfgang didn't relish the prospect. He knew the fate that awaited him if he failed.

Wolfgang had heard stories of people whose fingers had been cut off and whose hands had been badly burned, who were then stripped, scalped, bound to a tree, and tortured with a small fire. While the fire burned, the Iroquois danced in delight, singing and shouting around the shrieking victim. The more the victim writhed and screamed, the more excited the warriors became, until each brave cut off small pieces of their captive's flesh, and either ate it or threw it back in their victim's face. In a final horrific act -- and one of agony for the bound man -- they cut open his chest and removed his heart. The fire was built up and he was burned, then chopped to pieces and consumed.

Wolfgang looked to the west and saw a wild vastness of solid dark forest, and remembered what his old Delaware friend had told him. *Discipline came from within the man, and to survive one had to be both smart and strong.*

He decided to lead them on a long-distance showdown.

As Wolfgang hugged the deep shadows, he began a slow-paced, long-distance run to conserve energy. Fierce yells sounded over his shoulder, and Wolfgang decided he would collect his pack and bow-case then head south, to the crossing on the river and the Ohio country, in hope of losing his pursuers.

For a time Wolfgang managed to lose the Iroquois by continually changing direction -- always heading opposite the bluffs and cave. To cover his passage he used his standard ploy of climbing the rooted stumps of fallen trees, then scurrying along their trunks, careful not to dislodge any bark, hoping it would continue to buy him time. He avoided all patches of open ground. When finally he began his last sprint for the cave, he felt sure it would take time for the Iroquois to work out his trail. He had left his rifle hidden in the cave, and when at last he recognized the small, concealed entrance on top of the bluff, he slipped down into it feeling terrific relief.

Once he'd secured all his equipment and food, Wolfgang left the cave to run directly for the broad, shallow-riffled crossing and thought to himself, *I have to gain more time and distance.*

On the far side, he hid behind the long trunk of a large fallen tree in the shadows near the shoreline. He hoped to teach the Iroquois a lesson they wouldn't forget.

He could fire and reload five times in a minute, so he planned to let them all get into the crossing of the river shallows, then fire his first shot at 90 meters. He hoped to be able to kill them all before they reached him. He calculated: they would begin to charge after the first shot, but the water would slow them down. He judged the point in the river bed where he could fire his first shot while still allowing himself time to reload and shoot again before they could reach him.

Now he saw them quickly approaching the river. There were only four Indians, which was good but no doubt others must be searching for him, too. The fifth of this group had likely been sent to find and alert them.

Quickly Wolfgang cleaned and dried his rifle, then pulled out and checked several greased patches. He carefully selected his .490-inch lead balls, making sure each was slightly smaller than the diameter of the bore so he could ram them home quickly. Every fraction of a second would count. The .015-inch greased patches made the rifle a precision weapon increasing its range, accuracy and penetration. The greased patch acted as a gas check, giving the lead ball increased pressure behind it. At 300 yards, Wolfgang could hit his target 50 percent of the time with this rifle. At 200 yards, he could hit a man's chest every time. Wolfgang preferred to engage his targets at 100 yards.

Dumping the powder charge into the barrel, Wolfgang wrapped the ball in a greased leather patch, centered it over the coned muzzle and pressed it in with his thumb, insuring that the patch was equally exposed all around. It felt snug. Using short strokes with his ramrod, he pushed the ball down the barrel and felt it crunch against the powder. He tamped it securely once and saw that the muzzle was even with the mark on his wooden ramrod, indicating it was properly seated. He withdrew the rod. Thumbing the hammer to half cock, Wolfgang took a vent pick and placed it in the flash hole until it penetrated the powder in front of the breech plug. This would insure that the flash hole was open and allow quick ignition. The powder felt firmly packed. He removed the vent pick, wiped the pan clean and primed it a third-full with fine grains of powder. He reached forward and snapped the steel frizzen shut. The wolf's ears pricked up when it heard the click. Wolfgang checked the lock to make certain that there was a tight grip on the flint, and that the flint was sharp and not too close or too far from the frizzen.

Having rested and balanced the rifle level across the top of the log, he licked his index finger and held it aloft, checking the wind; a slight crosswind blew down the river. The log rest would help prevent his flinching if there was a slow fire due to the powder.

Wolfgang checked the leaves on the trees above and around him. There was barely enough breeze to rustle them; he estimated the wind to be four-to-seven miles per hour. He checked the larger leaves on the sycamores across the river. They barely fluttered. Any wind at all could affect his accuracy when shooting at distance: this crosswind would deflect the flight of the round ball about four inches at 100 yards, about two inches at 50 yards, a half inch at 25 yards. The sun was high overhead and would help his aim.

Then Wolfgang saw movement in the trees on the far side of the river, and the Indians erupted from the trees. Wolfgang noticed that the wolf was watching them calmly, and reminding him that like the wolf, he must always remain calm in critical situations.

All the same, Wolfgang felt his heart beating wildly.

He stared at the warriors' ritualized gestures bonding their relationship with the spirit world, heard their savage yells. Across the distance and above the sound of the breeze and water came the shrill tone of eagle-bone whistles and sharp, high-pitched scalp-cries. Squinting, Wolfgang could just make out the dangling, fluttering flash of yellow feathers. The Iroquois were calling upon the supernatural power of the thunderbird to protect them and overcome their enemy. Four colorfully painted, resolute warriors, singing their personal medicine song and already smelling Wolfgang's blood, now started across the river.

Not carrying rifles or bows, all were armed with two-foot carved ironwood war clubs with wrist thongs. Striking weapons. The lead man's club had a carved ball-head as large as Wolfgang's fist. The second carried the largest, a gunstock type with three large knife blades -- a weapon terrifically dangerous at close quarters. Seeing how the sun reflected on the brass-headed trade tacks decorating the stock, Wolfgang knew he must keep the Iroquois from getting close enough to use these punishing weapons. The last warrior looked to have a tomahawk. They would fight in limited numbers. Those watching were bearing witness to the spirit of the man and his rifle. Wolfgang's scalp was needed to dry the tears of their relatives.

The wolf, standing at the far end of the tree away from the expected noise of the rifle, now lifted its head back and howled, a long-drawn-out, melancholy, slowly rising and falling howl that abruptly cut off. The sound floated eerily, echoing and reverberating up and across the river, filling the valley:

OooOOOOOUUU.

It abruptly stopped, then repeated:

OooOOOOOUUU.

The Iroquois paused a moment, recognizing the wild, untamed eerie music, and understood the howling message of the wolf, which they regarded as an oracle. Now the wolf laid down in plain view of those across the river, staring, waiting.

Wolfgang remembered one of many stories his father had told him in Germany while training dogs: if a dog howled twice, a man was going to die. Seeing the Angel of Death approaching, the dog would then look at the person destined to breathe his last.

The wolf continued to stare across the river.

As the warriors reached his 100-meter range, Wolfgang reached up with his right hand and brought the hammer to full cock. The wolf's ears pricked up as it heard the hammer's click. Wolfgang could see his enemies' painted faces, half-red, half-black--symbolic of war and death. Slowly, Wolfgang snuggled the butt plate to his shoulder, took several deep breaths and let

out only a little of the last one to steady himself. He concentrated on a good sight picture -- the chest of the closest warrior, but slightly left, to compensate for the wind -- and gently squeezed the trigger. Flint struck frizzen...
Klatch!
The fine powder in the pan flashed and...
Poof!
The main charge exploded...
Boom!
Flaming powder from the pan stung Wolfgang's cheek and white smoke filled the air with a sulfurous smell. Wolfgang sat his rifle butt onto the ground and blew down the muzzle to rid it of any burning powder. The Iroquois watching across the river had just seen their lead runner's chest erupt in a shower of blood; the man then retched blood and flopped into the water, jerking in spasms.

Good, Wolfgang thought to himself.

Now the warriors began running across the river as fast as they could. Wolfgang reloaded quickly, again steadied the front blade into the rear "V" and settled it on the head of another victim.

The Iroquois screamed their war cries to still their fear and continued to run. Wolfgang touched the trigger and held his weapon steady.

Klatch! Poof! Boom!

A cloud of smoke blossomed and the lead ball smashed into the warrior's forehead; the man tumbled forward and convulsed in the water. The Iroquois, watching from the forest, saw the head of their comrade explode in a fine red mist as brains and bone spattered.

Just two left, Wolfgang thought.

Again the crisp, still August morning air was shattered by an explosion, then filled with a billowing white cloud of smoke. Wolfgang did not look at the rifle as he charged the barrel, ramming down wadding and ball, priming the pan, cocking and raising the weapon to his shoulder, and taking aim. The one warrior was closing in quickly across the distance. The high-pitched war cries from across the river rose in volume. The last warrior had already thrown his tomahawk and for a second Wolfgang watched it revolve in the air as if in slow motion. With a solid *thwack* it planted itself in the forward edge of a tree trunk, chips of bark flying. The Iroquois warrior was just starting to leap across the trunk of the downed tree, his knife raised high, when Wolfgang fired. Blood spurted from the warrior's face and throat, and his body collapsed. Quickly, Wolfgang moved away from the smoke and saw the rest of the warriors on the other side of the river watching. They began to scream oaths of vengeance and race both upstream and downstream.

Wolfgang frowned.

He knew the remaining Iroquois warriors would cross above and down stream to begin hunting him; he had hoped the dead bodies lying in the shallows would serve as warning not to follow.

Jumping over a tree trunk, Wolfgang loosened the tomahawk to examine it. It was well made, and he recognized that the head, made of steel, would be useful. The heavy handle was carved as if to fit his grip. A leather-thong loop hung from the handle. He hung it on his right side, storing his own tomahawk in his pack. He pointed the direction to the wolf. The animal gave a quiet "woof" and they were on their way.

He and the wolf were running for their lives through the shadows.

So far so good, he thought to himself. *I'll have to move fast to keep my pursuers from flanking me. I must get far enough ahead to allow the Iroquois to come together again and follow my trail straight west true to my earlier word to the young warrior he had let go. Then I'll double-back to ambush them. There are only six of them.*

Adrenaline coursing through his body, Wolfgang stretched into a long, strenuous running stride, but soon realized that he was wasting precious energy. He slowed and concentrated on regulating his breathing. The wolf ran just far enough ahead to stay out of Wolfgang's way, periodically looking back to make sure his master followed. The man was using a well-established elk trail that ran up and along a ridge to the west, and which eventually led to a large meadow.

As Wolfgang ran, he remained intently focused, his eyes scanning the surrounding timber. He watched all the deep shadows for movement, looking for darker shadows within the shadows.

He coughed and relaxed into his run, thinking. *I'll lead the Indians to the elk pasture leaving a visible trail across the open. The Iroquois will think I am waiting on the opposite side for them to enter the meadow. Suspecting me waiting on the other side and being cautious they will follow the inside edge of the timber around the open area until they hit my trail again.*

Wolfgang caught the wolf's attention the next time it looked back and by slapping his leg signaled it to run close at his side. The wolf stopped, waited, and then loped along beside him.

Wolfgang thought, *After crossing the meadow, I will fishhook back inside the edge of the forest and wait for them there on the near side, in the timber near a downed tree trunk. The Indians will stop inside the timber edge, group together, and look across the open meadow. Then they will decide to go around, using the trees as cover. While they are stopped and trying to decide what to do, I will kill as many as I can. I have an edge now, because they will be afraid of my rifle. They will be cautious.* He knew that as long as the Iroquois could see the straight line of his widely spaced tracks and deep toe prints, they would think that I am running hard ahead of them.

* * *

Wolfgang finally spotted what he was looking for: not far ahead, off his path lay a great downed tree trunk. He and the wolf took theirs position behind the tree trunk where a large limb had fallen, leaving them hidden from the approaching Iroquois on their back trail. Wolfgang pointed to the ground and ordered the wolf to lie down at the far end, where the trunk of the tree was clear of the ground, allowing the wolf to see. The animal lay down and curled its tail along its flank. Looking at the wolf, Wolfgang put his finger to his mouth and commanded silence. The animal's ears were pointed up, indicating he was alert and ready. The months of training the wolf were paying off.

Several times Wolfgang hyperventilated to catch his wind and regulate his breathing. He bumped the butt of the rifle on the ground, ensuring that the charge was seated, lifted the frizzen and checked the rifle's priming pan. Warm air held more moisture than cold air did, but for now the fine grains of powder were still crisp and dry. Wolfgang tapped the rifle on the lock side to bank the priming powder away from the flash hole, checked the position of his flint, pulled his ramrod and leaned it against the trunk of the tree so it would be at hand for reloading. Then he laid his rifle on the tree trunk pointed down the trail. His eyes had a menacing stare and his jaw was clenched, sweat glittering on his forehead and upper lip. His hands felt clammy as he wiped them on his pants.

Suddenly, from the corner of his eye, Wolfgang caught movement of the wolf's tail. Its ears were set stiffly forward in response to some sound Wolfgang could not hear, until blue jays in the trees ahead announced their coming. The wolf's head was tilted slightly, and its eyes concentrated in the direction of the trail. Its tail bristled upward with a crick in it, the wolf's nose wrinkled and its long canine teeth bared. The wolf glanced at Wolfgang, who put his finger to his mouth, commanding silence. Wolfgang took two deep breaths and relaxed. Then he concentrated on listening and watching.

Suddenly he saw a strange, surreal shadow, long and black, shift between the trees. An Iroquois was standing there checking the trail ahead. A number of moving shapes were approaching the scout. Wolfgang aimed carefully and fired. The warrior performed a brief two-step as blood spewed from his mouth and he spun to the ground. The Indians immediately fired into the smoke, but Wolfgang had already grabbed his ramrod and moved some feet away. He reloaded and left at a low crouch, hearing the noisy rattle of ramrods as the Indians also reloaded. Wolfgang knew his survival depended upon his ability to reload more quickly and quietly than his enemies. Running through the forest, he cut back over, and finally returned to the trail. Already the sun was setting in the west.

Wolfgang decided that the following morning he would again ambush the Iroquois. To avoid being driven by them into some predetermined location and surprised in ambush, he changed direction, turning south this time and maintaining a slow, steady pace, confident that the Iroquois, fearful of another ambush, would not follow so quickly.

Running down the ridge, Wolfgang left a detectable trail, wanting them to think he was in a panic. Stepping on the rocks, he crossed the creek then climbed the opposite ridge. His surroundings were steep and close: perfect for ambush. He would be looking down at his enemies when they approached. Wolfgang leaned against a large oak tree to rest. Wolfgang commanded the wolf to stay while he left to check the lay of the land. The animal let out a long sigh and laid its head on its forepaws, facing the direction from whence they had come. Its eyes fully open, the wolf's face eloquently expressed disappointment. Wolfgang was amused.

He explored a short way west. Rejoining the wolf, he opened his pack and took out meat for both. The night passed without any unusual noises or movement.

Chapter 8

Early in the morning there was light fog, a sign of good weather. As the fog was still lifting, the distant *caw-caw-caw* of crows sounded, signaling the Iroquois' return. The sun had moved one finger when Wolfgang heard the raucous cries of a blue jay. He could see a marked change in the behavior of every bird nearby; all were on edge. A short time later, he heard in the near distance the excited distinctive *tsik, tsik, tsik, chirrrrrrr -- siew, siew, siew* of a red squirrel scolding. *A warning signal.* The forest seemed to live and breathe with a life of its own.

The warning continued. All at once everything became very quiet. Wolfgang knew that the natural noises made by other wildlife rarely disturb feeding squirrels. Then he saw it: the slow, quiet movement of human forms. They progressed silently, a few steps at a time, from tree to tree. At each tree, they stopped, looked, and listened.

Wolfgang raised his rifle, fired, and ducked behind the tree to quickly reload. He didn't have to see if he had hit the warrior because he could hear the sound of a limp body rolling and sliding down the hill.

Moving away from the tree, Wolfgang took refuge on the far side of another large oak. He repeated this until he was over far enough so that the Iroquois could not see him. Led by the wolf, he ran higher up along the ridge to the west, through the chilly fog, zigzagging through the trees. The higher he went, the thicker and more claustrophobic the fog became until, disoriented, Wolfgang could hardly make out his surroundings. But it was lifting. After about 500 meters he turned and ran over the side of the ridge in the direction of the elk trail that he had left the day before. He slipped and slid, in the rugged slopes of the gullies. In the nasty descent between ridges, the wet brush and saplings battered his legs with each stride. They picked their way across the rocky streambed and scrambled nimbly up the side.

Finally, the boulders and downed trees gave way to a well-traveled elk trail. Wolfgang checked the trail for signs, but found none. He and the wolf watched and listened while resting. He kept watching the wolf; the animal showed no sign of hearing anything suspicious. They continued their slow run along the trail.

After running for some time, Wolfgang fell into a smooth rhythm. When a chilly wind developed, it not only lifted the remaining fog but also refreshed him as he loped through the stark landscape. The sun was one hand up in the sky when finally he and the wolf stopped to rest.

* * *

The shadows were beginning to lengthen. Glancing at the sun, Wolfgang knew that it would be near sundown by the time the Iroquois reached the elk pasture. Man and wolf would not rest tonight. The Iroquois were tracking him better than he might have expected. He had been told the Iroquois did not fight at night because they believed it important the shining sun witness their warrior spirit. *I will strike when they least expect it,* thought Wolfgang. The wolf threw back its head, and let loose a long howl. *OooOOOOOUUU.* The air fairly vibrated with the wail.

* * *

The old Delaware had taught Wolfgang to sneak up on an enemy, to move into the wind, day or night, and always to remain in the shadows. Wolfgang knew never to stop in the open, but to remain concealed by the earth's natural depressions with the sun behind him. At night he made sure to keep the moon before him so as to silhouette his enemy, and to move slowly, always stopping behind a bush or tree, next to a rock, or beside a tree in its daytime -- or nighttime -- shadow. To remain silent, he must be sure of the placement of his hands and feet at all times. He must hear, but not be heard. He knew the importance of moving in closely, rising out of the ground like a spirit, killing quickly, then melting back into the forest.

* * *

Wolfgang and the wolf circled their pursuers until they worked their way upwind in the manner the animal would hunt ordinarily. Before the moon rose, with the wolf guiding the way Wolfgang had glided from tree to tree, using the utmost caution and cocking his head to detect the faintest sound. When at last he knew he was as close as he dared get, he pressed the wolf to the ground and whispered in its ear to stay. Otherwise, there would be a chance that the animal's eyes might reflect the moonlight and give away their presence to the Iroquois guard.

Now, alone, Wolfgang went forward on hands and knees, in the soft, wet leaf mold. Noise -- the great betrayer-- carried better at night, and tonight a light breeze would carry it even farther. Though the Iroquois spoke in low tones, Wolfgang could now hear the low murmur of human voices in conversation.

Making his way slowly through the brush, Wolfgang concentrated on seeing and hearing in the thick shadows cast by the giant trees. Only the leaves overhead rustled with the wind's breath as Wolfgang's nostrils pulsated with the smell of their bear grease and smoke-stained bodies. He waited for the moon to come up behind the butt of a tree. Finally, in that great vault of inky celestial sky, there appeared the rising moon, and with it a myriad of stars. Small pale patches of moonlight shone on the ground, and Wolfgang could now count the men pursuing him: just three, which meant another group was somewhere further back along the trail.

Two of the men were lying down. From their breathing and slight shifting, Wolfgang knew their position. He watched and waited until he saw only one standing against a tree. He would watch this dark figure until the sentry's body became tired and slouched -- when Wolfgang knew the man's eyes would glaze and his movements become wooden.

Wolfgang saw the lone warrior's head turned away from him as the Iroquois listened to the classic, mellow *hoo, hoo-hoo, hoo, hoo,* of another night hunter, the great horned owl. The man remained vigilant for a while, but soon the slight shifting of his body told Wolfgang that caution had been sacrificed: the warrior was struggling to stay alert. Watching, Wolfgang saw the guard slump then straighten with a start as he caught himself dozing.

Now was the time.

Like a phantom, Wolfgang rose and moved slowly forward. Gradually closing the distance, he soon stood immediately behind the slouched shadow -- Wolfgang's eyes now fully adapted to the night, his gaze sweeping back and forth. Suddenly, with one rapid, desperate movement, he struck – lifting the man's head from behind, sawing the knife back and forth quickly across the throat to silence any shout of warning the man might attempt. Wolfgang held his victim above the ground as the Indian's feet flailed the air. He began to count. One... two... three... The warrior gradually grew still, having lost consciousness from loss of blood. Wolfgang held the stricken warrior suspended by his head and chest, and not even gurgling sounded. The warrior's feet ceased their movement. The warm blood soaked Wolfgang's upper body. He stood with the limp body, listening for the slightest sound. Nothing.

He laid the body down gently and took his place against the tree, making sure to leave no background of skyline above and behind him. He stood perfectly still. There were minutes of breathless silence. Wolfgang's eyes worked ceaselessly, scanning for the slightest hint of danger. Now he distinguished the motionless men lying in the deep shadows, and watched them on the ground for the slightest movement that would tell him they had awakened. They remained still.

Wolfgang made certain that there were no other deeper shadows of figures. He swayed his head like a snake so that his eyes could catch the light. He studied the position of the two sleeping bodies, and lowered himself to the ground where he could see ahead more plainly.

Slowly, he crept forward.

A moment later he had reached the nearer shadowed figure. There was a minute of breathless silence as Wolfgang identified the point where each man's collarbone stuck up beneath the skin. With a quick stabbing movement deep into each sleeping man, Wolfgang rendered them harmless: both men were dead with deep neck wounds, their black, pooling blood reflecting with a distinctive sheen in the moonlight. There were great gouts of arterial spray from the wounds. The air was now thick with the coppery smell of blood, feces, and urine--the stench of death. There was only a slight rapid intake of air and surprise, and the momentary rapid beating of the feet. This act would send the remaining Iroquois a message that he could outwit them and that they would never know he was there until they felt his bite. The agonized contortions of the facial muscles among these dead would inspire terror and awe.

OooOOOOOUUU. The eerie untamed music of the wolf startled Wolfgang. No matter how many times he had heard it --

the moaning howl celebrated their successful hunt -- the sound sent a shiver up his spine. Smiling grimly, Wolfgang knew the wolf had sent a message: the Iroquois would remember the time of the Red Moon.

Wolfgang collected their powder horns and shot and removed the flints from their weapons. Removing the two larger men's moccasins, Wolfgang and the wolf then returned to the elk and buffalo pasture to wash in a nearby creek.

* * *

The next morning, Wolfgang and the wolf watched and waited patiently. Before the sun reached its mid-point, he counted eight Iroquois below. From the safety of a tree's cover, he carefully took aim.

Klatch! Poof! Boom!

Moving quickly away from the drift of smoke, he stepped close to another tree and, facing his foes as he worked the ramrod, he began to re-load.

Pssst! Pssst!

The sound of close-passing lead balls filled his ears. But he was ready to fire again and he aimed low. A ball fired too low splattered leaves at his feet. He was able to fire four times before letting his rifle slip up against the log. In a barbaric frenzy, the remaining Iroquois attacked.

The braves' awful screams panicked Wolfgang. Tamanend's voice sounded in his ears: *"When you attack, yell wildly, meet the enemy quickly and violently, striking as many as possible while continuing to move."*

Now Wolfgang took his old mentor's advice to heart.

Gripping his tomahawk in his right hand and the large knife in his left, he ran with an awful yell to meet his enemies.

"EERRRGGHHH!"

Wolfgang ran into the first man head on, knocking him

The War Trail

into the path of another close behind and to one side. Both warriors went down in a sprawl. Wolfgang managed to roll and meet the closest thickset body, blocking the downward swing of an enemy war club with his tomahawk and the next instant ripping open the Iroquois' belly with his knife; Wolfgang twisted under the upraised arm and the Iroquois' life spilled out onto the ground. Not pausing, he met the last man in turn.

With a wild, terrible yell Wolfgang leaped deftly onto the man like a great cat, knocking him backward and riding him to the ground. The Iroquois was strong and of gigantic stature, and he managed to grasp Wolfgang's arms so that for a moment the mortal enemies stared into each other's eyes. But then Wolfgang wrenched his foe's arm sideways and with his tomahawk cut deeply into the warrior's forearm. Wolfgang's right arm, now free of the warrior's grasp, crashed downward with the axe and split the other man's skull. Wolfgang sprang to his feet just in time to meet a new rush by the first two warriors.

Dodging low to the ground and tripping the first running warrior, Wolfgang feigned a blow with the tomahawk but reversed direction, bent low, and stuck the long knife between the legs of the next warrior, slashing his thigh deeply. Blood spurted wildly as the warrior went down. Knowing he would bleed to death quickly, Wolfgang spun around to face his last opponent.

The brave had recovered into a fighting stance, but he was not going to rush Wolfgang again – Wolfgang understood this – so the two men stood facing each other, their faces immobile. With neither anger nor fear, they just looked at one another.

The Iroquois warrior saw how fast this gifted white warrior had successfully executed a complicated series of movements. The white man's speed and near-perfect coordination had caught them by surprise. The Iroquois noticed that the man's legs and hands did not tremble.

This fighter has control of his fear.

Wolfgang stared at the painted and ornamented war club. It had feathers at both ends and a single feather on the back, with the long sharpened deer horn pointed wickedly downward. Wolfgang looked into the eyes of the warrior and saw an extreme sense of calm. The warrior stood with his feet shoulder-width apart ready to move in instantly in any direction. His knees were slightly bent, and hands down, ready to move. Slowly crouching, Wolfgang laid his knife and tomahawk before him on the ground. Standing upright, Wolfgang raised his right arm skyward, palm forward, and clasped his hands together, left beneath right, indicating, "Peace."

The Iroquois, watching closely, looked the picture of ferocity, his head shaved and wearing only a Mohawk roach, his face painted from ear to ear with markings that Wolfgang understood. A black rectangle, running from his brow to the bridge of his nose, symbolized death, while a series of narrow red bands above and below signified war. Three vertical white stripes on each cheek indicated the brave cried for someone who was dead. He also wore a copper ring in each ear and in his nose, and fur armbands and garters. A sash crisscrossed his chest and a girdle wrapped around his middle. His leather moccasins were unadorned.

Wolfgang and the Indian stood staring. The warrior then put his elaborately carved deer-horn war-club into the back of his girdle. Wolfgang knew that if his enemy had put it into the front of the girdle, he still would be thinking of fighting. But now the Iroquois warrior responded with the sign of peace.

Wolfgang's hands motioned: he touched his chest, then extended his hand toward the warrior and back to his chest. His right hand, with palm upturned, moved from his mouth toward the warrior, signifying, "talk." They again stared into each other's eyes and in turn they talked. Wolfgang had to watch closely. Sign language was three times as fast as a person could speak.

    He made known what he had told the last young warrior on the far side of the Ohio:

    "I want to be alone. I have been a slave of the British and Americans. I go west, big walk. No follow. You speak great Otstungo Sachem. I kill warrior follow me."

    Wolfgang's hands continued to motion.

    "Stop war, your village future no happy. Much mourning. People sad. Warrior go war trail, many die."

    The Iroquois responded with signs acknowledging Wolfgang's message, then went on to convey, "Scioto River, short walk."

    Wolfgang backed away from the dead bodies and signed for the warrior to take what he needed and leave. The warrior walked toward two powder horns, one small and one large. After shaking each to judge the contents within, he moved toward his empty smoothbore rifle. He walked away into the forest and disappeared. Wolfgang thought that he would see him again. He knew that whether he had killed this last warrior or not, this area would soon become the starting point for the continued search for him. But Wolfgang believed it was right that he try to end this ongoing pursuit.

    He had to move a little farther west. He had obtained only one additional rifle. He saved all the flints for future use. Wolfgang knew that almost all Indians wanted the light, smoothbore guns because they could be used with either shot or ball. But he knew that these trading guns, with the brass, serpent-shaped side plate, were not accurate at anything other than close range. The one captured rifle was unloaded. He checked to make sure the lock worked safely and smoothly. Satisfied that the parts moved freely without any play, he brought the weapon to half cock and attempted to pull the trigger. It was a quality lock, because it would not fire. Any weapon that fired from half cock was dangerous. It was a good rifle. He ran an oily patch down the barrel. Wolfgang felt certain that any other warriors on his trail would have to return to the north to provide for their families during the coming winter, and that they would not resume their hunt for him until the following spring.

* * *

Wolfgang traveled mostly west by southwest through the rest of the Moon of Ripening, the Moon of Falling Leaves and the Moon of Winter, with a distance still to travel before he reached the Scioto River in the Ohio country. Remembering the Iroquois telling him that the Scioto River was just a short distance west, Wolfgang kept wondering what a "short distance" was to an Indian.

He found an unusual area in which to remain through the winter. It contained many caves, high cliffs, gorges, and waterfalls that fell over large sandstone formations. There was also a small forest of pine and hemlocks, surrounded by large oak, walnut, hickory, cherry, and maple forests in all directions. Planning ahead, Wolfgang cut pieces of resinous pine to dry through the winter for lighting the cave at night. After scouting the area for hunting purposes, Wolfgang settled into a small cave. Later, he would retrieve the cached rifles he'd left behind.

He hauled into the cave all the odorless burning wood he needed to provide him with fuel. The surrounding area had plenty of hickory, white oak, ash and maple. He spent time gathering all the acorns he could. He spent much time splitting, shelling, breaking them up, and leaching them in hot water. He would dry and then grind the acorn chunks into flour for thickening stews.

Finally, the second frost had arrived and curled the rhododendron leaves. It was time to hunt. The deer coats had already turned heavier, thick and hollow, into their hue of winter gray-blue. He came to realize that if the Iroquois were still looking for him, they would have to make a wide sweep through the country to look for sign--a lone trail coming out of or returning to a camp, and the smoke from a fire. To ensure that his tracks were covered, he made a habit of hunting just before a storm.

One day, after Wolfgang had returned from a successful hunt, the weather worsened and a cold front rushed in. In the dark and frigid nights, the temperature in the cave plummeted. Watching his foggy breath, Wolfgang would get up to put just enough wood on the fire to keep it going. He and the wolf listened to the ominous sound of the wind as it shook the bare, ice-covered trees. Man and beast now slept together, both hearing the loud cracking thunder of trees popping outside periodically. In this cave, Wolfgang began to dream again the spirit figure hidden by flickering flames.

He could sense that the dream was growing stronger. Wolfgang was aware that the Indians attached great importance to dreams. They foretold events about to happen.

Chapter 9

It was early spring of 1755. In an hour the sky would signal the start of another day. Wolfgang maneuvered west out of the Ohio Country. He crossed the narrow Scioto River, then the fork of the Miami River and Indian Creek, into the Illinois Country. At the Whitewater River, his quick eye found a dugout canoe made from a poplar trunk that enabled him to cross safely. The soil was warm and a dense carpet of bluebells covered the sun-drenched woodland floor, along the streams and floodplain. He traveled northwest into an area of limestone formations, caves and springs -- a good stopping place. Checking the billowing clouds on the distant horizon, he determined it would rain soon. He warily noted the low thickets of hazelnut bushes, and their wide spreading branches running along the edge of the woods, sporting limbs broken by feeding bears. An especially large male had peeled bark from a great number of trees to feast on their inner layer.

After a long winter without vegetables, he dug wild leeks from the moist soil. He hungrily watched a pot of them sizzle in bear grease as he worked by light of candlewood and lighted strips of shellbark hickory, casting molted lead into round balls. Later he would steam the leeks in their own juice. The pungent smell was overwhelming. The gray-green leeks were one of his favorite foods.

* * *

It rained frequently now. When the rain stopped for any length of time, the mosquitoes were suddenly everywhere, but the bear grease on the exposed areas of his body kept him protected from the voracious insects. The wind shrieked outside the limestone cave at night, and the wolf proved not only an excellent sentinel but also a great help in keeping warm. Man and beast lay awake side by side, staring out at the cold, wet night, listening to the wind and drumming rain pelt the forest. With the heavy downfall the creeks and streams ran high, and Wolfgang knew the flooding rivers would keep the Iroquois from looking for his trail for some time.

* * *

Late spring turned to early summer, and the sun appeared. Dogwoods blossomed, rattlesnakes emerged, and deer gave birth. The afternoons were hot and filled with pesky insects. During May and June, Wolfgang observed where a large boar had stood upright with his back to the trees and twisted his upper body to bite with his large canines, leaving long horizontal marks. The trunks of the maples, elm and beech acted as signposts of communication for the bears as the females neared estrus.

Summer passed as well. Wolfgang had remained in a cave near the mineral spring for much of the passing year. The season finally lapsed into the mellow and last lazy days of the Harvest Moon, the month when the full moon occurs closest to the autumn equinox. Mornings were crisp, with the afternoons warm and the evenings cool. Deer were plentiful and easy to spot as their antlers reached full development and the creatures remained in open country, feeding for longer periods to put fat on for the winter. The fawns entered their first autumn and grew out of their spots.

Nature, clinging tenaciously to life, had cloaked herself in riotous color, her luster but a prelude to the white shroud to come. The haunting stillness of the oak-maple-hickory forest was bathed in golden sunlight. The woodlands stood ablaze with color as the green leaves of oaks turned brown, sugar maples blushed scarlet, and the hickory turned a soft dull gold, masking the decay and musty odor of dissolution below. Small yellow blossoms of goldenrod painted the open hillsides and the sumac showed red. Ash and dogwood trees sparkled with berries. Occasionally, Wolfgang would stop in his work and take in the rich spectacle around him. The first frost had come and gone. These were the last sweet days of the season before the landscape started to turn gray.

* * *

Wolfgang scouted the moist soil of an upland mixed forest area for Indian sign. His measured breathing was nearly silent as he made his way stealthily to a virgin grove of tall, straight, wild black cherry trees. The berries were ripe. The fruit was dropping to the ground. But fruit would run through the mighty creatures quickly: The bear's would have to forage all day long to put on enough fat to last through the coming winter. Spoor was everywhere. Numerous round piles of bear-scats defined the area.

As Wolfgang approached the grove, he heard first the angry chatter of squirrels then the unmistakable sound of bear claws scraping the deeply fissured bark of the trees. *A climbing bear!* Now the creak and swishing sound of waving branches sounded in the distance; it sounded almost as if the trees were coming apart. Wolfgang proceeded cautiously until, looking ahead, it seemed he had stumbled across bear heaven: agile climbing black bears were everywhere among the spreading branches, feeding on the cherry crop. Woofs and growls emanated from amid branches dense and heavy with the ripening, marble-sized, purplish-black fruit. Wolfgang had never seen such a congregation of bears in one place. It meant that the bears would begin hibernating soon.

At the snap of a twig and a strange tinkling sound, Wolfgang turned and beheld the swinging head, lanky torso, and arrogant swagger of the biggest bear he had ever seen. The animal was no more than a dozen yards away. Its long head supported by a thick neck, it was covered with coarse, yellowish-brown hair and a large prominent hump between its shoulders with a large turf of hair. The bear was so heavily laden with autumn-fat that its stomach seemed to brush the ground as it shuffled along, snuffing the ground for fallen fruit. Its long talons tinkled as it walked. Remaining all but motionless, Wolfgang moved only his eyes. He realized this bear would stand well over eight feet tall, and, aware of a bear's keen sense of smell, he backed slowly away, without incident.

During the fall, Wolfgang and his companion tracked and killed two small bears for meat. From their pelts Wolfgang made a sleeping pad for the wolf, it had grown considerably. Several times Wolfgang saw young bears running in the distance and heard them crying. He also heard the loud popping of teeth followed by the *bah-bah-bah* bawling sound of yearlings. On those occasions, they cast nervous looks over their shoulders as they hurried from the area as fast as they could. Then came the huffing and puffing sounds of a large bear attempting to follow the smaller fast moving bear. Wolfgang understood that a large bear was nearby: Big adult bears would kill and eat youngsters. He always retreated from the area to avoid any confrontation.

He had seen fresh territorial markings on trees nearby clawed over the twelve-foot mark by a dominant bear. The scratch trees were visible from a distance, the darker, outer bark removed by body rubbing to reveal the lighter, inner bark. Five wide rows of parallel claw marks eight feet above the ground indicated a sizable animal and long, coarse, yellowish-brown hair clung to the bark. The big bear was marking his territory; Wolfgang also found large dark brown droppings with hair in it, the stool as thick as Wolfgang's ankle. Wolfgang could picture the beast -- a tremendous, grisly-looking bear that must feel as if he owned the world. Having sensed the man and wolf in his territory, it would be in an ugly mood. *This was not a black bear. This was a great grizzly bear. The hunter of men.*

* * *

As the season called the Hunter's Moon arrived, a soft, gentle, mist-like snow began in the shadowed morning light. Wolfgang listened to the sounds of geese honking overhead. Then a distant, raucous sound – *Gaaarrraaoobble-obble-obble* -- of a gobbler in a tree announced he was coming down soon. Deer tracks indicated that rutting bucks were chasing does. All seemed normal as Wolfgang stopped on a hilltop to rest.

Then, on his back trail, small birds flitted off in a small, white, burst of snow that cascaded from the pine where they had been perched. Frosted breath appeared beneath the still-quivering limb. Six Indians were moving at a slow trot as they followed his wavering trail. The tracker was well ahead of his companions. Wolfgang could see all half-dozen plumes of breath in the frigid air. He knew he would be easy to trail even in the sheltered places with no snow because the ground was wet and soft.

The tracker stopped and squatted to study the tracks more closely. He noted their sharp, fine edges: with no snow inside, they indicated the track had been made after the snow had stopped falling. He also noted that the tracks hadn't yet begun to melt outwardly from the print, and that their edges hadn't yet fallen inward. Standing, he placed his foot in the snow beside Wolfgang's print. The tracks looked the same: Wolfgang's was fresh. Wolfgang saw the tracker kneel and push one finger down into the track to test the point of greatest foot pressure to determine if it had started to freeze. The tracker knew the track had just been made a short time ago. Its maker was close at hand. Slowly his eyes lifted, noticing the fluid stride of a confident attitude -- a man who treated the wilderness like a friend.

Wolfgang saw the tracker's eyes following his trail up the hill, then suddenly meet his own gaze. Wolfgang saw the man's startled response, saw him shout; the other Iroquois scattered like quail for cover behind the trees, knowing all too well their quarry's ability with a rifle.

Wolfgang took off at a slow trot; he knew that his pursuers were tired and faced climbing the hill. He would gain time and distance. He planned as he ran.

All Indians feared and respected the bear. Wolfgang pondered how to use their fear to his advantage. He stopped running and listened for the familiar squeak in the dry snow that would tell him the Indians were coming. He leaned his rifle against a tree trunk to take off his bow case and pack. From his pack he removed his moccasin boots, which he had made from the hind legs of the bear in the cave the year before. He stood, secured his equipment and walked away. He stopped and looked back momentarily. Wolfgang was impressed with the tracks he had made. He had now transformed from a man to a man-bear.

* * *

The Seneca tracker stared in awe at the white man's tracks. Their quarry had sat down to rest -- and risen to walk away as a bear. There was no mistaking the prints -- the wide pad, the long, curved claws.

The tracker, a member of the bear clan, had deep feelings about bears that transcended his fear. He believed that the bear had a supernatural understanding of human language, and that his spirit went to the same afterlife as their own. The tracker motioned for those following at a distance to come to him. As his other bear clan followers came close, he pointed at the ground. The other five warriors stared down at the tracks; finally, the tallest of the group broke the silence.

"This white man whose friend is the wolf has great spiritual power," he said. "I feel a kinship with bears; somehow, he is both one of us and one of them."

There was another long pause.

"Him, two-legged man bear," said another warrior.

"I will no longer follow him," said the tracker at last, breaking the silence. "He is my brother. We share a blood relationship. The great nature spirit, Orenda, demands that we respect this person, who is our relative."

Without another word, the tracker turned and began retracing their back trail home. The others followed, each in deep thought about the spiritual power with which they had come in contact.

* * *

Wolfgang waited in ambush for the Iroquois for a day's time. When no one appeared, he circled well around the area where he had changed into the bear-paw moccasins he had fashioned from the animal he had killed, and which had served him so well, likely saving his life.

Finding the Iroquois tracks, he noted they were headed east, away from him. His eyes boxed the trail for an average man's pace and counted the number of tracks inside the box. Fourteen. Wolfgang was now sure that all six Iroquois had left the area. He followed their trail for some time, until he was doubly sure the Iroquois had gone for good. He and the wolf returned to their camp. With winter coming, they had hunting to do.

*   *   *

Ordering the wolf to remain in the cave, Wolfgang left on a short hunt. His moccasin boots, lashed to his legs, were absolutely silent on the soft leaves, and he moved slowly. While crossing a small creek, he saw a muddy roil along the edge. A deep bear track showed more than two hand spans long. It was wider than his hand was long. The long claw marks showed clearly. These were tracks of the great bear known to attack and eat men whenever it saw them. Bending to place his face close to the ground, he slowly inhaled through flared nostrils.

The smell of the bear was still strong.

Despite his foremost concerns, Wolfgangs' thoughts touched on his clothing after he had crossed the stream. The leggings and moccasins had been smoked and brain-tanned, protecting them from the frequent soakings they encountered, and Wolfgang had come to deeply appreciate the deer skin shirt the Delaware, Tamanend, and his wives had given him. Though most white men refused to wear buckskins because they found the clothes hardened into an uncomfortable shape, Wolfgang's attire remained soft and pliable even when dampened by rain or snow-this thanks to their having been tanned expertly and browned by smoking over oak and willow. The lower part of his shirt had been dyed a light green with birch bark. The soles of his moccasins had been made from the thick part of the elk hide.

As Wolfgang thought thankfully about Tamanend's gifts, a light breeze brought him a smell that snapped his thoughts back to the present. Detecting the pungent odor of deer, he propped his rifle against a tree and slipped his bow from its case. A moment later Wolfgang saw a buck stride along a field that bordered a grove of giant white oaks. Acorns would be abundant there, but the deer had no doubt been feeding on mushrooms as well. The sound of the deer told Wolfgang it was coming directly toward him, although the animal itself still remained hidden by the trees.

And then Wolfgang saw him: a swollen-necked buck looking for the does. The handsome beast's head was down and its tail pointed straight out.

Wolfgang eased the bow up to full draw and released the wooden shaft. The arrow entered the right side of the deer's rib cage, slanting deeply forward up to the fletching. The deer flinched then kicked into the air. It stood motionless for a heartbeat, and then walked away, seeming confused by what had happened. Wolfgang remained hidden where he was, watching and listening. The buck panicked and raced away through the oak leaves. Wolfgang saw its waving white tail as the animal disappeared from sight.

He followed his prey by listening. In the distance, a squirrel barked its annoyance at the deer, then a blue jay joined in. From the sounds Wolfgang tracked the deer's progress by the changing position of the tattletale.

Wolfgang would wait before following the drops of blood and leaf disturbance. He walked to the spot where the deer had been struck by his arrow.

A tuft of cut brown hair pinpointed where the deer had been. Searching further along the deer's trail, Wolfgang found his arrow on the ground, still intact. It was covered with bubbly, bright red blood, and from habit the hunter smelled it. The arrow had hit both lungs, and hit hard; the deer would soon die. As Wolfgang slowly followed the leaf disturbance, he saw the back of the tracks a little deeper on the uphill side. The deeper side indicated the direction of turn.

After a short distance, the blood trail abruptly ended, but the splayed tracks remained easy to see. The deer had traveled past a distant thick stand of evergreens and kept moving. The tattletale blue jay followed the deer, telling all. With no visible sign now, Wolfgang searched for the animal itself. He moved in close where he could watch and listen into the evergreens from a short distance. He could hear the animal's dying, rustling movements. Wolfgang crouched and peered in every direction, ending by looking ahead. He saw the creature now, and though its eyes had yet to turn green, it was clearly dead.

Wolfgang removed his rifle from his back and leaned it against a tree. Knowing that the smell of the deer as he cleaned it would attract any bears in the area, Wolfgang realized he must work fast. The smell of the animal's carcass would carry for several miles and many hunters had been killed or driven off while field dressing a deer or elk by the arrival of a hungry bear.

* * *

Wolfgang was working when an ominous quiet alerted him to imminent danger. He turned, looked and listened, but heard and saw nothing. He felt the hair on his neck stand up. The whooshing of a branch followed by a crunching of a twig confirmed another presence close at hand, and suddenly Wolfgang heard the dreaded faint sound of quick, heavy rhythmic paws padding directly behind him. He felt their vibrations and heard a tinkling sound. Bear claws! His nose flared, capturing the bear scent.

Wolfgang came upright on shaking legs and reached for the rifle with sweating palms, his heart racing. And there behind him it stood: the grisly spiritual totem, its broad face staring. Its intent was all too plain. The old bear's ears were hardly distinguishable, and Wolfgang froze momentarily to present no threat to the bear. He knew how fast the bear could move, knew also that running would trigger a response to pursue and kill. Wolfgang stood stock-still and averted his eyes, giving the bear a chance to leave. He looked down and let his eyes and index finger softly check the position of the flint in the jaws of his lock. He found the jaws tight and the flint properly positioned.

The yellowish-brown bear stood on its hind legs,

sniffing, slobbering, and glaring at Wolfgang. Its long claws glistened. Then the animal dropped to all fours, and issued a guttural grunt. It cocked its thick, blocky head, lifting its wide, blunt square snout. It coughed and loudly popped its teeth. Its lips curled, displaying its canines in warning, as it loudly sniffed the air. Wolfgang tapped the rifle on the side of the lock to bank the fine priming powder away from the flash hole. The bear's head swung back and forth. Again the beast stood and now began to snort, blow and drool.

As Wolfgang cocked the hammer, he knew he must remain calm: this bear was not about to flee. The stories of the great bear around the camp fires told of an animal that would deliberately stalk and attack without warning. A man hunting alone must be prepared to fight. Wolfgang willed himself to remain still to keep from seeming a threat to the animal, which now tossed its head from side to side in a slow rhythm. A horrible cacophony of snarls and growls building to a deep bawling roar escaped it jaws.

The bear again dropped to all fours, its belly nearly touching the ground. Then it cocked its head, shifting its ponderous weight forward. Its shoulders rippled as it swaggered toward him. Its hair stood on end, and every step was slow and deliberate. It slapped the ground with its paws, while continuing to pop and gnash its teeth. Wolfgang's stomach was sour with terror. Stringy slobber fell from the bear's mouth as its red-flecked, beady eyes stared at him. Seeing the animal's long claws, Wolfgang knew that a single swipe could bleed him dry in minutes. Then it happened.

Huffing loudly, the bear buttoned its ears back against its head, started a low moaning sound that rose to an awesome roar, and suddenly exploded into an attack. With incredible speed, the animal bounded open-mouthed toward him. Wolfgang hoped it was a bluff charge and that the bear would break off at the last second. Too late, Wolfgang saw the animal's accelerating speed and realized this was the moment of impending death. It was a full-scale, single-minded attack.

Wolfgang dropped to one knee and shouldered the rifle in a swift, practiced movement. Knowing that bears died fast if hit in the lethal area, he waited until he was absolutely sure of his shot. A mature bear has a thick hide and chest, and heavy bone structure. Wolfgang concentrated on the tip of the front sight, placing his point of aim just below the jaw. He squeezed the trigger. The pan powder ignited. He saw the .50-caliber ball strike the great beast in the chest just before the smoke puff from the pan charge completely obscured his vision. With a growling roar, the animal jumped to the side, spun around, and then fell and rolled over. It tried to rise but couldn't. Its front legs tore at the ground trying to propel itself forward. Then, screaming in pain, it managed to get up, took its first deliberate step toward him, and then another.

With its big head up, the bear of frightful size walked stiff-legged toward him. Short of breath from fear, Wolfgang worked quickly to reload. His mouth dry and heart pounding, he felt sick. Now the excited bear began a dead run right at him, its shoulders rippling, and foaming saliva flying from its mouth. Only steps away, the bear suddenly stopped, and rose up on his hind legs, looming huge, his paws extended. Wolfgang and the animal stared into each other's eyes. They were perhaps a body's length apart. No longer fully aware of himself, Wolfgang dropped the empty rifle, drew and raised his tomahawk. It was too late. A horrible roar sounded from the bear's open jaws, where its bared teeth showed as long as a man's fingers. Wolfgang moved back as the bear swung its right paw, knocking him down and rolling him backwards. He lost his breath, but raised both hands to try to shield his neck. The eyes of the great beast blazed and Wolfgang felt the animal rolling him over, smelled its foul breath as it bit and tore into him. Blood was everywhere. Wolfgang felt no pain; he felt curiously detached,

The War Trail

aware only vaguely of the claws ripping at his chest and thigh. The last thing he remembered was the fury in the beast's coal-black eyes and a glistening red inside the nostrils. Wolfgang's last thought was of how hot and strongly metallic his own blood tasted in his mouth.

Then, mercifully, he passed out.

* * *

Wolfgang slowly regained consciousness. He felt cold and weak.

Then he felt the pain.

The pain made Wolfgang gasp as it took hold of his arms and ribs. His legs trembled. His face pressed hard against the forest floor, he felt dizzy, and then realized that the bear lay atop him. Wolfgang couldn't move, could barely breathe. With a resigned calmness, he felt the blackness swallow him whole as he passed out again.

When he regained consciousness, he felt aware of a dull, rhythmic pain, which gave way to sharp, fiery pains shooting through his chest. His heart pounded. The bear was still on top of him. *Dead.* Wolfgang felt dizzied by the pain. In a crazy blur of clarity and pain, he saw hands reaching for him, pulling at him. Wolfgang was beyond exhaustion. His mind was reeling and exploding with sharp-pointed lights of pain. His wounded body and mind slipped into a shifting, hallucinatory state. Before he passed out again, in that heightened moment, he saw Indians.

Their breechclouts hung from their fronts and backsides and thigh-length leggings were fastened at the side with thongs and gartered with strips of fur just below the knee. Their moccasins had seams front and back, with large cuff flaps just like those of his old friend who had given him the Wampum belt. Though he couldn't tell how many, all the men were wearing two long braids and a scalp lock with feathers attached. They had facial tattoos. Wolfgang doubted his own perceptions. But these men looked like Delaware Indians -- the "Lenni Lenape," or "real men." It must be a dream. In that solitary moment when he thought he might be dying, Wolfgang watched the sky slip away. He heard the mourning howl of a wolf crushed by despair in the gathering darkness. The low sound rose, lingered and then died away.

Chapter 10

It was December, Moon of Long Nights. A monstrous full moon loomed ominously behind the great trees that towered over a small cabin. Smoke drifted from its rough chimney. Stripped bare and covered with snow and ice, the trees looked arthritic. A stream ran nearby where the white-trunks of birch, aspen, and willows grew.

An Indian runner burst from the forest, bent over and trembling from the hard run, struggling to catch his breath. He had come to speak with the Algonquian medicine woman, a sorceress, endowed with shamanistic powers.

The fearful runner announced himself and waited nervously. He had cause to be frightened: the light shifted eerily across two human skulls, one on each side of the doorway, each fixed atop a slender pole as if to guard the entrance. Their empty, glaring eye sockets and grinning teeth were unsettling. Inside the dark, open doorway, a face appeared to float magically toward him. It was the face of a woman, painted half-gray, half-black, with a black circle around the gray eye and a gray circle around the black one, each representing the moon.

"Speak!" commanded the apparition in a whispered voice.

"Our hunting party found a white man. He has many wounds from a grandfather bear, dead, fallen on top of the man's body. We are bringing him here," the warrior said in a torrent of nervous words. "He will be dead in a short time if you do not help him."

The woman listened silently, staring into the man's eyes. He shifted his weight awkwardly.

"We found an old Delaware seashell wampum belt with the man's possessions. Belt says friendship and peace; the man is a friend to the Delaware. We decided to help him. The hunters carry him a long time on the trail, he is a big man," the messenger continued. "The bear was dead before it could jump up and down on his body and brake all of his ribs." The man's face was a mask of awe at the triumph of a lone man over such a massive animal.

The sorceress listened, then posed but a single question: "Did anyone see a wolf?"

"Yes, a large wolf. It watched from a long distance," replied the runner.

The Sorceress nodded.

She had seen the wounded man in her visions: the one the tribes were calling Okwaho, the Wolf.

Turning from the messenger and returning inside, she took up a leather pouch and threw a handful of chopped, stinging nettle plant into water she had begun to heat for cooking. Stirring the mixture, she removed it from the fire, wanting it to cool by the time he arrived. She placed the metal poker in the fire.

She ground some of the rhizomes and roots of iris and blue flag into powder, and after mixing them with the rhizome powder of May apple and the dried root powders of poke weed and ginseng, she sprinkled the mixture into boiling water. She would use the tea to wash the wounds against infection, and after she had sewn up the man's body, she would apply the rest of the mixture as poultices. Then she soaked some gauze-like material in the strong cold tea made from the stinging nettles. In the event that she used all of the iris root and rhizomes, she also had collected comfrey, good for healing both inside and out, and marigolds, invaluable for open wounds.

Picking up a leather bag of sulfur crystals, the sorceress pounded it with a wooden mallet. The contents shattered easily, and when she was finished, she poured a small amount of the pulverized mineral into a mortar and ground it to a fine yellow powder; this she in turn set in an air-tight wooden container. Her hands worked with a practiced experience, and when the bag was empty, she was ready.

The hunters arrived not long after, looking in through the open doorway at the tall sorceress whose piercing, hooded eyes stopped them short. The four fearful men stood unmoving until she nodded at a reed mattress covered with deer hide. The spell broken, the men labored inside with their burden and laid the wounded man down. The sorceress was amazed at his size; most white men were much shorter. His hair was sun-colored. The sight of him was unsettling, though she could not have said why.

She reached for her sheath knife and began to cut his shirt at the seams, pausing momentarily to admire the remains of the thin, flexible, brain-tanned buckskin shirt and close-fitting deerskin leggings. If he survived he would need a new shirt and leggings, and this way she could obtain his size later.

"You stay," the sorceress ordered. "Help turn him. I will look at his wounds."

The warriors obeyed, fearful at being so close to her.

The wounds had cleansed themselves by bleeding. The sorceress now flushed and washed them with her potent tea. Passing her hand over his mouth, she felt a ragged and shallow breathing. His skin's bright pink color, caused by exposure, told her he was in critical condition, and she carefully checked the inside of his wrist for a pulse which proved weak. The rising and falling of his upper abdomen was a good sign.

"His spirit is strong; he will live," the sorceress told the hunters. She worried that the stranger had lost too much blood from the larger wounds. The mark of the bear, showed across his left cheek, his pale ribs were exposed, and his right thigh was deeply torn. She picked up the metal poker and touched it to the first of his wounds.

"*Fssssss.*"

She cauterized the wounds with a white-hot metal poker.

"*Fssssss.*"

Plumes of smoke rose with each burning as she seared and sealed blood vessels. The cabin soon reeked of burned flesh. In the smaller wounds she placed gauze-like material soaked in stinging nettle tea. Within minutes all the pulsing bleeding would stop. She poured some of the yellow powder into a gourd of hot water and stirred, and continued this until she had a paste. She packed the worst wounds with the paste prior to stitching them up, knowing the paste would help fight infection. She sewed some torn muscle together, closed all his gaping gashes, and wiped away the blood. The hunters, watching with rapt attention, were astounded to see how quickly she had stopped the bleeding, and were further amazed to see how well she had closed the wounds on his chest, shoulders and upper back.

When the golden-haired man briefly regained consciousness, she gave him sips of cool tea made from the powdered iris prepared earlier. The lily-like blue flag flower was good for many internal problems, she knew, its tea having a powerful corrective effect on human tissue. The rest of the tea she applied to his wounds to combat infection. More iris tea would be prepared for him to drink six times a day or whenever he was conscious.

Luckily, during the Moon of Thunder season, she had collected what she now needed most: pine sap. She built up the fire, placing balls of pine pitch atop it to melt, and put water on to boil. She applied the hot pine pitch to the smaller wounds, covering them and letting the pitch harden. *When the pitch hardened and is eventually gone, the wound would be healed.*

At a surprisingly close distance, the sorceress heard a

wolf outside growling. Smiling to herself, she said, "I will help him, Great Spirit."

Every year the sorceress collected her medicine from the soggy soil along and near the stream, where the pale yellow-green leaves grew. She would bleed the trunks of several of the trees and prop a shallow bowl under each of the tree's wounds; she always removed some of the larger limbs -- the willow wood was soft and easily cut -- and from these she would later strip the greenish-brown willow bark to use for bandages. She had cut twigs from the tree and had dug up some of the willow tree roots and had gathered a supply of mature cattail heads and moss. These supplies were all she needed to heal wounded bodies through the winter.

She poured hot water into the bitter sap and forced him to drink the willow bark tea, which would help curb his bleeding, fight the fever and kill the pain. She then set to work cutting up and grinding the tree roots into small particles. She soaked them in boiled water to use to wash his wounds. Along with the blue flag root and rhizome powder for poultices to fight against infection, she had comfrey, Saint John's wort, arnica and horse tail on hand for wounds, and echinacea root powder to combat blood poisoning.

The sorceress pressed the downy fluff from cattails into minor wounds to staunch the bleeding. For others she used the ground-up white-flowered, common yarrow plant to coagulate the blood. Herbal salves were applied to lesser wounds and bound with moss and spider web. Once Wolfgang's wounds were dressed, she began at last to relax. She looked at the hunters and commanded them to leave.

* * *

Wolfgang, no longer conscious, saw himself walking toward a light. He sensed he was in the shadow world. When he saw a horribly wounded man on the ground before him, he looked into the mangled face, and he saw himself near death, a demonic-looking angel hovering above, eating from his body.

"Jesus, hilf mir!" Wolfgang heard the man whisper– "Jesus save me."

Then a bright glow appeared behind the hovering demon and a beautiful, dark-haired angel materialized in its place. Wolfgang knew the man was safe. It all gradually grew dark again.

* * *

The second day Wolfgang slept fitfully. Again he dreamed of the demonic figure, this time dancing among flickering flames. Wolfgang awoke briefly to the sound of an unvarying and slowly beating drum; his mind slipped in and out of delirium, although for a moment his senses focused. He saw a small fire, which barely illuminated another presence. Wolfgang's blurred vision saw the sinister shadow looming above him reaching with cupped hands into the smoke of the flames and pulling the trapped smoke back over her head several times. She was using the smoke to carry her prayer up to the Creator, to help pull the white warrior to her. He wondered if he were still dreaming. At times the figure passed its open hands, palms down, over him while muttering. Wolfgang could make out only a dark, shadowy face illuminated by the glow of lurid tongues of firelight. A woman, he thought.

Her arms and hands stretched to the heavens, she moaned and chanted incantations to conjure up the spirits. She had fed the fire through the night to keep the malevolent spirits away. The sorceress was crying now for his spiritual and physical protection. She worried, and continued chanting to remove the bad spirits from his body and rid the evil wraiths that slithered through the night.

The witch saw his ice blue eyes briefly open and stare. They looked frantic, haunted and desperate, unsure of his surroundings and fully alarmed. She had never seen eyes that color. His face was white, haggard with pain and fatigue, but she knew this would pass. I will use the contents of my little Bearded Man brown jug with the yellow arnica flowers in brandy, but then decided against it: if his pain last long, large amounts would prove poisonous. She periodically turned him on his side and helped him urinate into an animal skin bladder. She examined the contents in the bladder, and saw that it was clear-a good sign. She smelled it and then dipped one finger in it and tasted it. It was not too saline. Another good sign of health!

His body was outlined with a thin red aura. She instinctively knew that he needed something more than a healer in his life. She also knew that if and when he healed, he would need more purpose in his life to continue to survive. She washed his wounds, changed the willow bandages, raised him up, and forced him to slowly drink more willow tea. Shivering, he awoke once, and felt a warm body next to his. Its heat soon put him to sleep again.

At dawn on the third day, Wolfgang regained consciousness. His mind was still a blur. He tried to make everything still inside his head; all parts of his body -- his forehead, cheek, neck, arms, back and chest -- ached. He felt dizzy and sick. His wounds throbbed with a deep, searing pain that exploded in his head. It was pain he had never felt before. He had to swallow to control his stomach and keep it from revolting. The shadow helped him to drink. In agony, he managed to swallow and lost consciousness again. Before his spirit collapsed, the sorceress saw the pain smoldering in his eyes like a fever. She also noticed a small, strange scar on his left arm, about which she would ask later.

* * *

At dawn on the fourth day the birds were singing as Wolfgang woke with a clear head and opened his eyes. He saw a figure sitting next to him. A woman. She was scraping the inner bark away from some twigs before putting them to soak in a separate wooden bowl of hot water. The shifting and dancing light of the fire was behind her, leaving her face partially concealed in shadow. He felt his hair starting to stand on end. He stared, for this was his dream figure. When she turned, lifted her head, and bent slightly forward, he saw her face plainly. There was no indication of emotion on her face, except for a subdued sadness on her unblemished skin.

Then she looked up at him, and their eyes met. She was momentarily watchful, as his gaze locked on her. Her eyes were hard to meet – dark, fierce, and frightening. He felt the strong personal force of her intense and strangely luminous eyes for tantalizing moments and saw the fiery temper to be roused within. He was mesmerized, and found pleasure in the watching. She helped him relieve himself, cleaned him and gave him something to drink. He felt himself become drowsy and then he slept.

He awoke weak from hunger and loss of blood. With his eyes still closed, he could smell the overpowering, musky leaf smells, as if all the smells of the forest and fields were concentrated in the cabin. He opened his eyes and looked around taking the measure of the one-room cabin he was in to be about twenty feet square. The logs fit closely, hewn on two sides and notched on either end to fit flatly against each other. A small amount of clay had been used to ensure the small cabin was air tight, but it had been built quickly. There was the odor of tanned hides all around. The floor was dirt, but covered with a woven reed-mat and on top of these were red summer-killed deerskin hides whose solid hairs were not brittle and could be used as rugs. Instinctively, Wolfgang felt that this was a German-built cabin. There were wooden pegs on the walls all around the room;

a short spear hung together with a small, round shield on one wall, decorated with small patches of braided hair from scalps. The skin side of the scalps was painted half-red, half-black. Nearby stood a quiver full of arrows and a small bow case. Wolfgang saw his rifle and powder horns hung up against the wall as well, with his pack suspended below. He saw no presence of another man.

The woman saw his eyes were open. The haunted and desperate look from the last time he was conscious was now gone; instead, his eyes shone clear and pleasant-looking. She was drawn into their ice-blue depths. His cheeks were pink and looked fresh. She liked what she saw.

He is so young and beautiful.

Wolfgang tried to lift his head up slowly to look down at his wounds, and felt knife-like pains stab through his body. He knew his ribs were cracked, and settled back. It hurt too much to move. From what he could see, the mottled bluish skin of his most severe wounds was packed with a salve made of spider webs and willow oil. The effort of moving had made him dizzy and his head began to throb, and he touched his face and felt where she had sewn his cheek; the area felt hard and crusted but was healing well. He closed his eyes tightly as spasms of pain shot through him; his ribs hurt whenever he took a deep breath.

The upper-chest wounds were wrapped and covered with wide strips of willow bark and doeskin. He was mostly numb and cold though his arms were throbbing. Wolfgang knew he was in the hands of a healer, but he was also aware that among the Indian tribes, a healer was considered just as capable of killing as healing. He knew that he was safe, for she had taken the time to braid a small handful of hair on both sides of his face, to keep it away from his wounds. He could hear the unsettling shifting sound of wind gusting outside, shaking and rushing around the walls and roof, sounding like spirits in distress.

She came to him, leaned forward quickly, and gave him

a foul-tasting drink. Wolfgang was vaguely aware that he was now at the mercy of a spirit form that stared at him. He could feel the sharp, glittering dark eyes, a reflection of the fire that burned with an intense light, as she studied him.

He could see she was tall with long black hair, broad cheekbones, and a patrician nose. Particularly striking were her piercing, vibrant dark eyes – deep brown, with an exotic, tantalizing tilt at the corners that seemed to hold secrets. She had a beautiful, full lower lip, framed by a delicate curved upper lip. He sensed she was strong-willed but not malicious unless provoked. A soft, deerskin dress covered her well-shaped, muscular, voluptuous body. Her breasts were large and showed proud nipples. Wolfgang could not take his eyes from her. The belt at her waist held one large and one small sheathed belt knife, the large blade with an elk-antler handle, and the smaller with a wooden handle.

She is eerily beautiful.

The sorceress observed his staring. She worried that communication would be a problem. Signing with her palm, all fingers extended upward, she turned her hand several times quickly at the wrist, signing. "Question"

"You know Indian sign language?" her hands asked.

Wolfgang clinched his fist and raised his index finger and quickly pointed it downward, meaning: "Yes."

She felt relieved. She looked forward to talking to him. Her hands motioned, saying, Moon, Night, then pointed to herself. Dark Moon. Wolfgang knew the literal meaning. Her name was Dark Moon.

She gestured again: "Question. You called...?"

"Wolfgang," he said.

"What Wolfgang mean?" her hands asked.

Dark Moon was in awe of the rapid movement of his hands, explaining that his name meant "Wolf going before."

Smiling inwardly, she mused, "A warrior whose coming

The War Trail

is announced by the appearance of a wolf."

She pulled the cooked, dark, bear meat out of the fire, and quickly cut it into small pieces. After letting it cool, she dipped each piece in melted bear's fat sweetened with maple sugar. She fed him with his two-pronged fork. Dark Moon mused: Wolfgang's appetite would improve as his pain diminished.

"I have wolf. Hungry. Deer meat. Take outside house," Wolfgang signed. "No see. Wolf there."

She was surprised to see that he worried about his animal. It was a good sign, she thought.

Dark Moon's hands motioned, "You speak Lenni Lenape?" The Lenape were an Algonquin-speaking tribe, her native language.

Wolfgang's hands gestured, "Yes."

She knew he would be here a long time. To her surprise, the thought made her happy. His belly full and his bladder empty, he slept.

* * *

The following day Wolfgang awoke to the fragrance of roasting meat. Dark Moon had killed a large five-foot beaver, which weighed almost 80 pounds. It would make many good meals. She had first quartered the animal then partly cooked it by boiling it in water. She was now roasting it over open coals. The flat, paddle-shaped tail was wider than a hand-span and almost three hands long. Only the base of the tail had hair on it. She had cut the fat tail off for cooking separately and impaled it on a sharp stick over the coals. As Wolfgang watched, the rough, scaly hide blistered and peeled away, leaving a clean white meat.

He enjoyed the sweet, fatty meat, which the healer had flavored with fennel seed and salt. It was soft and tasted like pork. She fed him, alternating between chunks of the tail and cuts from the body. He found the dark-colored body meat moist and delicious. After the meal, she gave him a piece of birch bark to chew on, explaining that it would help protect his teeth. Wolfgang found it quite pleasant.

"Where did you get your supply of salt?" he asked.

"From Shawnee traders who travel north and south from Chillicothe," she replied. "It is a large Shawnee town on the Little Miami River. The best salt springs are near a brine stream called Blue Licks on the South Fork of the Licking River, on the south side of the Ohio River, in Can-tuc-kee."

As she spoke to him, Wolfgang noticed her eyes were no longer hard.

The days shortened and the nights grew longer. It grew colder and one night the wolf appeared at the door. Locking eyes with the woman, the animal entered and stood staring, his eyes fixed on hers, and hers on him, in a silent and still conversation of death. As she looked into the oval, slightly oblique pupils, she knew it was a decisive moment for them both. Neither shrank from the other, but suddenly the exchange was over. The witch motioned with her head toward the door. Wolfgang turned and happily called the wolf to him. It responded, never taking its wild-looking eyes from the witch, and it shook itself vigorously – making both of them laugh at the shower of melted snow that sprinkled them. The wolf lay down next to Wolfgang, facing the woman: The animal seemed perplexed as it gazed from one to the other.

The sorceress, for her part, felt overwhelmed. She had never seen a wolf so large – he was as big as she -- and though he looked dangerous, he seemed also noble and very beautiful -- an animal not to be touched. Dark Moon found herself longing for the unbreakable bond of love, devotion and trust, a psychic bond that she sensed between this man and the wolf.

Dark Moon and Wolfgang continued talking, using

The War Trail

soothing voice and hand movements. She slowly told him scraps of the story of how she had come to this distant place.

"Indians, beyond reach of the white traders and their alcohol, were brave, honorable and religious beings," she began as she fished a large piece of meat from the pot and set it aside to cool. "Occasionally they had sought my help as a healer and as one who escorted the souls of the dead to the other world. My supernatural power is important in the religious rites of the Senaca, Wyandot, Shawnee, Conestoga, Delaware refugees, and larger groups of Miami Indians," she continued.

She put the cooled chunk of meat in front of the wolf's nose. The wolf took it gently. Wolfgang realized that she fulfilled the practical and spiritual needs of these people. The entire culture resorted to the supernatural to explain what they didn't understand. As she paused, Wolfgang told her of the warrior with the snake tattoo on his cheek.

"Iroquois believe it a symbol of wisdom," Dark Moon explained. She continued her story.

"I make sense of the unknown for them, such as weather. Any practiced sky-watcher could do this, by paying close attention to particulars of nature such as the colors of the sky, the moon's phase, clouds, stars, frost, dew on the ground, rainbows and lightning, the feel of the air and the way the smoke from the fire rose, drifted or hangs.

"Other signs in nature included the appearances of rising fish, high-flying or low-flying birds, the sounds of croaking frogs and noisy insects – all of which foretell weather patterns." She explained further. "Promoting the fertility of crops was largely a matter of shifting and clearing other areas to plant corn, squash and beans before the soil in one place became exhausted. A rich diet of good meat, vegetables and the right herbs, on the other hand, led to a longer life. Though simple for those with knowledge, doing these things brought us much prestige – but also much responsibility. Everything that goes wrong is blamed on the medicine man or woman. Many roaming hunters and their families died merely because they did not have access to one of us. Without proper diet, even breaking an ankle or wrist might be a life-threatening situation."

Dark Moon was silent for a moment, and then she continued.

"During the time of the Flower Moon, Strawberry Moon and Buck Moon, I gather medicinal plants needed to treat suffering people. Everything I need grows nearby."

Wolfgang knew that she meant during the summer time. Dark Moon paused to offer another piece of meat to the wolf. It finally stood, licked her hand and fingers, and gently took the morsel. The pause deepened into a long silence, and Wolfgang understood that the story was over for the day.

* * *

As Dark Moon tended to her injured charge, she found that, at long last, she was happy. Wolfgang's presence sent adrenaline coursing through her blood, and she made up her mind about him: he was good -- good for her. Dark Moon knew that dreams were often the shadow of something real, and she was aware that Wolfgang's second dream -- of seeing the evil spirit, or demonic angel as he called it, feeding upon his flesh -- revealed that he was at the turning point between life and death. Wolfgang was in awe of this beautiful woman, and he just sat, looking at her. Dark Moon returned his look stoically, but her spirit was smiling.

As time passed and Wolfgang grew stronger, he began to share some of his own story. Dark Moon would listen quietly as his eyes grew distant in the telling.

"My father was a hunter for the house of Baden. It was a four-floored castle with 105 rooms; it was called Neues Schloss. My father fell out of favor with his sovereign, and we were sold to a contractor for shipment to the penal colonies here in Nouveau Angleterre. Except for the convicts, they called us Redemptioners. We were each sentenced to seven years labor."

Here, Wolfgang's face grew masklike and expressionless.

"Like many others, my father died during the two month voyage, due to contaminated food and stale water. He was thrown overboard. With his death, I had to take on his duties as well -- fourteen years of labor.

"Luckily, because of my size, I was put to work cutting trees and building cabins like this one. Others went south to the sugar cane plantations," he said. "Many of the convict laborers and Redemptioners died of the Ager (malaria and typhoid) and malnutrition. Luckily, the Ohio Company of Virginia gave me the job of hunter before I became sick, thanks to my ability with a rifle. When my opportunity came to escape, I started moving west."

For many nights they talked and listened patiently with one another. Dark Moon told Wolfgang that more English colonists were moving into the land, and that they referred to the Indians as Mingos. The English displayed contempt and dislike for the Indians. Taking advantage of the treaties, they bought or stole land. They exhibited every intention of taking over the whole country. She explained that most of the Indians fought for the French, because they fought only for their fur-trading interest.

Now, however, both were smiling at each other, with the knowledge that the watching wolf had accepted her. The presence of the great wolf reminded Dark Moon of the growling sounds she had heard outside her door while Wolfgang was still unconscious, and she told him about it. Wolfgang smiled.

"Maybe he was guarding your entrance and warning the Azrael, the Angel of Death, to stay away."

Chapter 11

One day, while Dark Moon was boiling hardwood ashes in a pot of water to separate the lye from the pulp, the Delaware hunters who had brought Wolfgang to her passed through again, and stopped to talk. She noted their obvious fright when the wolf came from the cabin to stand beside her, its glare fixed on them as she motioned for them to be seated. None of them had ever been this close to a live wolf before. The animal added a powerful spiritual dimension to the mystique surrounding her and Wolfgang.

Dark Moon told her listeners that Wolfgang was also an animal – a two-legged man-bear and that he could change at will. Dark Moon fed the warriors' superstitious minds with this tale, knowing that the Delaware would recount this story to others, and that it would travel all over the country from campfire to campfire, growing with each retelling. She was hoping that with this growing renown, there was less chance of harm coming to Wolfgang in the future. They believed that she could even control the weather by bringing or stopping rain and snow storms, and that she could foretell events, such as his coming. Dark Moon also told everyone that she had just received word from those who secretly kept her informed that a great war had already started in the east, where the tribes aligned with the French were now burning the English forts and American colonies. Upon hearing this news, the Delaware knew they must return to their village. When they were gone, Dark Moon added raccoon fat and soapwort to the lye, and let it set for an hour. She was pleased with the response her tale had received.

"The center of Iroquois power is in the central position of the Onondaga nation," Dark Moon said, after the men had gone. "Distance offers no protection because their territory extends from the Saint Lawrence River in Canada to New Orleans in the south. To be safe, we have to go beyond the Mississippi River."

She saw that this information troubled him. Wolfgang remained silent. Dark Moon changed the subject then, and began recounting more of her own past. She had inherited her calling from her mother, Star-Watcher, who had been feared and resented for her power. This name was close to her mother's real name, but her real name was no longer spoken: to say it would disturb her mother's spirit. The daughter of a chief, she was well known for her strong medicinal powers and supernatural visions. Nothing was hidden from her. Everyone, including strangers, recognized her by the stars on the upper front and back of her dress. Although her family lived in a longhouse of logs, she preferred to live in a private *tipi*. After the death of her husband, people stayed out of her way. Whenever there was an incident with an animal, bird, or reptile, the people believed that it was Star-Watcher, who transformed herself back and forth. Out of a deep-seated fear of witches, they made plans to kill her, but a friend told her of these plans.

" One night, when the village knew that I was supposed to be with my grandfather in the long-house, they set fire to my mother's tipi to burn her alive. They listened to her screams, and later watched my grandfather bury her remains on the site of the tipi and erect a monument over her grave. No one knew she had escaped. It was one dark night not long after during the new moon when many sat gathered around a communal fire. My mother Star-Watcher suddenly made an appearance. Standing in the dark at the edge of the light, she beckoned to me. Having been told of this scheduled appearance beforehand, I silently joined her, and together we disappeared into the darkness. Throughout all the Indian country, the story has been repeated that Star-Watcher was resurrected by supernatural beings, and was escorted back to the world of the living. As we traveled south into the Ohio Valley, everyone stood in awe of us, knowing that my mother had control over good and evil forces. Those who encountered us modified their own behavior accordingly. She chose this isolated area to live alone with me. When people needed her help, they came to her and she gave it. As thanks, lone hunters often stopped and hung a deer or left choice cuts of meat in a place they would be easily seen. Now that my mother is in the spirit world, I continue on in her place."

Seeing that Wolfgang still remained silent after the story, Dark Moon signed, "What are you thinking about?"

"About the story you told. You said you were supposed to be with your grandfather," replied Wolfgang.

Dark Moon smiled.

"I was being initiated into the secret Midewiwin Society, the highly ritualized Grand Medicine Society. It makes contact with the spirit world and assures the well-being of the tribe," she said. She touched the distinctive beaded medicine bundle she always wore around her neck. "People recognize us by these. They hold our personal talismans. Our medicines have special powers, as you already know."

"Why were you picked?" Wolfgang asked.

"Because of my dreams and visions," Dark Moon replied.

* * *

Several days later, Dark Moon was examining

Wolfgang's wounds. The twisted flesh was now healing into yellow, pale blue, and reddish scars. His facial features had returned as the swelling had resided, but the scars would always show. As she re-applied the bandages, a messenger arrived inviting them to a special event.

Though Dark Moon knew Wolfgang was still weak and needed to rebuild his strength and flexibility, she decided he was fit enough for walking. It would be excruciating and exhausting for him, and he would have to walk hunched over with his sore ribs, but she would help steady him.

The Indian led the two to a large clearing, big enough to hold all the villagers. Wolfgang's interest turned to surprise as he beheld a straight, strong fifteen-foot post that had been set firmly in the ground with many tomahawked heads, mostly old, mounted on poles surrounding the area. He knew that the Delaware were going to torment and torture someone. He felt deeply distressed, knowing that he would have to hear and watch some prisoner's terror and pain. He noticed a fire burning a short distance away. Many long fagots had been arranged in a circle, one end pointing in toward the fire.

Dark Moon told him that those six-foot long fagots were hickory sticks that had already been burnt through. She saw his hand trembling, and could tell that he was distressed.

"You must put up with watching, for this is what happens when one is captured by the wrong people," she said firmly, catching the look of his uneasy, shifting eyes and stiffened face. "The ritual of torture is intended to give the victim the opportunity to display his courage and resolve. The heads on the poles represent those who were lucky. They were tomahawked. The rest are kept and used as slaves in and around the principal Lenni Lenape village of Goschachgunk."

Not long afterward came the echoing of yelps off to his left. The heads of the crowd turned, staring, eyes flashing brightly with excitement in the firelight. They slowly parted amid much shouting. A frightened, visibly shaken naked prisoner was brought forth. The coal-blackened captive was struck and beaten by everyone he passed. Being painted black meant he was condemned to death by torture. He was a white man of thin build and medium height, with brown hair. His wide, panicked eyes shone in the firelight as he anticipated the nightmare ahead.

"He's British. His fingernails had been burned out," said Dark Moon, adding that the first joint of each finger had then been amputated with a clamshell and that afterward the warriors had lacerated the stubs of his fingers with their teeth. As the chief gave a short speech, Wolfgang could see the captive was glistening with sweat despite the cold night. Dark Moon watched his jaws clench, his lips close tight and his eyes turn gray.

Now the Delaware began beating the man with sticks and fists. Dark Moon explained that after capture, this white man had been brought to the village, and was discovered as a known killer of peaceful Delaware Indians further to the east. He had killed women and children. His slow burning was to appease the spirits of those he had killed. Then the assembled warriors loaded their muskets with just powder, each man to fire it at the captive. Wolfgang heard the Delaware chanting repeatedly.

"Revenge."

He knew that having been dispossessed of their lands, the tribe had been forced to move further and further west. Many who had refused had been killed. Only a few of those who had worked with the British and Americans had escaped. The Delaware here now were intent on revenge.

The first powder-shots were at the captive's feet and they progressed up to his neck while he danced around, unable to break through the circle of his tightly knotted tormentors. The powder burns left red, raw bleeding wounds. The Delaware watched with delight, their eyes wide and their mouths open, as they loudly mimicked their captive's every sound with great enthusiasm. When the blubbering victim finally collapsed,

Wolfgang heard a smiling warrior ask loudly in good English how the captive felt. Then three warriors approached the doomed man.

    Wolfgang saw one warrior cut off an ear. The weeping prisoner lost control of his bladder and bowels. His urine flew in every direction, while his bowels released excrement that soiled his legs. The crowd was greatly amused. Many mockingly held their noses and laughed. The second warrior then cut off the other ear. The last one knocked the captive to the ground, grabbed him by his queue and cut it off. He quickly grabbed a handful of hair at the top of his head, and with two quick circular thrusts with his knife, loosened the skin. With one foot against the man's shoulder, he swiftly pulled the scalp loose from the top of the head with the loud characteristic flopping sound, scalping him. The abundant blood vessels in the rest of the scalp sent rivulets of red running down the victim's face and onto his chest and back. A savage noise echoed through the air as the warrior lifted his face to the sky, raising his tomahawk in one hand and the scalp in the other to the sky.

    "Aaawwwwooohhhhhhh."

    The sound was quickly taken over by a delighted chorus of other warriors, which echoed through the clearing: *"Aaawwwwooohhhhhh."* The latter part of the scalp halloo rose to a higher octave than at the beginning.

    The prisoner sat up, blood streaming down his torso. His eyes were wide open and his lower lip twitched visibly with acceptance of his fate. Wolfgang could see the victim's pulse pound in his neck as the warrior shook the blood from the scalp in his face. The Delaware were screaming in delight, feeding on his pain and suffering. In shocked silence, Wolfgang forced himself to watch. His senses tingled as he felt the short hairs on the back of his neck rise.

    "His scalp will be treated, strung, and stretched on a black hoop," explained Dark Moon inexorably. "A yellow flame

The War Trail

will be painted on the skin side to show he was burned alive."

The captive's hands were bound behind him. He was taken to stand in the center of the watching crowd. Four large women held him down briefly, while a fifth moved in quickly and with a long knife removed his genitals. The skin of his testicles would be made into a souvenir pouch. When the laughing women were finished, several warriors took turns, cutting small pieces of flesh from the victim and eating it before him or giving it to the dogs to eat. The crowd imitated each scream of his until it was drowned by the rage and fury of the crowd. One end of a long rope was tied to the post and the other end to the ligature between his wrists. The white man was able to move around the post two or three times and return the same way. The Delaware went to the fire and took up the fagots with one end burning brightly. On every side of the prisoner the Delaware, one after another, applied the burning ends of the fire sticks to his body. Even the cronish old women excitedly took part. His genital area, buttocks, armpits and back of his knees were favored targets. He ran around the pole in an attempt to escape, much to the captors' delight. He ran as far as the rope allowed and back again. The Delaware allowed him to run and dance for their entertainment.

Now wood was brought, assembled in a great pile and placed in a circle four feet beyond the upright pole. Branches were covered with pitch and animal grease. Dark Moon explained that this distance would greatly prolong the captive's slow-roasted torture. The squaws carried boards of coals from the fire and threw them over the top of his head. Other squaws threw them at him. Soon the victim's running area between the pole and the ring of dead wood was carpeted with live coals. Wherever he moved, the soles of his feet were burned. As he hopped about, the Delaware roared with delight.

Wolfgang wanted to shoot the man, but Dark Moon warned, "Show nothing on your face. Watch. This punishment must be burned into your memory if you wish to survive," she continued. "The victim failed the test of the gauntlet, because he was a weakling. If he had been brave, they would have eventually killed him and eaten his heart in order to transfer his bravery to themselves."

Finally, torches were thrust at the outer branches. Wolfgang heard the crackle of dry wood catching fire. He saw the great circular pile of wood burning four feet out from the pole. Soon the flames were licking hungrily around the prisoner's feet while his eyes were smarting and tearing. He started hacking and coughing, as his throat grew tight. Struggling for breath, doubtless dizzy, the prisoner shuddered from the rolls of harsh, acrid, heat searing smoke. Wolfgang heard a peculiar, hair-raising animalistic sound, faint and distant, beginning to build from the searing pain of the captive's burning lungs. It became sharp and shrill, then erupted into high-pitched screams of hideous pain and agony. The man was outlined in the heart of the swirling flames. Tongues of lurid yellow-orange flames were leaping and glimmering all around the circle, the reflection lighting the amused faces of the watching and mimicking crowd. Oily, black smoke charred the air. The high-pitched wailing of the man now rose higher and higher, dominating the roar of the flames. His pleading, stinging eyes briefly burned into Wolfgang's as he danced grotesquely in a frenzy of panic and excruciating pain. The warriors pantomiming the sounds and movements of the victim now became more excited and animated.

There was a brilliant flare as the prisoner's remaining hair fluttered up and caught fire. His head was briefly surrounded by a halo of gold as his screams began to subside. His skin blistered and burst. The intense heat and smoke from the blazing inferno was beginning to envelope the captive. Pillars of hellish, crimson flames burned hot and glowed radiantly. Pitching and dancing, the wild flames leapt high. Smoke shot up as the crackling fire started to consume and blacken the lower part of his body. The skin on his thighs cracked and oozed blood. The faint, sick-sweet smell of raw meat cooking filled the air. The screaming sound of hell and the fire became a continuous roar, as ash and flying sparks drifted and floated upward. The Englishman somehow still stood, his fire-blackened arms lifted upward. The melting palms of his hands were hanging down to his forearms. His steaming shoulders and torso were twitching, bubbling, blistering and growing black. His face was now badly burned. He was already blind. The pain already destroyed his mind. The still-living body fell and rolled over and over, trying to escape the excruciating pain. For a moment, the screaming torment ended. Then he got up again amid the vibrant pillar of flames. There was only the silent vision of an open-mouthed head frozen in place. His eyeballs exploded. Wolfgang realized the man's nightmare was almost over as he finally crumpled into the wall of flames. Then to Wolfgang's surprise the writhing captive got up and start walking blindly around the pole again as if unaware of the pain. There was now the strong smell of burning flesh in the air.

Now began the incessant rhythm of drums. Delighted and howling, the Delaware were watching and smelling. Their shadowy faces dimly lit by the flames. Some started a frenzied dance around the flames, flailing their arms and legs wildly and pumping their feet in ritualistic rhythm. The fire had risen to a roar amid the fearful and blood-chilling war cries of the possessed warriors.

Wolfgang could hear the heavy, rhythmic stamp of feet and the rattling sound of deer hooves tied around the waists of many warriors shaking the night. They lunged with lances and raised their tomahawks to the ferocious hammering beat of their deep-voiced drum as they felt the power of the sound. The Englishman finally sank to a kneeling position, remained that way for some moments, and then pitched forward, sending the red-hot embers flying in all directions. Flames leapt around the blackened form until -- pop! The sound came of his head exploding. Eventually, as the fire died, all that was left were the charred bones of arms and legs that had drawn up blackened, almost indistinguishable from the fuel itself--the remains of a body that had been burned beyond recognition. The Delaware were still dancing with a promise of the war to come as Dark Moon and Wolfgang finally left. The fire had died down to glowing coals and just a few flickering yellow flames and smoke.

* * *

The rest of the cold winter, Wolfgang motivated by the man burned at the stake, worked at regaining his strength and getting himself fit. He felt more determined than ever that his enemies must be shown no mercy. He was determined not to allow himself or Dark Moon to be taken.

Dark Moon told Wolfgang that the people of the Indiana and Illinois country were preparing for war together with the French, who had established a line of forts and farms from Quebec to New Orleans in order to secure the Ohio valley as a right-of-way to their Mississippi trading posts and block British and American expansion. A Catawba Indian named Tanacharison, a leader of the Delaware Indians in the Allegheny-Ohio country had started a war with the Virginian George Washington, by killing a French officer, Ensign Coulon de Jumonville de Villiers. The Delaware had lost their lands because of the man named William Penn, and now their chief, Teedyuscung of the western Susquehanna Delaware, was raiding isolated white settlers in those areas.

* * *

The two maintained a quiet existence, hunting with their bows and trapping together through the winter and spring. It was a happy time. Dark Moon's skill was greater than Wolfgang's in most things, except for the rifle. Many times at night he took the opportunity to instruct her in its usage, teaching her the importance of cleaning the bore soon after firing, and explaining how the corrosive salts in fired black powder combined to draw moisture and would rust the barrel, making cleaning very difficult. He showed her how the action of some flintlocks fires faster than others, showing her how to test the mainspring that powers the lock and to check for gaps in the pan and frizzen cover. He told her that the most accurate rifles fired instantaneously, because their parts were in good condition.

He demonstrated the intricate process of loading the rifle, putting two lead balls in his mouth and pulling the plug out of the horn with his teeth, pouring powder from the horn into a hollowed out bone that served as a measure. He cupped the muzzle with one hand and poured the powder with the other, let it drop, lifted the horn and reinserted the plug with his teeth. Centering a tallow-greased patch over the muzzle, he leaned over, spat a ball into it, and pressed it down into the muzzle with his thumb. Then he pulled his ramrod and in three measured strokes, seated the ball, pointing to the mark on the ramrod that indicated the ball was properly seated.

As Dark Moon watched Wolfgang's measured movements, she realized that his commitment to mastery of the rifle was deeper than any man's she had ever seen. There was something different about this man. She found herself aware of his every gesture, and felt how his presence made her heart beat faster.

It was the beginning of April in 1756 that Wolfgang realized they must leave before the Iroquois came looking again.

Chapter 12

Already up and down the Appalachian Mountains families had vanished. Redemptioner homesteads had been burned to the ground, crops and livestock, destroyed when Wolfgang and Dark Moon returned to the village to trade her cabin for horses. She decided that they would trade for three animals. The third one would be used as a pack animal to transport their few belongings and Wolfgang's captured weapons. Those weapons would make excellent trading material in the French fort at Vincennes on the Wabash River.

* * *

Dark Moon studied all the available horses for a long time. Turning her attention briefly to Wolfgang, she said, "When trading or stealing horses, it is important to watch and observe which horses are friends, because they will occasionally be tied to one another. If they fight and stay mad at each other for a long time, they will wind up throwing our pack load all over the country and destroying what little we have. We must always talk nicely to them to gain and keep their confidence and trust." She was silent for a long time as he observed her and the horses. Again looking him in the eyes, she said, "An ill-mannered horse is dangerous to handle." Finally, Dark Moon centered her attention on just three animals and pointed them out to him.

Wolfgang saw that the three she had chosen were sturdy looking and thick in the body with especially strong straight legs. "Why those three horses," asked he. "They stand quietly, a good sign that they will be little trouble on the trail." Wolfgang watched and listened to her approach the first animal talking to it. *HUNH. UN-hunh. Unhunh. Unhunh.* He was stunned as he saw the horse answer her by lowering its head to her hand. As he watched, Dark Moon put her nose and mouth to that of the horse. Then she was again talking very low as she slowly and closely walked around the horse with one hand on its back where she could see Wolfgang. She said in the same low voice, "I checked its back with a light but firm pressure to see if it would drop. We can ride this horse bareback." She ran her hands down each leg and picked up each hoof. She straightened up, and looking again at him, said. "A packhorse must have short, wide cannon bones and short, moderately-sloped pasterns. One with long pasterns will cripple more quickly than one with short pasterns. He must not be too large or too small, have well-defined withers, well-developed hindquarters and a short back."

Dark Moon again went and faced the horse. Then she easily opened its mouth to check its teeth. Taking its lead rope, she walked each horse forward on cue with a clucking sound and a gentle pull. She again cued the horse to stop with a slight tug. She repeated the entire process with each horse. Wolfgang watched closely everything she did with each horse. Then Dark Moon took the large leather ropes off. From around her neck she grabbed one end of the dry single rope she had hanging there with her right hand and carefully shifted it around to the back of her arm. She placed her arm over the horse's neck and let the line drop from her hand, reached down with her left hand and secured it with a tie around the neck behind the jaw. She then twisted the running end one complete turn and lifted it over the horse's muzzle as a nose loop. "This is your rope halter." She said. "When the lead end is pulled pressure is transferred to the neck loop. Before packing and unpacking, you tie the horses up short and high to a tree."

Dark Moon selected a sawbuck packsaddle made from the forks of elk horns with carved wooden side bars. It must be padded to keep from rubbing and making sores up the back of the animal. "In hilly country this breast collar will prevent the pack from riding back on the horse." When she walked back, she hooked up the britchen strap and said. "This will keep the pack from sliding forward when going downhill." Then she cinched the animal up. Picking up two side packs, she hung an empty one on the on each side. "When you pack these bags, they must balance so they will ride evenly. Anything you put in them must not rattle. Anything that will rattle must be padded. Otherwise, the horses will spook and take off at a full run, and throw all the gear over a period of miles, until they stop running from fright." After they completed their trade for the animals, Dark Moon tied the packhorse in to her mount and told Wolfgang to follow behind the pack animal at a distance and to watch.

* * *

Dark Moon led the horses back to the cabin through all the muddy spots and creeks along the way. She was happy to find that the horses did not side step. When they approached a stream, the horses did not show any signs of anxiety. They did not balk at the unfamiliar water crossing either. She was happy that the animals did not focus on their feet but kept their head and attention on the intended direction. She knew they would present no trouble on the long trail ahead, because they all had a steady gait.

* * *

Dark Moon showed Wolfgang a small piece of rope

spliced back into its other end. "When you put the horses out to graze, you lift one front hoof, put it through the loop, twist the rope three or four times and place the other hoof in the loop at the other end. The horses can move around, but slowly, and cannot roam too far." She showed him many mufflers for the horse's feet to eliminate deep tracks and sound, which would otherwise warn of the presence while moving. Giving him a serious look, she said, "You must become adept at watching the ears and turn of a horse's head. They will see and warn you of a strange and threatening presence if you pay close attention. Watch me closely and I'll show you how to mount a horse quickly." She grasped the horse's mane and rope rein with her left hand at the withers while bracing her left forearm against the horse. Facing to the rear, she took one quick step with her left foot and used her momentum to swing her right leg up and over the hindquarters. Wolfgang was surprised at how easily he mounted by using her method. "To dismount safely," Dark Moon continued, "You put your weight onto your hands, swing your right leg up, back over to clear the horse and slide down on your right hip, then land on both feet facing forward." Following her instructions, he dismounted and grinned. Dark Moon said, "An elk hide pad will provide a better grip for a well-balanced ride, as long as you maintain shoulder, hip-and heel-alignment, and use your thighs to maintain balance."

* * *

The wolf traveled the trail ahead at a short distance and would return only when there was a dangerous presence. Dark Moon would stop the horses, lead them into cover and stay with them if he returned. Using a brushy tree drag to eliminate tracks, Wolfgang brought up the rear. He watched their back trail, cleaned up and disposed of any horse droppings along the way. They left as little sign of their passing on the trail as possible.

Dark Moon thought that Wolfgang was an "instinctive" hunter with a mystical awareness of what went on around them at all times, and was well pleased with this man. They would stop early enough to cook, while it was still daylight, so that at night they could go without a fire. They were well armed and vigilant.

Chapter 13

It was an early afternoon in late July of 1756, the time known to the Indians as the Buck Moon. Wolfgang and Dark Moon, who had been traveling through the rolling woodlands for nearly four months, crested a tall hill to behold a breathtaking panoramic view. Bare hills rose in the distance, the land stretched before them, and to the northwest hung a haze of smoke over what must surely be a large village.

"The Piankashaw Indian village of Chippecoke sits on the east bank of the River. The French call it the Ouabache River. The Miamis call it waapasshsiki siipiiwi - 'bright white' river. The English call it the Wabash River. Vincennes is in the chain of forts established by the French from Quebec to New Orleans. It is located at the site of the village. The Piankashaw are an Algonquian speaking tribe. Across the river is the Illinois country," said Dark Moon, pointing at that direction.

The travelers felt heartened to think they might soon rest. Upon leaving the forest, they traveled past fields of livestock where crops of corn, wheat, squash, beans and tobacco told them most of the men would be out hunting buffalo. Dark Moon was delighted to observe deer and blackbirds around the cornfields. At this time of year, it indicated that the young cobs were in the milk stage, when their moisture content is the highest. The silking strands of corn were being wind pollinated. Continuing onward, the travelers reached the Indian village at last. Across the river lay the Illinois country. They planned to cross in October when the water was slower and at its lowest level; this would leave a natural barrier between themselves and any would-be pursuers.

"The Piankashaw belong to the allied tribes of the Illinois Confederacy. The main bands of the Illinois are the Miami, Piankashaw, Kaskaskia, Kahoki, Michigami, Wea, Peoria, and the Mascouten," said Dark Moon, proudly reeling off the list

They continued onward to the village. Upon entering its outskirts, Dark Moon and Wolfgang saw perhaps three-dozen tipis and a lesser number of cabins. Tribeswomen who had been tending their chores moments earlier -- carrying water in buffalo-skin bladders, squatting to scrape hides, thrashing seeds and tending fires to dry strips of meat -- all stopped to stare.

Dark Moon approached a stocky woman who stood beside a fire.

"Where chief's tipi?" she signed.

The woman pointed, but said nothing.

Wolfgang and Dark Moon made their way to the center of the village, where a large tipi rose taller than the rest.

"There," said Wolfgang.

* * *

Wolfgang and Raven Wing, the medicine man summoned by the chief, smoked in silence. Now Wolfgang handed the well-worn wooden pipe back to his host with both hands. Dark Moon sat inside the tipi's entrance patiently, respectfully, as befitted a woman in such company.

When Raven Wing had had enough silent reflection, the chief spoke: "What brings you here?"

"My woman and I are traveling west," Wolfgang began. He told them the length of their journey, their destination, and their adventures so far.

Dark Moon noted the expressions on the Indians' faces as they looked upon his scarred visage; the listeners' eyes made it clear that they were impressed.

Wolfgang finally said: "We left our horses in a secluded area to the northeast, beside a creek. May we camp there?"

The chief nodded.

"May we also collect corn?" Dark Moon added. When asked why, she replied promptly: "For food and medicine. While the young cobs are in the milk stage, the corn silk is ground into powder. The powder will help the aged pass water."

She saw that she had impressed the old medicine man with her knowledge and made an influential friend, as she had intended.

"There's a smallpox outbreak among the Delaware due east," said the medicine man abruptly, eyeing the pair with suspicion. From the visitors' obvious surprise, he seemed reassured that neither carried the scourge. Then Dark Moon said: "This white man cannot catch the smallpox. A scar on his left arm protects him."

The old man's eyes became wide in surprise.

"Can this be true?"

Dark Moon assured him that it was. "But only the white man has this medicine," she added. The chief and the medicine man looked at each other. "This is powerful medicine," said the chief. The medicine man's eyes suddenly grew large and a smiled creased his face. He turned and spoke briefly to the chief whose eyes suddenly came up and studied Dark Moon and Wolfgang. "Now we know who you both are. It is better that no one else knows of your presence." said the chief. The medicine man continued to smile and stare.

"You must travel with great stealth, for the Iroquois are everywhere," the tribal healer warned. "They destroy whole villages, torturing and killing. They take women as slaves and raise young children as Iroquois."

"This man has outwitted Iroquois trackers before," replied Dark Moon. "We'll be very careful."

The conference over, Wolfgang and Dark Moon made ready to leave. Before the two departed, the medicine man pronounced solemnly, looking at Wolfgang: "You are a man of great spiritual power."

* * *

Dark Moon felt especially pleased to see that in several abandoned, overgrown fields nearby, wild buckwheat grew. She knew that grinding the little black seeds would yield delicious flour for battering meat and fish, but she also knew that she and Wolfgang must not remain here long. Sometime before the harvest the men would return from hunting buffalo in the northwest. After the crops of corn, beans and squash had been gathered, many of the Indians would scatter into their assigned areas of the surrounding country to live and hunt in small family groups through the winter. The area they camped in would be too crowded for safety.

* * *

The late afternoon shadows had grown long when Dark Moon put water on to boil. She found her hand-net and large basket and moved to the creek. Picking a number of ramp flowers whose seeds she knew she could use later. She approached the shallow bank and listened: the hardly audible dainty *"sip,"* and louder *"slurps."* Then aggressive *"roll."* Fish were feeding on the surface of the water. She watched a soft, slow, slurring sound of a wake moving across the surface of the water. She wandered on the bank a little, picking some leeks for seasoning, until she saw small burrow chimneys rimming the shore. Recognizing these as made by crayfish, she knew it would be a good starting point for her search for dinner. A woodpecker banged on a snag nearby. Hearing no other sound, Dark Moon let her eyes study the loosely piled debris in the water.

Patiently she watched the shallow water. There was a sharp disturbance. Squinting through the sun's glimmering reflection, she discerned a large carp digging for crayfish. A sudden pumping action and one of the smaller fan-tailed creatures shot backwards, leaving a trail of mud puffs as it darted out of the cloud to escape danger.

Dark Moon tossed her fish net and trapped the fish.

Other mud puff trails led to an overgrown grassy embankment. Suddenly Dark Moon spied a large crayfish, big enough to cover the length of her hand, moving slowly, toward the darkness. Crayfish shunned daylight, hiding from larger finned predators under the bank in the grass hanging into the water; there they would remain until night, when they came out to forage. Dark Moon watched the four legs on each side move, the menacing claws poised at the ready.

Now she unrolled her net, five-hand-spans wide. Large sticks at both ends provided handle grips. She moved into the waist-deep water and carefully approached the grassed-over bank. Her arms at her sides, the net before her, she slipped it into the water beneath the grass, and brought it slowly up in short, upward pumping motions until it cleared the water. Large and small crayfish wriggled atop it. Folding the net in half, she returned to the bank and transferred her catch to the basket. There was still enough light to make a second trip and she entered the water again. She and Wolfgang would not go hungry.

Ready to go, Dark Moon stood. But suddenly a great stillness enveloped her and then -- blackness.

Her eyes rolled back into her head.

And now her mind saw the shadows of figures: a large woman wearing a hat... a tall man... a much smaller man... and a third man wearing a wolf's cap. How long the images remained she could not have said, but when the light finally returned, the sky had gone a deeper hue and leaves skittered across the ground.

Dark Moon was afraid, but she would say nothing to Wolfgang until she knew more.

* * *

The following day, while the wolf was away roaming, Wolfgang and Dark Moon set out for the trading post. Since early morning, she had been plagued by a sense of impending trouble borne from the previous day's vision.

En route they came upon a warrior. Recognizing him as a Shawnee, Dark Moon asked him the location of the French fort. Pointing down river, the Shawnee replied that it was named Poste de Vincennes. Once they had left him, she whispered to Wolfgang that she had been surprised to see the Shawnee since the tribe was known to be hostile toward the French.

As the two walked, they saw many flatboats being poled along the river near the shoreline. They had been told that some of the bateaux going up river were transporting lead to Lake Erie from Kaskaskia on the Mississippi River. Pointing out an Indian with a roach and small red feather dangling in the back, Dark Moon explained: "He's a Miami warrior. Do you see the way he wears only a red breechcloth and moccasins with a central seam in the front? This is their way of dressing during summer."

Upon nearing the fort, Wolfgang was surprised to see rows of whitewashed houses along the banks of the Wabash River. The travelers passed a log structure, which evidently served as the Basilica of St. Francis Xavier. Here Jesuit priests stood talking earnestly to Indians. Wolfgang and Dark Moon saw a stone church being built by Indian slaves that belonged to the Jesuits. A number of horses stood tied at the trading post, their tails swishing.

Chapter 14

Wolfgang and Dark Moon entered the French fur-trading outpost, set two of their captured rifles on the counter for trade, and stood still, waiting for their eyes to adjust to the gloom.

Gradually they made out the shop sutler, his clerk, and a group of four people -- three men and a woman -- sitting at a table with a deck of playing cards. Wolfgang wasted no time on pleasantries.

"These rifles are for trade for items we need: powder, lead bars for making bullets, and linsey-woolsey cloth," he said.

"They are valuable," the sutler replied, gazing appreciatively at Wolfgang's well-made rifles.

The sutler looked hard at his scarred face and seemed startled by both the stranger's imposing stature and his unmistakable aura of self-assurance. But it was the rifle carried by Wolfgang that the French sutler noted most.

Most men carry only muskets -- and cheap, poorly made, ineffective weapons at that. Rifles are valuable: in the hands of a skilled marksman, they were much more accurate than muskets, and from a longer range.

The sutler knew that on the frontier there were three kinds of guns: military guns, trade guns, and a third, least-common kind -- rifles of superior quality. The two rifles for trade were of superior quality. He could see the rifle the German carried was an instrument of rare quality, excellently forged, its frizzen bridled and its furniture cast in brass -- clearly made for rugged survival conditions. The rifles offered for trade were fine weapons that would fetch a good price, but he itched to get his hands on the German's rifle.

Then the sutler eyed Dark Moon, who was taller than most men. Her glittering eyes -- at once piercing and hooded, showing no emotion -- remained inscrutable.

Turning once again to Wolfgang, the storeowner motioned for a clerk to wait on them as the clerk put away scalps he had just bought. Wolfgang knew that both the English and French sought after scalps; the British paid forty pounds, but Wolfgang had no idea what the French paid.

Walking up close to the clerk, Wolfgang looked into his face. The clerk saw the fierce, ice-cold blue eyes within that lean, strong face, and felt unsettled – it was like staring into the visage of a beast of prey. The clerk swallowed nervously, and blurted the first words that came into his head.

"Are you German?"

Wolfgang offered no response.

"I thought you might be from one of the two German communities down on the Arkansas River," the clerk continued. "Ahh... what brings you here?"

To Dark Moon's surprise, Wolfgang replied in fluent French: "Trying to stay away from the British and Americans."

That was all the encouragement that the talkative clerk needed. Immediately he plunged into a monologue, explaining that soldiers, traders, farmers, and Jesuit missionaries from Canada had settled into this village in 1702, and that the Frenchmen had built cabins and married Indian women. Wolfgang pointedly started perusing the trading post's shelves. The oblivious clerk continued to chatter, about how the English and Americans used their allies the Chickasaw, Creek and Cherokee to disrupt French trade routes, and about the capture and burning of the French fort of Vincennes by the peaux rouges. Only half-listening to the clerk's patter, Wolfgang let his eyes roam the room. He noted closely the big man and his three companions at the card table. The tough-looking woman wore a perpetual grimace. The big man seemed to be studying Wolfgang's rifle, its lock and barrel excellently forged, its frizzen and its furniture cast in brass.

Turning his attention back to the clerk, Wolfgang felt troubled to hear of so much warfare in this new land, but he and Dark Moon were here for supplies. He pointed at linsey-wool clothing. Made of linen blended with wool, it was perfect for wearing beneath buckskin clothing during winter. He also selected an adze, a frow and mallet, and a double-bited axe -- all indispensable tools. Next he chose two carved wood porringers from which he and Dark Moon could eat, along with a slender, pointed iron spit for roasting meat over a fire; a metal wedge for splitting wood and logs; a bullet mold; some tallow candles; and some Carolina Gold rice and fancy Castile soap. Finally, indicating some small, carved wood drinking cups and a small coffee mill, he told the clerk to hold these items until he returned for them later.

Feeling Dark Moon's light touch at his sleeve, Wolfgang turned to see her nod at a shelf that held an assortment of neatly cut pieces of tree bark, all of them labeled.

"Which do you want?" asked he.

When she pointed at one, he read the label, "Jesuits' bark" in French. "For fever," she explained.

"How much do you need?" he asked.

She lifted her right forearm, palm down, and moved it in a tight horizontal circle from right to left. All! Wolfgang looked back at the clerk and said in French, "Tout."

She caught Wolfgang's eyes and knew that he was bewildered.

"It's from the cinchona tree in Bolivia. Ground into

powder, it yields the highest quinine content for the most resistant cases of malaria," said the clerk, looking at Wolfgang.

Dark Moon also pointed out some fist-sized brownish and yellow crystals.

As Wolfgang looked at her, She said, "It is the healing powder." "Sulfur," added the clerk.

Wolfgang again noted the others in the room. The three men and a hard-eyed Iroquois woman were all dressed in dirty buckskins, well armed with rifles, a brace of pistols and a large butcher knife. The tallest man, fully as tall as Wolfgang, stared at Dark Moon with lust in his eyes. He also noticed Wolfgang's rifle. A smaller man and a half-breed sat at the table with cards in their hands, playing a game of whist.

Wolfgang sensed that the others had stopped to watch and listen to his conversation with the clerk. Looking at the foursome, Dark Moon recognized these footloose frontier rogues.

The apparitions from her vision, Dark Moon mused, already worrying.

She knew they were killers. Long before Wolfgang had come into her life, Dark Moon had heard stories of four frontier marauders who slaughtered wantonly and ceaselessly, their only common denominator the well-honed skill with which they brought death. She had also heard of their rape, torture and murder of young local women that had instilled fear in the nearby inhabitants.

Dark Moon could smell evil's presence in the four. They were wicked and empty inside and brought out the worst in each other. The only way they could feel alive was from the fear they instilled in others while taking their lives.

Dark Moon saw that though the woman wore a tri-cornered hat, her face was scarcely visible beneath its brim. The loudest and most vocal of the group, she was, as its leader, unsmiling, with intense, flinty eyes. A slight lifting of her head allowed Dark Moon to see the points of the smallpox scarred face where the woman's character dwelled. She had a thin unpleasant mouth. The eyes were surrounded by white, revealing a maniac temper. Briefly, a light, dancing amusement showed on her face as she stared at Dark Moon. Then she lowered her head, holding her face in shadow again.

The smallest man, a Frenchman, with wide shoulders and deep chest, had a springy muscular tension and looked the most dangerous, in his own sinister way. His face was rough-hewn and weathered by years of outdoor living. His eyes looked like dark holes punched above a short beard and mustache. The man lived solely for the joy of killing – in particular the thrill of seeing the terror in a victim's eyes as he or she begged for mercy. To the Frenchman, that thrill was almost sexual. In his eyes, Dark Moon saw a flashing vanity when he glanced at her.

The third of the group, the half-breed, had the features of a fighter, with a brutal, coarse-grained face and high cheekbones that left his eyes hollows of darkness. Many on the frontier looked upon half-breeds as notoriously savage. This man, wearing a wolf's cap and cape, had been a warrior kicked out of his tribe for excessively enjoying intimate physical contact through torture without tribal approval.

The fourth and final member was a powerfully built tall man. He had strong looking arms and enormous hands. His eyes were small, cold, and rat-like, his chin was square, his mouth full. None of the bulk appeared to be fat. He had killed many and his once, roughly handsome face bore many long, ugly scars. He sneered as if convinced of his own superiority. Now, as his cold, gray eyes arrogantly, lasciviously studied Dark Moon, his teeth flashed like blades as he smiled at her.

Dark Moon knew it was this last man who presented the most danger to she and Wolfgang. Wolfgang saw that her eyes outwardly showed nothing -- no emotion whatever. But he noted her right arm remained hidden behind her back, and immediately knew that her hand gripped her large knife and that she was very dangerous at this moment. Thus Wolfgang was silently warned. As he turned his head, he saw the Frenchman also staring. Fighting to control himself, Wolfgang felt the thick cords of his neck bulging.

He knew he must get Dark Moon away from this trading post.

* * *

The half-breed quietly got up and went outside. Soon after, the small man also rose and left, followed by the Iroquois woman.

Outside, the half-breed checked the cinches on the horses as if in preparation for their departure. Upon leaving the building, the smaller man turned and stood with his back to the building's wall, just opposite the door. A few minutes later the Iroquois woman joined him, positioning herself on the opposite side of the door. None of them noticed the small groupings of Indians seated in the shade of trees a hundred yards' distant, their attention focused on the doorway.

Dark Moon appeared from the building's dim interior. As she blinked at the bright sunlight, she suddenly felt a stunning blow to the back of her head and crumpled to the ground.

Wolfgang, meanwhile, was still inside, watching and listening to the clerk. He saw the man's eyes go wide with surprise, but no sooner had he registered the other's reaction than he felt a blow at the back of his head, delivered by the big man bringing the butt of the flintlock down on his skull. Stunned, Wolfgang fell to his knees. Even as he fought to remain conscious, he heard a quick shuffle of feet moving toward the door and sensed a darkening of the room as the big man momentarily filled the doorway, then was gone.

Wolfgang struggled to regain his focus. Spots swam

before his eyes, and then suddenly a torrent of cold water doused his head. The clerk, Wolfgang realized, using the emergency bucket kept behind the counter in case of fire. He was grateful.

The shock of the bracing liquid helped clear Wolfgang's mind. After he shut his eyes, he forced them open again. He shook his head to clear it and pulled himself resolutely to a standing position. The clerk stood immobile, a look of intense consternation on his face. Wolfgang's rifle was gone, but he made his way unsteadily toward the door, where he looked out, then stepped from the building.

The horses were gone. Scanning the ground, Wolfgang saw the animals' tracks, which led back toward the village.

Chapter 15

Wolfgang saw a large crowd of Indians assembled ahead. Dark Moon was still nowhere to be seen, but all at once he saw the outlaws -- mounted, obviously ready to flee, but kept at bay by armed warriors. Then he spotted Dark Moon, two braves helping her from a horse and untying her. A lone figure stood nearby: the old medicine man. His eyes locked with Wolfgang's; he must have seen the outlaws abduct Dark Moon and ordered the rogues stopped.

Closing the distance, Wolfgang saw the medicine man joined by the chief. Across the distance the hands of the medicine man gestured in the universal language that the rogues were his, to do with as he wished. Wolfgang approached closer and stopped a short distance away. He felt the familiar rush of adrenaline that always coursed through his body before a fight, and removed his shirt so his opponents would have nothing to grab onto. A murmur passed through the crowd. All could see the long, jagged, semicircular lines of white and pink scar tissue that stretched from his face and shoulders down to his chest -- clearly the marks of a great bear. The bear was a religious symbol of immortality and strength to all Indian tribes, a reflection of the Great Spirit; all the beholders realized they were in the presence of a warrior of truly great spiritual energy and power.

Wolfgang signed to the medicine man: "Give the big

man his knife and send him to me."

Again a murmur swept through the crowd. Those in front immediately sat so that those behind could also watch. They studied the tall, raw-boned man, his clear blue eyes and shoulder-length blond hair, and his ominous, dead-serious face.

oooOOOOOUUU!

All heard it: the haunting, dismal howl of a great wolf nearby. The crowd stirred, now even more alert. This was not the time for wolves to howl.

oooOOOOOUUU!

An omen!

Wolfgang saw the Indian crowd part and then close again behind Dark Moon, as the very large wolf walked up to her and stopped between her and the four rogues. The animal's opalescent yellow eyes stared at the big man. Its hackles rose as it uttered a low growl, baring its ivory fangs.

In a state of deep calm and with a grim, magical smile, Dark Moon addressed the large man and his cohorts in French.

"You are all about to die. The wolf has just foretold it. His mournful cry has summoned the spirits of the dead for you."

All eyes in the crowd watched her command the animal to lie down. Immediately he obeyed, though remaining alert with his head up. Murmurs swept through the crowd, repeating all that Dark Moon had said. The eyes of the warriors locked first on the wolf, then Dark Moon and finally Wolfgang. The crowd slowly became aware that this man was the one the Iroquois called the 'two-legged man-bear."

Now the large man found himself facing Wolfgang. Dark Moon saw that there was no sign of emotion on Wolfgang's face except for his eyes, which had darkened to a penetrating gray. The Frenchman's eyes were locked on Wolfgang's. The Frenchman held his knife in a slashing position with his thumb laying flat along the handle of the knife, nearly to the base of the blade, instead of being hidden in the grip and laid over his index finger.

    The French rogue approached cautiously, one step at a time, his eyes squinted and glaring.

    Wolfgang felt his stomach knot and his mouth go dry. His muscles tightened as his breathing and heart rate quickened, his limbs now slightly shaking. He accepted these symptoms, breathing deeply several times to calm his mind and body as the old Delaware warrior had taught him.

    In his fighting stance, Wolfgang crouched with knees bent and feet spread to shoulder-width. He faced his opponent on an angle, one foot behind him to keep his body flexible and mobile. His right hand held the bone-handled, double-bladed knife in a hammer grip ready to strike at the arm, groin, stomach or throat. Dark Moon's pulse quickened at the glinting from the long steel blades in the light. She noticed that both men had long, double-edged, razor-sharp pointed fighting knives they could thrust into vital areas to make you bleed inside. She marveled at Wolfgang's self-confidence and radiating power. His left arm was raised to act as a shield against any stab or thrust. Wolfgang watched the other man's eyes, which would telegraph his move. They widened and bulged. His opponent's muscles tensed as he looked where he intended to strike, and his upper lip drew back in a snarl. Wolfgang knew the first move would be coming the next instant.

    The Frenchman's left arm shot out in a stabbing motion. It was a feint, but Wolfgang anticipated it and moved to the right. The blade found only empty space between his rib cage and left arm. Instinctively he moved again, and the rogue's knife flashed forward only to miss the target. Then the large man slashed on his backward move, fiercely and accurately. Wolfgang felt the blade open his flesh and scrape the bones of his ribs. The Frenchman backed off and raised his knife so that Wolfgang could see the blood on it. The man raised it to his mouth, licked it clean with his tongue and smiled wickedly, expecting Wolfgang to choke at the sight of his blood on the knife. Blood seeped down Wolfgang's leggings. He didn't feel the wound, but he felt the blood running. The three restrained rogues, watched in fascination. Dark Moon felt chills at the roots of her hair -- but she also saw the mental transformation on Wolfgang's face. She saw the beast within her man surface.

Wolfgang knew he had to finish this before the loss of blood made him light-headed. He remembered the Old Delaware's knife-fighting instruction: evade your opponent's line of attack, and disarm him immediately by countering his knife-hand with a determined knife-strike of your own.

Wolfgang's eyes fixed fully on the gleaming weapon in the Frenchman's hand, with its thumb still extended. Then he forced his eyes away from it to his opponent's eyes, which signaled a sweeping slash. Leaning his upper body slightly back, he avoided the knife yet kept his balance. The blade barely missed his face. Wolfgang's left arm shot out and pushed the Frenchman's arm farther in the direction it had been traveling, sending his opponent off-balance. Quickly, stepping forward, he butted his forehead sharply against the Frenchman's face, and heard the sharp, telltale crunch of his enemy's nose breaking. As the Frenchman stood momentarily stunned, he brought his knife blade up on the inside of his opponent's beefy forearm, grasped the arm with his free hand and tugged it downward against the knife blade, slicing deep into the veins that fed the other man's strength.

The Frenchman's eyes went wide with surprise. Blood now pouring freely from his nose covered his teeth, which were bared in pain and hatred. As the man's arm went limp, his nerveless fingers dropped the knife, which fell to the ground amid the pattering blood. Wolfgang stepped back and watched the cursing giant, whose shirtfront was turning rapidly crimson.

Dark Moon was impressed by Wolfgang's quickness, and momentarily relieved, but she was upset by his sense of fairness, which kept him from killing the Frenchman when he had the chance. Instead, Wolfgang again assumed his fighting position -- his knife reversed this time, with blade running back along the underside of his forearm. Wolfgang watched him remove his neck scarf and, bite one end between his teeth, to wrap and tie it off around his forearm. Grinning, the wounded giant picked his knife up in his left hand and moved forward, showing his determination and confidence. He seemed totally relaxed as he smiled at Wolfgang, showing his bloodstained teeth. Wolfgang's pulse quickened. The Frenchman still held the knife with his thumb extended along the handle and blade. Dark Moon saw the Frenchman's white-colored face, and knew that no matter how much confidence he had, he would lose.

Wolfgang felt sure the Frenchman would try to end the fight by using his enormous strength to make a stabbing penetration. Sure enough, the rogue stepped forward and shot his arm straight out at him. Wolfgang responded by moving with a rattler's speed and precision, turning slightly to his right, stepping inside toward the giant and bringing his knife sharply up. His gleaming blade sliced off the Frenchman's thumb. Shock registered on the man's face, which went waxy white. His eyes bulged as he stared at his amputated thumb on the ground. Once more the knife had dropped from his grip, and now Wolfgang knew he had to end the fight.

Dark Moon thought that the fight was over and that Wolfgang would back off and let him live. As she watched, though, he quickly reversed the knife in his hand and struck the Frenchman's temple with its bone-pommel, stunning him. Again reversing the knife, he stabbed repeatedly into the rogue's stomach and chest cavity, twisting the handle and pulling it across and out with each strike. Blood with air bubbles spurted from the chest wounds. His life energy ebbing fast, the man sank to his knees sighing. Blindness, shock and unconsciousness set into the dying man. Using the Frenchman's collarbone as a guide for the tip of the knife-blade, Wolfgang plunged the knife deeply once more. He twisted it and made a cutting withdrawal. Blood gushed and spurted upward and out several feet in a continuous stream as the Frenchman fell forward, rolled over and lay sprawled on the ground, legs jerking, blood spurting from his wound. As he died, his body shuddered and spasmed, his glazed eyes stared up at Wolfgang. Everyone could hear the deep fluttery death rattle and see the release of tension from the body.

Wolfgang put his knife away and slowly looked up. The sun was marking high noon. Dark Moon looked into his steady, expressionless eyes. With his lips drawn back like a wolf, he was waiting for the next victim. He turned toward the chief and the medicine man and signed: *"Give the small man his knife."*

Wolfgang waited. He could see the wicked gleam of the knife. When the Indians pointed the way, the man obeyed without a word. Dark Moon felt the chill of fear. Wolfgang could see the little man's eyes light and a grim, cruel twist come to his lips.

With the knife in hand, the man stepped confidently forward. As he drew near Wolfgang, a minute tightening of his mouth telegraphed his intent. Wolfgang perceived the smooth flow of motion and downward, diagonal slash, and leaned backward ever so slightly as the other's knife-blade came within an inch of Wolfgang's thigh. His opponent followed up with a backward horizontal slash that targeted Wolfgang's stomach. Wolfgang smoothly avoided the attack. The Frenchman made a quick stabbing feint, forcing Wolfgang to leap back. Again the Frenchman's knife-arm shot quickly forward, thrusting for his foe's heart. As Wolfgang jumped back, both his arms shot downward, palms side by side, and his thumbs locked to the index fingers forming an open "V." Catching the Frenchman's wrist, Wolfgang stepped sharply to his opponent's right, lifted his arms overhead and turned, twisting his arm in a downward motion. As the smaller man flipped onto his back, Wolfgang heard the wind go out of him. Still gripping the arm, he kicked the Frenchman in the side of the chest, then punched downward with one fist to the man's sternum and felt it crack. Holding the man's weapon-arm with one hand, Wolfgang drew the knife from it with his other hand, and rolled him over onto his stomach. With a hard single stomp to the nape of the neck, on the knobby ridge of his spine, Wolfgang's foot shattered it with such force that everyone heard it. Instant brain death followed. The watching crowd saw the blade flash as Wolfgang flipped the knife to his other hand and plunged it into the other's chest.

Dark Moon's eyes grew wide and bright with pride as the crowd went wild. Her man had fought twice in single combat for her. She turned to look at the two rogues left, just in time to see the Chief sign to the prisoners' guards to kill them by knocking their heads with war clubs. Running to Wolfgang, she signed that he be taken to a shaded area nearby and laid on a reed mat.

* * *

Wolfgang's wounds ran two hand-spans in length, longer than they were deep. Though inner tissue was exposed, the edges were smooth. Dark Moon thought he had been lucky not to be stabbed. As she studied his wounds, she felt sorry for him, but proud. She was not worried, because she knew that he would recover quickly under her care, though he would be sore for a good while. Since her medicine was far away, she asked the medicine man for supplies.

He first handed her what she needed to stop the bleeding: powder from the roots and leaves of the stinging nettle plant, which she was relieved to see. She washed the wounds.

When I apply the root power to the wound, it will contract the tissues and blood vessels, stop the bleeding almost immediately and cleanse the decomposing flesh. She mused to herself as she administered the powder. *I'll boil nettle leaves in* water to soften them and lay them over the smaller cuts. They will check the flow of blood from the surface wounds almost at once, but I cannot leave them too long. Otherwise, blisters will form.

After sewing up the wound, the medicine man handed her two poultices, made of dark blue juniper berries, to help the injury heal quickly. These pea-size berries will heal small wounds almost overnight. He had had his assistant prepare these as the fight started. Then she requested that the assistant peel a patch of bark large enough to cover the wound from a slippery elm, soak it in water, and bring it to her.

As she worked, Dark Moon thought about how quickly and violently Wolfgang had ended the fight. His timing, accuracy and seemingly fearless attitude had shown him a fighter to be respected. He was big, but his opponent had been bigger, and still Wolfgang had won. Recalling him stabbing the big Frenchman at the end, she knew this scene would be imprinted permanently upon her mind. He had defended her honor without hesitation. Her eyes went liquid with love. She knew that she would always love him. While applying a poultice, she looked into his blue eyes shining upon her.

When she closed her eyes and rubbed her fingertips over his chest, she felt great energy emanating from him, and then saw visions. She trusted her developed capability of sixth sense; an enhanced intuition, which allowed her mind to see these brief impressions and foretell that she was forever linked to this man on life's trail ahead.

* * *

For two days, Dark Moon made Wolfgang remain lying down most of the time. She watched his body fight the fever that had raged within his body. She fed him a warm, strong tea of ground apple to help him sleep. A poultice of chamomile covered his wounds to drain them of infection. Whenever he needed to go out to relieve himself, she helped him to his feet. Every other day she removed the poultice to check the wound, allowing it to air, then applied the slippery elm's softened bark over the wound. The sizable injury, with its stretched and tightened skin, hurts. Dark Moon mused. But when the bark dissolves into a viscous slime, it will feel cool and allay the inflammation. The old Piankashaw medicine man was greatly surprised to see how quickly and effectively the slippery elm and poultices worked their wonders. It was as if Wolfgang's great knife wound had healed itself overnight.

* * *

His fever broken, Wolfgang awoke slowly to the smell of cedar smoke. Wild, yellow flames crackled and jumped as shadows danced. He saw Dark Moon sitting facing him with her legs crossed. Her arms were straight and her hands were resting on the inside of each of her knees, her palms faced upward. Her head was tilted slightly back and her eyes showed only the whites. He realized the spirit of the sorceress was heavily enveloped with visions. His body shivered at the sight. Exhausted, he watched her face, a mask of horror. He kept wondering what she saw, until finally he fell into a deep sleep.

In her vision, Dark Moon saw the Iroquois burning a village, killing its people and taking its children back to the lands of the long-house to raise only the fittest as tribe-members. Her mind moved among broken and dismembered bodies lying in gory piles. She could smell the faint odor of things rotting.

* * *

The old medicine man visited Dark Moon while Wolfgang was sleeping. He informed her that everyone was grateful to them for helping to get rid of the four French rogues. But he warned that they should leave before the French authorities decided to arrest Wolfgang. "Cross the Illinois country by heading southwest to the French-speaking towns on the Mississippi: Kaskaskia, St. Genevieve, Fort de Chartres, and Cahokia," he said. "The French have built another settlement in the Missouri country at St. Genevieve, just across the river and a short distance north. When you get there, you can trade for whatever you both need." He was silent in thought for a while and then he resumed: "Avoid Cahokia since the French are still maintaining hundreds of slaves there. You will know before you see or reach the Father of Waters, for there will be a bluff and the rest will be flood plain and swamp."

* * *

By August, Wolfgang was recovered and ready to travel. Just before they started their long trail once again, Wolfgang, overcome with curiosity, asked Dark Moon why she had bought all that bark back at the trading post, and where it was now. "It is for what you call the 'ague,'" she said with a rare smile. "I have already broken it down into a smaller bags for ready use."

Chapter 16

It was September 1756, the month known as the Moon of Falling Leaves -- the autumnal equinox, a time when the sun rose directly in the east and set directly in the west. The sun's ever-decreasing sunlight made each day shorter and colder, urging millions of birds to migrate south. Pale yellow, wind-tossed leaves adorned the silver maples along the bank of the nearby creek, and the round, dark purple fruit of the hackberry trees growing in the wet bottomland areas showed ripe. Turkeys and squirrels fed busily on the pea-sized harvest in and around the warty, gray-brown tree trunks. The antler growth of whitetail buck deer was complete and rubbed clean of velvet. They now became loners and were aggressive with each other. Black bears went on feeding binges, and the elk had begun bugling and gathering harems.

    In this forested land, interspersed with prairies, connected by buffalo trails, Wolfgang and Dark Moon together with the wolf sat in a large grove of oaks. Both noted with appreciation the conical forms and wide-spreading branches of a grove of red cedar trees amid a limestone outcropping at the edge of the grove. They spent a month moving slowly through the country looking for a good place to stop. This far south, it would be more wet than cold. They decided to spend the winter here.

    They chose a fire site and cleared it. Wolfgang stripped

thin, shreddy, ruddy-brown cedar bark from a young tree and wound it into a bird's nest for tinder. Dark Moon collected fuel. Wolfgang returned to the fire site, and using the steel of the tomahawk, began striking sparks from a piece of flint into some dry grass and fireweed. Soon he had smoke, and then, moments later, a red-hot glowing coal. Quickly placing the glowing sparks into the bird's nest of red cedar, he blew on it gently until it smoked and finally burst into flame. He added shavings and twigs until a steady fire burned.

Wolfgang and Dark Moon soon had the hindquarter of a young deer cooking, along with a grouse she'd packed with sassafras leaves. The mouth-watering smell made Wolfgang not mind the wait, and he noticed that the wolf, too, seemed to love the scent of roasting meat.

*   *   *

The next morning Wolfgang helped Dark Moon collect young hickory saplings in the forest. After she marked off an area approximately twelve by fifteen feet, they placed the large ends of the sapling into the ground, one every two feet around the marked area. They planted each one two feet into the ground, and dug them in, working on opposite sides, pulling and bending the tops into the center and lashing them together with thin strips of young walnut bark. Then they placed an outer frame of saplings a hand-span from the inner frame. They built the sleeping platforms next to the wall on both sides.

The two cut the dark gray bark from mature elm trees and secured them to the inner and outer sapling frames to enclose the wigwam. Bundles of grass and leaves were tamped down between the frames for insulation. Mud was plastered around the fire hole at the top in order to accommodate the fire at the center of the structure. Over time, the mud would become hard-baked and black.

In the evening the air turned cold as soon as the sun went down. Wolfgang and Dark Moon sat out in the dark, embraced by a deep and abiding stillness that closed in around them like talons. Listening to the night's sounds, which told them all was well, they stared into the sky.

"The Algonquian see that rectangle of stars as the Sky Bear," said Dark Moon quietly, pointing at the Big Dipper. "And that handle of three stars as the three hunters who trail the bear and kill it. Its blood is what turns the leaves on the trees crimson."

There was a pause as both stared up into the night sky, admiring its beauty.

"Let's go hunting together tomorrow, early," said Wolfgang, knowing they needed meat.

"You must hunt alone. I must prepare the wigwam and supplies for the harsh weather to come," answered Dark Moon.

* * *

Man and wolf had listened to the sounds of the elk vocalizing and bugling for hours. The short, high-pitched, ee-uh sound of straying calves was answered by the husky eee-ow's of attentive cows. Then came a low rising, resonant pitch, with an extended shrill high squeal. It then broke off, ending with a series of deep, gravel-toned-grunts of a full bugle.

OOooEEEeeeeeeeeeeeoooo, OUGH, OUGH, OUGH.

It was the unmistakable full-throated sound of the herd bull, meant to intimidate the younger lone bulls. As dawn broke, the elk, with bellies full, started heading for the timber.

Wolfgang moved from tree to tree in the shadows, just inside the edge of the timber, using every blown-down tree for cover and avoiding sunlit areas at all cost. He paused between steps to vary his stride, taking a long step, then a short one, and alternating slow and quick ones. He knew that hunters would alert squirrels by their rhythmic patterns of walking--a gait no other forest creature used. Hearing the constant plopping sound of the high-energy mast crop falling to the ground, Wolfgang knew he had to be careful not to step on an acorn.

He caught the scent of rutting bulls--a rank, pungent smell. Spotting the sun shining off the polished, ivory-tipped rack of the herd bull, he admired the animal's heavy rack, which swayed back and forth as the bull tossed his head or walked gracefully among the cows to answer the challenge. The love-pealing challenge was answered from five different directions. The herd closest to his side of the timber edge was now edging slowly his way. Movement revealed a cow and her yearling calf standing in the grass close to him. The elk were unaware of Wolfgang.

He selected a pale-colored arrow from his quiver, knowing the wood was hard, strong and very heavy. Having quickly checked that it was straight, he knocked it on his bowstring. The heavier arrow would be stable, dampen noise and penetrate well. Ready for the yearling, he waited motionless.

The release was smooth. The soft twang of the bowstring and the viburnum-shaft flew straight and with great force, sinking deeply. Wolfgang kept his arm extended until the yearling leaped into motion from the shock of the impact. It crouched and lunged slightly forward, then whirled almost instantaneously. Its head and ears swiveling on alert, the animal disappeared in a shower of leafy humus into the hardwood forest with an amazing burst of speed.

Then Wolfgang heard the yearling cartwheel and slam into the ground. He listened to the sound of the animal struggling to get up. It continued to thrash the ground, but growing weaker and weaker, until there was silence. Wolfgang continued to wait and watch.

Chapter 17

Dark Moon knew she needed to make a large stew. There was no telling when Wolfgang would return. Carefully she emptied her fire case and opened the neck of the deerskin tinder bundle to arrange her tools in the order she would need them. She placed a dry bark coal-catcher down first, then set the fireboard, where the notch was over the bark, to one side.

Lightly lubricating the hollow of the bone socket, which served as her hand grip-with animal fat, she knelt on her right knee and placed her left foot on the fireboard. Putting the bone hand grip on top of the drill, she applied gentle pressure downward with the heel of her hand, and holding the bow with her right hand, she sawed back and forth, using its full length spinning the drill on the fireboard as fast as she could. The drill burned into the fireboard, producing a smoldering black dust that formed her coal.

To start the fire, she transferred this red-hot coal to the mixture of fine, dry dead grass and shredded cedar bark, though she also used birch bark. Easily peeled birch bark was one of the best materials. It burned even more readily than paper and lit even when wet. Blowing gently produced flames.

Now Dark Moon began to feed the fire with small, crooked twigs, which she had collected from the lower levels of the tree. Breaking and crushing the stems, she patiently fed them into the fire, which began to crackle and leap with an orange brilliance, as she breathed their wintergreen-like smell.

Increasing the size of the twigs, she followed up with oak, which produced minimal smoke or ash, was long lasting, and its aroma barely detectable. She adjusted the tripod over the fire, then browned the meat in the pot and poured water into it. There was no sound except for the hissing of sap from the burning wood.

* * *

Outside the doorway, in the growing darkness, a small bird talked -- a nuthatch. Carefully Dark Moon listened to the low, single-pitched, nasal notes -- *whi-whi-whi-whi* -- and knew from long experience that the next sound would be a single ank, to locate its mate. But when instead there was a quick pair of notes -- *ank-ank!* –an alarm call, she felt a pang of anxiety. Then in its jerky flight it alighted above her head on the side of the entrance and climbed around, and upside down, and was looking at her — *ank-ank!* She realized the bird was talking to her. It had actually flown inside and talked to her.

An omen, she mused, worrying about her man.

She knew it meant that someone would die -- a prophecy. She shivered with apprehension and alarm. The little bird flew out and was gone.

All her people knew that when birds talked to you, someone would die. She sat brooding for a long time. She listened harder for a few moments, but there was only silence. The air seemed to crackle with danger. A distant, low-pitched sound -- *"cuk----cuk----cuk"* -- came from the forest. It was made by chipmunks from their burrows and was repeated by others in a slow beat, warning of an intruder. Then closer, a chipmunk made a loud chatter in a chipping sound, followed by the rapid-fire trilling sound of warning. She continued to listen. It grew dark outside. Acting on her premonition, she removed the pot's lid. As steam wafted up, she quickly dumped the contents of a small deer skin bag into the stew, scraped the contents from a small wooden container into it and gave it a quick stirring.

When she got up to get more wood for the fire, she vaguely detected the dull thudding vibration of moccasin covered feet. She stooped and slipped through the door. When she straightened, she saw nothing at first. She stood still watching and listening. Then she detected a set of earrings, nose ring, and eyes reflecting the light from her door way. She could barely make out the warrior standing in the deep shadows perhaps ten steps away.

As her eyes adjusted to the dark, she made out the red-painted head and face. The eyes were still set in the darkness as he drifted toward her. There were others. She now saw the wide black painted rectangle of war paint extended from the brow to the bridge of a nose across both eyes to the front of both ears. Three thin, black, painted streaks extended downward over both cheeks. They wore a Mohawk-style roach, complete with porcupine and deer guard hair on top of their red painted shaved heads. Two angled turkey feathers were attached. The closest warriors' entire body, she now saw, was painted black. He wore only a leather breechclout with short ends held in place with a leather belt and moccasins. Ireohkwa.

Dark Moon's eyes detected that the moccasins were the one-piece type, with the seam down the front. There were black-painted faces with red around the eyes, and another face painted half red, half black. All the faces were a combination of colors and shapes.

Dark Moon knew who they were: *Ireohkwa.* Iroquois.

Chapter 18

As the grim, tight-mouthed faces of six Iroquois warriors stood staring at her, Dark Moon took a deep breath and fingered the rawhide lacing at her breast. She felt as if her heavy spirit were trying to hide, and could not get enough air to breathe. The sheer, silent intensity of the six pairs of luminous, empty eyes-alert to her every movement-held her frozen. The warrior's lean, near-naked bodies shone with bear grease, and their heads were bald except for their scalp locks with two turkey feathers. They carried their bedding over one shoulder, and muskets or bows in their hands.

Dark Moon felt a coldness creep upon her.

"Who are you?" the first warrior signed.

Dark Moon's observant eyes read subtle emotional messages: the lack of muscle movement around the men's glaring eyes, their turned-downed mouths, tight lips, and slightly flared nostrils. Their body language showed their arrogance and contempt. Dark Moon knew intuitively that they were intent on killing. And she knew also that her only chance for survival relied on her thinking and acting normally.

"I am Singing Bird. My man is hunting," her steady hands replied. "I have food prepared."

She knew they could smell it. The leader, who had briefly seen the look of terror in her eyes, turned to one warrior and ordered him to stand watch. Then he motioned for the warrior closest to the wigwam to go inside. The warrior ducked inside and shortly reappeared.

"There is the smell of two people in the sleeping robes," his hands signed. "A shield, spear and bow. The wigwam is newly built."

The leader motioned them all inside. Gathered inside the wigwam, the warriors watched Dark Moon thicken the stew. Stalling for time, she told them it must boil a little longer before it was ready. As she prepared mugs for her guests, she felt secretly thankful for their arrogance: when it came time to eat and she did not join them, rather than grow suspicious, they would assume that she, aware of her lowly place, knew she must serve them first.

On the night of the full moon, during the time of the Flower Moon, what Wolfgang called May, her deft fingers had collected and dug her roots. With great care and cunning she had compounded this poisonous potion. She knew that they would never survive this last meal: the poison morels and mixture of ground and water hemlock, castor bean, pokeweed and mountain laurel she had added would guarantee that.

The mushrooms needed a few more minutes to cook, or they might cause the warriors to vomit their food, and then they would kill her immediately. As for the taste of the poisonous mushrooms, the parsnips in the stew would cover that. And once her unwelcome visitors' abdominal pain set in, there would be nothing they could do. They would be unable to help themselves and would die a slow and painful death. But, she would help them along their way.

The Iroquois wolfed down their meal. Scarcely had they finished, when they broke out into a cold sweat. The first sign of alarm appeared on their faces. With less time than it took to eat the meal, nausea and salivation set in, accompanied by fever. As Dark Moon watched, their bodies suddenly went rigid and as their hands tried to grip their weapons, their eyes filled with understanding, panic and hatred. But too late: the warriors tried to speak, in vain, as they gasped for breath. They vomited blood and began to shake with violent convulsions and in gut-wrenching pain. Doubled up with severe stomach cramping, they lost control of their bowels. Dark Moon watched her victims' last act, of falling to the floor with legs thrashing as their respiratory systems failed. Lungs filling with their own blood, they were drowning as she watched. Pain-stricken eyes met the witch's in disbelieving terror. Now unable to move or talk, the leader knew that the deep dark eyes, which looked into his belonged to the one whom they were hunting.

Dark Moon waited for them to begin hallucinating. When the leader could no longer see the vicious fury of her glinting, predatory eyes, she drew the large elk horn-handled knife at her back from its sheath. Her hand came up behind his head. She placed her arm around the leader in a deadly embrace, and started the slice behind his head and drew it in jerking motions toward the throat. Blood spurted everywhere as the victim tried to pull away. She grimaced and forced the blade deep. She continued to saw back and forth through the muscle and pulsing arteries. She let him pull away slightly so that she could more easily continue the cut across the throat. Blood spilled down the front of his hide shirt. His eyes wide with panic, he struggled in futilely. Dark Moon let him go and kicked him in the side, forcing him away from her. Now she bent slowly forward to the next paralyzed victim, looked deep into his eyes, and thrust her arm forward and cut the throat open wide. With lightning speed she hacked another warrior in the head. The other two were already in a coma and near death. Both were too incapacitated to do anything but die.

Dark Moon took down her small shield and spear and went out the door into the shadows. She stood silently, listening and watching, until she saw the lone warrior standing guard outside.

"Your friends and leader are already dead," she said. She paused a moment to let that sink in. Then she continued: "You can join them or go home. Their relatives need to know what happened to them."

She waited, unmoving, until she heard the quickly retreating steps of the fleeing warrior.

Chapter 19

Early the following morning, Wolfgang glided from tree to tree, stopping at each to search for apparitions lurking in the shadows ahead. To cover any noise, he moved only when the wind gusted. When, finally, he was within a hundred yards of the wigwam, he saw the wolf ahead. The animal looked agitated, standing stock-still, staring intently ahead and lifting its nose. The wolf's bristled black hair extended from his shoulders down his back and his bristled tail pointed straight back. Wolfgang knew the animal smelled Indians.

Wolfgang also felt the tickle of his hair rising on the back of his neck as his nose caught the sweet, metallic odor of blood. He saw a fluttering of wings. Several birds were perched atop a stake. A head was mounted on it. Suddenly he recoiled in horror. They were pecking the eyes and skin from the skull. He recalled the skulls Dark Moon had outside the cabin they had left far to the east. Wolfgang advanced until he was face to face with the grisly vision. He realized that Dark Moon meant to instill a sense of dread and terror in the beholder. He pointed the wolf off in a wide circle so that they would approach from another direction. He followed the animal until it came upon the Iroquois trail, when it stopped and looked back at him. When he examined the ground carefully, he saw the darker color of upturned disturbed leaves contrasting with the lighter bleached color of the undisturbed forest floor. At least six Indians had passed this way.

Completing the circle, Wolfgang came upon the last head, and saw Dark Moon. Wolfgang sounded the whistling *"Kee-kee! Kee-kee!"* of a young gobbler. Her head turned slightly, signing that it was clear. She had decided not to tell Wolfgang the story until she was more at ease with the telling; he would ask no questions until then, trusting that she would tell him what he needed to know.

* * *

It was December, the season known as the Moon of Long Nights. It was the time of the winter solstice when the sun rose in the southeast and set in the southwest, making the nights long and the days short. The next two months would be the coldest and wettest of the year. The threatening weather would foul their rifle barrels, resulting in hard ramming if they were to use them more than once. Wolfgang knew that the gunpowder wouldn't burn cleanly in damp weather and that it was better to leave it stored in their horns, keeping their rifles clean and powder dry for an emergency. Wolfgang and Dark Moon did not venture far from the wigwam. They had plenty of meat, having hunted with their bows and killed another elk, several deer, and three fat bears that they had rendered into cooking grease. They also had plenty of maple sugar.

* * *

During January the season known to the Indians as the Moon of Snows, the rain came for many days. The wind was ceaseless. Wolfgang and Dark Moon spent much time working together, busily preparing hides for leather clothing. Winter was the best time for stretching, drying, and scraping the hides till they were thin and light. In the below-zero weather, they freeze-dried the hides. The leather expanded in the cold air, which helped break down the skin's fibers. Dark Moon had saved the brains of the animals they had eaten, and would use them in the final preparation, by boiling them. She soaked the hides overnight in the brain barrel, where the brain tissue's fatty acid broke down the natural glue that bonded animal hide fibers together. The leather so-treated proved smooth, soft, and supple.

She also boiled animal hooves, skimming off and saving the little bubbles that came to the surface. Applying a light coat of this warm oil also helped keep the hides, clothing and footwear water-resistant.

Wolfgang showed Dark Moon how to hand-cast undersized lead, rifle balls with the mould. The roundball had to be fifteen-thousandths undersized from the fifty-caliber bore for easy loading.

During this time, Dark Moon finally told Wolfgang what had happened when the Iroquois came. She left much to the imagination; her story instead revealed her skill in the art of poisoning.

"The early spring is an easy time to find everything. When the leaves are budding, I explore swampy areas and wet meadows near streams to find the small, whitish, heavily-scented flowers of water hemlock that grow abundantly. When mature, the whole plant is poisonous, but the roots are where the poison is concentrated," she said. "I dig under and around the hemlock plant, then pull it easily from the wet ground to get the whole bundle of chambered tuberous roots. I bleed the fleshy root-stems of their poisonous, yellow, oily sap, which is one of the substances I had added to the Iroquois' stew. Every season I collect a great volume of delicious morels to add to our food. I also gather false morels, which are terribly poisonous. Merely chopping them finely and sprinkling them over a victim's food guarantees death by liver failure."

Wolfgang understood and was grateful.

* * *

By June 1757, again on the move traveling west, Dark Moon and Wolfgang were nearing the town of Kaskaskia when she stopped to question a local Indian woman working her corn, bean and squash field.

"Can we trade for lead and salt in this town?" Dark Moon signed.

The bent old woman quietly stared. Then her index finger of her right hand touched her thumb -- the universal "yes."

"Where I make camp?" Dark Moon's hands signed. She noted the old woman eyeing the freshly killed deer across the travelers' horses.

"Me-Little Bird Woman," the old woman hands rapidly gestured, introducing herself. "I go house. You come." Looking at the horses, Little Bird Woman signed, "Plenty grass water."

From the old woman's hands, Wolfgang and Dark Moon learned that most of the boats unloading at the dock on the river were carrying lead and salt from the French mines on the western shore further north. That lead ore was melted into bars at the mines then transported by horse to the river, whereupon it was next brought here to Kaskaskia. Lead shot was produced across the river, and salt was mined across the river at Saline Creek, due southwest.

Upon their arrival at the campsite, Wolfgang and Dark Moon unpacked their horses and walked them to the meadow. They hobbled the horses' forelegs with rawhide straps fitted to their pasterns, allowing the animals to graze but not wander too far. She walked to the wet part of the meadow, looking around.

Dark Moon found tall cattails. Known to her people as hood-wort or mad-dog weed, the plant's dull-blue flowers bloomed in pairs this time of year. She dug up a number of them and washed them in the creek, then positioned them in the shade to dry. She mixed in a weak portion of ground roots from her stock of yellow root, called golden seal, and moccasin flower, known as lady slipper. Later she would chop and ground up the whole hood-wort plant, including its yellow roots, to make tea.

* * *

Inside the wigwam, she told the old woman to rest and that she would prepare the meal for the party. Dark Moon also asked the woman if she was troubled by any physical ailments, and Little Bird Woman said she was restless at night, unable to sleep well and was suffering a slight heart pain.

"Don't worry," Dark Moon said, smiling. "Tonight, after I serve you tea, you will sleep well."

As Little Bird Woman was drinking her tea that evening, the wolf showed up at the door. Dark Moon saw the old woman's eyes go wide, but before she could speak, Little Bird Woman smiled.

"I now know exactly who you are," she signed. "When I saw the magical talisman around your neck, I thought so, but I was not sure. Now I am. You are the Algonquian medicine woman Dark Moon, and your man is the one called 'Okwaho,' the warrior of the Red Moon."

Dark Moon could see that the old woman was greatly pleased to have them as guests.

The following day, Little Bird Woman was all smiles. She had slept well. While Wolfgang and the wolf scouted up river, the women walked into Kaskaskia town, exchanging information and gossip.

Dark Moon explained to her new companion that the ingredients of the tea were best picked at this time of year when the plants flowered. Hood-wort would help her heart condition, act as a sedative, enable her to sleep, and keep her liver healthy, while goldenseal would stop infections, slow bleeding, and clean the system, acting almost as a cure-all herb. The yellow root would help many things, but the heart especially.

The old woman complained that the French traders had turned the local Illinois Indians into a people lacking tribal standards because so many had become drunks. Drinking the white man's firewater dulled the senses and impaired the judgment of many strong warriors, and created a thirst impossible to satisfy.

Dark Moon knew they must start across the Missouri country in order to put time and distance between themselves and their enemies. They stopped and talked to a friend of the old woman's, an old Osage warrior. He told her that she could fastest travel the open hills and plains country, abundant in buffalo to the west. Because so many tribes were hunting the animals, there would be many eyes watching, and their travel would be noticed. Many villages were located there because the Three Sisters crops -- corn, squash, and beans -- grew well in the area's dark, loamy soil. In the open hill and plains country, they could expect to run into the Osage and Missouri, as well as their enemies the Sauk, Fox, and Kickapoo Indians.

"You travel west until you come to the western plains country. It's an open country. You'll know it because of the flinty limestone and shale rock formations. Then travel northwest," the old Osage warrior's hands said. "Each night the Great Bear star constellation would point the way, then you must travel until you reach the Missouri River. The country is open and the plains tribes see anyone crossing."

"Manitou, the Great Spirit, will make his wishes known," replied Dark Moon.

Chapter 20

It was July of 1757, the month known as the Buck Moon by the Indians – the time when they first observed the soft velvet antlers emerging from the foreheads of the buck deer. The summer had been abnormally hot and dry, and the crest of the Mississippi River had fallen steadily since early June.

Little Bird Woman took Dark Moon to see the Kaskaskia Indian chief Jean Baptiste Ducoigne. When they met, she told him all she knew about Wolfgang, who was scouting upriver. The old chief was much impressed, but greeted Wolfgang and Dark Moon with a warning.

"Don't let Wolfgang go to the trading post. They will immediately know him as a stranger, and his size will give you both away," he said in a kindly voice. "A message runner has just arrived from Vincennes before our talk – Monsieur Tisserand de Montcharveau, the military commander of Kaskaskia, has been ordered to arrest your man. I will see that your supplies are obtained."

"The French and Iroquois are vengeful, relentless and cruel," replied Dark Moon. "We will pay you for the supplies, of course."

The chief nodded in acknowledgment.

"Two packs for your horses will be placed in one of the two canoes to cross the Mississippi River. They will contain cones of brown sugar, a five-pound bag of raw coffee beans, a finger-candle lamp, and other essentials as well: needles, fishhooks, beads from Europe, French and English wool blankets, German silver trinkets for both men and women, and a small jug of brandy," he replied.

Dark Moon knew these items would be useful for trading farther west.

"Obtaining salt will be no problem – there are many salt springs across the river near the place where the Saline River empties into the Mississippi River. You can stop and boil down your own supply or trade for it," the chief continued. "There are many limestone caves in the Ozark country. There you can find all the necessary ingredients for making gunpowder. Go upstream until the muddy water clears below the bluffs, and you can easily pick up lead in the streams."

He told her where to obtain gunpowder across the river, adding that they could also watch how it was made.

"The French have been producing it locally since I was a young man," the chief said. "Anyone can do it, but it's very dangerous. The Wazhazhe or Ni-U-Ko'n-Ska, as they like to be known, is the dominant tribe on the Ozark Plateau. You may know them as Osage. Their villages can be found along the wooded river valleys. Their name means 'Children of the Middle Waters.'"

He showed the hand sign for Osage, bringing the backs of both hands with fingers extended and joined back behind both ears, and moving his hands downward sharply. Dark Moon understood, it meant "shaved heads."

"They are great warriors," the chief went on, "conducting raids in all directions and frequently attacking the French. You must watch for raiding Chickasaw coming up from the south. They claim much of all those lands, and the Sauk, Fox, and Kickapoo are warlike tribes and very aggressive warriors. They live far to the north and can always be expected to raid most of the year south along the Mississippi River into the Ozark

Plateau."

* * *

When Wolfgang returned from his trip, he told Dark Moon what he had seen. "Not far upriver, I crossed on a small ferry to the west side and walked across long, narrow wheat fields into the French town of St. Genevieve. Everywhere I went there were large fields of wheat growing in the black soil of the cleared flood plain. There're many vertical-log houses built up off the ground, with double-pitched roofs. They're well furnished. Their porches extended all the way around each house. African and Indian slaves were everywhere. The blacks worked at the horse-powered gristmills, and also at the loading docks on the river. I learned that the wheat loaded on the flat-bottomed bateaux was shipped down river to New Orleans. I stayed only long enough to gather that information, then crossed the river again."

Dark Moon could see Wolfgang's glaring eyes and furrowed brow. Her concerned gaze noted the storm raging in his face as he told of the lines of newly-arrived black slaves standing around waiting, their necks linked together with heavy rope, moving in a long file to scattered destinations where they would be put to work, clearing timber in all the valleys for farmers. His own experiences of captivity fresh in his mind, Wolfgang felt a deep sympathy for the men. Dark Moon put a hand on his shoulder, but said nothing.

* * *

The next day, when it was again time to travel, Wolfgang was surprised to see Dark Moon dressed and ready for their journey. In skin-tight leggings and a breechcloth that left the thighs uncovered, she was dressed as a warrior. Laces ran up the outside of each leg, from her ankles to her waist, and her leggings were worn open at the bottom. She wore high-topped moccasins, ornamented with porcupine quills.

"Why do you dress that way?" Wolfgang asked.

"Because I'll be riding the horse," she answered simply. Wolfgang kept staring at her, but she ignored him.

She has no idea how beautiful she is, Wolfgang thought.

They crossed the meandering river in two canoes, Wolfgang and Dark Moon paddling one and two Osage warriors paddling the other that carried their horse packs. The horses swam. They paddled in silence beneath a sky full of river birds, finally reaching the thirty-yard-wide mouth of Saline creek. As they entered the marshlands, they saw great pools of shade and heard only the heavy rustling of leaves overhead.

Having traveled some distance further up the brackish creek water, passing great cottonwood trees well over a hundred feet tall, they came at last to a gravel bottom where they might land. After helping them round up the horses, the Osage left. Wolfgang and Dark Moon packed up the animals and followed the Saline Creek trail around miles of cane brakes, high-grass marsh land, islands of timber and great bodies of standing water.

After a time, they came suddenly upon the unmistakable straight line of a bluff, which had been impossible to see from a distance. They followed a trail up a small creek valley through the low limestone hills.

At a limestone cave, Wolfgang and Dark Moon encountered black slaves working for a French overseer. Because the Frenchman was drunk, they were able to trade with a black slave for powder. The old slave said his name was Louis, and that he had worked there all his life. He walked them some distance from the mine, talking about black powder, explaining that the size of the powder particles determined how fast they burned.

"Small grains burn faster," Louis said. "The big ones

burn too slow to shoot accurate."

Wolfgang was silent a moment. Abruptly, he asked, "Do you wish to be free? You can come west with us."

Louis shook his head.

"I have a wife and two young girls. They're better off here than out in the wilderness. It's dangerous, unknown country out west."

Louis gave them a keg of powder.

"It must be turned over every few days," he cautioned, "so the saltpeter, charcoal and sulfur won't separate. Saltpeter settles to the bottom." He reminded them also that after periods of wet weather they must empty the keg to sift the powder and make sure it was dry.

"Wait for a hot day," their friend advised.

As he and Dark Moon left, Wolfgang could see tears shimmering in the old man's eyes.

Chapter 21

After some days' travel, Wolfgang and Dark Moon were in rough wooded hills and valleys covered with oaks, cedar and hickories. There they came upon a working mine and traded for lead. Afterward they made their way to the edge of the forest. At its fringe, they watched and listened for sound or movement. All seemed normal.

Ahead lay a long, broad expanse of high grass that they must cross. Beyond the field was a screen of timber, and beyond that, the trail winding its way up through the rocky dry bluffs of a southeastern slope.

As they approached the nearly waist-high grass waving in a strong breeze blowing from behind them out of the southeast, they both had the uneasy feeling they were being followed. They watched and listened, but everything seemed normal. They started across.

Suddenly the wolf, leading the way up ahead, stopped and stood motionless in the middle of the trail, his nose up. When the animal looked back at them, Wolfgang's sixth sense was tingling. Quickly, he and Dark Moon tied off their horses.

The wolf's head turned toward one side of the trail, then the other. He raised his hackles and extended the hair on his high carried tail. Wolfgang read the signal: an unseen presence lay ahead. When his master gave him a silent arm and hand signal to go, the wolf left the trail to merge into the ominous shadows of the trees and turned. He obediently lay down to watch.

After seeing the animal's alert warning posture, Wolfgang felt an ominous chill and a presence on their back trail. The hair rose on his arms and neck. He dropped into a crouch, cradling his rifle. He was startled to see a beautifully feathered roach with something shiny attached floating fast toward him. Dark Moon stepped to the side, her rifle swinging up to the ready. Meanwhile the warrior, without moccasins, ran silently toward them, his face painted red with yellow vertical marks and his chest sporting a tattooed serpent. He wore only a breechclout with his leather belt.

Wolfgang's eyes caught on the silver dangler between the warrior's nostrils. Feeling a hot rush of adrenaline and the familiar hollow of fear in his stomach, he raised his rifle and fired.

Klatch! Poof! Boom!

The lead ball crashed through the warrior's right eye, leaving a black crater and exploding out the back of his head.

"Got him!" cried Dark Moon as the warrior flopped and rolled, stilled forever. Now shadows emerged from the trees -- two more, plumed and painted, walking slowly on each side of the trail. With raised muskets, they stood in plain sight. More movement stirred in the trees beyond the two warriors in the open. Then other Indian warriors emerged, silhouetted against the dark forest and staring in their direction.

Dark Moon ran to the horses for her shield and spear. Wolfgang could see the guns pointing, some with a feather suspended and swaying in the wind. A small puff of priming smoke rose above their locks. Wolfgang saw it followed by muzzle smoke.

Booooom!

The deep-throated sound told him they were shooting smoothbore muskets -- notoriously inaccurate -- and Wolfgang felt a slap of wind as a musket ball passed near his head.

The next moment a howling war cry sounded from the warriors, screaming themselves into readiness.

"After your first round, start reloading for me," he instructed Dark Moon. He forced himself to ignore the screams of the oncoming Chickasaw and concentrate on firing. He fired and immediately shifted away from the dirty smoke. A warrior staggered with a hole in his chest. When Dark Moon fired, another collapsed. Standing beside Wolfgang, she handed him a fresh rifle, snatched away his empty one, and began to reload even as he again took aim.

Klatch! Poof! Boom!

A warrior running toward them pitched forward into the grass, twisting in agony.

Wolfgang heard and felt the wind of several arrows singing past his head and shoulders as he lifted his rifle to take aim. He saw and heard a ball splatter through the grass in front of him -- a near miss. Quickly, Dark Moon poured a measure of powder down the barrel then desperately rammed the wadding and ball down as Wolfgang had taught her. Sprinkling a few fine grains of powder into the pan, she handed him the loaded weapon.

Dark Moon, turning to watch the advancing Chickasaw, heard the solid click of the hammer falling.

Klatch! Poof! Boom!

Smoke belched from Wolfgang's pan and muzzle. Again her pulse quickened as she loaded, rammed and primed the other weapon.

Wolfgang raised the rifle, fired...

Klatch! Poof! Boom!

Quickly they exchanged rifles.

The Chickasaw were leaving a trail of dead behind them. Wolfgang brought the hammer to full cock and raised the rifle to his shoulder, but before he could pull the trigger, a sharp, searing pain tore through his leg. He winced and sucked air through clenched teeth. With horror, Dark Moon saw an arrow piercing his leg. He waved her away and, again sucking air deep into his lungs, raised the rifle to his shoulder. He half-exhaled and held steady, applying pressure to the trigger.

A warrior's war cry was choked off as the ball bit into flesh and bone. The victim threw out his arms and collapsed into a rolling tumble, as only the dead fall.

Both Dark Moon and Wolfgang realized that they would not be able to kill all the Chickasaw. He felt a searing pain in his left shoulder, as he thrust his rifle out to her for reloading. She saw that his shirt was now wet with bright blood.

Wolfgang signed to the wolf. Instantly the animal bounded up to sit beside him in a defensive posture, its muscles quivering, its yellow eyes staring back down the trail, toward the onrushing warriors. Then, all at once, arrows flew from behind Wolfgang and Dark Moon toward the Chickasaw. He commanded the wolf to lie down.

Looking back, Wolfgang saw a line of four grim, silent warriors behind them -- Osage identifiable by the bright blue paint streaks on their faces. Shrieking their war cries, the line of warriors charged into the open to finish off the survivors in hand-to-hand combat. But now more Chickasaw appeared, outnumbering the Osage.

Knowing that Wolfgang, with an arrow in his leg, would be unable to fight hand-to-hand, Dark Moon handed him the now-loaded extra rifle and shouldered her shield and spear. He saw her gaze become suddenly wild, hard, and bright, and her lips move as though she were chanting. Her nostrils flaring, she was performing a deep-breathing exercise to relax and gather her strength and power. Then a blazing intensity in her eyes signaled her intention. Even as Wolfgang realized her plan, her screaming war cry pierced the air when she bent low to the ground, coiled like a great snake, and charged.

Wolfgang watched, amazed, but also frightened for her

safety. The Osage warriors had killed all the Chickasaw but one, a warrior with a tattooed snake running the length of each arm. As Wolfgang and the Osage watched, Dark Moon came to a stop just out of reach of the Chickasaw.

Her shield arm held close to the left side of her chest, her head down and the lower part of her face hidden by the tough buffalo-hide shield, Dark Moon kept her chin tucked to protect her throat. Slowly she and the Chickasaw began to circle, countering each other, their shields floating in a flexible rhythm with their bodies to avoid each other's line of strike.

The Chickasaw tested Dark Moon with a feint. Quickly ducking his head and bending his upper torso, he shifted his shoulder with the upright tomahawk and grunted as he moved forward, whipping it downward. Dark Moon bent low and forcefully thrust her leather shield upward at an angle, checking and deflecting the blow of the ax. She emitted a blood-chilling yell to intimidate her opponent and punctuate the strike. She took a quick, smooth step forward as her right arm explosively thrust the spear forward and upward beneath his shield.

Dark Moon's spear pierced and passed all the way through the warrior's body. His strength leaving him, the opponent remained standing but bent over. His eyes and mouth were opened wide in shock as his hands grasped the wooden shaft protruding from his lower belly. She jerked the spear backward, but not far enough. She released it and still crouched, quickly circled the warrior, whose arms and legs were jerking wildly, as he sunk to his knees. Only her eyes and the top of her head showed over the shield. All watching the close combat noticed the stunned and shattered eyes of the surprised veteran Chickasaw warrior. A loud *"UUh-aaaahhhhhh"* escaped his throat just before Dark Moon closed on him. His eyes, now full of horror and pain, bulged as her knife started high on the left under the ear, and passed deeply across his throat. Dark Moon used her shield to block the spewing mist of blood, pumping out in a furious stream. Then a thicker arc of blood pulsed up and outward, signaling the dying beat of his heart.

The jerking warrior, able only to gargle and spray blood, tried to turn. With her foot, Dark Moon shoved him violently to the ground. Wolfgang watched as she and the four Osage mutilated the wounded survivors. He heard the sucking sound as the scalplocks, complete with ears, were savagely and easily removed from the dead victims' heads. Then the Osage stopped to watch the tall, well-proportioned Dark Moon walk around the side of the dead Chickasaw and look deep into his eyes, and quickly stabbed each of his eyes so that he could not see his way into the next life. Sensing no danger from the Osage, she returned to Wolfgang's side. All the Osage took notice of her shield, with its braided hair scalps around the edge of the shield, and knew that they were in the presence of a formidable woman of great power. They also knew that they had not only witnessed a great seasoned woman warrior in action, but also a man extraordinarily skilled with a rifle.

After giving the sign of peace, the Osage slowly approached them. The wolf, rising to a standing position, issued a low warning growl, its head lifted, and four paws planted.

The hesitant Osage stopped where he was, and spoke with sign language that he was of the Ni U Konska Osage. Venturing no closer, he regarded the woman tending her man but also watched the wolf. The animal continued its deep-chested, low rumbling growl. Its hackles were raised stiff and high along its back, lips curled back and exposing gleaming white teeth. Its ears stiffly erect and forward-pointing now, it sent an unmistakable warning to the Osage: this wolf would sink its teeth into anyone it thought a threat.

Wolfgang sharply signed and spoke for the wolf to sit. The animal instantly obeyed.

The warriors were greatly impressed by Wolfgang's control of the animal. Still slightly confused, the animal continued to emit a low growl as its wild, intelligent yellow eyes fixedly scrutinized the assembled warriors. The Osage avoided making direct eye contact, knowing a direct stare is a threat to the wolf.

Finally, accepting them as friends, the formidable beast wagged its black-tipped tail and sat, alertly watching.

Wolfgang had been hit with two arrows. Dark Moon examined his leg wound first, and found the arrow had passed almost through, barely missing the bone and the vital artery. She unpacked her medicine bag from her horse. Asking the largest warrior to help him take the weight off the wounded leg, she opened up his leggings. The arrowhead was just barely peeking out the backside of his leg. She knew that the dry sinew wrapping that secured the arrowhead to the shaft would gradually loosen from contact with the hot, wet blood, and that would make matters worse. She gave Wolfgang a piece of thick leather to bite down on against the pain. Giving him no time to think about what she was about to do, she swiftly bent and gave the arrow shaft a sharp push. Immediately its head became visible, sticking out the backside of Wolfgang's leg. Dark Moon deftly notched the shaft behind the arrowhead's sinew wrapping and snapped it off. Then she placed her left hand on his leg, and with her right hand gripped the shaft as close to her left hand as possible, jerking it out clean. Wolfgang hissed around the leather scrap clamped tightly between his teeth.

Signing to the large Osage to lay Wolfgang on his left side, Dark Moon stuffed the wound with a mix of common yarrow, spider webs, downy fluff from cattails and a fine powder from the roots and leaves of nettle; these would staunch and coagulate the bleeding. Then she bound the wound with a clean sash. She was relieved to see that the other wound was much less serious.

As Dark Moon worked, the Osage watched in amazement. When she was done, the large warrior asked by sign language if she were a woman shaman -- a medicine woman. She knew the risk of replying: if too many people died under a healer's care they were sometimes put to death by being cut to pieces then widely dispersed, to prevent them from using their power to reassemble and practice the mystery of their magic on the people.

Nonetheless, she replied honestly.

"Yes."

She met the warriors' gaze.

Each man wore his hair in a small roach with a scalp lock with the rest of his head -- including his eyebrows -- shaved. Each had vertical lines tattooed on his red-painted face and his ears split with small rings attached. Each also had a nose ring. Only one warrior wore his hair long and restrained by a light tan-colored headband made from the underbelly fur of an otter. All were naked from the waist up, with horizontal lines tattooed on their chests and arms to signify acts of bravery. The leather belts around their waists were a hand-span wide, with sheath knives and small pouches attached. Their beautifully tanned deerskin leggings were fringed with scalp locks, split above their moccasins. Beaded garter strips were worn below the knee. Breechcloths with short flaps barely covered the crotch.

The biggest Osage warrior signed to Wolfgang and Dark Moon. Right palm up, he shook it back and forth.

"Question."

He continued to sign, his fist in front of his mouth and extending his forefinger again at her while moving his hand forward.

"You called."

Her expression hard and watchful, she signed back, holding extended hands in front of her body and crossing the right hand over the left hand. Then she made a curved thumb and index of right hand to form a moon, and held it in their line of vision where the moon should be on high.

"Dark Moon."

She pointed at Wolfgang and held her right hand with palm outwards near the right shoulder, first and second fingers extended and separated and pointing up. Then she moved her hand several inches to front and upwards.

"Wolf."

The Osage pointed his right thumb at his breast. Me. He extended the fingers of both hands and compressed them in front of his body and opposite each other. He moved them further apart but still opposite each other. *Big.* He then made two fist palms inward, raised them to his head and extended both forefingers. *Buffalo.* His right hand, balled into a fist, came up in front of his face, palm in and forefinger pointed straight up. *Male.* Dark Moon now knew that the big warrior's name was Big Bull.

The Osage began to talk among themselves, and then stopped. Big Bull signed that they had heard many stories of the man known as Wolf. Looking at Dark Moon, Big Bull signed, "Him two-legged man-bear?"

"Yes," Dark Moon replied.

One warrior turned from the group and ran back along the trail. As he ran away, Wolfgang saw his upper shoulders tattooed with concentric circles. The elder Big Bull, the fierce-looking, bold-faced man, signed and spoke to make himself understood to all.

"We know you. You Algonquian Sorceress. Him have mark of great bear. Friend of wolf. Dark Moon kill Chickasaw war chief. Him Tattooed Snake."

He pointed and signed the names of the others with him: Fox Eyes. Spotted Deer. Him run up trail. Him called Flying Man. Wolfgang had already noted that the runner had been lean, of medium build, and looked to be very fast.

Wolfgang sensed the physical power of the big Osage warrior. Fox Eyes, on the other hand, seemed particularly alert.

The longhaired warrior, his gaze darting constantly, had a gunstock-type wooden war club decorated with brass trade tack studs and a wide, bloody blade, its handle-grip wrapped with the skin of a large rattlesnake. The warrior's Osage orange wood bows were well made, and Wolfgang noticed the arrows were tipped with a white-colored arrowheads. Quartz.

Shifting his gaze to Spotted Deer, Wolfgang noted friendly eyes and a sincere-looking smile. Wolfgang and Dark Moon both felt convinced they were in safe hands.

With his penetrating eyes on the two strangers, Big Bull signed, "Flying Man go village. Tell chiefs you come. Spotted Deer take Wolf and Dark Moon village. Me, Fox Eyes stay. Watch trail.

"We have already heard all the stories," he added, smiling.

"Wolf ride horse. Signed Spotted Deer. Him hurt. Move slow."

Big Bull explained that the village was located on a tributary of the Osage River and would take ten days to reach.

Dark Moon helped Wolfgang onto his horse. Once mounted, he pointed at the wolf. Lifting one paw, the animal whirled with incredible speed and ran ahead. Standing by her mount, Dark Moon turned to Big Bull, extended both hands, palms down, and swept them out and downward.

"Thank you."

Chapter 22

The first evening on the trail, they stopped by a stream, where Dark Moon spotted the distant, luminous silver-white bark branches of ancient sycamores. Knowing the old trees were often hollow, she rode the horses toward the tree. She was pleased, easily finding a hollowed sycamore; it was gigantic in girth, and offered space enough inside for them to camp. Luckily its cavity faced to the west, out of the wind.

After making Wolfgang comfortable, Dark Moon led the horses first to water then to graze. After checking their backs for sores and their hooves for cracks, she hobbled the animals to limit their wanderings while eating. From a short distance away, she watched them graze, focusing on their eyes and ears. She knew that their ears would twitch at the first sign of danger. *For now, it was safe.* Later she would return and bring them to the camp to tie them for the night -- to prevent them from being stolen but also so they would be ready for immediate use if necessary. Returning to Wolfgang, Dark Moon cleaned his wounds and administered a comfrey poultice from purplish-blue, yellow, and white flowered plants she had found in the moist places along the stream.

During the night, she fed him a tea made from the dried roots of the purple coneflower to prevent septic infection. Spotted Deer remained on watch. Only once did the horses smell and hear something prowling, and then Dark Moon went to speak gently to them and to touch them. Before the beginning of morning twilight, Spotted Deer softly spoke to her, saying that it was time for them both to be on their guard. During these quiet hours, Dark Moon reflected back upon the time she had spent with Wolfgang, and realized that she had never known such happiness as that which Wolfgang brought when he came into her life.

* * *

As sun-up arrived, Dark Moon watered the horses and took them to graze, again hobbling them. Returning to prepare them all a meal, she was happy to find that Wolfgang's forehead and the back of his neck felt normal to her touch; just in case, she made willow tea and made him drink it to fight wound inflammation, and fever. She pulled out a small coffee pot and the little coffee mill and ground some beans for Spotted Deer. The Osage was amazed at her skill with the horses, for his people had very few of these animals. He was also impressed by the way she noticed the horses' attitudes and conditions. He was well aware of the power of other Indians far to the west, rich with many horses. The animals improved their ability to hunt, make war and move their camps easily. Spotted Deer liked horses, even though they left tracks and dung an enemy could easily follow.

He watched the circular motion of her hands as she prepared the coffee. The smell of the fresh-ground beans was wonderful. When Dark Moon handed him a hot cup of coffee laced with sugar, she watched his eyes and smiled at his reaction. He made the small turning motion that she had made while turning the crank of the mill to grind the beans, and smiled. Spotted Deer liked this woman.

* * *

The party crossed through large, bronze-colored natural prairies of thick bluestem grass, which rose above their knees. Spotted Deer turned and pointed into the distance. He hand-signed, closed hands with his wrist at the top and to the forward side of his head and stuck both of his curved forefingers up in the air like horns. *"Buffalo."*

Dark Moon turned to tell Wolfgang there were buffalo ahead. Sure enough, before long, they spied a few old buffalo bulls -- the only creatures to be seen or heard except for the shrill, thin skree of a distant hawk high above dipping and soaring.

Hours later, they climbed through dry soil hills into hundred-foot stands of short-leaf pine. Smelling the warm, resinous aroma, Wolfgang couldn't help admiring the towering trees' straight trunks, covered with rosy-orange plates of bark. Around many of the looming giants the ground was trampled and the tree trunks showed signs of horn-and head-rubs. The thick air was rank with the musty, acrid smell of the living wall of a large herd, a mixture of dung and the musty wool of hairy bodies. Noticing small, bare, damp depressions in the open grassland, Wolfgang saw round, flat manure pads; their guide said it was buffalo wallows. Wolfgang stopped to stare at the buffalo tracks, and thought that they looked like cow tracks.

When they started across another bluestem prairie, they could hear bulls roaring and bellowing, the sign of the buffalo rut, and a low rumbling and bawling, all of which grew steadily louder as they continued. Spotted Deer warned that, since it was almost time for the bulls to breed, it would not be safe to pass too close: the animals were unpredictable, surprisingly fast and dangerous. Small black birds swooped in the distance. Spotted Deer signed that they would soon see buffalo. The sun hung directly overhead when they neared the top of a rise, and Dark Moon and Spotted Deer stopped. Dropping to all fours, they crept up to the top.

Below, they saw the grand sight of a prairie covered by hundreds of fat-rumped buffalo, most of them lying down. Over each group presided an immense, powerful and savage-looking bull.

"The herd's calmness indicates that the animals believe no one is hunting them. A good sign for us," Dark Moon signed.

The party passed only close enough then to see the huge beasts stare belligerently at them and to hear them snuffling and biting off mouthfuls of grass. Spotted Deer said that passing so close to the herd would allow their back trail to disappear under the many hooves as they moved aimlessly around. Wolfgang's leg hurt, but the sight of hundreds of buffalo, and their sheer size, took his mind off his shoulder and leg. He saw the slobbering nostrils dilate as they tried to draw in their scent. A few shook their heads, unafraid, and continued cropping grass. Wolfgang was thankful. A rutting bull would need little provocation to turn ugly and destroy anything in its path.

The earth trembled beneath the weight of so many hooves. Wolfgang and party knew that any hunter, suddenly caught in the middle of a herd, would wind up beneath those hooves. As they passed the herd, playful calves held their tails half-cocked, then suddenly kicked their heels in the air, gave chase to each other, then stopped and wheeled without warning, occasionally butting heads.

Traveling along the top of an open ridge, Wolfgang saw a low point, two miles away, which could only mean a creek, stream or river. Before long the party had passed the herd. The three soon reached and entered the shadows of oak trees. As they continued, Wolfgang recognized white and bur oaks. Moving through the trees, stopping often to watch and listen, and feeling comforted to hear only the sounds of birds, Wolfgang pointed to light-colored worn spots in the wide, thick, grayish fissures of bark on the oak trees; Spotted Deer, nodding, pointed in turn at the long, slightly kinky brown hair stuck in the bark. They both understood: buffalo. *A rubbing post.*

The branches of the tall, dark trees, so closely spaced that they mingled overhead, produced a deep gloom that left the open ground all but devoid of brush. As the sun now neared the unseen western horizon, Wolfgang knew it would grow darker quickly -- and cooler, though right now he felt uncomfortably hot. The combination of pain and fatigue left him feeling haggard as they moved with little sound. The forest became thick with brush at ground level. They were nearing a stream, and began to see walnut trees. Tall cottonwoods, sycamores, and elm rose ahead. Spotted Deer stopped.

"A trail leading to the village is nearby," he signed.

Wolfgang was impressed by their guide, who showed so much caution even though he was so close to his village, located beside a small creek flowing into a natural cove. Wolfgang's eyes focused on the lazily flowing waters. But all at once his vision blurred; he shook his head, but when his vision blurred again -- accompanied now by light-headedness -- he realized he suddenly could barely see.

Her eyes registering alarm, Dark Moon realized Wolfgang was fever-wracked and exhausted, and would likely soon slip from his horse. His skin looked dry and flushed and, feeling his forehead and the back of his neck, she found it much too hot. She knew she must find a place to tend to him quickly.

Dark Moon called out to Spotted Deer and signed for him to hurry back. The guide took one look at Wolfgang and grasped the horse's halter. Flying Man appeared on the other side of the horse and helped Dark Moon hold Wolfgang in place as the small party hurried into the village.

The warriors who met them beat snapping, snarling, hungry-looking dogs away. Clicking his teeth, the bristling, stiff-legged wolf was crowded by the village dogs. He quickly killed two of the wolfish-looking dogs and the rest slunk away in fear. Never had the people of the village seen such a great wolf, tall, heavy, longhaired and broad-headed. Groups of small, naked children gathered and gawked. Dark Moon saw the curious looks of the men and women directed at her attire.

The familiar village scents of wood smoke, earth, bark, sweat, and roasting meat filled Dark Moon's nostrils. She saw that the Osage lived in rectangular wigwams positioned under the protective cover of trees. She was overjoyed at the sight of the straight, columnar trunks of a grove of elm trees, which she identified from the diamond-shaped ridges of their bark, and which stood well over a hundred feet tall. Their huge girths and overhead limbs swept outward in vaulting arches to form a great dome of interlocking branches high above the village shading and protecting it in all weather.

In order to begin tending to Wolfgang quickly, Dark Moon asked Spotted Deer to have someone bring her the inner bark of an elm. She needed it to begin ministering to her companion's wounds. I will ground equal amounts of golden seal root and the inner bark of slippery elm into powder and apply it directly into the wound. That will heal him quickly.

Chapter 23

It was the Moon of Ripening in 1757. As Wolfgang rested, Dark Moon told him about the village; it lay on the bottom of ridge along the Osage River near Big Buffalo Creek, which entered the river from the northwest. Two miles downstream across the river ran Little Buffalo Creek, while immediately across it rose steep, timbered bluffs.

Wolfgang's mind was now clear. He was sitting up in the wigwam, sipping tea Dark Moon had made for him this evening.

He said, "The aches and stiffness in my shoulder and leg didn't bother my sleep."

"That's because you have been drinking my brandy," she answered. "You have been asleep for two days."

When he looked at her doubtfully, she nodded.

"I boil yellow arnica flowers and its ground roots together. The oil from both added to the brandy takes away the pain."

As he tried to get up to one elbow, she propped him up with one of their packs, and brought him a cup of broth. He drained it and asked for another.

"Rest one more day," Dark Moon said. "Tomorrow I'll help you go to the stream to bathe and get some exercise. The wolf has been like a lost soul. He scent-marks the area around the wigwam to warn off the other animals. I have seen him with his leg raised against the shelter. None of the village dogs will come near here. Each evening he comes and peaks in the door. He waits for me to give the command 'come.' He tiptoes in and stares into your sleeping face and then accepts meat from my hand. Then he goes outside and makes a long mournful howl, setting off all the village dogs." Wolfgang watched her laugh. *She is so beautiful.*

Then he said, "I dreamed there were two wolves in our lives."

"Big Bull has a large female wolf, the only one in the village," answered Dark Moon. She realized that there was a true spiritual bond between the wolf and her man.

* * *

The people of the village got their first real look at Wolfgang as he limped through it to wash himself at the creek. The wolf ran to him the moment it spotted him. They stared as the animal ran in circles around the stranger, whining and leaping in a frenzied, ecstatic display. When the beast stood upright, resting its forepaws on his master's shoulders, mouthed and licked his face with obvious affection, the villagers were astounded. They were in awe of the spectacle of a medicine animal known for its stoicism and power, yet behaving like a fawning puppy. Surely this wolf -- larger than any the Osage had ever seen -- must speak for Wolfgang and Dark Moon to the spirit world.

The villagers were also struck by the magnetism of the beautiful woman, who moved always with an innate grace. Though her frequent, friendly smiles showed beautiful, even white teeth, anyone who looked into her dark eyes saw a mysterious black pit that plainly was no place to linger. She seemed older than her man, but her exact age remained a mystery. And at night around the fires, when Dark Moon and Wolfgang were elsewhere, the Osage warriors told again and again the story of her hand-to-hand fight with the Chickasaw war chief.

After several days, Wolfgang went to gently exercise his leg and arm, and found himself being greeted by everyone. He considered them the finest and proudest-looking Indians he had seen, aside from the Iroquois, whom he did not like. The women wore wide belts with knives and were adorned with earrings, bracelets and tattoos. They all smelled of columbine seed.

During the next days, everywhere Wolfgang went, he found their ruddy faces with glittering eyes smiling at him. From the way he carried himself, they recognized him as a predator -- one who had lived a solitary life in the great eastern forest and had survived. They could tell he was dangerous.

* * *

One day the warrior Big Bull called upon Dark Moon and Wolfgang to inquire about the latter's condition and to give them fresh meat. Later, as Dark Moon examined his wounds, Flying Man visited. The warrior laughed and talked as he signed:
"Wolf big stabbing teeth kill quick. Two bad dogs. Soon knock head. Make stew."

All the time that Flying Man talked, his eyes roamed the wounds, old and new, which covered Wolfgang's body. He well knew he was in the presence of a great warrior. His visit was short, and after he left, Flying Man went directly to Big Bull, Spotted Deer and Fox Eyes to discuss this new man. Later, the smiling women of Big Bull, Fox Eyes and Spotted Deer came to talk with Dark Moon, bringing with them dandelion, water cress, young stems of cattails, wild onions, fruit, berries, and morel mushrooms as gifts. Feeling the kindness and warmth of these tall, handsome, tattooed people, Wolfgang and Dark Moon knew they liked the Osage.

By the time Wolfgang was recovered, he had decided

what to do with his five extra rifles. He presented one to the chief, and the others to the elder warrior, Big Bull, and his three followers -- Spotted Deer, Fox Eyes and Flying Man. He included full powder horns as well. When he gave them to the men, he did not forget to tell them that these had belonged to great Iroquois warriors.

*   *   *

The warriors of the village having recently returned from a raid against the Chickasaw with many scalps, the little old men of the village invited Dark Moon and Wolfgang for a scalp dance.

Escorted by Big Bull, Wolfgang entered a large structure in the center of the village and was shown where to sit. After the warriors had recounted their exploits by chanting and dancing, the women came forward.

Wolfing and Dark Moon watched the scalp-dance as firelight shimmered on the roof overhead. Dressed as warriors for the dance, the Osage women were naked from the waist up, their exposed skin painted and striped. Bear grease, mixed with soot painted across their eyes, signified their defiance. They carried fresh, gory scalps strung out on the end of small saplings and brandished tomahawks. These they waved high in the air as they sang and danced in a circular frenzy, feeling the loss of loved ones.

Dark Moon explained to Wolfing that this dance -- a showy display accompanied by the sound of throbbing drums, rattles, and pounding of feet -- allowed the women of the tribe to release their anger and tension. Piercing screams, whoops, and wails pervaded the night, as the songs described the taking of the scalps. The dance lasted until well after the moon had risen.

The Osage Hunkah war chief present represented fifteen clans of the Earth People, who were symbolic of leaders in war.

He was greatly impressed with Wolfgang and his gift of the rifles. The chief signed that these weapons were exactly what his warriors needed, since it took less time and effort to cast a lead ball than to make an arrow that was straight and true.

The chief explained to both that the Meshkwakihug, or "red earth people," were called the Fox by the French.

"The Fox and their allies, the Saux and Kickapoos," the chief went on, "will soon move southwest from the Wisconsin Valley and the northern Iowa country, along the Mississippi, then disperse west during the Moon of Ripening or Moon of Falling Leaves to winter and hunt the prairies. We can expect many problems."

The chief added that the alliance would permit them to war with the French and Illinois tribes. The French wanted the lead mines that belonged to the Fox across from the northern Illinois country. The Fox, Saux, and Kickapoo together had many more warriors than the Osage people. The chief therefore had need of the longhunter called Wolf, who spoke his woman's Algonquian language.

"To prevent surprise," the chief said, "you will be with just one of many small groups that will watch and protect our land. The Wolf will accompany a party consisting of Big Bull, Spotted Deer, Fox Eyes, and Flying Man. You must watch south of the Missouri village at the joining of the Grand and Missouri Rivers. The Fox, Saux, and Kickapoo all speak Algonquian. If you wish to remain the winter with us, you will serve as one of my wolves." The chief continued, "You and a few others will be my eyes and ears, and warn me of any raid. Dark Moon will remain with the village, helping our medicine man. He will soon go to the spirit world. You must teach them about the fire stick"

The chief directed his attention toward Big Bull, Spotted Deer, Fox Eyes, and Flying Man. The four warriors' eyes were intense. The chief's voice sounded grave as he said: "You must learn to do this thing with the fire stick. I, too, shall go and learn."

"You must send warriors to collect more powder from the French mines," Wolfgang replied. "They should wait for the French overseer to be drunk or absent and then ask for the black slave named Louis. Show him the sign of the Wolf for his help in obtaining more powder."

Wolfgang instructed the warriors to wear long-sleeved leather shirts the next day to minimize the chance of being burned by a spark. Before breaking up and going back to their lodges, they agreed to meet at the edge of the village at mid-morning.

*   *   *

The four Osage warriors believed that Wolfgang's rifle was endowed with magical powers. The stories of this brave man's adventures, especially his war with the Iroquois, were spreading fast, told around the night fires of all the tribes in the whole country. The Indians of the territory, known to the Europeans as New France, believed that the Iroquois needed his scalp to dry the tears of their many mourning relatives.

The next morning, when they assembled at the edge of the village, Wolfgang asked for three pumpkins. Lifting one, he gestured for Flying Man and Big Bull to carry the others as he led the way to an open area some distance from the village. Setting the pumpkins on a downed log, he led the men some thirty yards back. He reached down, broke off a stalk of grass and stuck it into his mouth.

"We all know the purpose for our gathering," Wolfgang signed. He unslung the rifle carried diagonally across his back and showed the Osage how to adjust the sling and buckle.

He said, "It's easier to carry the weapon long distances across your backs when you have to move fast on foot through open country. When you're moving slowly through the cover of

The War Trail

forest and brush, you should carry it at the ready, always expecting an enemy. When you're running through forest and brush, you should carry it in one hand below waist level for good balance and to avoid brush."

Next Wolfgang showed them the firing mechanism. "We call this the battery." He explained that for loading, the steel frizzen must be open and the cock or hammer, in the down or fired position. "The white man calls this part the dog's head or 'cock' because it resembles a cock rooster's head. The cock has a piece of flint in its beak wrapped in elk skin." With the stalk of grass he first pointed to the flint and then the steel, and then to the trigger, telling them that when he pulled the trigger, the correctly positioned flint hitting the steel frizzen would cause sparks and the contents of the barrel would explode. Wolfgang unscrewed the dog's head and showed them how the dark, flat-topped flint was shaped for its purpose.

"The beveled edge of the flint is always up, with the cutting edge on the downward side," Wolfgang said, pointing. "Each of you must always have several extra flints, because a good one lasts only about fifty shots. It might even break apart after just one shot. Without flint, the rifle is useless."

After everyone had examined the flint thoroughly, Wolfgang replaced it, showing how to use the screwdriver to tighten the screw. He told them that this screw that held the jaws of the cock holding the flint tight must always be checked. Before loading, Wolfgang pointed to the end of the ramrod below the muzzle of the rifle, and explained that the cupped brass end was for ramming the ball down the barrel. He pulled it out and flipped it around, showing them the two marks on his ramrod.

"I'll tell you what these are for in a moment," Wolfgang said.

He took up his powder horn, the large end enclosed with a wooden disk and the small end kept in place by a close-fitted wooden plug, which he now removed. Pouring two-and-a-half drams of black powder into his hand, he showed it to them. "A dram is equal to 60 grains of powder," Wolfgang said. "You must use this much each time, never more, never less."

He poured it into the barrel, and then removed a lead roundball from his bullet pouch, wrapped it in a greased scrap of thin deer hide, and pressed it into the muzzle of the barrel with his thumb. "For accuracy load the tightest fit you can get in the barrel," he said.

Wolfgang removed the ramrod from the barrel hoops and used it to ram the ball into the gun as far as it would go. Tamping the charge, he said, "This is to be sure the round ball is properly and firmly seated on the powder charge and that there is no trapped air left in the charge."

Leaving the ramrod in the rifle, he pointed at the remaining mark on it at the muzzle.

"And this mark indicates the ball is properly seated."

He removed the ramrod and leaned it against his leg. Withdrawing the stalk of grass from his mouth, he directed their attention to the pan placed behind the rear sight, above the end of the barrel. Then he identified for them the very small touchhole, which connected with the inside of the barrel. Next he slowly used a flash-hole quill to open the channel of the flash-hole, and then showed them how to prime their rifles. He placed the hammer at the half-cock position and poured a small amount of priming powder into the flash pan, taking care not to cover the touchhole with powder. If it was covered with powder, he explained, the ignition would be slowed. "Prime the pan only half-full," he said looking at them

Wolfgang emphasized that it was important now not to cant the rifle to avoid spilling the powder. He closed the steel frizzen. The powder in the pan was now protected from the wind and dampness.

"This must always be the same," Wolfgang said. "The

frizzen is made of steel and the flint that strikes it will cause the spark, which ignites the priming and then the barrel charge."

He showed the warriors quickly how he could make fire with a piece of flint and his steel tomahawk, while telling them that the frizzen was made of the same metal as the tomahawk. The warriors said they would be more careful in the future to watch for steel tomahawks carried among their enemies. In their eyes, he could see that they also desired steel tomahawks. He continued with his demonstration.

After walking fifty paces, Wolfgang turned, dragged the dog head on the hammer back to full cock, shouldered his rifle, aimed, and fired. They saw the flash in the pan, and the smoke beyond the muzzle of the rifle -- and the pumpkin exploded. Having told them to hold their rifles steady while firing, he made them practice at twenty paces until they could hit the pumpkins. Satisfied, he set up a large piece of a remaining pumpkin and told both men to walk with him a hundred yards away. As he walked, Wolfgang loaded and at a hundred yards he turned, steadied, and fired. They saw the slab of pumpkin shower into pieces. Then he told the Osage to wait where they were, while he walked forward and picked up a pumpkin piece that was two hands wide. He walked it out as far as 250 yards, propped it up on a log and walked back.

As they watched him, the Osage seemed nervous. Wolfgang said the piece of pumpkin was nearly the size of a man's chest. Again the Osage watched as he aimed and fired. The piece appeared not to move at all. They all walked toward it and saw a hole through its center. Expecting a trick, the Osage asked him to do it again. They walked back, their eyes showing suspicion. Wolfgang turned, aimed and fired. Now the warriors ran to the target and beheld the second hole. He watched them whoop and dance in the distance when they realized what had been done. Their eyes shining, they were beaming with smiles when they returned to Wolfgang, for they recognized the gift of magical power he had offered them.

"It is important to use this greased patch for accurate long-range shooting," he further instructed. "In emergency situations, such as an enemy getting too close, you must load without the patch. Since your enemies can shoot four or five arrows in the time it would take you to reload your rifles, you must keep your enemy from getting within arrow range.

"A flight of arrows well shot will unnerve anyone," Wolfgang continued. "You must not let your enemies get close -- which means you must learn to shoot these weapons well."

He also told them that since they would consume gunpowder quickly, they must always have a good supply and that they must practice from the distance they had first fired, then from seven paces back, then seven back again, until they could hit at 100 yards.

"When shooting at men, aim low because when you get excited, you will tend to shoot high."

Wolfgang said they must practice reloading now until they could hit two charging warriors before the two could cover that distance.

Wolfgang told the Osage that they would not be able to load as fast as he could because it took lots of practice. But the barrels of their rifles were much longer and more accurate at a longer range, if they practiced. Wolfgang saw the light of recognition in Big Bull's eyes, and he knew that this man would work hard at mastering his weapon. He then instructed each warrior to mark his ramrod, so he would know when it was unloaded or loaded. Asking them to sit together a few paces behind him, he worked with one at a time, making sure the others watched closely. As they took turns firing, they all watched each other's odd behavior as each missed the target. They laughed at one another's reactions, their eyes stunned by the initial flash in the pan, followed by the thundering boom, and their noses filled with the cloud of sulfurous smoke. They realized that they had looked the same to each other, and had to think about overcoming these sensations and practice making the weapon work for them. Muttering to each other about Wolfgang's calm, steady demeanor when firing the rifle -- and his accuracy! – the chief and warriors knew they must master this challenge.

Wolfgang removed his small spiral-shaped metal worm from the inside of his stock and twisted it onto the wooden end of his ramrod. He then attached a slightly moistened patch to extinguish any lingering sparks and changed to a clean patch to oil their barrels. Setting the muzzle down on a piece of leather, he told them all to watch the end of the barrel. He used a small metal needle flattened at one end with a sharp edge, called a vent pick, to insert and clean the touchhole to insure fast ignition for the next shot. As his hand slightly twisted, they all heard and saw small pieces of hard powder drop onto the leather. Wolfgang said that this must always be done when they find the time, because if the little hole clogged, only the powder in the pan would ignite and not the charge in the barrel; their charging enemies might well have time to kill them.

Wolfgang found a large, downed tree for them to kneel behind and rest their rifles on so that the force of the explosion would not throw off their aim.

* * *

Each day, he worked with one man at a time, always checking the fit of the cock to the lock, the flint in its jaws for sharpness, and the position of the dropped sparks at the end of the throw, all of which were critical for a quicker lock time and accurate shooting. He explained that a combination of the quick lock time, the long sighting plane and balance was what made these rifles accurate in offhand shooting at long range. As the Osage became better marksmen, he had them stand to fire their rifles by using the side of a tree to steady their aim. Knowing they were now familiar with the basics of the rifle, Wolfgang told them they were doing so well that it was time for them to develop on their own.

First, however, Wolfgang would give them one last demonstration. He picked three tall, straight trees some distance apart -- the width of a man's shoulders -- and took the group up to inspect the trees. Upon each tree he used his tomahawk to blaze the bark as a target. These marks were palm size. As he walked away, he told them to remain where they were and to stay alert and watch, for he would leave them briefly. Wolfgang walked away and disappeared into the woods.

After some time passed, the Osage began to wonder and mutter among themselves. Suddenly, they heard the patterned, almost silent fall of fast running feet. They all turned their heads and saw Wolfgang, almost upon them, coming fast, his rifle held in one hand. They were surprised to see him so close without having heard him coming. He seemed much taller, and more intimidating. He ran smoothly and quietly, his eyes forward, looking ahead at the horizon. His running style was efficient, with his body alignment straight, his shoulders carried level and low. His face and hands were relaxed. He ran directly toward a downed tree trunk. Then he swerved away and back again and cleared it with one arm extended to the trunk.

The Osage realized he would pass between them and the identified target tree. When Wolfgang was almost between them and the tree, they saw him lift the rifle across his mid section, steady it with the open palm of his left hand and fire. Wood flew from the tree. He continued to run with the rifle. Before they knew it, his tomahawk had flipped end-over-end and planted itself in the center of the next target tree at chest level in the middle of the blaze. He continued to run while reaching for his knife. Quickly, it flipped end over end and planted itself in the blaze mark.

Wolfgang stopped, turned and walked toward the watching Osage, who were now whooping and yelping. He, however, remained unsmiling as he fixed his gaze firmly on each of them, his eyes showing the penetrating intent and assurance of someone older. The Osage understood that this was not just some showy display, but a quick-witted demonstration of survival. Together they all walked up to the first tree and saw the hole at center mass, chest level. Then they walked to the trees to recover his tomahawk and his knife. As he primed and charged his flintlock, he looked at them.

"There is much to learn, practice, and teach your other warriors," he said. Wolfgang saw the fire in their eyes and knew they would practice.

"I have seen the truth of why there are so many stories about you and the Iroquois," said Big Bull.

Wolfgang nodded.

"At a long distance, kill as many of your enemies as you can, then move away. Use the terrain, which offers the best cover and concealment, avoiding the trails. Also use the cover of dense woods, folds in the ground, creeks in the ravines, and hills to retreat to another concealed firing position. Observe your enemy from pre-planned observation points. You must avoid skylining yourself. Stay away from the crest of the hills. Always change your direction of travel. This is most important when you are caught in open, high grass. Once at a new position, reload quickly and wait to make another well-aimed shot to kill. Before the smoke clears, you must again be gone. When your enemies realize you are gone, they will give chase. You must plan for this, since during this chase you will kill many enemies even as you seem to run away. Eventually they will lose heart."

When Wolfgang paused in his instructions, Big Bull asked what the traders would want for a rifle.

"The Indian must pay twenty beaver skins for a Trade gun," Wolfgang replied. "The white man can trade this same way or pay twenty-five dollars for a good Pennsylvania rifle."

He pressed his thumb into the rifle's muzzle and explained that the weapons sold by white traders were not all the same. Indians to the east chose the fusil, a cheaply made smoothbore with a light barrel, which could be carried comfortably all day. Loaded with a single-round ball big enough for large animals at close range or with smaller balls of shot for large birds, the fusil worked well enough. But it was a bad choice for warfare.

Wolfgang removed his thumb and showed the barrel grooves impressed upon it. Drawing a circle in the dirt, he said, "This was the smoothbore -- the type all your Indian enemies carry. In war, a single well-placed lead roundball directed by a rifled barrel will win your fight. The rifle can shoot much further, allowing you to reload before your enemy can get to you. The British and Americans give their allies, the Chickasaw, rifles to fight the French. These rifles I have given you were taken from Iroquois warriors. When you kill an enemy, you must try to get all his weapons -- and powder horns, flints and shot -- but the rifle is the most important."

Big Bull again asked, "Who made these rifles and where can we get more?"

"These were the best made. That's why I held onto them until I decided to give them to you. They were made far to the east, in Lancaster, the birthplace of the Pennsylvania rifle. They are transported over the Allegheny Mountains to the Three Forks, then down the Spay-lay-wi-theepi to Chief Monakaduto's village of Chininque for trade. The English call it Loggs Town. It is there that the English trade with the Delaware, Cayugas, Senecas and Shawnee tribes. You'll need supplies for the rifles as well. The traders will give you three flints for one beaver skin, and four skins would get you a pound of powder. Since black powder is dangerous to make, you can buy or trade for it at Kaskaskia. Make sure to get it from the black men who make it near the mines, or simply take it. Tell them that is the price for letting them live on your side of the river."

* * *

After seven days' practice, the chief and his warriors were ready to hunt on their own. The chief ordered each man to bring back a deer, elk or bear to the village. Just a short time later, all had succeeded; the hunting proved much easier with the rifle and everyone was happy with the plentiful game.

After eating their evening meal, the men assembled in the chief's lodge, the largest in the village. While Dark Moon made them coffee strongly laced with sugar, Wolfgang showed how to care for the rifles' firing locks.

The chief said, "Longer than anyone can remember, the Iroquois have carried on a series of wars against western tribes. Now the French have come, and also the Spanish, and soon will come the British and Americans. We kill all coureurs de bois attempting to go through our territory to trade guns with our enemies--the Taovaya, the Kadohadacho and Kitikiti'sh." He paused and nodded to Dark Moon.

She leaned forward to Wolfgang and whispered, "The Kadohadacho are known as the 'real chiefs.' She continued, "The Kitikiti'sh are the raccoon-eyed people. The French refer to them both as the Taovaya, and they live to the south and southwest of here."

When the chief was sure Dark Moon was finished, he said, "The Taovaya trade weapons to the Commanche for horses. We must obtain more rifles, and our younger warriors must learn to use these weapons well."

Wolfgang worried. *There are so many hostile tribes spread across this land.*

Chapter 24

It was October 1757, the Moon of Winter. The Chickasaw scout had been heading north through the autumn-colored hills for two hours, his gaze ever shifting. He had followed the high ground above what was called Rainy Creek, then turned northwest after a night's rest at a cave near a natural spring. As he advanced into the wind, the distant scream of a large hunting cat reached his ears. The scout felt relieved that by the time the sun set on his left side, he would be within sight of the Osage village.

* * *

The mountain lion had first begun following the Indian out of curiosity. When the huge tom first spotted the Chickasaw, he had been merely returning to his deer kill to feed. But as the Chickasaw drew closer to the remains, the beast became possessive. Eyes and ears forward, he followed silently, moving on stealthy, padded feet, to within fifty yards of the unsuspecting man.

And suddenly the killer's yellow eyes ceased to watch with mere curiosity. Now the lion glared, for the man had found its kill.

* * *

The Chickasaw had just found the cut in the land, which told him Little Buffalo Creek lay to the east, when he noticed the buzzing of flies above a mound. The metallic scent of blood associated with death enveloped him and he stood perfectly still, his eyes scrutinizing his surroundings. Slowly, he approached the remains and kneeled.

Flies had arrived but barely: no eggs yet appeared nor had decomposition begun. Tense and alert, the scout studied the kill. The large, partially eaten buck was covered with debris, and a wide bite mark showed at the base of its skull. The remains were of a lion kill. He smelled the rank scent of the mound where the lion had urinated to cover its kill and warn off other predators.

* * *

The lion's muscles rippled as it silently stalked within fifty feet of the man. As the animal crouched motionless, eyes forward, belly low to the ground, its rear legs began pumping. Then it sprang.

Claws digging into the earth, the animal burst forward with blurring speed, covering forty feet in two bounds. The birds had stopped singing and the insects no longer buzzed. The Chickasaw's senses caught fire his eyebrows and eyelids raised, his lips drew back and his face pinched fearfully. The scout heard the slight sound of something rushing toward him and felt the earth's vibration, even as he began to turn – too late. The forest god's had called his name.

The lion slammed a powerful shoulder into the strange creature, hooking its claws into the doomed man's shoulder. The other clawed paw grasped the human by the nose of his face and pulled its head around to the backside. Long, scissor-like canines, designed for piercing and tearing, caught the victim at the top of his neck. Then they closed tight in a loving embrace around his spinal chord at the base of the skull. The spine was crushed and broke, the head almost severed.

There had been no sound in the first moments following the warrior's death, and now the only noise to break the forest silence was the rasping of the great cat's tongue as it licked thirstily at the victim's neck, drinking the blood. Then, it disemboweled its victim and rolled the stomach out and away. The cat ate the liver, heart and lungs. When its blood meal was over, the animal's back teeth, shaped for cleaving muscle and cracking bones, sheared the smaller bones of the rib cage, which the creature easily swallowed. Covering the body with forest litter, it urinated on the mound. The cat left, but he would return.

* * *

When the sun came out, it brought the first crisp frost and a chill that spoke of winter. It was good weather for hunting. Wolfgang and Big Bull knew that any tracks they found would be fresh.

The two men left the village, taking their time in leading their two pack horses up the ridge due south. After traveling less than a mile, they came to a large clearing with a small lake. The sounds of water birds were almost drowned out entirely by the high-pitched squabbling of waxwings in the sumac. Wolfgang picketed his packhorse at a point where he could see the river flowing from the west. Big Bull said he would picket his own packhorse a half-mile away in an open area as they separated.

* * *

The buck first appeared to Wolfgang as it strutted along a field edge next to a grove of giant white oaks, picking its way through the abundance of acorns scattered beneath the trees. Easing the bow to full draw, he smoothly let the wooden shaft go and saw it enter the right side of the animal's rib cage, slanting deeply forward up to the fletching. Then the buck raced through the oak leaves and collapsed.

It was a fat buck. In a gesture of respect, Wolfgang placed his hand on the deer and thanked the animal for its life. Now it was time to find Big Bull.

* * *

A faint buzzing of flies alerted Big Bull to something dead. He quickly found the remains of the Chickasaw scout. A cavernous hole gaped in the victim's upper torso. Great claw marks showed on the face and left shoulder, and tooth marks revealed that the cat had come from behind and severed the victim's neck.

The mental vision of the scout's death haunted Big Bull. He knew that lions often returned to a covered carcass. He realized that as long as the lion remained in this territory, no one would be safe. He would have to hunt the cat. Now would be the best time, for the lion would quit roaming, continuing to return to its victim to feed until not even scraps remained or until the flesh turned rancid.

Big Bull scouted the area, gradually moving uphill along the finger ridge, when suddenly he spied fresh tracks in the bare, damp earth: something had recently crossed the trail here.

He knelt to scrutinize the bent blades of grass and one well-defined print. Both indicated the direction of movement: a round pad and four toes. There were neither wind-blown signs of aging nor superimposed footprints of ants, mice or bird tracks. The track was fresh. The Osage warrior noted the distinctive curved ridges between the heel and toe pads. He also noted the track's depth and the wide spaces between the pads. It was a very large cat. As Big Bull knelt for a closer look, a tremor ran through him. Studying its direction toward the large rocks, he thought that they would serve as a good hidden observation point. The normal forest chatter of birds and squirrels had ceased. The inexplicable and ominous silence awakened Big Bull to imminent danger. He stopped and listened. The forest was talking to him.

* * *

Dropping silently to the ground, the predator pricked its hairy ears forward to catch the sound of the man. The wide yellow eyes then followed the man, its nose gently sniffing the air. With its ears back, the great carnivore decided to attack. He moved his long, heavy legs stealthily and silently, and flowed forward over the damp grass, keeping low to the ground. The cat used every bit of cover of the ground folds, trees and boulders, never taking its eyes off the hated man. The lion hesitantly placed one huge paw before another, molding sensitively to the ground litter in its stalk. Now within striking distance, the cat dropped to its belly and with swift purpose, watched.

Big Bull became aware of the stink of the cat. An odd sensation and then a tremor ran up his back. He turned his head slowly and saw it. The warrior felt an instinct to flee. The animal switched its tail, its ears pitched forward. In the sunlight, the vertical slits of its yellow eyes never left him. The flattened ears now showed its intentions.

A frightening grimace wrinkled the cougar's whiskered face as it emitted a loud wicked hiss, clamped its eyes to mere slits, and crept closer. Big Bull could see the four immense canine teeth. The tail of the man-eater now whipped violently and his hide seemed to ripple as he gathered himself to spring. The crouched lion began pumping its rear legs, up and down, unsheathing its claws, ready to make the final rush. It suddenly sprang forward. Big Bull drew, and took the frontal shot. The arrow flew. In two amazingly swift bounds, the cat was upon him.

The hunter's legs shook and though Big Bull clutched his knife, there was no time to act as the five large claws on each of the cat's heavily muscled front paws gouged into his chest and shoulder. The cat's terrifying squalling filled the air as the three-inch long, razor-sharp claws of one paw gripped the man's shoulder. Big Bull's head snapped back in reflex as he plunged the knife into the man-eaters chest. The force of the cat's attack knocked him over with great force. The cat and the hunter rolled together several yards downhill. The animal ripped long red stripes in the flesh of Big Bull's thighs. Its hind feet searched for his prey's belly. He felt the cat's teeth grate along the top of his skull and then immediately loosen as the animal tried to find a firmer grip.

* * *

The terrified screaming of the horse tied nearby startled the lion, causing him to release the man. He spit, snarled, and then shrieked. Suddenly he stopped and stood still in a half crouch as the hunter rolled away. The cat's attention was momentarily on the horse. Feeling a trembling paralysis, Big Bull stopped and stared. He caught his breath as he stared into the wide, golden eyes of the great cat reflecting the sunlight. He came to his knees and felt for his ax; he slipped his hand through the lanyard, not wanting to lose the weapon when the cat attacked again. Standing on shaking legs, Big Bull slowly raised his ax arm as his other hand gripped his long, bloody fighting knife. The great cat with muscles quivering, shuffled forward quickly, and launched itself into the air, aiming at Big Bull's shoulders and head once more. Big Bull grunted as he brought his arm downward with a whipping sound.

There was a dull wet thud as the ax blade fell on the cat's

skull. Instinctively, its paws dug into Big Bull's shoulder and neck, holding them for the lasher claw and bite that would never come. The force of the cat sent them both rolling. Big Bull tore himself from the cat's grip. Thinking the cat was only dazed, the warrior got to his knees and struck the lion's head again and again. The animal's body trembled and stiffened. It was dead. Big Bull knelt on the ground on his hands and knees. He could hear only the sound of his blood hitting the ground. His chest and shoulders crisscrossed with lacerations, he had to stop the bleeding before he fainted. He was very cold when the first spasm of pain jolted through him. His breath was short and labored. As he sat up against a tree, he thought about how his whole life had been a struggle.

* * *

Dark Moon was in the swamp pond near the village stream, up to her waist among the arrowhead-shaped leaves that rose above the water harvesting tubers. The tubers were at the end of the long subterranean runners, sometimes a few feet from the plant. Dark Moon would dislodge the thick potatoes with her toes and let them float to the surface. She would crush most of the starchy, egg-sized tubers into flour for bread, or for thickening soups or gravy. The rest she would bake, boil, roast, or fry with their evening meals. Wolfgang liked the cooked nutty-flavored tubers with meat drippings and fat.

Suddenly, she felt strangely unsettled and waded out of the water. Turning slightly, she stared to a distant place, cleared her mind, and felt the subtle shift as her breathing slowed and her awareness sharpened. Muddled images flickered before her inner eye.

Several of the women near the stream saw Dark Moon standing still facing the direction Wolfgang and Big Bull had traveled. They approached her from the front, close enough to see her face, and stopped.

Her eyes were rolled up into her head so that only the whites showed. Her gaze was fixed on some distant point. The women felt frightened, aware that she was now possessed of the spirits. As they began to hurry away, they heard Dark Moon begin a pitiful, bone-grating wail to the sky, as if dread had seized her heart. She had seen the shadow of a large man attacked by the great cat. The hair on the napes of the women's necks rose. The eerie wail also woke the wolf from his slumber and within moments he was by her side, his eyes searching and muscles twitching.

"It is time to find Okwaho," Dark Moon said.

She commanded "Come!" and the big wolf trotted behind her. Hurrying back to her wigwam, she packed her medicines, a water container and some food. Quickly she went to the pasture, put a halter on a horse, and un-hobbled him. Then she led him and the wolf back to the stream.

The three women had been joined by others, all of them talking excitedly. With a terrible, wild look, Dark Moon said, "I'll need help."

As the village women watched silently, she pointed across the stream.

"Okwaho," she said to the wolf.

The animal crossed the stream and cast about, circling. Finding Wolfgang's old trail, he looked back at Dark Moon. The village women were amazed to see her mount the horse with a single bound and motion for the wolf to go. Several women hurried away to inform their men. Dark Moon urged the horse to follow the wolf, which had vanished like smoke.

As more villagers joined the others, all sensed that something terrible had happened. Spotted Deer, Fox Eyes, and Flying Man now appeared, armed and ready. They started to the trail pointed out by the crowd. Dark Moon was already well ahead as Flying Man crossed the stream, but he was not worried

The War Trail

since anyone could follow the trail of a horse.

* * *

Wolfgang had been letting his eyes do most of the walking as he pulled the horse along packed with the deer, when he suddenly became aware of something very wrong. Moments later, reaching a clearing, he was dumbstruck by his first sight of Big Bull.

The Osage warrior's body, lying amid the leaves, was torn and covered with ugly, bloody gouges. Wolfgang dropped the horse's lead rope and rushed to the fallen man, his mind was racing, wondering if Big Bull was still alive. When he saw the wounded man breathing shallowly, he tried to think of what to do for him. And then, suddenly, the wolf was there. The beast padded toward the lion, sniffed, then softly padded over to Big Bull, staring and sniffing at him, too.

Slowly Big Bull opened his eyes and saw a dark form -- the wolf's face. Their eyes locked and stared in the conversation of death. He heard the wolf make a low squeaking sound, as if calling him back. Once again his eyes closed and he briefly passed out. The warrior's spirit felt lifted. The wolf turned, raising its head, his ears rotating. Then Wolfgang heard a horse, and he knew it was Dark Moon.

When Big Bull opened his eyes again, he saw another shadowy form: Dark Moon, he realized, looking into his weary face. As the red, life-stealing flow ran from the warrior's eight largest wounds, she quickly cut the leather shirt away. For the first time, he looked deep into her glittering dark eyes, which he found full of spiritual power. Aware that the gods talked by signs, he suddenly felt all would be well. He also felt that Dark Moon and the wolf, were each other's spirit helper and that they were calling him back.

"Build a small quick fire, and heat water in this small

pewter cup," Dark Moon ordered Wolfgang. "Go to the creek, fill the small iron pot with water, cut bark from an alder and put it into the pot to boil."

Big Bull's lacerations and puncture wounds needed to be washed and stitched closed. His head injuries were especially bad, covering his face with blood as they bled freely. He could still only see a shadowy silhouette through his blood-caked eyes. She opened her medicine bag and started arranging her tools and containers.

When Wolfgang returned, he and Dark Moon both began to wash out Big Bull's wounds with the alder bark concoction. She hoped it would prevent the foul-smelling creeping sickness. The bite marks resembled gunshot wounds. To some she applied powdered root of the stinging nettle plant, and to the deeper, penetrating wounds, she applied dried root bark powder from the black cherry tree. Upon application, they quickly stopped the bleeding, but she still worried about the creeping sickness under the skin. Then she cut hair away from the head wounds and rinsed them again. After stopping the bleeding, she worked quickly at sewing him up with a bone needle and sinew.

Dark Moon knew that Big Bull was at the limit of his endurance. He was in excruciating pain. His eyes revealed that his body had quit, although the spirit still lived in the eyes. She took the small cup of warm water from the edge of the fire and mixed the ground powder of leaves and seeds from the henbane plant. This powerful narcotic will relieve his pain, enabling her and Wolfgang to get him back to the village with minimal suffering. Once he is back, I can use the spirits of arnica from the little brown jug for his recovery. A few drops of the oil and resinous substance in the brandy, administered six times a day, will help Big Bull tolerate the pain while he recovers. In the days ahead, I will use fly maggots to clean the wounds; since they eat only dead flesh, and will prevent his wounds from festering.

Dark Moon and Wolfgang had just finished loading Big

Bull onto a horse to rush him back to the village when the wolf alerted them to movement on their back-trail. Wolfgang took cover next to a tree, then spied Flying Man, Spotted Deer and Fox Eyes quickly approaching.

The Osage took a quick look at Big Bull, then, loaded the enormous lion on a carrying pole. The brave Osage warrior would return home to be honored. Leading his own horse, still packed with the deer, Wolfgang whistled low for the wolf. The animal was off, scouting ahead for possible danger. Making his way with his companions, Wolfgang thought of his first real friend in this new country, the Delaware warrior, Tamanend. For a moment he once again felt the comfort of loyal comrades.

The party finally arrived back at the village, which was now a mix of noise, smoke, and general confusion. People scrambled for a look at their famous warrior and were stunned and horrified by his condition, blood still oozing from his wounds. Big Bull was carried into the wigwam, and his two wives and Dark Moon remained inside. Before she lowered the deer-hide flap to the entrance, she asked for the old village medicine man and his young helper to join them. While Dark Moon and the two wives tended to Big Bull, the old medicine man sang and chanted to Wah'Kon-Tah Above and the Wah'Kon-tah Below, the supreme spiritual creator and force of the Osage universe, manifest in sky and earth respectively.

Each day Dark Moon pulled the willow bark away from the wounds, sniffed at them, and cleaned them. To ease the pain and swelling, she applied a paste made from the milky sap leaves and stems of the Wapato found in the marsh. She also made her patient drink a Wapato tea to further promote healing. For many days, Big Bull experienced a confusing mix of sights, sounds and feelings, as he drifted in and out of consciousness.

Through the winter, Dark Moon and Wolfgang supplied Big Bull's family with meat. They spent evenings sharing both provisions and stories. It was on one of these nights that Big Bull revealed a different story entirely -- about the Pawnee Morning Star -- that most caught Dark Moon's interest.

"Early in the morning on the longest day of the year," Big Bull said, "as the morning star rose, the sacrifice of a virgin painted red would take place by arrow and knife. The upright wooden frame she was mounted on would then be torched. Then the whole tribe celebrated with singing and dancing. After the second hoeing of the corn and the Morning Star ceremony, the Pawnee set out to the south for their first big buffalo hunt of the year."

Chapter 25

It was the season of the Green Grass Moon, April of 1758. Clouds drifted like veils over the full face of the moon. Big Bull led his small scouting party of Fox Eyes, Spotted Deer, Flying Man, and Wolfgang on a northward course, following a ridge top through rolling hill prairie country and formidable sandstone formations.

As it grew light, they heard the soft chuckle of birds leaving their roosts to feed from time to time. They also heard the *brrrrrr* of flushing birds ahead. Mottled gray-brown birds resembling chickens, but with sharp tails, abounded, but rarely cackled when flushed from the trees. Along the ridge-top, wide-spaced bur oaks dappled the area with shade. Because the trees were broad and tall, it was an area almost void of undergrowth and carpeted with short, sweet grass. Herds of deer and elk were plentiful and could be seen in all directions. The scouting party also saw scattered groups of buffalo resting and grazing. The animals gave no signs of having been hunted, even though they had seen rock shelters with soot-stained roofs from campfires.

Wolfgang saw an old malformed oak. "When the tree was young long ago, it was bent down and held with a rock," said Big Bull, watching him. "That marker tree gives the direction of the path to the Missouri village," he continued, "Many trees like that are used for sign-posts. They mark tribal boundaries, show direction, locations of creeks and rivers, act as hiding places, and are used for hiding messages." Wolfgang and the Osage saw tracks and trail markers of other Indians: bark chipped away on tree trunks, bent trees, and knotted bunches of grass-tops pointing in different directions were all too apparent to them. Big Bull pointed at a split bush stem with a broken end resting in the crotch of a tree–the sign of a message nearby.

Herds of deer and elk were plentiful and could be seen in all directions. The scouting party also saw scattered groups of buffalo resting and grazing. The animals gave no sign of having been hunted, even though they had seen rock shelters with soot-stained ceilings from campfires.

They stopped at a small lake surrounded by marsh where they felt safe from ambush, for in these park-like flats they could see well in all directions and they had no fear of rattlesnakes. They ate their pemmican and resumed their travels, moving all day until finally they saw the terrain falling away on both sides. Ahead lay their route of travel. The large gap and abundant downy cottonwood seeds blowing on the wind told them they were getting close to the river and the Missouri Indian village. The wind-borne downy seeds gave the view a wild autumnal quality. As they continued north, they knew the Missouri River was now on their west, north, and east side. The river was still invisible, but the wide gap all around in the terrain showed its course of flow.

Toward evening, they arrived at the point of a ridge above the river finally reaching a point from which they beheld a gentle sloping of the ridge top. The village appeared in the grassy flat below. In the distance rose wide, crumbling bluffs. Big Bull pointed out the Grand River below, to their right front, amid the cottonwood groves, where it appeared to flow in from the north. Ahead of them to the west, north, and east sat a large open flood plain. Gesturing, Big Bull explained: "The Missouri River bottoms are rich farmland, but aren't always dependable because the river periodically floods. The river flows southeast and eventually empties into the Mississippi."

Wolfgang estimated the northern bluffs across the river were four miles away. From the point where they watched, the western bluffs were three miles away. The northeastern bluffs he estimated at six miles. The black shapes of waterfowl showed on the water, with geese, ducks and herons appearing plentiful. The party remained alert and watchful through twilight, but they had heard only the natural sounds -- the strange winnowing sound of droves of running snipes, of loons wailing *"Haoo-oo-oo,"* then cackling maniacally in the twilight, the drifting of a great bird. They also heard the whirring of feathers cutting the air on near silent wings, and spotted the silhouette of an owl hunting silently overhead. *An evil omen.*

* * *

Early in the morning, long before sun-up, Wolfgang and the Osage crept to the top of the ridge and peeked over. The mist from the moist air along the river kept them from seeing far, but there was the pungent scent of wood smoke and, beneath it, the stench of cooked flesh. When the sun came up, it was just a dim glow through the light gray overcast, and the Osage party could barely discern the village. A faint acrid odor of burned wood now told the story. Flocks of water birds and land birds around the village were scattering into the sky as if alarmed. Dogs below barked in alarm. *Something was wrong.*

Then the Osage saw flames begin to shoot up in the air amid smoke and floating ash. Wolfgang cocked his head and heard distant sputtering and crackling sounds -- the noise of gunfire. *Many guns.* Even from a distance, the bright flashes were visible. Wolfgang and the Osage listened and watched for a long time, knowing all too well what was happening. He suddenly remembered Dark Moon telling him of her vision of a burning village. A crushing agony enveloped him as he heard people shouting and screaming, saw them running wildly about, hunched low, shoulders forward, in animal fear. The crop fields were on fire everywhere. A continuous volley sounded, then a pause. Sporadic firing began again. A battle raged in the village.

Wolfgang looked toward the sun to check the time. It was the second hour of the afternoon, and still the villagers were sprinting about, terrified. Finally, toward evening, the buzzards began circling slowly overhead. Wolfgang and the Osage watched and listened until night fell.

* * *

"We call them 'Seven Hunters.' They are past their middle-of-the-night position," Big Bull said, pointing to the constellation (Ursa Major). "Come – it's time."

As Wolfgang and the Osage followed a narrow finger of timber and brush downward, he felt his heart pound as he slipped through the underbrush as silently as smoke. The party proceeded in single file until, nearing the village's perimeter at last, they moved up and lay down within arm's reach of one other. In the darkness of the quarter moon, every other man slept, only the reflection of the eyes of those awake giving a hint of their presence. The murderous howling, followed by the screams of women and children bawling for mercy while suffering from unspeakable tortures, lasted all night. As the Osage watched, the northern warriors, their faces suffused with murderous glee, butchered every beast and dragged older children away to be disemboweled. The agonized screams and weeping of young girls rent the night as, their arms and legs pinned to the ground, they suffered the searing pain of brutal penetration by warriors driving their hardened manhood into them. Bathed in blood, other warriors threw babies into the air and caught them on the tips of their spears or hacked them, while airborne, with tomahawks. Wolfgang and the Osage warriors soon heard the shrill, staccato yelping of coyotes that began to gather, smelling the blood.

Finally moonset, the darkest hour just before dawn, arrived. All the Osage were awake, watching and listening. Their anticipation grew with the light of day, and before long they could discern the mad-eyed Fox warriors in detail. They saw their red-dyed deer-hair roaches decorated with one or two feathers, their shaved heads with circular patches, locks of long hair hanging, indicating revenge, and their sashes wrapped around their mid-section with one end dangling. The marauders wore fitted, thigh-length painted leggings fringed below the knee, and soft-soled flap moccasins. They were bare-chested, their skin painted red or black or white on their shoulders, arms, and upper backs -- indicating scalps previously taken.

As the Osage watched, the enraged, frenzied Fox, Saux, and Kickapoo systematically dismembered many live victims. As the enemy warriors walked near the edge of the brush, they saw their painted faces, with yellow, red, and black stripes showing on the lower half of each visage.

Lying beside Wolfgang, Big Bull pointed to a group of distant warriors and signed: "Sauk."

Wolfgang marked the red-fitted breechclouts secured by leather belts. Some of the invaders wore hip-length, grease-blackened leggings decorated with a narrow band of porcupine quills or scalplock fringes. The attackers' shaved heads were colored red with black stripes on the lower part of their face, and their eyes were rimmed with red.

Now close beside Wolfgang, Big Bull explained: "Those older Fox warriors with one or two eagle feathers attached to their roach are for acts of bravery."

Glints from the sun indicated that they also wore earrings. The white hands painted on their body's symbolized enemies slain in battle.

Pointing out one group, Big Bull signed and spoke in a

low voice.

"Kickapoo -- the unconquered people. The tribe had traveled and plundered from the Great Lakes to Mexico, and from the Great Plains to the Three Forks," Big Bull continued. "They are great raiders, well trained and disciplined. The warrior societies are small. They hate all white men, whether French, British, Spanish, or American, and like the Iroquois, they cook and eat human flesh from all body parts. As a tribe, they are cunning, and as individuals, they are among the greatest warriors and fighters in all the land. They would never surrender, determined, instead, to fight to the death."

Wolfgang remembered Dark Moon telling him of the Kickapoo during the long winter nights he had been recovering from the Great Bear. "Kickapoo" was an Algonquian name for he moves about. Wolfgang had seen one Iroquois warrior who seemed to be a leader among these tribesmen. Big Bull pointed out two warriors -- one young, the other older.

"The young warrior is Kiala, leader of the Fox war party, and the older warrior is Black Hawk, leader of the Saux warriors." Big Bull explained that Black Hawk's father destroyed a Michigamea tribal village, on the "Great River," just as here. He had killed all the men and the women, and children he didn't kill were sold into slavery. The village's unarmed old men and helpless women and children had suffered the brutality of the tomahawk and scalping knife. Now up close, Wolfgang listened hard. Whenever the enemy warriors fired their weapons, he heard the distinctive clack-whoosh, of their muskets, indicating that their weapons did not fire fast, and therefore were less accurate. Men could be seen staggering, disemboweled, trying to hold their bulging guts from falling out. The desperate, hair-raising animal sounds and horrific screaming of people being tortured continued to fill the air. It raised the hair on Wolfgang's neck, and he could barely stand listening to the forlorn terrible screams of the women. He began to rise from the ground, but Big Bull's strong hand stayed him. "No, not yet, there are too many," Big Bull said, his eyes gleaming. "Wait. It will be over soon." He observed Wolfgang as he wrinkled his nose in disgust.

Looking at Big Bull, Wolfgang spoke directly and strongly.

"We must have vengeance for these people."

Big Bull's face was impassive, except for his eyes.

"Yes, I agree," he said.

The remaining houses were set afire. Roofs began to steam, smoke, and then erupt in flame. Wolfgang and the others heard the rush and crackle as tongues of lurid yellow-orange flame shot skyward with a roar, and the structures caved and crumbled, pillars of resinous black smoke rising high into the sky. Huge curls of light ash and hot, flying sparks drifted and floated up on super-heated air and then downward as they cooled. The strong, sweet smell of burned human flesh was everywhere.

And then at last it seemed over. The raiders formed into two groups. With prisoners, the larger Fox war party headed north. All the log canoes were used to transport the raiders and prisoners across the river, below the entrance of the Grand River, where the channel was deeper and faster. Since the river was but a half-mile wide, Wolfgang and the Osage could plainly observe the Fox warriors, departure. They heard a shouted command, followed by pivoting grind of feet moving away.

Now Big Bull led the Osage into the smoldering village. Flies buzzed noisily, drawn to the scent of death, and turkey buzzards overhead swooped low. From the tracks leading toward the river, Wolfgang and the others could tell that some of those in the war party had been wounded and were bringing up the rear. Tracks and trails of blood and their tapered ends pointed the direction of movement. Some footprints were not as deep as the other, signaling a leg wound. Those with a shorter pace accompanied by drag marks indicated more serious wounds, incurred by the village warriors' fighting back. Dead bodies lay in mangled heaps. Many women victims were in the fetal position, broken faces pressed to the ground and mothers still clutching their dead babies in front of them. Confronting the brutality of the Iroquois, Wolfgang understood the rage and malice the whole frontier was experiencing far to the east. He felt a deep hatred for the Iroquois and their allies, those who smiled as they killed.

    The raiders seemed to have spent some time in the village -- perhaps a day and a half. The bodies of those recently killed were waxy looking, with bluish lips and nails, but their limbs were still flexible. The pungent, sour-sweet smell of putrefied flesh was strong. In others, rigor mortis was just setting into the face and neck. In most of the bodies however, the stiffening process was complete, all the way to the legs, meaning they had been dead for part of a day and all of the night. Some of the naked women who had only recently been killed showed a white, thick, sticky material between the legs. Wolfgang and the Osage recognized that they had been raped before being killed.

    Now Wolfgang felt as if the dead were talking to him, their eyes no longer reacting to the light. When he lightly touched an eye, it did not react to pressure. It was softer than it should be. He stared at the slitted, slightly clouded-over dull bluish-gray eyes. They were dry and sunken because the color was cooked from them. Their noses and lips were burned off, showing bone and teeth. Many of the bodies were burned down to the bones, fingers and toes, had been burned off. Others were burned only enough to split the skin. Birds had already eaten the eyes out of many of the corpses. The bodies were stiff, and had started to decompose and stink. Their skin was dry and discolored. The stale, moldy stench of rotting flesh, hung heavy everywhere. Some bodies were bound to upright poles. Many unburned bodies lay in old blood, hardened and turned black.

Their hands tied, these victims lay in awkward, gore-splattered tangles of arms and legs, with the dry ground darkened from puddles of blood that had soaked into the earth.

Many had marks on the skin around their hands and feet, showing they had been bound and tortured, then cut down to make room for those to be tortured next. The inflicted cuts on the bodies were ragged and gaping. Sightless eyes stared up at nothing, stone war-clubs having ended their lives. Their faces were now bloated by injury and death. Almost all the dead had released their body waste front and back due to their terror before dying or at the time of death. The dead were disfigured and eviscerated. The fish-and meat-smoking racks were empty, looted by the raiders for extra provisions.

* * *

Checking the perimeter of the village, Wolfgang and Fox Eyes saw that the tracks of the smaller party of enemy warriors headed south. The enemy war party was staying in the cover of the low ground and avoiding the higher open ridge. Big Bull withdrew the Osage back up the hill to watch from above those who crossed the river and to make sure they kept traveling northeast. The raiders had moved to the north of a large cut-off lake. The Osage could hear and see ducks and geese noisily rising and settling, disturbed by the passage of the distant prisoners and enemy war party. The lake appeared to extend for more than two miles to the south.

Finally, pointing toward a spot some six miles distant, on the horizon, Big Bull said, "It's the point of a large, flat-topped ridge that runs to the northeast. There is a good trail that they will use to travel to their villages on the Rock River and the bluffs on the Mississippi River further north."

He paused for a moment, before he continued.

"Many of the prisoners will be tortured, burned and

eaten along the way. Others will be adopted into the tribe."

Dogs and crows were feeding upon the decomposed bodies. Everything of value had been taken or destroyed in the fire. From the small stores of food that the marauders had overlooked, Wolfgang and his cohorts gathered all the corn and jerky they needed for their return-trip south.

They all realized that the enemy war party heading south could only mean that their destination was their own Osage village. Big Bull knew he had to follow the scouts that had split off from the raiders. Pointing to the trail, he said, "Fox Eyes, scout their trail. Flying Man will accompany you and act as your runner to keep me informed. We will travel more behind."

The two then left, running at a punishing pace, to get ahead of the Fox war party. Both would be able to follow the progress of the allied enemy scouting party, always maintaining visual contact with their last man. A strong runner accustomed to long distances, Fox Eyes knew he could quickly close the distance then pass around them unseen. Upon leaving the village, he followed their enemies' tracks closely. Sharply focused, he looked as far ahead as he could. The way the feet impacted on the damp soil and left deep clear prints with sharp edges told him that these men were carrying weapons and heavily laden packs. Fox Eyes followed in their trail for a short distance.

Turning to Wolfgang, Big Bull said, "Fox Eyes can move so slowly and quietly," He appears suddenly in your midst, out of nowhere, like a spirit ghost."

Big Bull mused that the enemy war party had traveled southeast to the first creek that flowed into the Missouri River. It was fast and tumbling. It was here at the mouth of the creek that the Iroquois-led scouting party would camp, within sight of the river, and remain in the cover of the tree line.

* * *

The next day, the enemy scouting party followed the creek upstream for a short distance to the point where the first creek fork came in. Then they continued on that branch, which, they well knew, would serve as an accurate guide for moving straight south to its main watershed.

* * *

Fox Eyes and Flying Man were lying close to the trail. Fox Eyes had his ear to the ground. He could hear the vibrating earth sounds of the approaching men. He lifted his head to watch and soon heard the rhythmic, dull thud of soft, padded soles. The enemy scouting party passed a short distance away. Fox Eyes and his partner knew if they remained perfectly still, their enemy stood little chance of seeing them, though they both could smell the enemies' sweat and smoke-soaked bodies that passed by.

Waiting quietly, Fox Eyes watched, listened and smelled the air as his enemies followed the twists and turns of the watercourse. The two hidden scouts knew the Fox had been on the trail long enough to be tired, which would make them clumsy in their movements and, in turn, noisy. Disturbed insects, flushing grouse, startled deer, and the small campfire had all helped Fox Eyes keep track of the war party at a distance. Now and then when he had not observed the party for some time, he approached the creek path to check their tracks on the trail to be reassured that they were still all together. Fox Eyes' let the terrain dictate his pace as he moved, crouched, his weight forward on the toes for better balance and control. His pace was dead slow; his eyes and senses did most of the walking. Alert to any sign, he registered everything in his peripheral vision. Flying Man followed behind at a short distance.

Suddenly, off-trail, swarming insects caught Fox Eyes' attention. His senses were on fire as the northwesterly breeze brought the fetid smell of human excrement to his nostrils. This was the best indication that the enemy party was still ahead of him. Standing perfectly still in the shadow of a great tree, he moved only his eyes and stood listening. Only when he was sure he was alone did Fox Eyes move slowly again until he stood a step away from the spot where a man had squatted, relieved himself hurriedly, and covered it. The place was easy to see, for the man-made patterns were between him and the position of the sun well past its zenith. Fox Eyes looked at the darker colored imprints in the leaves where the warrior had compressed them. The undisturbed leaves, lying loosely on the ground with plenty of air space, were visibly lighter. He also noticed the dark-colored, flattened imprint where the rifle, leaning against the tree within hand's reach, had rested. Those pressed down imprints were easy to detect, for they reflected more light. Uncovering the spot and poking the pile with a stick, he found the droppings still soft and moist. A light touch with his finger revealed its warmth, indicating that little time had passed.

As Fox Eyes proceeded further down the trail, his eyes caught the swarm of butterflies drawn to the crusty, clear mark of a hole where another man had urinated. The un-faded leaves torn off the surrounding brush indicated that their enemies were only a short distance ahead.

Continuing slowly along, Fox Eyes boxed the trail in his practiced mind's eye and measured off an average two paces, and counted the number of moccasin prints within that space. He determined there were still eight warriors walking the trail.

Suddenly Fox Eyes' senses told him there was danger. He stopped, and so did Flying Man. Instinctively he concentrated on reading the surrounding terrain closely, observing every detail as his eyes swept the side creeks, gullies, and slopes of the hillside. The trees were large and the screening scrub was thin. Traveling slowly, every tree had to be cautiously approached. His eyes sharply focused, carefully peered into the deep shadows of surrounding brush, timber and rocks on either side of the trail capable of concealing death. Fox Eyes realized it was altogether too quiet and that somewhere ahead other eyes were watching. He knew that he could only remain unseen by using his head. He began to move forward, slowly as a shadow. Remaining in the deep shadows, he sought the watchers from the vantage points that commanded the trail route.

* * *

He now felt a premonition of impending danger and knew the spirits were with him. A scolding blue jay was his second warning. He stood silently, his senses alert, and placed himself in the watcher's position. All at once he caught a reflection in the cover of some large trees across the hard sandy creek bed ahead. Suspicious of dark shadows, he changed his position slowly. It took a while to pick out the outline of a deeper shadow within a shadow. Slowly the detailed form of a warrior, half hidden by the side of a tree in the deep shadows, emerged to his eye. The man was standing very still. Then Fox Eyes heard a scolding squirrel pinpointing another area.

He thought to himself: *"You can always depend upon the blue jay or the squirrel, just as the rest of the forest does."*

To his trained ear, the light breeze carried the sound of a carelessly handled musket. When Fox Eyes caught the faint movement of a man scratching his ear. Then he caught the flicker of an eyelid in the shadows. He carefully withdrew to a point of greater safety.

Now was the time to send Flying Man to Big Bull.

Chapter 26

Flying Man reported to Big Bull that although he and Fox Eyes had remained unobserved, the Iroquois-led allied scouting party had suspected their presence and was lying in wait for them.

"Lead the way," Big Bull replied.

The Osage and Wolfgang used a deep section of the dry, sandy creek as they moved up to Fox Eyes' position. They stopped long enough to daub themselves with red war paint. Then Wolfgang watched the Osage paint horizontal lines on their chest, circles on their shoulders and vertical lines on their face, and encircle their eye sockets. Each warrior wore a red dyed horsehair roach, except for Fox Eyes, who wore his hair long. The roach ran from their scalplock from above their forehead to a short tuft of hair at the back of their neck.

The surrounding terrain occupied their full attention. Dark timbered slope kept them concealed from their enemies in the forest on the other side of the creek bed. Its banks were not steep. He knew their enemies were close – within rifle range. He reminded his companions that their rifles were more accurate at a longer range than their enemies' weapons, the smoothbore muskets.

The Osage scanned in all directions, straining to see into the thick, foreboding shadows, watching uneasily but attentively. Wolfgang could see that, like himself, the Osage could sense the

Fox, Saux, and Kickapoo. Fox Eyes pointed out to everyone the enemies he had already detected.

The stillness of their surroundings settled in. Wolfgang determined that they had traveled seven miles. By now there was no doubt what the enemy scouting party's mission was: to scout the Osage village, then return to their own people to begin planning and preparing for a raid. Big Bull had decided to kill this allied scouting party.

Holding the rifles upright alongside their protective tree trunks, Wolfgang and the four Osage scanned the woods for protruding musket barrels. They studied the trees and terrain to plan how best to rush to engage their enemy. They advanced as close as they dared by crawling, until finally the five stood upright to begin moving quickly from tree-to-tree for cover, knowing they could be seen.

Booooom! Booooom! Booooom!

The reports sounded ahead as sparks flashed and flickered in the gloom. Clouds of smoke belched from pans and muzzles; grey-white blossoms hung thick, staining the air.

Wolfgang's pulse leaped. Judging from the guns' sound, they were all muskets. A ball ricocheted off a boulder, whined off through the air and smacked a tree behind him. Several muskets fired shot, which hummed and pattered nearby through the branches. He realized the enemy had suffered a number of misfires. Counting the number of enemy muskets by their blossoms of smoke, Big Bull commanded that after the next round of firing, they would charge into the ranks as fast as they could run.

"Our howling rush will unnerve them!" Big Bull shouted. "Fire only when you are among them – then use your knife and tomahawk!"

They continued, advancing from tree to tree, as more muskets fired in unison, followed by the whine of lead balls.

The enemy warriors worked to re-load quickly, but the

The War Trail

Osage line whoop sounded from one end of their skirmish line to the other, and the group rose in unison and charged like the wind of death. They raced across the shimmering sand and out into the splattering trickle of water in the wide, mostly dry creek bed. They did not slow when they screamed their war cries, hoping to panic their enemy. Running over broken ground helped them avoid the arrows now filling the air. Arrows whispered, hissed and whined through the air, smacking the branches all around closely.

The enemy stood its ground.

Wolfgang spotted one enemy warrior bending his bow. Quickly raising his weapon to his shoulder, Wolfgang let his finger squeeze the smooth trigger. The rifle exploded. Wolfgang felt its stock punch his shoulder. The next moment, as the rifleman darted from beneath the telltale smoke-blossom, he saw a warrior lying spread-eagled, his blood pooling into the ground from a mortal head-wound.

Wolfgang ran on, dropping his rifle against a tree. The charging Osage warriors watched the curling serpentine smoke from the rifles drift slowly away as they ran. Amid the hideous war cries, the Osage charged through the protective screen of brush, and fired almost point blank at their foes. Many fell before the warring parties quickly switched to hand-to-hand fighting. Piercing shrieks of anguish and rage ensued as warriors grappled.

Slowly the tide of battle turned. Confronting tomahawk, war club and knife, the Fox, Saux and Kickapoo faltered. Spotted Deer blocked the deadly blow of a war club with his own club and stabbed quickly with his knife, killing a Saux warrior similarly armed but slower by the blink of an eye. Swinging his tomahawk at a smaller warrior, Big Bull struck Fox warrior at the side of his head and the enemy dropped wordlessly.

Wolfgang stood, panting, when suddenly he felt

someone's eyes on his back and the hair on his neck and arms rose. Wolfgang spun to behold a tall Iroquois warrior standing with head high and chest thrust in a haughty, insolent manner, a silent challenge. *He's big, very big, a good two inches taller than me,* Wolfgang thought. As all the others' hand-to-hand battle was finished, only Wolfgang and the Iroquois warrior – the light of slaughter still in his eyes – remained facing one another.

"You are the warrior of the Red Moon" – the Iroquois spoke with rapid hands signs – *"the one called Two-legged Man-bear, brother of the bear and wolf. I have been looking for you. I am called Bear Killer. You killed my brother."*

The rest of his scouting party having been killed, Bear Killer drew his knife and brandished his tomahawk, his eyes unafraid and glittering with hatred. The Osage stepped back to watch and Wolfgang wondered why they didn't help him. Then it dawned on him: having heard so many of Dark Moon's stories about him, they wanted to see this hand-to-hand challenge. Wolfgang's eyes darkened into a hard gray, and his lips drew back like those of an angry wolf. Now rolling his shoulders and arms in a constant movement, the sneering Iroquois warrior danced in place, shifting his weight from one foot to the other. He feigned several striking blows with each of his weapons in a mocking show of defiance to distract Wolfgang as he closed the distance between them. The Iroquois' knife would pop in and just as quickly be retracted. Wolfgang tried to maintain a distance so that the full extension of his opponent's arm could not reach him, a gap that would let him avoid a disabling thrust at his vitals or a wounding stab at an arm or leg. Slowly they circled, remaining mobile, stabbing and thrusting without effect, looking for a weakness. But Wolfgang could see the Iroquois was determined to work closely.

Suddenly, Bear Killer gave a yell and took the initiative with the attack. He charged without hesitation, raising his tomahawk. Wolfgang came up with his own tomahawk and blocked the downward swing. His left hand, meanwhile, forming a V-shape, caught his opponent's hand just below the wrist, blocking the Iroquois' upward swing with the knife. His strong grip prevented Bear Killer from arching his hand and cutting Wolfgang's forearm. He now extended his tomahawk and arm higher until he had Bear Killer's locked above him. The Iroquois' head was slightly turned with the grappling strain, and Wolfgang saw his opportunity. He head-butted the Iroquois just above the front of the ear, momentarily stunning him.

Then Wolfgang spiked his opponent high on the groin with his knee, swiftly followed by turning his body to the left and kicking his enemy's left knee with his right leg, before quickly disengaging himself from the warrior. The kick was so vigorous and well directed that it sent the warrior staggering, but not before Wolfgang felt a warm splash. He had received a minor cut on his upper thigh. The Osage, seeing the Iroquois' mobility slowed, began to clamor.

* * *

The fight had an almost paralyzing effect on the watching Osage. They watched closely as the two combatants lunged, grappled, slashed and hacked. The more the two sweated, strained, grunted and gritted their teeth, the more animated the Osage became. They witnessed the staring eyes of the Iroquois warrior become wider until they were bulging. Blood spurted and drained from both combatants.

* * *

Wolfgang danced out of arm's reach. The Iroquois turned and faced Wolfgang with his legs spread, favoring his left leg. Wolfgang drew his knife with his left hand and waved it. He felt sweat beading his brow, and his hands trembled. There was no hesitation in his opponent's eyes. Wolfgang saw the mental-transformation taking place in Bear Killer's eyes and knew he would attack. The limping Iroquois made a feigned lunge with the knife in his right hand, causing Wolfgang to sidestep the wrong way, to the left, to avoid the enemy's tomahawk. The Iroquois then pulled the knife back in a forceful, sweeping slash. Wolfgang realized this was the second time he had made this mistake, and he felt a sharp pain in his right side. Hearing the Osage muttering, he knew the Iroquois was attacking with the tomahawk. Wolfgang managed to dance backward, narrowly avoiding its swing and the following swift, striking knife slash. With a flick of the knife, he quickly sliced his opponent's extended tomahawk arm as it completed its arc. He saw the shattered surprise in Bear Killer's eyes. The Osage cheered loudly. The deep slicing wound to the enemy's forearm muscle disabled him, causing him to drop his weapon. Hearing the Iroquois immediately break into his death song, Wolfgang chose to follow up with a quick second and final strike.

A wild animal sound issued from Wolfgang as he moved forward quickly and made a downward diagonal slash at his opponent's upper right shoulder and down across the upper chest, opening his shoulder and chest muscle. The enemy's mouth hung open and his eyes became glassy as he swayed. Wolfgang quickly followed with a backward horizontal slash, opening the warrior's stomach. The thunderous din from the Osage came to him:

"Kill, kill, kill !!"

With the tomahawk in his right hand, Wolfgang struck downward onto the warrior's skull. As he wedged it loose, it brought fragments of bone and brain. He smelled a bony odor, and stood back. Wolfgang's chest was heaving for air. His opponent's blood covered him from his head to his leggings. The blood spurting out of the Iroquois's head, mouth and body wounds, sent the Osage into a frenzy of dance steps and war whoops. All the Osage were deeply impressed with the focused and smooth pattern of Wolfgang's fighting moves. They had learned by watching, and were now aware that there was something else you could do with your head at close quarters: you could strike with it. The Iroquois' face was set in the eternal, reposed rigidity of death, now food for the birds and forest critters. Big Bull checked Wolfgang's two wounds. They were better than they looked, but bloody. The wound on his thigh was small, but the cut on his chest was long. His ribs had prevented a deep wound, but Big Bull could see bone. He could also see where the wound from the blade became shallower, as it continued its sweeping arc toward the stomach. Handing Big Bull a small deerskin bag, Wolfgang told him to put the powdered root contents into the wound. As both watched their surroundings and talked, his bleeding stopped. Soon after, Fox Eyes brought a large strip from a slippery elm soaked in the creek and used it to cover the wound. They bound his midsection with his waist sash. Big Bull knew that Wolfgang would not approve of taking his foe's ears with the scalp. He grabbed the scalplock decorated with a piece of seashell, and cut only a small circle in the skin around it. As he pulled, it created a sucking sound, resulting in a loud smack as the dripping scalp pulled free. He walked back to Wolfgang and smiled.

During the battle, only Wolfgang and Spotted Deer had been wounded, the latter with a knife wound smaller than Wolfgang's along his ribs. The Osage all stood looking down at Wolfgang, smiling. He in turn looked up at the Osage

"This is the second time I have made this same mistake on the same move and received a wound," Wolfgang said. "I won't make it again!"

"We will have many stories to tell at night," said Big Bull, smiling.

Chapter 27

Over the winter months, when they were not hunting, Wolfgang helped his friends obtain the tools for their rifles. He demonstrated how to use the ladle for melting lead and casting shot and lead balls. They acquired napped flint and bone arrow points from the old men of the village serving as master nappers. At night while telling stories, Wolfgang and his Osage friends went through dry, tightly bound stacks of arrow shafts that had been allowed to dry straight. They selected each for proper weight, durability and straightness and then further straightened the wooden shafts by applying bear grease, heating, and eyeballing them with finger pressure. There was talk about how much more time was spent on obtaining and preparing the materials for bows and arrows than on maintaining a rifle. Carefully they cut the notches and rounded them for nocking and tight fits for the stone and bone points. While sorting turkey feathers, the Osage laughed at Wolfgang's use of scissors. They applied cut feathers with hide glue and wrapped the forward part with sinew. They also wrapped the shafts behind the flint arrow points to keep them from splitting, and applied heated pine pitch to seal the sinew from moisture. The finished arrows were checked for straightness, and spun in the palm of their hand to make sure that there was no wobble. Each was shot to insure it would fly perfectly true.

They discussed the news from runners that the Spanish settlers had abandoned the northern territory of Texas because the raiding Kiowa, Comanche, Apache, Kansas, Omaha,

Pawnee, and Ponca now all had guns. As always, they also talked about the ever-advancing American settlers crowding the French lands, and also about the British arming and inciting their enemies the Chickasaw. Wolfgang knew the Osage worried about their future. He advised them to save their gunpowder for war and hunt with the bow. That winter the hunting was good.

*   *   *

Now it was spring, 1759. The days during the Grass Growing Moon became longer as the sun continued to shift toward the northeast. The emerging leaves were coppery-colored on the cottonwood trees. Summer was fast approaching. The longer days and shorter nights allowed the heated ground to keep its warmth, and it grew warmer each day. Now would be a busy time on the high plains for the tribes recovering from winter. Everyone would be out gathering or raiding for food, horses and slaves.

The time had come for Dark Moon and Wolfgang to leave. The entire Osage village wanted them to stay, but for the safety of those villagers they had come to love, they had no choice. If the French learned where they were, they would direct their Indian allies against this village.

Big Bull, Spotted Deer, Fox Eyes, and Flying Man would see them safely on their way to the bluffs across the Missouri River where the Nemaha River flowed into the Missouri.

"From there on, trees are sparse," said Big Bull, "and the rolling hills are covered with tall, waving grass. The sky will swallow you up."

"What kind of trees will burn smokeless?" Wolfgang asked.

"The plains' cottonwood does. It leaves only a fine powdered ash afterward, which is easy to conceal," Big Bull said. "During the winter you can feed the horses the inner layer of bark, twigs and foliage. They like it.

"Deer prefer to bed in the cottonwoods," he continued. "The bucks will be found on the islands in the streams, in young stands of immature cottonwoods on the outside perimeter of old stands of the trees, closer to the stream. There you'll also find the willows and rose bushes. Turkeys will roost in the mature stands."

Big Bull's wives were busy telling Dark Moon that during the approaching spring, the young chestnut-colored leaf and its greenish, catkin-like flowers – thick with yellow pollen emerging at the tips of gray twigs – could be made into tea to stop scurvy, fight fever, and relieve arthritis. On and on they went, detailing the miracles of the cottonwood tree as she listened attentively. "Ahead, to the west," Big Bull continued to Wolfgang, "you will see Big Blue River, flowing north to south. You'll see the entrance of a large creek on the west side of the river – Turkey Creek. Keep to the east side, along the higher ground. Eventually, you'll come to the Platte River. The nearest village will be an Oto Indian village at a sharp bend in the Platte River, a hard day's travel to the east. Those earthen lodge people are constantly sick from contact with the French traders." Big Bull was silent for a moment.

"Take my female wolf. She already belongs to your big animal. Nothing can part them." He said.

Big Bull went on to give Wolfgang further information and instructions – that fuel would be scarce except for buffalo chips, which burned well... that there would be little rain and running water to the west, where the grass was much shorter... that by traveling straight north from the Platte River they would come to the Elkhorn River, running northwest to the southeast... and so on.

He reminded Wolfgang that they should avoid being seen, and that hunting grounds were sacred to any tribe.

"If strangers are found intruding there," Big Bull said somberly, "they'll be made into slaves – or, worse, will be tortured, scalped and killed. They spare only crazy people or medicine men. Once you have come to the pine-covered ridges, travel northwest into the mountain forest of He Sapa. The tallest mountain will be what the Lakota call Inyan Kara – sacred to the Lakota and Cheyenne. Travel north, then, to Mato Tipi. Beyond this is what the French call the Belle Fourche River. Buffalo country. That is as far as I have traveled in my youth. It was here in a valley, just beyond the Belle Fourche River, that I saw the white wolves."

Suddenly, Dark Moon gave a strange look.

"The place of one of my visions," she murmured.

Chapter 28

Wolfgang and Dark Moon were drawn upwind, following a mysterious, sweetly scented fragrance that pervaded the air, until at last they beheld groves of oak, hawthorn, plum, and crab apple trees. Clusters of pink and white blossoms caught their eye. Bees hovered everywhere. They had reached the east side of the Big Blue River at last. They rode down into the trees, stopped and dismounted to rest, feeling safely hidden under the canopy of craggy branches overhead. Dark Moon set the horses out to graze in a grassy hidden pasture and hobbled them. A short time later, Wolfgang left to cross the clear, gentle, slow-moving water of the river.

* * *

Dark Moon fished and gathered fresh greens. The gullies were full of broad-leaved plants and low shrubs that included wild roses, gooseberries, chokecherry and service berries. She noticed the increased movement of deer and realized that the does were selecting their birthing territories to drop their fawns. A few trees in the gully were full of sharptails. They were sitting in the shade, watching for danger, and their *ducka ducka ducka* cries were often heard as she moved about. She knew they could be easily harvested for a meal with a throwing stick. When Wolfgang returned, she would cook some of these big birds, stuffing them with sassafras leaves.

In this way two days passed until Wolfgang returned,

reporting that he had traveled as far as the Little Blue but found no suspicious sign. He had discovered where countless horses had passed through the grassland, stomping the trail to a fine dust – it was the great Pawnee Trail, which ran north to south – but the travois skid-marks were not fresh.

"That must be their trail to the buffalo hunting grounds to the south," Dark Moon said. "Big Bull told us about it. We must stay away from there and move north instead of remaining on this side of the river."

As they ate their meal and gazed at their surroundings, the wonderful, pungent aroma of damp earth reminded Wolfgang of the German farmers. *What might they do with country like this if it were not so wild?*

They rested several days, before continuing their journey. They crossed broad flower-filled grasslands covered with tall buffalo and gramma grass. The only trees visible were cottonwood forests along the riverbanks and islands of the Platte River. In almost every direction they saw buffalo. When the herds ran, the earth trembled beneath their pounding hoofs and the air filled with dust. Wolfgang and Dark Moon didn't need to see the creatures to know they were there. Even when the terrain obstructed their view, the thousands of swarming birds flying above the herd – feeding on insects in the air and on the animals' hides – made the herd's location apparent. The two travelers took care never to venture into the path of the beasts, which always ran in a straight line and could outrun a horse, but the two enjoyed watching the young calves scamper and bounce about.

* * *

One moonlit night on the trail, amid the unearthly, drawn-out howling of wolves, Dark Moon asked Wolfgang when the first day of summer, the longest day of the year, would arrive.

"June twenty-first," Wolfgang said. "The day before the sun begins to move further south each day – the latter part of the Rose Moon. Why do you ask?"

"Because that is when we shall steal horses from the Pawnee," Dark Moon said.

Wolfgang just stared at her, speechless.

Dark Moon explained that they would travel faster with an extra mount apiece and that the best time to steal the animals would be just before the Skidi Pawnee began to round up their horses and pack their tents to move south for their summer buffalo hunt.

"Everyone attends the Morning Star Ceremony," she said. "It culminates in the human sacrifice of a virgin captured from another tribe as the 'Morning Star' starts to rise. All the Pawnee will be there to see it."

Wolfgang was impressed by how thoroughly she had thought the plan through.

* * *

Wolfgang and Dark Moon had not seen the wolf or its mate for days when, as suddenly and silently as spirits, the two animals appeared. But their worried expressions and body language signaled danger ahead, and Wolfgang pointed in a direction for the wolves to proceed; effortlessly, they were gone on their mission. Meanwhile Wolfgang and Dark Moon rode with their noses into the wind, their eyes moving constantly, in search of anything that seemed not to fit. For two more days they rode – until the absence of tall, waving grass became the first hint of an abandoned village up ahead.

When close-cropped grass and dried horse droppings appeared, and the air changed to one slightly odorous, Wolfgang and Dark Moon weren't surprised to spy a large area denuded of grass ahead.

Entering the abandoned village, they closely observed the large, round, earthen lodges. Now Dark Moon dismounted and, walking around a lodge, observing how they were built. She saw that small tree trunks had been set in excavated holes to support the rafters, which in turn supported each structure's roof of laid-over willow and earth-covered prairie grass. The lodges' interiors would be cool during summer, but with the central fire hearth, its smoke hole directly above, they would be warm in the winter. The travelers examined the round, blackened areas of old campfires and teepee rings outlined by stone circles. Inside each circle were sunken, circular blackened hearth pits lined with rocks used in cooking. The travelers also noted an abundance of flint chips in and near every lodge. Seeing the drag-marks of the travois moving off to the northwest, Wolfgang and Dark Moon would follow later at a distance further east of the lines of travel.

Dark Moon's eyes carefully searched the ground. Finally, she found a long, slender and stout pole. She moved around back and forth, tapping the ground.

Watching curiously, Wolfgang said, "What are you doing?"

"Listening to the sound of the pole striking the ground and feeling the vibration in the pole. There is a grain cache down here."

She immediately stopped and began digging with one of several buffalo shoulder blades that were leaning against the wall of the lodge. Then together they uncovered a pit insulated with grass, inside of which lay meat, vegetables and grain. She removed only what was safe for the horses to carry, and immediately fed some of the stored grain to the horses.

* * *

A day later, Wolfgang and Dark Moon spotted the wolves sitting atop a low ridge. The animals' posture and alertness warned of human activity nearby.

They camped at the bottom of the ridge. That night the four saw a glow in the night sky they recognized as a sign of an Indian village. Though the travelers remained hidden all the next day, at night they followed the glow across the prairie as far as they dared, picketing their horses at last well downwind of the camp. Early the next morning a gray smudge showed on the far horizon – a sign, an indication of morning cook fires. From the amount of smoke, the two knew that they had located a large village. It was on the southeastern shelf of a small plateau above a wide terraced valley, exposed to the sun, but protected from the northwestern winds. Surrounded by a natural spring, the village was free from floodwaters. It also offered a view in all directions so that the Pawnee could easily defend against any surprise attack from approaching enemies.

Dark Moon and Wolfgang observed a narrow forest of cottonwoods, mulberries, ash and box elder trees along the banks of the Platte River. The gooseberry bushes were leafed out. Women of the Wolf Tribe tended their corn in the mouth at the moist bottom of a ravine in the hills.

Among the lodges, favorite animals were tethered close at hand to each warrior's lodge. Wolfgang and Dark Moon continued to watch the village for two more days and nights. They saw the horses graze east of the camp, and also saw the fog set in early each evening. They studied the terrain for an easy approach and then a quick departure with the horses they planned to steal. Now they would wait and watch.

An hour before moonrise, the wolf led them close to the guarded horses. With her keen sense for night sounds, Dark Moon listened for anything unusual as she and Wolfgang approached the hilltop. They heard dogs barking and yowling at a distance, but detected nothing close-by. As they edged over the hill, a smell came to Wolfgang: not strong yet – the camp had only recently been established – but easily discernible. He could see the winking glow of smoking pipes as men sat around the fires, and the shadows of women crossing back and forth past the flames as they worked. The smaller, fast-moving figures were children still at play.

Continuing downstream, Wolfgang and Dark Moon discovered hundreds of horses grazing in the lush pasture. Working their way around, to keep downwind all the time, the two moved from a smaller group to a larger one. Several animals, interrupting their eating, lifted their heads to look their way and snort, but the two moved slowly, speaking softly, and the animals did not toss their heads or bolt.

Having discovered that the Pawnee had hundreds of horses, Dark Moon and Wolfgang spent two days watching and studying the animals from a distance. She especially listened for breeding stallions that would be active until early autumn. Though it was dangerous to be anywhere around the Pawnee horse herd, they knew they must move among the animals to earn their confidence before stealing any. Dark Moon studied how selected animals walked or ran, but she rejected many just from watching how they just stood: some had too-narrow chests, or hooves that pointed in or out, and others stumbled, or caught a rear with a front hoof. Also excluded were those with conformation faults such as straight hocks, which would cause an animal to become easily lamed. Finally, her eyes found the right conformations in a small group of horses standing close to each other. They were switching their tails to protect each other from the flies. They all had strong hind legs and good hock construction.

Each evening, Wolfgang and Dark Moon enjoyed the glorious colors of twilight and watched the blue daytime sky turn to the vibrant oranges and reds of sunset. Then after dark, Dark Moon would strip herself of clothes, clean herself with a wet rag, and rub her skin with sage, herbs, and a little horse manure on her arms and legs. She would chew fennel seed to sweeten her breath. After she felt sure that her body and breath would not smell offensive to the horses, she disappeared among them, leaving Wolfgang alone, shivering in the cool nighttime hours.

* * *

"What is it that you are doing each night?" Wolfgang asked on the second evening. "Getting the horses to trust me," Dark Moon replied. "How do you know where those you have chosen will be each night?" "Within the herd, each horse has its own place to sleep. No matter where the herd is moved, each animal will be in the same general location relative to the rest of the herd." Wolfgang was amazed at her knowledge. Several days passed. The big night finally arrived.

Charles A. McDonald

Chapter 29

In preparation for this night, Wolfgang and Dark Moon had fasted all day so that their body odor would be less discernable to the horses. Since dusk they had been watching the two night herders guarding the horse herd. Once it became fully dark, Wolfgang and Dark Moon spotted those men by their foggy breath. They had lain preternaturally still in the chilly early morning hours, and now they chewed a little potato. The last quarter moon hung above, partly hidden by clouds, and a cover of light patchy mist crept across the ground.

After much concentration, Dark Moon pointed out three mares: a mouse-colored one, a dappled gray, and a dull, grayish-brown animal. She noticed the three were alert: Whenever a coyote or wolf ventured nearby, the horses raised their heads and watched. Not part of a harem group, they were evidently good friends in comfortable harmony with each other, and their movement indicated their hooves were in good condition. Wolfgang and Dark Moon would have no trouble leading them away. She studied the periodic mutual grooming among them that maintained their social ties. The dappled gray led the others to water and grazing areas.

"There is much to be gained by having horses well-matched in age, size and disposition," she whispered.

Seeing the horses feed down into a draw, she directed Wolfgang to stay where he was but to whistle if he spotted danger; she would go alone to inspect the horses further.

"But why should I stay and watch?" Wolfgang asked.

"Because horses can be most dangerous," she whispered in answer. "If they smell fear or are handled roughly, they will kick you to death, maim you or roll on you and bite savagely." She explained further. "The harsh voices of men seemed to frighten horses, they respond best to women's voices." Wolfgang knew she was always right.

"Just watch and learn," she said. "When you see or hear me coming back, go get our other horses."

Dark Moon now had but to wait until the moon, in its last quarter, rose in the early morning. When it did – the clouds again partially covered the shrinking moon – she advanced in the shadowed late night, crushing glistening blades of grass beneath her silent footsteps.

Far out among the herd, she finally found the animals she had selected earlier. The horses' keen sense of hearing – along with ground vibrations they had sensed – warned them of a stranger's approach, but Dark Moon whistled in a soft, low tone, soothing the high-strung animals. She was pleased that none of the surrounding horses were shivering fearfully, and felt lucky not to hear any telltale snorts or aggressive squeals or screams of a stallion nearby. Speaking soothingly, she slid her palms lovingly over the animals' bodies as she moved ahead. Although a few surrounding mares, their heads up, neighed their displeasure, Dark Moon knew the animals she would lead out had shown a head-down posture, a sure sign of compliance.

Listening for any low nickering that would warn her of a stallion courting, Dark Moon was relieved to hear only the distant squealing of a mare as a stallion sniffed her. She didn't worry about the younger stallions, which were on a more distant fringe of the herd, fearing the older, vicious, dominant stallion.

Most of the surrounding animals were too old, too young, or too temperamental, as shown by their laid-back ears.

Horses too fat or thin would affect stamina and performance, and Dark Moon didn't want those too wild or strong-mouthed for a hand, toe or heel to guide. Having found the three animals she had watched from a distance, she eliminated a fourth: Its eyes were wide in the moonlight. She was fast-looking, but carried her head too high, the sign of a "stargazer" that would have difficulty seeing where she was going and be hard to control.

Watching from a distance, Wolfgang was amazed. Dark Moon moved without making a sound or alarming nearby horses. He saw her make her way close to the three selected horses and squat on the ground. Judging from the position of their heads and their keen noses, the horses were aware of the intruder but not alarmed. Dark Moon continued to wait, carefully watching the horses seize the grass with their front teeth and, with a quick jerk, nip off the stems, dropping nothing from their mouths. She knew that horses that dribbled food didn't chew properly and wouldn't have the energy or stamina for long trips. But these were young, healthy animals seemingly without any problems. In the moonlight, they looked lean and healthy. She spoke to them in the deep guttural language of their own. HUNH, UN-hunh, un-hunh, un-hunh.

Dark Moon was pleased that the dappled-gray and dun horses, their ears pricked forward, allowed her to walk up to them. As she talked to them, her hands began to stroke the dappled gray leader, which turned and extended its head toward her. It whinnied in its soprano tone, speaking a kindly greeting, and Dark Moon watched the horse's ears, which were well forward in greeting. Then the two other horses followed, crowding up to her. She was happy to see the friendly response, but knew a greeting could change to a threat if the ears suddenly flattened back. Careful not to let her hands move too quick, she checked for running noses, a sign of bad lungs due to respiratory disease, then gently blew breath into each animal's nostrils, showing affection and bonding with the creatures. Letting her hands run over the crest of each horse's neck, she walked around the side of the horse, and felt along the line of its back. There were no back sores, and were not sensitive to pressure. "Good." She found each animal's fleshy back flat with no crease down the middle, their withers well-rounded, and each mare's neck and shoulders blending smoothly into its body. She could feel the ribs but not see them, as her hands acted as a medium of conversation through skin pressure, through which the horses, watching her the whole time, sensed her love for them.

They all had a slight ridge over the loins and a faint outline of the ribs. She felt the prominent fat around the tail-head. Sliding her hand down their legs, she felt the tendons and ligaments but no swelling or heat from inflammation in the lower legs. She then lifted their hooves, one at a time, to check for cracks, sloping pasterns, corns, or injuries from its hind feet over-reaching. She felt their coronary bands for heat. There were no cracks in their hoofs; they were in good condition. Their feet and legs were exceptionally good. In the daylight there had been no unnatural bobbing of their heads. She felt no swelling around the hock, from excess fluid. *Good*, she thought, *these animals had not been overused.*

Dark Moon waited until the moon was clear of the clouds, then expertly inserted her fingers in the space between the incisors and grinders flat on top of the tongue, to open the horse's mouth. She slid her thumb under the tongue and turned it up to the roof of its mouth for examination. She repeated this with the other horses. They all stood quietly. A good disposition was imperative to her selection. The half moon provided enough light for her to make out that each horse had a full set of healthy teeth. The solid enamel dipped down deeply into the pocket of the tooth, showing the black centers. Only the first four teeth had dark spots. The four canine teeth were present. The young mares were four years old, and already broke. She was pleased that she had chosen well. In another year, she thought, they would be fully developed and able to stand harder work.

Dark Moon's low voice and hands were caring and calming on the animal's bodies, and now she made friends by scratching their sensitive withers. The feel of the hair along their back told her these three had been used, and when she put her arms over each horse's back, pressing with her weight, she could see they were already broken to riding. Speaking softly, she placed a soft rope halter on the dominant, dappled gray. She then slowly fed each of them maple sugar as she gently tugged on the rope, while making a soft clucking sound. The horses did not exhibit spooky behavior at the sound of nearby coyotes and wolves that moved among the herd, nor did they raise their heads in fright nor point their ears. Until the moon was clear of clouds, she remained with the three horses among the herd then walked them slowly back toward Wolfgang. The horses raised their heads at the sight and smell of Wolfgang and the other strange horses, but Dark Moon knew how to soothe them. She used her halter and made it quickly into an emergency bridle. When she mounted the dapple gray and urged it into a sprint, she felt the power of its mighty hindquarters.

Dark Moon felt excited as her mount filled its lungs with a burst of speed. With little urging, the three mares leaped quickly away from the herd and fled silently through the light cover of fog, which she knew, would help muffle any sound, not to mention... making it impossible to see any distant object. When they turned their heads to look back, Dark Moon and Wolfgang were surprised that, as far as they could tell, no one was following. Dark Moon was thrilled. She had briefly noticed how their stolen horses carried their tails – high, clear of the hind limbs, proudly and gracefully arched. They crouched low over the horses' withers, the grip of their knees giving the animals powerful rhythm and direction, flowing in harmony, the hooves pounding in unison over the rugged terrain. It seemed the further they went, the better these animals ran.

*   *   *

Eventually Wolfgang and Dark Moon reached the Platte River. Driving the older, reliable horses ahead of them, they urged the new animals to plunge in. The horses splashed the shallow water in all directions as their feet sank deeply. Lifting each hoof, they made a sucking sound and left only small, circular depression that quickly filled with water behind them. The current would soon hide their crossing point. Dark Moon smiled inwardly because the younger horses had shown no fear of the water.

Stopping on the opposite side to drink, Wolfgang and Dark Moon found the water silty. After leading the horses slowly and steadily up and across the lowland hill bordering the river, they came upon a stretch of good grass. They hobbled the horses, and let them graze and rest. To Dark Moon's delight, the horses had not even begun to sweat. Listening to their breathing, she heard no asthmatic wheezing; the animals were sound, with good wind stamina. She again inspected their hooves since they had a long trail ahead.

The early morning fog had gradually disappeared as Dark Moon scrambled back up to the top of the bank and listened for drumbeat sounds of hooves in pursuit. They saw the dim light of dawn now exposing their back trail and felt satisfied no one was following close behind. The sun had not yet risen. As she turned, facing east, she noticed a white brilliant star.

"The Morning Star," she said, as Wolfgang's eyes followed her arm and saw the bright star in the pre-dawn sky. "It is the star you call Venus." She added that Mayan star-watchers far to the south had worshipped the bright star as a very dangerous warrior called Chac Ek – a God who might bring omens about the future." They remained on high ground above the river, watching their back trail.

They walked back toward the six horses and stood

looking at them. "Look at their shapely heads, the broad width between the eyes and their wide nostrils," said Dark Moon. Wolfgang said, "What does that mean?" Dark Moon replied: "Intelligence and good endurance. Horses express themselves through body language, and you must learn to read that language by watching them constantly. When gauging their fear, brace, stiffness and discomfort, pay attention to the position of their ears, the eyes blinking, the lips licking, the throw of their head, and front-leg movement." She pointed approvingly at the broad shoulders, well-rounded ribs and straight profiles of the new horses. She stood and watched as the animals settled down to cropping the buffalo grass. All six horses were good. She unpacked some corn from the abandoned village and portioned it out to each horse.

* * *

Together Wolfgang and Dark Moon slowly approached the mouse colored horse – a fine, strong mare with tremendous muscles, and a deep, powerful chest. Dark Moon noted, *This horse will be a strong runner. Its beautiful, chestnut-colored eyes are expressive of her good mood.* Wolfgang said to her, "I wish to be your friend." The mare turned her head and whiffed inquiringly. Then the horse softly whinnied, and stretched out its neck and head with the lip-raising posture, in effect asking for the hand he held hidden behind his back. He was amazed that the horse knew he held pieces of hard maple sugar.

"She can smell it," said Dark Moon.

Wolfgang also admired the mare's deep-muscled girth and powerful hindquarters, which were the source of its physical prowess and would be an asset in the mountains. Walking to the front of the horse, he noted the well-rounded barrel. The animal had sturdy, straight legs and feet in proportion to its size and weight.

Watching the horses eat, Dark Moon pointed out to him that she knew they were content because they ate with all four hooves touching the ground, head down, and tail swinging gently. The dun, a dull grayish-brown animal, was also beautiful with its black ears, muzzle, mane, tail, lower legs and dominant black dorsal stripe.

Together, Wolfgang and Dark Moon again scrambled back to the top of the ravine to watch and listen. Satisfied the Pawnee herders hadn't yet missed the stolen horses, the two again mounted up and soon fell into a rolling lope. For two days they rode on the west side of the Elkhorn River, continually checking the land around them. At first the only troubling sign was a dark cloud in the distance to the northwest, but then a second troubling sign appeared: The buffalo and antelope, all up and feeding. Dark Moon felt anxious to move because the buffalo gnats, flies, and mosquitoes had become active, feeding on the travelers' exposed skin mercilessly. Just before dark the winged pests swirled, bit, stung, crawled, and worried them all to death. To reduce their flailing, swatting, and scratching, they avoided the brushy draws and rode into the wind, away from the herd. Then she found Sweet Flag growing in a marshy area. When she collected a leaf and nibbled it, the pungent taste verified that it was what she was looking for. She directed Wolfgang to harvest the long narrow leaves and rub the animals thoroughly with them.

"When you finish, rub the exposed areas of your body with the bruised leaves too," she said.

The fresh aromatic leaves indeed proved a great insecticide and he immediately noticed that the insects left them alone.

"You know much!" he said to Dark Moon, smiling.

* * *

As the two made their way through the open, rolling and green-carpeted hills shrouded with beautiful prairie grass and flowers, Dark Moon pointed out how well their older horses had fared: Having filled out with added weight from the good grass, the animals looked beautiful. Though the riders hadn't seen the two wolves for some time, they saw plenty of other wolves, always near the buffalo herds and constantly testing them.

Most of the huge, horned beasts were too agile to become easy prey. They watched a small number defend themselves as a group. They observed a cow running through the herd pursued by several bulls, Wolfgang and Dark Moon realized the rut had started. Soon a string of tending bulls was strung out behind the running cow. When she stopped running, fights developed among the males. The human observers could hear the terrific shock of their butting heads, the knocking of horns and also see them tossing their heads in uppercuts. Most of the fights were not serious, but the power of two huge animals was striking. Their bodies rippled in visible waves as they plowed the prairie with locked horns, driving first one way then the other. Then, as Wolfgang and Dark Moon watched, one bull succeeded in knocking down another. The upright bull slammed into the downed one, hooking a horn into his opponent's belly, to rip flesh. The fight's massive winner claimed the cow.

As the herd continued to move, the wolves spotted the injured bull and gave chase.

Dark Moon and Wolfgang knew a horrible death lay ahead.

The wounded bull still dazed and bleeding from its belly, soon stood encircled by the wolves, which took great care not to be kicked or pierced by the animal's horns as they charged and parried the isolated animal to tire it. The buffalo desperately resisted but eventually, exhausted, he became defenseless. As several wolves distracted the bull by slashing and biting its flanks, one large wolf seized the nose and held on, and another grabbed the throat. Two more flung themselves at the rear legs. The powerful jaws of the other wolves were now savagely biting and slashing at the desperate bull's hide. Then they began shearing it away. The bull was now partially eviscerated. As his entrails began to emerge, a large black wolf grabbed and pulled out the rest. Other wolves began gobbling up the entrails while the bull still stood. The victim stamped and snorted as his flesh tore. Nervous shivers shook his body as he began to wobble on his feet. The bull, a bloody mess of lacerations, tired from the loss of blood, just stood as the wolves literally ate him. Soon his hide and flesh were hanging in strips and his tongue had been bitten off. The great animal, blinded, was being suffocated from the wolf clamped on his throat. He dropped and was devoured by the wolves alive.

"The wolves gave the bull a slow death," Dark Moon said, "but not as slow as it would have suffered from infection of its belly wound." Still, the two agreed that the violent attack had not been pretty to behold. During the rest of the day, either a lone wolf or several wolves periodically ventured close to observe them. The animals would trot along side them for a time, then gone.

"Don't worry about them," Dark Moon said. "We have the smell of the wolf upon us."

As the two continued to ride, an almost perfect stillness enveloped them. They discussed how deer, like antelope, consistently traveled downwind, ignoring the air currents revealing their presence but trusting their eyes in these open spaces, to keep them safe from possible danger.

"Would you prefer having to overcome their vision or sense of smell when hunting them?" Dark Moon asked.

"Their vision," Wolfgang replied immediately.

"Me, too."

"I've noticed antelope don't move at night," Wolfgang said. "When they bed down in the evening, they're always in the same place the next morning, unless a predator makes them move. When we stop tonight, let's watch the nearest antelope herd bed down, and sneak up on them before dawn."

Dark Moon agreed.

They continued onward. Wherever they looked, they saw that the landscape in the open light showing a gold and pale green color that looked evanescent toward evening. The time seemed endless beneath the open sky. Finally, toward evening, they saw ahead a narrow creek meandering swiftly through high, grassy banks. A nearby marsh flanked a small lake, and the only sound above the gentle wind was that of raspy red-winged blackbirds, the long-beaked, white-black-brown mottled willet birds in evidence everywhere near the lake. Swallows were diving and dipping as Wolfgang and Dark Moon reined in at the creek to make camp.

* * *

Passing through the low, timbered area, the two hiked up to the bluff. Then they watched a small herd of antelope moving down wind. The animals were using their eyes to see ahead and by keeping the wind at their back, they could sniff any danger that might approach from behind. At last light the antelope finally bedded down.

"Antelope are the most beautiful animal I have ever seen," said Wolfgang.

He pointed out a dry coulee a hundred yards down wind beyond them, which ran from the river, well up into the flats.

He continued saying, "The wind is blowing from the northwest, and the evening and night air will move downhill toward the valley floor. Early tomorrow morning, while it's still dark, we can approach them closely. The wind will carry our scent away from the herd, and the coulee will mask our sound and movement."

* * *

Dark Moon followed Wolfgang closely in the dark. She felt that there was a magical sense about him. He was an excellent hunter. As dawn broke she watched him move out from the coulee behind a large clump of sagebrush and slowly push the muzzle of his rifle through it. She preferred to watch her man's actions than observe the kill. She saw his concentration narrow on the closest doe as it ambled along a few steps, stopped to nibble at tips of the sage, and continued on. The herd was relaxed, unaware of danger. When the animal turned its head and looked away, Dark Moon saw Wolfgang calmly take a deep, controlled breath, let out a short one, and come to a natural pause as he squeezed the trigger. The sudden flash of the pan and explosion sent the rifle stock recoiling into his shoulder, and she heard the resounding slap of an animal solidly hit.

Even as remainder of the herd bolted, Wolfgang and Dark Moon remained still for a time, studying the surrounding terrain for movement that might indicate anyone had heard the shot. Finally, satisfied, they stood. Approaching the fallen animal, she quickly field-dressed it as he continued to watch for enemies. A short time later, when the heart and liver had been returned into the animal's body cavity, Wolfgang lifted the doe to his shoulders. Then the two re-entered the coulee and made their way back to camp.

After hanging and skinning the antelope in the shade, Wolfgang and Dark Moon went to the stream to bathe. When they returned, they spied the two wolves laying in the dark shade, though the animals immediately bounded playfully out into the light to greet them. After a rough-and-tumble greeting, the animals laid down to watch their human friends attentively.

While Dark Moon cooked the liver for their breakfast, Wolfgang split the antelope carcass with an ax and placed the pieces separately on the ground. He looked at the wolves and motioned for them to eat. As Wolfgang and Dark Moon enjoyed their own meal, they watched and laughed at the sounds of the wolves devouring the carcass.

* * *

As Wolfgang and Dark Moon rode through the tall, bluestem prairie grass, the sky above showed clear and beautiful. The air felt humid. The horizon grew dark with a distant storm. She noticed a troubling sign as the birds flew low to the ground, and just then a strong gust hit them from the west. It felt cool and good, quickly ridding them of the gnats, but it continued to grow stronger. Now the small dark cloud they had seen on the distant horizon was a great, ominous-looking, black sagging wall bloated with fast-approaching rain. The wind continued to pick up until they heard it as a low howl, and they knew they must search for cover.

Far ahead they spotted a lonely, cone-shaped hill with a ridge behind it that quickly leveled out with the prairie. The near side of it would protect them from the storm closing in around them like a liquid curtain. Inside the dark clouds, an eerie glow showed as lightning cracked the sky.

As the whistling wind picked up, it became a menace. Grass and seeds flew through the air at great speed. Drawing closer to the hill and ridge, Wolfgang and Dark Moon saw a dark spot below an overhang – when suddenly hail began to fall. Pellets of ice, blown with great force, hit and stung them as they rode through the box elder, red cedar, wild plum and chokecherry around the base of the hill and up the side. Dismounting quickly, the riders led the six horses up and into the cave. Dark Moon hurriedly collected kindling along the way.

Inside it was cramped but the party was safe. Wolfgang and Dark Moon took turns going out to collect not only dry twigs and dead branches but also buffalo chips, which they piled onto a blanket. The hail became larger and beat the ground viciously, covering it with an icy, white sheet, as the sky outside grew darker. A silent streak of lightening flashed far in the distance to the south, illuminating the landscape. "Lead the horses as far back into the cave as they can go," said Dark Moon. She pulled head covers out of one pack and joined him covering the beasts' heads.

As they sat and leaned back against their packs to rest, his arm encircled her shoulders and pulled her close. Together they watched the storm. The rain outside looked like jewels when the lightening flashed. Knowing that their back trail was now eliminated, they felt a little more secure.

Then the two heard a distant rumbling come closer and closer. The earth began to shake and the sky became bright with flashes of lightening. A panicked herd of buffalo came stampeding across the landscape. Wolfgang and Dark Moon pressed closer to each other, knowing how lucky they had been not to be caught out in the open. Then suddenly, the storm was gone. The sun was now only one finger above the horizon in the west. They went out, climbed almost to the top of the hill and studied the terrain in all directions. Only a few dead buffalo lay fallen across the prairie. Satisfied that it was as safe as it could be, they led the horses out of the cave and down the hill, and hobbled them for the night. The air smelled fresh and clean. Having waited for darkness, Wolfgang walked out to the nearest buffalo cow with the wolves and salvaged the tongue and back straps. He cut a hind leg off the dead animal, split it for the wolves and left them at the carcass. By the time he returned, buffalo chips were burning hot and slow.

Chapter 30

It was still the early part of the Moon of Thunder. Wolfgang and Dark Moon, continuing their travels by night, relied on the Fixed Star as their guide. Because it wasn't dark enough to see the stars until near midnight, they always took a good fix on direction before stopping. Traveling this way was safer since they needn't worry about being seen.

Each evening the nighthawks and swooping bats announced the dying of the light as Wolfgang and Dark Moon listened to a familiar, ancient language: the seductive wails of howling wolves, changing in pitch as the animals assembled for the hunt. The drawn-out, single notes rose sharply as each animal strained for volume, and tapered to a moment of tremolo. Later in the evening came the shrill, staccato yelping of coyotes.

The nightly celestial light-show included falling stars streaking across the late-night sky. Wolfgang and Dark Moon felt awed by such beauty. The stars looked so large, white, and sharp, the travelers felt they could reach out and touch them. They both were always quick to locate the familiar pattern of seven stars that depicted the Great She-Bear: four stars that formed the scoop represented a bear, and the three stars of its handle were three hunters stalking her. The itinerant couple took comfort from that most prominent configuration in the northern night sky, which appeared slightly to the northeast during winter.

The earth bears were immortal, Dark Moon explained,

coming to life again each spring when they emerged from their den. And like the celestial bear, they continued their life cycle around the Fixed Star. Wolfgang and Dark Moon, too, followed the direction of the Fixed Star, indicated by the celestial bear.

"The souls of the dead dwell in the moon," Dark Moon said, gazing skyward. "It has the power of rebirth."

"I like figuring time the way the Indians do," Wolfgang said. "Keeping track of the four phases of the moon in their complete cycle – the New Moon, First Quarter Moon, Full Moon, and Last Quarter Moon, each separated by about a week. The 7-day-old moon signifies the moon's 'age'– 7 days after the New Moon: the First Quarter Moon. The Full Moon occurs 14 days after the New Moon, and the Last Quarter Moon is 21 days old." They continued to ride side by side. Wolfgang went on. "When I look into the night sky and study the moon and stars, I feel the wonder of this world. I feel lifted spiritually. I feel the hand of God."

In the dark, Dark Moon smiled to herself.

Riding by night, the two star-watched and moon-gazed in wonder, while by day they rested under the relentless summer sun. During the day, Wolfgang and Dark Moon were surrounded with an endless sea of luxuriant, waist-high leafy, blue-stemmed grass that stretched from horizon to horizon. The only sound was the slight whispering sigh of the wind. The only movement was the shifting back and forth of brightness and shadow from the shifting clouds. The soft and slight swaying motion of the grass made it appear like a living creature. To Wolfgang, it was the month of July. To the Western Indians, it was known as the Moon of Thunder or the Blood Moon. The heat was punishing. Creeks had dried to a trickle and the water they found was bitter, ruined by alkali poisoning. Forcing their horses away from the bad water, they rested often in the shade of dry creek banks.

Dark Moon was worried.

The animals were near the limit of their endurance.

The War Trail

With heads held low, the horses plodded, scuffing their hoofs as they ambled along in short strides. They were puffing, their tongues hanging out. By now the riders had given the animals the last of their water, and though the sun sat low on the western horizon, Wolfgang and Dark Moon felt white foam forming in the back of their own mouths as well.

"We all must have water soon," Dark Moon said. "If the horses die, we will have to drink their blood to survive."

She could not stand the thought of losing these animals, but already her own tongue was swelling in her mouth, her throat was dry, and her lips were parched and cracked.

Slowly, they continued north.

Then, later that evening, it came: a sudden breeze. The horses whinnied and began to stamp and sidestep, and Dark Moon knew they smelled water. Immediately she and Wolfgang mounted and gave the animals their head. The riders didn't worry about direction since the animals' ears were pitched forward toward the Fixed Star. Though only grass showed from horizon to horizon, the horses' heads had come up and, with nostrils wide, they quickened their pace. Dark Moon and Wolfgang knew they must be close to water – a lot of water. All at once, they could smell the change themselves.

The wild, wind-raked landscape began to change as the wide flats, separated by gentle, undulated dips and rises, became higher and steeper. Finally, from their moonlit vantage point, they could see thick cover in the distant bottom ahead, where a silvered stream braided the tall cottonwoods.

At the stream Dark Moon first checked the water as Wolfgang held the eager horses back. Cupping her hand, she brought a handful of the sparkling liquid to her mouth and cautiously tasted it. She smiled, pointed down and signed by holding her right hand flat in front of her left breast and briskly moving it horizontally from left to right.

Water. Good.

Wolfgang understood and released the horses. Moments later they smiled at each other as the animals drank greedily.

In the days that followed, the horses cropped the tall, rich, blue-green-stemmed prairie grass, and their weight increased with remarkable speed. Looking around them, the travelers beheld low plains covered with luxuriant grass and a tremendous variety of wildflowers. Much of the area was dotted with small lakes and marshes fed by springs, while on the higher ground stood tall, yellow prairie sunflowers. Dark Moon pointed out purple cornflowers and black-and-gold black-eyed Susan's blooming everywhere.

* * *

Wolfgang and Dark Moon decided at last to travel during the day. Several times they came across signs of Indians' horses, but these were old. One afternoon as they rode, listening to the calm whisper of their horses' legs moving through tall, thick grass, they came to a large, cleared area filled with small, earth-rimmed craters. Pausing, the riders saw many small rodents perched sentinel-like on the rims. As Wolfgang and Dark Moon approached, each small animal flipped its tail, sounded a high-pitched warning, and dove into its burrow.

Dismounting, the two walked their horses through the area in zigzag pattern. When they reached the far edge of the colony, they stopped to rest and watch the amusing creatures. Dark Moon turned to Wolfgang, smiling, but instead of a smile saw his face blanch, as he stood motionless.

Following his downward gaze, she found herself staring into a pair of wicked black-and-yellow eyes.

"Don't move," she whispered hoarsely, her right arm inching slowly toward the cased fighting spear attached to her saddle.

Wolfgang kept stone still, staring at a rattler bigger than

any he had ever seen. He felt unable to shift his gaze from the snake's frightening eyes as it swayed to and fro, gathering itself to strike.

Suddenly Dark Moon's spear darted, pinning the creature to the earth. Wolfgang jumped back.

"Sometimes they don't rattle." She said.

She held up the body, which was as long as he was tall. He watched her bleed the yellow venom into one of her small containers.

"For our arrow-heads," Dark Moon said. "Against our enemies."

Though they continued on their way immediately, Dark Moon worried about this incident. Seeing that Wolfgang was shaken, she felt it was an omen.

Finally, after traveling for some time, she said, "Do not worry. I can treat a snake bite if there is need."

* * *

The two travelers began to watch for a place to stop. Again the horses were showing signs of needing water, but there was something else they were paying attention to. They walked with their heads straight in front of their bodies, though the startling sounds of small birds flushing ahead erupted often. The birds cried shrilly and flew up, then dipped, fluttered, and flew away low over the grass. The horses paid no attention except for flicking an ear now and again, keeping track of the birds' flight. Dark Moon recognized this ear movement as sign of the animals' alertness, and she smiled, pleased with these horses.

At length, Dark Moon and Wolfgang noticed the mounts paying close attention to the northern horizon. They stopped. Studying both the terrain around them and the distant skylines, they saw nothing to explain the horses' excitement, and decided to continue onward. But there was no denying that the animals' thin ears were pricked forward, and something imperceptible to Wolfgang and Dark Moon seemed to be alerting them. Wolfgang stuck a finger into his mouth and then held it aloft. The wind was from the northwest.

Whatever sound had excited the animals remained inaudible to the riders. But then, in the distance, the sky was suddenly filled with black birds surging, wheeling, and diving ahead, low in the sky. Wolfgang and Dark Moon stopped to watch. The next moment the sky became empty as the birds descended, all at once, as if on command. The riders' mounts began to dance from one foot to the other. Dark Moon bent forward and whispered in a pleasant tone into her horse's ear, and Wolfgang did the same. Whatever alerted the horses covered a large area, indeed. Wolfgang pulled his long rifle out of its carrying case, sat it across his legs and checked the priming. The six horses kept their heads up. They appeared slightly excited and began to neigh periodically.

By now the two realized what lay ahead.

Chapter 31

An unseen buffalo herd was moving ahead of them. A small grove of tall cottonwoods laid ahead – a sure sign of ground water. When Wolfgang and Dark Moon finally reached the grove, they made their way through the curtain of wild plum, hackberry, chokecherries, elm, and box elder to the open ground under the old trees. There was ample shade, fuel, and good water. They remained several days and allowed the horses to regain their strength before resuming their journey. It was here that Dark Moon showed Wolfgang how to prepare an ointment for themselves and the horses, which was good for an entire day at a time, when applied. The main ingredient was the natural oil from marigolds, sweet flag, and dog's tongue, which would repel flies, mosquitoes, gnats and midges that followed the buffalo.

Days later, a short time after the sun was half a finger above the horizon, Dark Moon and Wolfgang at last heard it - an almost inaudible rumbling, as of distant thunder which would not stop. Then a distinctly musky, bovine scent reached them.

The two looked at each other and nodded, sharing the same thought.

"It must be a large herd," Dark Moon said.

Sure enough, the rumbling grew louder until they both topped a small rise. Then the land on the far side opened before them and their eyes beheld a stupendous sight: a vast, heaving, dark-brown mass of shaggy-haired buffalo stretched across the sand hills.

Each animal's back and head were covered with feeding blackbirds, some showing red on their upper wings, some yellow, some brown-headed or bronze-colored or with a purple sheen to their head and a greenish tint to their bodies. The birds' hoarse croaking, the bulls' bellowing, and the continuous sound of flies filled the air.

Slowly Wolfgang and Dark Moon advanced, watching the herd, especially eyeing the huge, enraged bulls. During this their rutting season, these bulls battled on short, powerful legs, shoving, pushing, and kicking up dust in every direction as the tufts at the tip of their tails fluttered in the breeze. Transfixed by the violence and mortal blows, the two saw some bulls give up and others continue to fight even with gaping wounds. Still others lay dead or dying from infection of earlier wounds.

Wolfgang was amazed by the size of many bulls. Standing on all four legs, their humps rose taller than he stood, and their weight was easily double that of any of the horses. The thick fur on each beast's hump accentuated its bulk, and the animal's forehead stretched three feet across between his black horns.

When the battle between the two nearest bulls ended, Wolfgang and Dark Moon could hear the feeding herd biting off mouthfuls of grass and chewing as the beasts drifted slowly northeast.

With the constantly changing position of the sun as their guide, the riders continued northwest, and in time the buffalo were gone. When the sun showed half a hand's breadth above the western horizon, they decided to make camp for the night. Seeing a coyote trot up from a depression ahead, they rode toward it and found a dry, narrow stream.

The open ground had good grass and the travelers found a spring bubbling among a dense wooded thicket. Bright red berries identified the thicket as chokecherry. Wolfgang and Dark

Moon felt surprised by the number of deer that lived out in these open spaces, with whitetails abundant in the brush thickets that edged every coulee they encountered. Refusing to leave these small patches of cover, the deer remained hidden.

Once Wolfgang and Dark Moon had unloaded their horses on the parched, hard-packed soil of the ravine at the edge of their camping area, she groomed and inspected each animal for sores and wounds. She hobbled the horses to keep them close. She fed each a little corn. Then she turned them out to the grass, planning to bring them in close to the spring just before dark. The camp would provide good security, and the ravine would hide a small fire. As she and Wolfgang collected wood from the nearby thicket, they knew that the slender yet heavy chokecherry wood would provide a smokeless fire to cook their meal.

The sun hung low as Dark Moon checked the horizon in all directions. In the east, there was a rainbow. Pointing at it, she told Wolfgang that the colors always showed in the same order: red, orange, yellow, green, blue, indigo, and violet.

"A rainbow in the evening indicates continued fair weather for another day," she added.

Wolfgang was impressed by her forecasts.

After eating, they felt tired from a full day's riding, and fell asleep in the soft glow of a small fire that would soon be but embers.

* * *

Suddenly Dark Moon was awake. She had heard a faint sound from the far side of where Wolfgang lay. Though she now looked past him, she saw no looming shadow or other such presence. In the moonlight she saw only Wolfgang asleep. She lifted up on one elbow. Nothing. But then the faint sound returned – a low, horrid scraping sound edging nearer – and something caught Dark Moon's eye, her keen peripheral vision detecting a long, thick, muscular shape.

Realizing what it was, she froze, as still as death. The tip of the rippling undulation that was closest rose slightly from the ground, and the huge snake – whose scales she had heard slithering across the hard-packed, dry sand – moved nearer to Wolfgang, raising its head up slowly, swaying slowly to and fro. Dark Moon made out the great snake's large, thick, dark coils, its heavy, evil-looking wedge-shaped head poised near Wolfgang's exposed arm, the black, forked tongue flicking in and out to test the air. Fearful that waking Wolfgang would cause him to move, Dark Moon reached slowly for her bow case to flip the creature away, but then a movement at the corner of her eye caught her attention. Wolfgang was shifting position in his sleep.

In an instant the scaly head darted forward, its deadly fangs latching onto his forearm.

Wolfgang started awake even as the snake released its hold to gather for another strike; he rolled, and the lunging rattler missed. Dark Moon flipped the reptile away with the bow, the thrashing body striking the far side of the bank then sliding to the center of the dry creek. Tightly coiling into its defensive posture, the great snake, head cocked, sounded its fearful, nerve-jangling warning rattle, but Dark Moon was up. Reaching for her great knife at her back, she darted in and swiftly severed the serpent's head in one backward swing. As its body rolled and danced in a tortured snarl of coils, she turned back to Wolfgang, who sat stunned.

"Sit up with your back against the bank!" she ordered. "Keep your arm down and don't move!"

Locating the two small fang punctures at the end of each row of scratches quickly, she saw that the holes pulsed blood. Hurriedly she snatched up a piece of flat leather and tightened it around Wolfgang's arm just above the wound – not so tightly as to stop the arterial flow, but enough to slow the poison's absorption. Then she built up the small fire. She placed their two water-filled pewter cups near the flames and turned back to him.

"This will hurt," she said briefly, drawing out her small knife.

Taking firm hold of his forearm, she cut once across each hole – deeply enough to allow the wound to bleed out the venom, though not so deep as to affect nerves or blood vessels. Then, as the bleeding slowed, she covered the swelling wound with her mouth and alternately sucked and spat out the fluids. She repeated the action, tasting the acid, yellow venom mixed with Wolfgang's salty blood.

For a quarter-hour Dark Moon did this. Finally she tied a strip of cloth as a second tourniquet just above the first, which she now removed. Wolfgang watched her stir a small amount of powder from one of her medicine containers into a cup of water. Seeing that her fingers had a tactile memory all their own as to the proper amount, he told himself he was in good hands.

"Do you feel a strong dryness and tightness in your mouth?" Dark Moon asked.

"Yes," Wolfgang said, hearing his speech slurred.

"Do you feel pain in your arm yet?'

"Yes."

The local swelling was moving up the arm. She made him drink the hot contents from the cup. It tasted both bitter and sweet. As she cut another set of incisions above the first, she told him that the powder was snakeroot and that it would increase his circulation.

Dark Moon sucked on the new incisions. She stopped only when she no longer tasted the acidity in his blood. Pouring a different powder into a second cup, she concocted a thick paste, which she smeared over the wounds.

"This is Rattlesnake Master," Dark Moon said. "It is used when Senega is not available."

Warning him not to get up for any reason, she checked

to be sure of a pulse in the wrist of his injured arm. For the rest of the night she watched him closely for signs of difficultly in breathing. But his muscles hardly spasmed and his heartbeat remained strong. She felt surprised to see few blisters and little inflammation, and knew that the snake had either expended its venom on a previous victim or had not been able to inject Wolfgang with a full dose.

The next morning when Dark Moon awoke, she found Wolfgang standing over her, smiling.

"How do you feel?" she asked immediately.

"Weak – but better than last night."

For two days more they remained at camp, until she felt sure he was strong enough to travel.

*　*　*

All day they traveled, moving beneath beautifully clear skies. Coming up over a range of hills in the soft early morning light, they saw a river just ahead, and a line of large cottonwoods in the distance, with high bluffs rising beyond them.

Through a break in the trees they caught glimpses of sun-dappled waters exploding with brightness. Slowly they wound their way down the gentle incline of the hillside cliff, through the dark timber of cedar, bur oak, yellow pine and black walnut. Crossing a small creek, they soon found themselves back in the sunlight along the bank of a beautiful river. Dark Moon and Wolfgang remembered being told by the Osage that the Ponca and Omaha Indians called this river the *Ni obhatha ke* (Niobrara River), meaning the "Spreading Water River."

The river was some 400 yards wide, with a few deep channels but for the most part shallow, with sandbars showing the way across. Cottonwoods lined both banks and also stood on the islands in the river.

Stopping in the tall streamside grass along the near bank

opposite a large island, Dark Moon and Wolfgang studied a stand of massive cottonwoods. The bright, clear water flowed in a slow current, and the only sounds came from humming grasshoppers and cottonwood leaves rattling in the summer wind. Having decided to camp on the island, they watered the horses, then splashed across the rock and sand - strewn bottom to their home for the night.

"I don't think the French will venture up the Niobrara," Wolfgang said. "They'll see that though in some places you can walk across it, in others it's over your head and isn't navigable by anything larger than a canoe."

* * *

Once they had made camp in the large grove of cottonwoods, Wolfgang took the horses into the water to lead them a short way upstream, to a pasture hidden amid the tangles of heavy brush and small trees among the taller cottonwoods. Dark Moon watched Wolfgang until he was out of sight. She then busied herself with obscuring their horses' tracks and setting up camp.

A while later, she checked the sun and judged it to be mid-morning. Observing the gentle swaying of the tree limbs and the dance of the many leaves, Dark Moon stood in silence. She surrendered herself to nature's power, listening to the rhythm and heartbeat of the natural forces around her.

But all at once she realized that there was an ominous absence of the normal chatter of birds and chipmunks. Her instincts alerted her to imminent danger, and she now sensed she was not alone.

Charles A. McDonald

Chapter 32

Dark Moon froze momentarily, then, turned. Amid the trees, at a distance of about thirty paces, she saw the painted face of a warrior staring directly at her. Bare-chested, he wore a mid-thigh-length breechcloth. His thigh-high leggings had fringed side-seams and were painted with black horizontal stripes. He had braided hair with two horizontal feathers. Dark Moon recognized him for the predator he was. Then a second bare-chested warrior appeared. This one had vertical red stripes on his leggings and a single upright feather in his hair. Both warriors stared at her. Before she could turn, the soft swish of leggings brushing through grass sounded from off to her right. As she turned to escape, she was overwhelmed by a blur of motion and sound. She reached for the large knife at her back, but immediately felt a vicious blow to her arm from behind. Then another blow – this time between her shoulders – knocked her to the ground. She raised her face from the dirt and tried to collect her arms and legs beneath her body to make a quick sprint. She felt a shattering pain as a savage blow struck her head. The thought of Wolfgang flashed through her brain even as she saw a starburst of color. Her consciousness slipped away and then... darkness.

* * *

When Dark Moon revived, she got up slowly. The effort made her slightly dizzy. Her head felt swollen and her body ached. Her hands were tied and hanging loose in front of her, already losing feeling and prickling with a growing numbness. She briefly tested the cords binding her hands, but quickly ceased. She was tethered behind the horse of a warrior who was watching her. She noticed the warriors all wore three braids, one on each side and one in the rear. Their white horses were painted with hoof and hand prints. *Older warriors. They belong to a military society. The hoof markings symbolize successful horse raids. The hand prints for touching an enemy warrior in battle. They had all counted coup.*

Seeing she had recovered, he began spitting invectives at her. Dark Moon reasoned that she would soon be on her way to their village. *A prisoner.* The warrior's hands motioned. "Me called Crazy Thunder." His glittering eyes moved over the shape of her body.

Dark Moon remained stoical and silent. Her stomach twisted with revulsion, but she willed herself to remain still and calm. *I will not panic.* She fixed her piercing eyes on the surly faced warrior and detected the ferocity of hatred in his eyes. Arrogantly he looked deeply into her eyes but saw no fear. He quickly turned and mounted his horse. Then he jerked Dark Moon forward, forcing her to run to keep herself from being dragged behind the horse.

* * *

Dark Moon plodded along through the *Ni obhatha ke*. She had to be careful not to trip in the long moss growing in much of the stream. She saw Crazy Thunder wearing her own big knife. Reaching the far side of the stream, he jerked Dark Moon off her feet coming out of the water. Then he stopped his mount and sat looking back at her. Suddenly he leaped off his horse and rushed to her. Drawing the knife, Crazy Thunder brought the blade to her face and slowly pressed until blood ran down her cheek and trickled down her neck.

Dark Moon didn't utter a sound. She only kept her eyes fixed on him, her pupils shrinking to pinpoints. As her ancient eyes burned deep into his, he jerked back despite himself with a shiver, suddenly overwhelmed by a premonition of doom. His eyes opened wide, he clenched his jaw, his lips drew back tight toward his ears, as he gasped for breath. Fear twisted his gut and crept up his spine. The glitter from his eyes was gone, his fear turned to panic. Crazy Thunder quickly backed away from Dark Moon.

The other warriors stared in stunned surprise when he resheathed the knife and mounted his horse. He jerked the leather rope hard and the party resumed a faster pace.

Dark Moon resolved that she would kill Crazy Thunder before this was over.

Whenever the warrior jerked the tethered line, Dark Moon had to raise her bound hands sharply to keep her balance. But she knew she must maintain some slack in the line in order to keep from being jerked off her feet. After a time her tied hands became numb, which made her clumsy. She maintained the pace for a long time, her throat dry from thirst. Her eyes wild and hot, she now had to run faster to keep up. She knew that if she stumbled and fell, she would be dragged.

Finally, with the setting sun, they arrived at the village. Dark Moon's wrists were stained with blood. As the warriors led her to an empty tipi, she passed the spread-eagled figure of a man staked to the ground. He stared up at her. A few people kicked and spit at him as they passed, muttering the word, "Psa."

Inside the tent, uncomfortably bound, Dark Moon knew she must sleep if she were to think clearly the next day. Staring up through the smoke hole in the tipi's top, she saw a lone, winking star.

An omen, she thought - and knew that Wolfgang was on his way.

At last, she slept.

* * *

Daylight splashed across the floor of the tipi as its flap was flung open. Dark Moon felt rough hands grab her, and the next moment she was dragged outside.

Full daylight had arrived. Her bonds were removed so that she could talk with her hands. She stood momentarily, blinded by the sun, but when her eyes adjusted, she saw a silent, hostile crowd standing before her. She could tell the village women were awed by her size, for she was larger than many of the men. She noticed most of the women wore their hair parted in the middle and hanging over their shoulders. Their dress was simple – a wraparound skirt and poncho top with painted designs. They wore moccasins, decorated in great detail with porcupine quills. The villagers remained silent, staring at her. Dark Moon read the contempt on their faces. She saw Crazy Thunder standing nearby, his face twisted in a leering grin.

Standing erect and showing no fear, she gazed at the largest hard-eyed warrior standing before her. She used her hands in the universal language:

"Who are you?"

"I am Iron Cloud," the warrior signed. Then, lifting his right hand in front of and parallel to his neck with the palm down, he made a quick cutting motion. She knew this signified cutting off heads, and that they were the Oceti Sakowin, known as the People of the Seven Council Fires. The Lakota.

Dark Moon remembered the French refer to these people as the *nadouessioux*. Little adders. She also recalled Big Bull's remarks that most of the Indians she and Wolfgang would encounter along the Niobrara River would be close to the

Missouri. Midway along the Niobrara and further west a great drought had lasted many lifetimes, making that area uninhabitable.

As Iron Cloud's hands gestured, Dark Moon saw them refer to the three divisions of the Ocheti Shakowin – the Dakota, Nakota, and Lakota. She knew that this former drought area was now occupied by the seven bands of the Lakota – the Sicangu (Bois Brule), Oohenonpa (Two Kettles), Itazipacola (Sans Arcs/Broken Bows), Miniconjou (Those who plant near the water people), Sihasapa (Blackfeet), Hunkpapa, and the Oglala. She also understood that these people were protecting their land and their hunting territory – their new settlement. She also remembered that the Ocheti shakowin meant the 'seven council fires.' She and Wolfgang had been warned about traveling along the Niobrara, because of the Lakota.

The movement of Iron Cloud's hands continued to say that the Dakota are further north, and the Nakotas further east. Far to their northwest is the land of the Crow.

"We Lakota belong to a warrior society, and are the western-most band, known as the Pte Oyate, the Buffalo People. Our warriors are brave and spread out widely across the country to the west, but they come together each summer for their Sun Dance," he signed.

Now Iron Cloud, gesturing rapidly, seemed to confirm Dark Moon's thoughts: We are Lakota and our band is the Sicangu. She knew that these people, the Burnt Thighs band, lived in small groups.

Then the warrior raised his right palm to his shoulder, motioned it back and forth, and pointed his index finger at her, drawing his hand back to his mouth with his fist closed. Then he again pointed at her. Dark Moon understood the question:

"Who are you?"

"I am the Algonquian Sorceress, Dark Moon."

She answered slowly, for effect. She knew that the

prisoner staked out on the ground was listening and watching, too. In her peripheral vision, she noticed the warrior Crazy Thunder leave the group and enter a lodge nearby where his white horse stood tied.

Good, she thought. *Now I know where to find my knife – and my enemy.* She resolved once again that before she left, Crazy Thunder would die.

"How did you get into this country?" Iron Cloud's hands asked.

"I was flying over the land and landed at the river to rest," Dark Moon's hands motioned in answer.

Their fear will give Wolfgang time to find me.

"Where did you come from?" Iron Cloud signed. "The River of Sorcerers." Her hands said. "The white man calls it the French River. It runs into the great lake of the Huron's from the north. Your old people know of it."

Staring, the crowd began to murmur amongst themselves. Seeing many suddenly became fearful at her answer, she knew they would need to talk about this among themselves for some time. She also knew that before the village council members had finished talking about her, she would be gone.

* * *

The day was growing short when Wolfgang returned from hiding the horses upstream. He kept an eye on the westering sun as he scanned the trees. Shafts of gold were already illuminating their tops. The low areas would soon harbor the deep, black shadows of night. He was suddenly startled. *Dark Moon is gone.* His heart was pounding in his throat. Then his eyes fell upon an unknown set of prints near the stream. They were closely spaced, telling him that those had been made by someone moving slow, creeping and using stealth in approaching the camp. He well knew Dark Moon's prints. They were smaller and narrower. He compared the prints to his own, and the depth told him that they were the larger, rounded moccasin tracks of a large man. *An ominous sign.*

He followed the prints until he came to a place where he found horse tracks, scuffle marks and small drops of bright blood that were now turning dark. The blood color told him that these Indians had a good head start. His drawn face turned white and his breathing became hard. The strain showed on his face as his body began to tremble with anger. A guttural bellow of pain and frustration erupted. Fighting to control his emotions and the pain he felt, he tried to concentrate on thinking. Those tracks plainly show there where three men, with three horses. They attacked Dark Moon, and forced her to the ground, tied her and led her away. He feared her imminent death. His fear evaporated. He became calm.

Wolfgang knew he must locate the wolves quickly. Taking a deep breath, he tilted his head back and let out a howl, "oooOOOOOUUU." Then quickly he packed their belongings and readied the horses. He would not have the light much longer, and he must determine the direction she had been taken.

Returning to the horse tracks of Dark Moon's captors, Wolfgang found the wolves sitting, waiting. From their tracks around the area he could tell that they had already sniffed out the situation. The trail was cold but he knew that for the wolves, this posed hardly a challenge. The animals could follow a cold trail easily.

Wolfgang pointed in the direction the horse tracks led, and the two wolves eagerly set out on the trail.

Starting out at a good pace, they made a brief stop several times during the night. At times Wolfgang watched the great wolf sniff the cold trail, lick rocks and bits of brush, then snuff the freshened, pungent scent with low nasal snorts before throwing its nose into the wind and bristling.

As he had done many times, Wolfgang reflected how

wise it had been to save the wolf from the bear so long before.

Across the dark, silent terrain the wolves never faltered. When the pair stopped finally, Wolfgang stopped, too. Staring into the darkness, he neither saw nor heard anything unusual, but both wolves held their heads up slightly, as if scenting the wind. The next moment Wolfgang smelled it too: a faint scent of fire smoke.

Chapter 33

No sooner did Wolfgang catch the first whiff of smoke than both wolves raised their heads and howled. Their long, lonely wails were answered immediately by the barking cries of a large number of dogs in the distance.

The enemy's camp, Wolfgang realized. He continued onward, following his four-footed guides until he saw the village at last. He carefully found a place to hide in a dry gully where he and the horses could remain out of sight.

All the next day Wolfgang watched the village, waiting for nightfall. At one point he saw Dark Moon roughly dragged from a *tipi,* untied, and positioned before a large group of people to stand talking with hand gestures to a large warrior. This went on for some time until another warrior tied her once again and led her back into the *tipi.* Moments later the warrior exited, letting the flap drop. Wolfgang pictured Dark Moon lying bound in the dirt, a captive.

He could only watch and wait.

* * *

Wolfgang's eyes snapped open and stared at the night sky. He had been asleep for some hours, the Big Dipper now pointing to midnight. He had lain between the wolves, knowing they would warn him of danger, but now it was time to move. It had grown cold. Wolfgang lay awake and listened; there was only silence. The early darkness still held the light at bay. The darkest hour presaging the coming dawn would soon be upon him. He counted upon the guard or guards to have become inattentive and neglectful in watching.

    Wolfgang knew he must hurry, while the village still slept.

* * *

    Clouds covered the moon as Wolfgang silently made his way. He could hear and smell a storm in the distance, and felt the wind picking up. Noise in the open country travels far, but the ground was soft. Any sound he made would be dull, and would not carry, but he did not intend to make any sound. Perhaps, when he had freed Dark Moon, they could use the storm for cover by riding toward it. The two wolves pointed their noses toward the village just ahead. Tuning his senses to capture the slightest noise or movement, Wolfgang ghosted across the plain. Nothing seemed to be stirring, but he felt the hair on the back of his neck rising.

    The two wolves stopped and sat. With their heads tilted, they were listening and watching in the same direction. When Wolfgang performed a slow scan of the area, the sensation of a presence grew stronger. He wiped his hands, moistened with sweat, on his leggings. He strained his ears, listening for any sounds in the darkness, and for moments he shut his eyes to better sort out the night's sounds. His nerves and concentration of attention were sharp from long experience. Sweat beaded on his forehead, but he resisted the urge to wipe it away. He savored the chill as the sweat dried on his back. A faint whisper came to him; the sound of someone passing gas. Then Wolfgang saw the shape of a head as the Indian leaned over and partially exposed himself to the horizon and a weather-whitened tipi. The man was sitting in the shadow of the tipi, but the light brown color of his deerskin clothing was now easy to see at a distance.

After watching for some time, Wolfgang determined there was only this single guard. Suddenly, he saw movement. His senses sharp, he heard the scrape of a foot on the ground. The guard's dark form was now moving quickly in his direction, coming nearer and nearer. Both wolves slowly lowered themselves to the ground, heads erect, ears pointed. Wolfgang crouched, his hand on his tomahawk, but then the guard stopped, turned suddenly, and squatted. A moment later Wolfgang heard the man relieving himself. From the sound he heard, Wolfgang made his judgment to move.

He placed a hand on each wolf, bent his head down to their ears and commanded: "Stay."

Moving as slowly as a spirit rising from the ground, he drew in close. Choosing each step with care, Wolfgang gripped his tomahawk and raised it high, then brought it downward sharply. A loud *crack!* And the enemy, who had been about to rise, staggered and collapsed.

Wolfgang set his foot on the back of the Lakota's neck to jerk the axe free from his skull.

*   *   *

The long, sleepless night had been exhausting to Dark Moon, who lay stiff and sore in the dark *tipi*. She tried to shift position to ease her discomfort. She had gone without food and water for so long that her stomach had stopped growling.

Then the ominous stillness was broken. Dark Moon's body stiffened at the sound of faint movement as the guard moved from the entrance toward the rear of the *tipi*. She turned her ear to follow his steps. His sound stopped. She heard him relieving himself. But then, suddenly, there came a dull, meaty thud of something striking flesh and solid bone, followed by the near-silent sound of a body dropping to the ground. After that, an ominous stillness prevailed. Then the flap to the entrance was gently moved aside and in the gloom a menacing animal rhythm of movement half-entered and paused to inspect the scent. Suddenly, a familiar tall shadow stood beside her. They could not see each other well, just their dark shapes, and the shine of one another's eyes. Then the wolves licked her face. Dark Moon freed, hugged both wolves to her. She knew that both wolves had followed her trail here in the dark, leading Wolfgang to her.

Dark Moon pressed one hand lightly to Wolfgang's chest and told him to give her his knife. As he watched in the dark, she went out and cut the other prisoner free and told them both to wait. Then, keeping to the darkest shadows, she slipped ghostlike from lodge to lodge like so much mist moved by the wind. At last she stopped beside one *tipi*.

Kneeling beside its closed entrance, Dark Moon carefully lifted the cover. She slipped into the darkness and knelt, closing the cover behind her so as not to present her silhouette if the occupant awoke. It was dark, but the weather flap at the top was open to allow a little light, and she also saw a faint red glow from the coals of the fire in the center of the floor. She remained still and listened. Finally, she detected the steady, easy breathing rhythm that told her Crazy Thunder was deeply asleep. As she listened, she determined that he was alone. His breathing continued steady, easy and deep. Any change in his breathing rhythm would tell her he was awake. Her slow-moving, searching hands found her cherished long knife, and her stern face now stretched into a broad smile. Listening to Crazy Thunder's breathing, Dark Moon added a few small, unburned twig ends around the fire into the coals and turned toward the sleeping figure.

Dark Moon could smell him. Carefully she crept forward, her hands exploring slowly ahead of her. Finally, she stopped and remained still, kneeling beside him and listening to

The War Trail

make sure his deep rhythmic breathing went unbroken. There was no restless movement from the warrior lying on his back. Her long-fingered left hand now hovered over the lower part of his body, lightly touching and feeling its heat. From his body rhythm, she would know instantly if he awoke. Her left hand continued to search and follow his dark form upward along the contour of his chest. Her large curved blade was in her right hand. She grinned hungrily as she leaned over and found his throat, then the hollow behind his collarbone.

Dark Moon waited until the smoldering twigs erupted in flame. She wanted her enemy to see her. She placed her left hand lightly over the top of his chest, just below his chin, and applied pressure. The warrior's eyes opened wide, showing perplexity, then shock as he saw Dark Moon's smiling face hovering above him. He was transfixed and arrested by the piercing, hooded eyes. He felt as if her hand were like a warm current of paralyzing fear flowing through his body. Crazy Thunder's eyes became desperate and frightened, and his heart raced. A ringing in his ears cut off the outer world as, barely able to breath, he gulped for breath. He saw her eyes brighten. In that moment, the knife blade, poised and centered behind the collarbone, sank deep. Dark Moon leaned away from the flow of blood as she held him down. The spasms convulsed him, and his feet silently drummed on the buffalo padding, his body fighting the oncoming eternal unconsciousness. The rich scent of warm blood filled the air.

* * *

Wolfgang had begun feeling uncomfortable as he wondered where Dark Moon had gone and what she was doing. Then the wolves sounded a low warning. Wolfgang peered again in the direction she had gone, and saw her approaching figure leading a white horse.

Dark Moon returned his knife, and handed the prisoner a knife, ax, bow and arrow case, along with a small case of fire-making material. She positioned herself so that the freed man could see her hands. She signed rapidly, saying that the Lakota warrior, Crazy Thunder, would no longer need them. Then she signed, "Who are you?"

"I am Two Bulls," the young warrior signed.

"Psa," said Dark Moon. Her hands signed, asking for the word's meaning.

"It is the Lakota word for Crow People," replied Two Bulls.

"Do you wish to go with us?" Dark Moon's hands asked.

The answer was yes.

Quickly and silently, Dark Moon, Two Bulls, and Wolfgang walked toward the horses.

Ahead, in the dark, the frightened animals nickered in alarm, their hoofs having sensed the vibration through the hard ground. They settled down once they smelled Dark Moon's scent and heard her soothing voice speaking calmly to them. Wolfgang knew that in the darkest hour before dawn, they would have to push their horses until the first gray stain of predawn. Two Bulls was given the dull grayish-brown horse. All three knew that their use of time and the terrain would determine whether they succeeded in staying alive.

* * *

A short time later, Wolfgang, Dark Moon, and their new traveling companion watched from a high point to study their back trail. They saw the first sign of their followers: far in the distance, a small group of Lakota traveled at a fast trot, their horses' hooves kicking up tiny puffs of dust. The three had just reached the top of the last large hill and the still-distant, deep coulee – their last obstacle – lay ahead.

When they reached the bottom of the hill soon thereafter, Dark Moon signed for the others to walk their animals to rest them. The tiny party hadn't gone far, though, before their horses – feeling the earth tremble more strongly with the deep, drumming vibration of reverberating hooves – turned to check the skyline. When the three riders looked back, too, they beheld a sight that quickened their breath.

In the early morning sunlight, the Lakota, their bodies and faces painted, sat stoically atop their horses, forming a skirmish line atop the hill. Wolfgang counted thirteen warriors – too many to fight.

"Come!" said Dark Moon curtly, wheeling her horse. Wolfgang and Two Bulls followed, all three now racing once more toward the deep coulee.

As she rode, Dark Moon saw a rainbow in the west, a sign of approaching rain. She also knew that they must traverse the gap in the prairie before the Lakota caught up.

It became apparent all too soon that they would not make it – that there wasn't time to follow the narrow trail down through the deep gap then up the other side. If they tried, they would only make targets of themselves. The Lakota's fastest mounts would catch them, and the other warriors would arrive soon thereafter.

"This way!" Dark Moon shouted, swerving her horse away to the west. The others followed even as she rode to within 100 yards of the gap, wheeled, reined in and dismounted.

"We're going to teach the Lakota a hard lesson," Dark Moon said. "Now is the time to show our power."

Dark Moon signed to Two Bulls, "Just watch but be ready to go."

She grabbed the rifle from her horse and began to check it. Wolfgang realized what she had in mind: that the only possible escape would be to demonstrate the long range of the rifle to delay the Lakota, then jump the horses across the large wash in the open prairie behind them. As he stood ready, he looked at Dark Moon and for the first time saw the blood on her clothes and body, the knife wound and deep purple bruising on her beautiful face. He knew that he would not miss.

* * *

Knowing their quarry was trapped against the gap, the Lakota just sat motionless on their horses for some moments before screeching their war cry, and starting to walk the horses forward. Then, abruptly, they broke into a canter. For a moment Dark Moon could not help noticing the Spanish horses' beauty, their necks gracefully arched and their tails flowing high and gaily. The Indians rode bareback, controlling their animals with knee pressure, and many rode without a bridle, leaving both hands free to use their bow and arrows.

"Be careful not to hit the horses!" Dark Moon warned, as she yanked the ramrod free of her rifle's thimbles.

Although Wolfgang knew the horses would be a surer target and would put their riders afoot, he would aim as she directed. He had no intention of causing her any anger or sadness if he could help it.

As the volume of their war cry rose, the Lakota divided to ride left and right to face their quarry in a large semi-circle. Their blood-chilling, chant-like war song sounded loud in the still air and was meant to churn the stomachs of their intended victims. *"Aiee-aee-aee. Aiee-aee-aee. Aiee-aee-aee."* The Lakota would not charge en masse. Each small group of individuals would be trying to outdo the others, attacking in their own way.

Wolfgang knew he must shoot long range – if he waited longer, the Lakota would get close enough to overwhelm them. And he knew that by keeping his enemies at a distance, he would make them fear the power of the long rifle. Dark Moon would load for him. He was worried because he would have to use patched balls for accuracy, which would slow the reloading process. The build up of black powder deposits inside the barrel would permit him only a few long-range shots at a time before he had to clean the barrel again.

The Lakota war party all sat, naked except for loincloths and moccasins. Ready to charge, their horses began to snort and dance impatiently.

Four Lakota warriors walked their horses out in front of the others, and stopped them. They would be the first. The horses shook their manes, pawed the ground, and pranced, holding their heads high. Their eyes rolled and their tongues lolled in an effort to charge. The four on the line sat still, watching.

Finally, with their war whoops rising in volume, their horses skittered forward. They broke into a lope, then leapt forward at a full gallop, their hoofs slewing up prairie sod as their riders broke into a *yip-yip* ululation.

Charles A. McDonald

Chapter 34

Wolfgang, Dark Moon, and Two Bulls felt the earth shudder beneath the pounding hooves of the four charging Lakota horsemen. The other nine Lakota yipped and howled in encouragement. Two Bulls marveled at his new companions, who looked so calm as they stood watching their enemy quickly approach.

"They think they're out of range," Dark Moon said.

Wolfgang studied the tops of the gramma grass movement for breeze direction. He wet his finger and held it up for further direction. He could feel only the lightest current on his face, but decided to hold his point of aim slightly to the left and a little bit low. He worried that his rifle was sufficiently cleaned and oiled, for the first round from a clean-bored rifle generally shot high, often missing completely. He knew he would have to adjust his aim to compensate for this. Once the barrel was fired, he could aim dead on.

Wolfgang saw the white eyes and bared teeth of the oncoming galloping horses and heard the pounding of their hooves in his ears getting louder. The fierce, wild-faced riders screamed their war cries as they closed the distance.

Dark Moon pulled the loading block from her shooting pouch as she watched Wolfgang closely. He reset the hammer to half cock and flipped up the frizzen to check the priming powder. Satisfied, he lowered the frizzen protectively over the pan and drew the hammer back to full cock. The warriors' furious shrieks and howls grew louder as they grew closer by the second.

Returning the long rifle to his shoulder, Wolfgang took a deep breath, mated the front sight to the rear sight, and let his trigger finger creep slightly. When he was perfectly lined up on the first bobbing figure with a split-horn buffalo bonnet with a waving half tail, he squeezed the trigger. The big curved hammer snapped forward.

In an instant, the sharp black flint struck the frizzen successfully, spraying a little burst of sparks over the exposed powder of the pan. Its fine grains flashed... small red sparks flew upward amid a small puff of white smoke... and, as the distant, watching warriors sat silently, the rifle bellowed a roar. Wolfgang and Dark Moon quickly shifted position away from the sulfurous smoke. They saw that the greased patched roundball had done its job. It had struck the leading charging warrior just below his chin in the top of his chest. Amid a spray of misting blood behind him, he was knocked backward off his horse. He rolled several times, and lay still.

Dark Moon saw the surprised look on Two Bulls' face when she handed Wolfgang a loaded rifle, then checked the flint of the empty rifle for sharpness. Gripping the powder-horn stopper between her teeth, she pulled it free and started reloading. She was well aware that they could not afford a misfire.

Again the rifle bellowed thunder, followed by another spray of blood. The second warrior wearing a wolf hide headdress rose from the back of his horse, dropping his weapons as his arms flung up and outward. The air was tinted now with a sulfurous stench.

Bringing up the rear on slower mounts, the two remaining Lakota stopped their charge at the thunderclap of sound. Confused and afraid, they rode to their two dead comrades who were lying on the ground, their arms and legs still jerking spasmodically. The two riders sat staring at the dead. Wolfgang knew well what they were looking at: the fat, blunt, heavy .50 caliber roundball, a dependable hunting load, expanded at low velocity, and had torn large holes in man or beast.

Quickly he handed the empty rifle to Dark Moon. She, in turn, handed him the reloaded one. The Lakota were so surprised at the long-range accuracy of his rifle that they were unwittingly giving their foe ample time to reload.

* * *

The warriors sat watching, stunned. Dark Moon checked the thick, square piece of gray-black flint in the cock. Its forward edge had a ragged appearance. She quickly loosened the top jaw screw and slipped the flint out. She pulled her tool pouch from her bag and removed the small hammer and flint napper. Then she gently tapped several times along the edge of the flint, sharpening and straightening its edge and put it back. She lowered the cock slowly to check how the edge of the flint met the face of the frizzen. Not satisfied, she swiftly loosened the top jaw screw to reposition the leather-wrapped flint slightly forward, and screwed it finger tight. Again she lowered the cock. This time she was satisfied. Making sure the flint would not move, she tightened the screw a bit more. Putting her tools back, she removed the vent pick and cleaned the vent hole. Satisfied again, she poured a measured amount of powder.

Dark Moon positioned the first of the rounds in the seven-hole loading block, a convenient time-saver, over the muzzle. Using her short starter, she inserted the patched ball. To keep from breaking the ramrod, she grabbed the wooden rod fairly close to the muzzle and rammed, using short, precise pushes until the ball was seated on the powder. She found the tight fitting greased patched lead ball a little harder to load into the deep-grooves of the rifle with each shot, because of the black powder fouling the barrel. But the rifle shot more accurately. The tighter the fit, the more difficult it was to load. She loaded the frizzen pan with the small horn used as a priming flask for faster ignition.

Finally aware that they needed to keep the Lakota at a distance, Dark Moon thought that if they got too close, she would load balls without a patch to save time. She turned her head and checked the distant group to their left front, and told Wolfgang to look to his left. One small group, having recovered from the shock of his demonstration, had become more determined. The Lakota horses bunched their hooves and started into a gallop, and the warriors raised their loud war outcry in chorus as they started forward.

Wolfgang carefully took aim at the wearer of an eagle feather bonnet with a single tail and squeezed. When the cloud of sulfurous smoke cleared, he was amazed to see two Indians on horseback side-by-side fall. Again the others stopped their charge and sat stunned, looking at their fallen warriors. One of the two started a weak but audible death-wail.

Dark Moon quickly handed Wolfgang the loaded rifle and said, "One young warrior lost his nerve at the closeness of the shot and dropped from his horse."

Now they saw him crawling back the way he had come. The watching Sioux looked bewildered. In tumbling another warrior with a roach headdress from his horse, Wolfgang again broke a charge.

The build-up of burned black powder residue had made it harder for Dark Moon to ram the ball all the way down the barrel, so after the fourth shot, she decided to forego the patches. Glancing up, she saw the bodies spread over the grassland. A shrill staccato war cry alerted Wolfgang to the direction of the next charge.

"It's time to leave," said Dark Moon.

The threesome mounted their animals and Dark Moon told Two Bulls to bring up the rear. She hoped the white horse would have the confidence to follow them.

At a full gallop, the mounts charged the chasm head-on. The horses' ears swiveled back, questioning their riders, then, receiving encouragement, swiveled them forward again. The three let the horses have their heads to select their own position to make the jump. Leaning forward, Dark Moon spoke into the ear of her animal. At the same time, she let one hand gently stroke it, urging it to take the lead and embolden its spirit to make the others jump. Her legs urged it forward. She felt the animal respond. Seeing the horses' eyes focused forward and their ears sharply pricked, Dark Moon knew they were concentrating. A short distance from what looked like disaster, the other horses, following her, stretched their legs farther and farther yet, devouring the ground in huge strides. She felt as if she were drinking the wind. The animals summoned up an almost unimaginable reserve of stamina and courage from each other.

They reached a point about four feet from the dry wash when they could no longer see the obstacle. Dark Moon knew that this was where the animals might balk, throwing their riders. But the next instant they were floating on air, in a great arc taking them well across the wide, deep prairie gap. They landed hard and skidded, digging into the ground with their hind legs and nearly sitting their hindquarters into the ground into a spectacular sliding stop. They had all made it. The white horse had followed the others.

Dark Moon was laughing, overjoyed with the performance. Deep down, she had known that she could always reach the spirit of this animal. Wolfgang was shaken at first, and was greatly amazed at her reaction to the jump. She was the most talented and extraordinary woman he had ever met. He also saw that she was completely thrilled with joy and glorying in the willingness, strength, and speed of their companion horses – her family.

The three riders whirled their fiery horses around and trotted back a short way toward the edge to watch their pursuers. The Lakota had reined in well away from the prairie cut and sat their horses, displaying a sudden lofty indifference and staring with studied calm at their enemies. Wolfgang knew that his rifle's long-range accuracy had served its psychological value once again.

He also knew that their lives depended upon keeping the barrel clean, and that only hot liquid would dissolve the powder residue. Telling Dark Moon to ready a dry patch, he set the rifle butt-down in front of him, stepped backward and leaned the rifle back until the muzzle was level with his crotch. Then he lifted his breach cloth and aimed a stream of urine down the barrel. Since his bladder was full, he had no trouble filling both rifle barrels. When he was done, he used the patches to swab them both clean.

While tending to the rifles, Wolfgang gazed across at the mahogany-skinned warriors sitting on their horses. The Indians, in turn, were watching him. Wolfgang noted the war clubs and axes hanging by each man's right knee, and the buffalo leather bow and arrow case worn around their waist on the left side. Small buffalo-hide shields hung behind their left legs. Wolfgang realized these men fought on horseback like men he had seen in Europe in his childhood.

Finally, the three riders were ready to leave. Wolfgang and Dark Moon each raised their arm in friendship, greeting, and good-bye. Their eyes were directed to a chief wearing a double-tailed eagle feather headdress, then turned and walked their horses away. Two Bulls merely glared at the Lakota. The wolves were nowhere in sight, but their howls sounded in the distance.

* * *

After they reached their camp and gathered the remaining horses, the three headed south. A dark sky was developing and swollen clouds hung low and heavy. A chill wind from the northwest whipped their backs as they took to the trail. They were hoping the coming storm would help cover their trail through the open grassland.

They had traveled only a short time before strong winds and heavy rain, enveloped them, stinging their heads and hands. Then they came upon a large buffalo herd, slowly moving west. Two Bulls stopped Dark Moon and Wolfgang.

"We must ride through the herd," his hand gestures said. "It will be dangerous because if they are frightened, they will stampede and trample us or a bull could suddenly wheel around on us. We might die."

Dark Moon answered by lying on the back of her animal and urging it forward. Wolfgang and Two Bulls followed her example. They turned sharply into the herd.

The three rode slowly through the seemingly indifferent buffalo. They maneuvered their horses in a zigzag fashion through the herd, knowing the tracks of the great beasts would wipe out those of their own unshod horses and confuse any pursuers. Dark Moon and Wolfgang also knew that the heavy rain would wash away any remaining tracks.

They prayed as they lay on the backs of their horses and rode among the rumbling, shaggy manes of the sacred beasts. Wolfgang estimated that many of these animals weighed over 2,000 pounds. He saw that the bigger buffalo were eleven feet long. Laying their heads on the withers of their horses, they observed that many buffalo stood six feet tall at their formidable shoulders. The longest hair on the older animals was on their heads, covering their eyes. The three rode through the crowding, snuffling herd without resistance. The buffalo merely opened up space, appearing to know that no harm was meant to them.

When they reached the other side and were in the open again, Two Bulls' hands moved rapidly, saying, "I did not hear one threat grunt or bellow. The Great Spirit and the Buffalo God watched over us."

Seeing another storm developing in the distance, they felt themselves a part of something much greater. The dark underbelly of the sky threatened to open up anytime. Breathing deeply, they smelled that brassy, penetrating scent that usually preceded an imminent storm. Every lightening flash made them shudder and they felt sure the spirits were angry. The three travelers now rode north again, toward the river, through the passing wind and rain. And finally, the storm was in the distance and the rain stopped, though ominous gray clouds still hung low, blocking the sun.

Two Bulls began to talk about himself and his people, his hands gesturing rapidly.

"Our tribe calls itself the Absaroke, 'Bird People.' The French call us Gens de Corbeaux, 'Crow People.' Our most sacred objects are the Tobacco Society bundles that carry our tobacco seeds, for the tobacco plant is sacred to my people. We believe the practice of the tobacco ceremony enables us, the Crow, to overcome our enemies and to multiply and grow stronger."

Wolfgang and Dark Moon remained silent, listening.

Two Bulls' hand movements explained, "I'm a warrior belonging to the Fox Society. I was captured about the same time as you, Dark Moon, on a horse-stealing raid."

Then they rode in silence for a while. Two Bulls was thinking and feeling somewhat intimidated by his two large, laconic friends, especially by the tall, muscular, beautiful woman with dark, piercing eyes. Even just riding close to her, he felt her power overwhelming. He had often thought of his earlier encounter with her that dark night: the dark figure looming over him had made him fear she was going to kill him. Instead, she had cut him free.

He also secretly admired the small fighting-shield on her horse, decorated with many scalps, and the fresh one belonging to Crazy Thunder now stretched and drying on the willow loop. She had brought it back when she returned from the darkness in the village. He abruptly stopped his musing as she now looked at him and began to talk with her hands. She described in great length Wolfgang's battles with the "rattlesnake" people far to the east, and his fights with the French.

* * *

Each day Two Bulls noticed Dark Moon's routine.

Walking part way toward the horses, she would stop, stand still, talk to them in their language, and also use whistles and squeals. They would come to her, seemingly from love. The bold primary mounts came first, nuzzling and sniffing her. Dark Moon offered her love to each horse individually, talking into its ears while her hands moved lightly, lovingly over its body.

Once Two Bulls looked toward Wolfgang, who in turn nodded and smiled as he went about the business of preparing their gear to be packed.

"She is like the Gatakas," Two Bulls said, watching each horse mysteriously take his place in the string for the trail. "She possesses the 'horse power.' The Gatakas steal horses far to the southwest from the Spanish and trade them to my people."

Like the Crow's allies, the Gatakas, Dark Moon clearly had the gift of being able to speak with animals. Two Bulls knew there would be much to tell to his people when he returned to his village. Sensing that Dark Moon was not unaware of his silent, admiring appraisal, Two Bulls signed quickly to cover his thoughts, "Where did you get these horses?"

"We stole them from the Pawnee," Dark Moon replied,

smiling.

    Two Bulls laughed. He knew he would have more good stories to tell when he got home.

Chapter 35

The three traveled more slowly now, but still stopped often to watch their back-trail. When they reached the hills overlooking the Niobrara River, they changed direction again and turned west. They followed the southern range of hills paralleling the river. The limitless expanse of the new land stretched Wolfgang's imagination.

It was now the Moon of Ripening, the month Wolfgang still remembered as August. Already a bitter nip hung in the air. Streaks of high, feathery cirrus clouds – another sign of winter coming – raced across the sky. With the fast-approaching fall weather, the travelers began to consider where they would spend the winter, a place that would allow them to hide from their Lakota pursuers.

As they rode, Dark Moon felt thankful. There were no trees whose spreading branches might obscure the Great She-Bear. During this season, the constellation sat low on the northern horizon.

They changed direction to due north again to confuse any pursuers. When they reached the dark rim of the canyon, they stopped for the night. The following morning, in the gray light, they walked to the rim and found themselves on the edge of a towering cliff looking down into a large sandstone canyon. The river below ran from west to east. They observed a beautiful forty-foot waterfall, where a stream flowed into the Niobrara.

Continuing west, they came upon a deep, well-timbered canyon that opened some 200 feet below them. At the bottom lay a large, channeled tributary creek, which fed the Niobrara from the south. They gazed down in wonder at the largest body of water they had ever seen while crossing the prairie. Watching a tree float leisurely in the current, they knew the creek had a steady flow. Shifting red sand channeled the beautiful, calm-flowing stream, which did not appear particularly deep. After studying the landscape long enough to feel sure they were alone, they were ready to make their way down to the creek and up the other side.

"How beautiful the trees are," Dark Moon said, looking down at the rich sight of pine, cedar, juniper and a large grove of beech that crowned the top of a sixty-foot waterfall. The white trunks of birch trees sported leaves turning yellow, orange and red. Along the spring-fed creeks and river stood cottonwoods, ash, hackberry, cedar and plum trees. In the distance on the far side of the canyon they could make out the black, oval shapes of several bears. The party continued, following the river upstream.

By the time the sun had moved two hands across the sky, they had ridden some nine miles. As the landform rose above the river, they perceived a series of hidden waterfalls ahead. They paused to look back, and beheld a stark landscape of undulating hills covered by wildflowers, gramma grass and buffalo grass – a sight they would find vastly different from what lay ahead. The sky in the west was blue-black.

* * *

Wolfgang, Dark Moon and Two Bulls rode along the rim until they found deer tracks and droppings that indicated a game trail, then began the descent. To preserve their horses' stamina and to safeguard the animals' general soundness, the riders dismounted to walk them down the steepest grades.

At the bottom, the three remounted and looked for a place to enter the water that was shallow enough for the horses to see bottom. Using her reins and leg pressure, Dark Moon positioned her horse to face the crossing, then drove it forward to allow both hers and the other horses to relax and drink for some moments. When her horse started pawing, she drove him forward again, now aiming at a point that offered the shortest swim to the far side. Wolfgang and Two Bulls followed. Having crossed the creek, the trio dismounted. Testing the creek water, they found it good.

Both Wolfgang and Dark Moon wanted to put the creek between themselves and their enemies. After scouting the area thoroughly in all directions, the trio decided to remain here through the winter, for there were plenty of rich bottoms with grass for the horses. It was growing cooler, raining off and on, and very soon the snow would fly.

Meanwhile, they suffered a passing storm. Heavy cloud cover and a gloomy, slanting rain dampened their mood. It was almost impossible to see. It made them feel safe, however. Then the storm was gone and so was any trail that they had left behind.

That night, watching a distant lightening storm from the ridge bury itself in the hills to the west, they felt amazement at the colors of flashes that danced above the storm. They were unsure of what they were seeing. The distant bolts showed red, purple and blue as they shot into the sky on the horizon, making them feel it must be a sign to remain where they were for the winter. And indeed it was. The next day, scouting the surrounding area, they found there was much to recommend such a course: across the prairie above the canyon roamed buffalo, elk and antelope aplenty. Along the steep slopes, breaks, canyons, and gullies bordering the creek and river valleys, both turkey and bear were plentiful. Wolfgang and Dark Moon were surprised to see more deer in the river bottom than they had ever seen in the eastern forest.

Two Bulls looked at the two and, signing with his hands, he said, "Winter time, prairie deer and elk come canyon stay, no wind. Good hunt." His hands continued, explaining. "Spring time, many fly come canyon. Deer go prairie, much wind."

Having found a place to spend the winter, they decided to kill some buffalo for meat and fresh hides. Immediately Two Bulls set about procuring four ten-foot wooden shafts, which he began to scrape and shape. He asked Wolfgang and Dark Moon meanwhile to help fashion four large, flint lance-heads. Once they found the necessary flint, they sat with a hammer stone and used an antler to flake bits off, shaping several large spearheads with finely honed edges.

* * *

Two Bulls had led Dark Moon and Wolfgang some distance south from the canyon out onto the prairie. Having reached a small high point on the plain, he decided he was close enough. Dismounting, Two Bulls dropped to his knees and pressed an ear to the ground, though he could feel vibrations also through his palms and the bones of his knees. Sure enough, he perceived the slight tremble and faint sound of hooves. *There!* He quickly mounted. Now came a rumble of thunder in the distance. The mares became excited. Dark Moon and Wolfgang whispered to the animals, as their hands tried to calm them. When she shifted her gaze, she noticed that Two Bulls strangely could barely control his dun. As the trio gazed in that direction, they saw dust rising into the air. Then magically the landscape turned dark. The rumble grew louder and louder. Then they saw a rising cloud of dust. As far as they could see, the plain appeared black without any breaks in it. The land appeared to be in motion, with the black moving mass coming closer and closer. *Buffalo.* A solid wave-like herd was moving quickly in their direction. It was so dense that it presented a uniform blackness.

Now, the ground trembled under the impact of thousands of thundering hoof-beats, as the herd started changing direction away from them. The three gathered the horses in close and silently watched the oncoming herd.

Now they smelled the stench of the great herd, as the huge, shaggy-animals swept past them grunting. Those in front were frothing at the mouth. The three riders could not take their eyes from the great beasts. The wickedly gleaming black eyes and rattling horns were unnerving. The edge of the herd swerved away from the three again as they passed. Keeping one hand on their horses, the riders spoke quietly to the shivering animals. The dust was now suffocating, clouding their vision. The roar of pounding hooves drowned out all other sound. Then the herd stopped. Two Bulls knew that the buffalo had not been hunted. The grayish-brown dun mare with its black extremities was excited, holding its head high. Its ears were pricked forward and its eyes were wide and rolling. It pranced and whinnied, pulling at its leather halter, and wanting to bolt forward. Dark Moon observed Two Bulls smiling with great joy.

He signed to his companions to carry the extra lances and follow him. As they approached, Dark Moon began to take notice of his horse prancing proudly. She could tell the animal was happy and excited, even as it grew increasingly impatient. Dark Moon and Wolfgang saw that the dun mare had had its leather halter removed.

Two Bulls signed for the others to follow close behind, to watch and learn. The Crow warrior caught up with the herd and guided his mare with his legs to the first fat young cow with a large round rump amid the crackling sagebrush. It was grazing slightly apart from the herd. Two Bulls was quickly astonished, as the captured Pawnee mare took over, separating the cow from the herd. He realized he had a trained buffalo hunter under him. He felt exhilarated, knowing he was rich. He tilted his head back and screamed a piercing cry of joy. *"Aiiiyeeeee!"*

Two Bulls leaned into the wind as the dun mare directed the cow away from the herd, causing her to begin a panicked run. The herd began to run. Again came the sound of hooves and the clatter of clicking horns. The terrible thunder of pounding hooves was beginning to distance themselves from the lost cow and three riders. The clean rush of air bathed Two Bulls' face as the mare's smooth, powerful rhythm carried him in pursuit.

He slowly drew in alongside the panicked cow, positioning the tip of his lance behind the animal's shoulder blade. He waited for the forward surge of the shaggy beast until the left front leg went forward and the ribs reached their maximum separation and permitted passage of the lance behind the shoulder blade. His arm cocked, the sharp point drove forward deep into the chest cavity and heart. Frothing blood coming out through the mouth and nostrils told the story. The cow went down, and moments later he was galloping alongside another young cow. Two Bulls listened to the breathing of the mare and realized that she was not even breathing hard.

Dark Moon and Wolfgang saw the cow tumble. They caught up to Two Bulls to give him two lances and he was off. They watched the skilled horseman at a full gallop over the rough terrain pursuing the rear of the herd again. Soon they heard the distant shrill sound of the Crow warrior's cry. Another young, fat cow went down to her knees, bellowed and rolled over.

"He strikes the running animal when it is stretched out in stride. He drives the lance between the ribs when they reach the most separation," Dark Moon shouted at Wolfgang, never taking her eyes from Two Bulls and his mare.

Two Bulls' horse had summoned up an unimaginable reserve of energy, and before long, four buffalo lay still on the plain. Wolfgang and Dark Moon rode toward their friend, who was waiting for them obviously pleased

"It seems so easy for you," Wolfgang signed.

"Why are you smiling so much with such an impatient horse?" Dark Moon's hands gestured toward Two Bulls.

"Because her strong-mind horse. You give me good horse. Her buffalo runner," his hands replied. "Her big medicine. Now go home. Me kill many buffalo. Winter time family no hungry. Small brown horse run long time. Horse run, her float on air.' Her good wind. No want stop run."

Dark Moon realized that he was right. The horse was valuable, a trained buffalo runner.

Two Bulls excited about his new horse Dark Moon had given him, now seemed inpatient. He pointed to the northwest. The manner of his gestures said, "I go home. My people. Trail twelve sleeps."

There was silence now between the three. He saw the disappointment on their faces, and realized that they liked him and would miss him.

After a short silence, his hands indicated, "In the Moon of Awaking, you see purple and white flowers. You go northwest to big mountains. See the buffalo jump on flat ground. Follow smell. You see big, red hole in ground. Many buffalo die there. Then see big cottonwood trees. You see pine, oak, and juniper hills. Come big rock. Lakota call Mato Tipila. Travel north. See Big Cheyenne River Valley. Go north. West you see forest ridge. We call Bear Lodge Mountains. East, see high open ridge prairie. See grass and sage. See lone high butte. You halfway to river. River turn southeast. You see my village. Winter gone, you travel quick. Moon of Roses time Lakota make big ceremony there."

Wolfgang and Dark Moon knew he was referring to the month of March, and to the harbingers of spring, when the purple pasque and white-petaled bloodroot flowers bloomed. The Lakota would start preparing to hold their spiritual rituals there and honor the summer solstice.

Two Bulls' hands continued to express, "Rock hill, you

will know."

He pantomimed.

"A giant bear scraping its claws, cutting distinctive grooves on it," he explained.

Dark Moon gave Two Bulls a small leather bag.

"Use this on future wounds," she signed. "Take white Lakota horse, you travel fast, two horses."

He thanked her. They watched him ride away on the dun, leading the white horse. Then Dark Moon turned to Wolfgang.

"Do you still have tobacco and seed?"

He looked at her and smiled.

Chapter 36

To Dark Moon, it was the Moon of Awakening. According to Wolfgang's calculations, it was March 1760. The winter had been long and hard. The two sat huddled before a fire, talking. Outside, they could hear a warm wind howling through the timber.

Dark Moon, staring down at the fire, said, "The evening star in the west has become less bright."

"Mercury," announced Wolfgang,

"Mercury," Dark Moon replied.

After a pause, she continued.

"The morning star is bright and now sets low in the eastern sky."

"Venus," replied Wolfgang.

"Yes, Venus," Dark Moon agreed, watching Wolfgang closely. "The air is gradually getting warmer. The snowdrifts are almost gone. It will continue to get warmer. Soon it will be spring."

The two great wolves lay, listening with their eyes closed, their heads resting on their paws and their ears cocked.

"In the days ahead, there will still be light snow and rain to hide our trail. We'll have to travel on the ridges, because the low areas will be too wet," said Wolfgang, acknowledging her unspoken suggestion. "The Lakota will start looking for us now."

They gazed at each other silently, eyes locked; both knew it was time to go. The wolves looked up suddenly, smiling as if in agreement.

* * *

Dark Moon and Wolfgang made their way beneath a bright quarter-moon. They found the tree they had marked early in the winter for such an occasion. They both could see the water level of the river was rising dangerously.

"I'll go first. The river will soon be a raging torrent," said Wolfgang.

They could both hear the sound of cracking ice upriver.

"Soon it will be full of trees and debris," Dark Moon replied.

They quickly stripped, tied their clothing in bundles and secured them on top of the horses.

"Go," Dark Moon said. Wolfgang urged his horse into the water without hesitation.

There was no wind in the canyon, but the sound of cracking ice covered the snorting of their swimming horses fighting the current. They crossed the moonlit river and reached the riverbank before the water got too high.

* * *

Well after the quarter moon reached its apex, they reached the top of the other side of the river. The stars were still sparkling in the sky. They located the sky bear, found the star-that-does-not-move, and followed it. Joyfully, they rode northwest. When they stopped at a high point, the first crimson tendrils were spreading across the eastern sky. Their eyes searched the skyline in silence. As the stars disappeared, the two riders remained motionless in the pale light, waiting patiently for sunrise.

The higher parts of the hills were filled with buffalo. Wolfgang and Dark Moon watched closely for signs of the Lakota. They gazed at a magnificent, pine-covered white cliff with rugged buttes that rose on the skyline. The sun now rose directly in the east and set directly in the west. Dark Moon, who had been watching the orb's movement each day, was happy that the three-moon period of cold in this northern part of the land was finally ended.

As he carefully kept an eye on the horizon for anyone on horseback, Wolfgang felt constantly amazed by the scenic wonders of this largely uninhabited land – a land whose native inhabitants lived in harmony with nature. Here in this western wilderness, for the first time in his life, he felt a sense of how small and insignificant he was, in this land that seemed to go on and on forever.

The blooming pasque and bloodroot flowers painted the land purple and white. For twelve days, the two moved through this sweeping, rolling expanse where blossoming grasslands reached to their horses' withers.

* * *

The sun had reached its zenith in the blue sky as Dark Moon and Wolfgang were giving the horses a rest break. Lying flat on her back between him and the wolves, she listened to the munching sound of their horses grazing contentedly nearby and also watched a prairie falcon overhead. All at once the raptor began to keen. The normal sounds of gentle snickering, chewing, snorting, tail-swishing, and stamping of hooves ceased. Dark Moon and Wolfgang stiffened in alarm. The wolves raised their heads above the grass, their ears pointed forward. An instant later they were running, bellies low to the ground, rushing to the edge of the hill and staring down. Dark Moon and Wolfgang eyes cut to the mares that had stopped grazing and raised their heads. They both became alarmed as the animals' ears pricked up slightly forward and started twitching. Their noses were thrust out and their nostrils were dilated. "Many horses come," said she. The two quickly rose and went over to the mares. She spoke in a deep-chested, low soothing guttural tone: *Un-hunh-unhunh-hunh-hunh.* The mares whickered gently in reply and nudged her. Dark Moon and Wolfgang gently rubbed their necks. Then put their hands on the soft muzzles to prevent their blowing or neighing and giving away their position. They saw no one yet, but trusted the animals' highly developed instincts to detect a distant unseen danger.

Dark Moon glanced sharply toward a rapid series of loud, excited guttural calls down the hill. Raising her head, she saw, a large, black and white bird flying away in the distance. To warn Wolfgang, she motioned her right hand, making a fist. Then she extended the first two fingers, showing the back of her hand, and swung it outward to exhibit the palm. *Enemy close!* He checked his rifle. Still seeing nothing, she continued to watch the wolves and study the horses.

Huddling close, the mounts had sensed other horses in the distance – Dark Moon was now almost sure of this. Both wolves glanced back over their shoulders at their masters. Now Dark Moon's keen-eared dappled gray turned its head to look at her with an ear cocked. It then emitted a loud snort and pivoted the cocked ear forward and slightly left. She realized the animals had heard something upwind. The mare emitted a second loud snort, but because it stood still with head erect, she knew that whatever had alarmed the dappled gray was still distant. She made a low-toned, continuous hissing sound through her lips and teeth to soothe the creatures. "SSsssssssss." A band of spooked cow elk emerged from the timber below at a swift trot, their noses held high. Dark Moon knew that they were always quick to warn of the presence of an enemy. She cautioned Wolfgang to remain still. Her eyes searched the wooded area below, and then she pointed to another emerging movement.

In the distant cottonwood timber lining the creek below, Wolfgang glimpsed shadowy forms moving slowly on horseback. The animals labored beneath bulging packs, and when the distant pack train stopped, one rider detached himself from the group to ride to the edge of the timber. Dismounting, he scanned the land ahead and found himself staring directly up at Dark Moon and Wolfgang, who now saw him to be a white man. He waved, beckoning them to come down.

"He's a French or Spanish trader – with tattooed Indians," said Wolfgang to Dark Moon without turning his head.

Observing no indication that the traveling party meant them any harm, Wolfgang and Dark Moon trusted their instincts and began to approach the party warily.

The trapper, a grey-bearded man wearing Indian-style leggings and shirt along with a beaver cap with a black bill in front, turned out to be French, traveling with six Indians in his company.

Wolfgang and Dark Moon spoke with him and learned that the Black Hills, from whence he and his companions had just come, was a three-day ride from here in the foothills. The journey would bring them to Crow Territory. The trapper said he had seen some Lakota during their travels – a fact that Wolfgang and Dark Moon were not pleased to learn.

The talk turned more general, and the talkative trader spoke about the land and the tribes that lived in it. He said that the Spanish had been trading horses to the Shoshone tribe for years in the Shoshone country far to the west. The horse had changed the Indians' way of life, enabling them to be mobile, extend their hunting territory, and make war. The Crow then began to raid the Sioux and Blackfeet for horses, and sometimes raided to the south to steal horses from the Ute Indians.

"What of the Iroquois east of the Great River?" asked

Wolfgang.

"In the few years you say it took you both to travel to the far west," the Frenchman replied. "The sun was setting on the power of the eastern Indian tribes. Much has changed."

He explained that, largely due to the British conquest of Quebec in September 1759, the French and Indian War had been over and that the Iroquois were no longer a major threat. The Ohio country, where Wolfgang and Dark Moon had begun their journey, was now a battleground where all the displaced tribes were warring with the settlers, who were taking Indian lands at an alarming rate.

Dark Moon and Wolfgang exchanged a look. Each knew what the other was thinking: their decision to leave the Ohio country had been the right one.

"And who are the tattooed people with you?" Dark Moon asked, gazing toward the warriors.

"The Pique," replied the Frenchman with a smile. "They are the Caddo and Wichita, and we call them the Taovaya. The Wichita have the most extravagant tattooed marks and designs – from head to foot, as you can see."

Looking into each Wichita warrior's face, Dark Moon saw a line extending downward from the corner of each eye. Even their eyelids were tattooed.

"The designs symbolize honors won in war and hunting," the Frenchman continued. "The two with fewer tattoos and the odd frontal-shaped heads are the Caddo, known for eating people."

Nonplussed, Wolfgang asked, "What is the land like beyond this point?"

The Frenchman pointed.

"To the northwest, beyond the Black Mountains, lies the Big Cheyenne River. We French call it the Belle Fourche River. The mountains to the west of that river are called the Bear Lodge Mountains. The grasslands follow next, and beyond, the Big

Horn Mountains. Then, *Les montagnes de pierres brillantes* – the Shining Mountains, named for their forest's blue, green and gold colors in late summer. It is a place of streams, vast mountain meadows and high peaks. They seem to rise straight out of prairie country. It is a place named for the Ah-sah-ta, the Big Horn sheep, though great herds of buffalo, elk, antelope and deer lived there, too. It would be a good place to live and hunt," he added.

"Who lives in the Big Horn Mountains?" Wolfgang asked.

" We French call them *Les Corbeaux* – the Crow Indian tribe," the trapper replied, his hands making the sign of flapping wings. "They named themselves 'Absanokee.' It means 'Children of the Raven.'"

He explained that there were three bands of Crow; the River Crow, who live along the Musselshell and Yellowstone Rivers; the Kicked-in-the-bellies, who live in the Big Horn Basin; and the Mountain Crow, who occupy the Upper Yellowstone River, Bighorn Mountains, and the Valley of the White Wolf.

After the trader and his Indians had talked and shared food with Wolfgang and Dark Moon, the party took their leave, their horses plodding off in the direction the two had just traveled. As the sun dropped below the timbered ridge to the west, Dark Moon and Wolfgang had already killed a cow elk and set up camp in the cottonwoods.

* * *

Wolfgang and Dark Moon continued their travel north-westward at an impressive pace, but they both had the unsettling feeling that for the past several days eyes had been watching them. Riding toward a ridge up ahead, they looked back and beheld a chilling vision: *Indian riders.*

It was the Lakota from earlier, closing in behind them.

Dark Moon had foreseen in her vision their reaching the Valley of the White Wolf, but now she wondered if her vision had been wrong. She felt empty inside, for she knew she could no longer live without Wolfgang. Reaching the ridge – their only hope of an escape route – could well mean the difference between life and death.

She and Wolfgang pressed their mounts uphill, eating ground as hard as they could.

* * *

Surmounting the crest of the ridge, the two paused to study the Lakota trailing them. By keeping to the heavy cover as best as they could, they hoped the pursuers might not catch them.

Two scouts were in the lead. When Wolfgang and Dark Moon looked back from their elevated position at perhaps a mile's distance, with sinking hearts they saw the Lakota find their trail.

In the open, the couple knew, they would be entirely defenseless. They proceeded forward at a brisk clip, hoping to reach the high, timbered mountains due west, where they might hide.

They hurried their horses through grass that brushed knee-high until finally they reached the top, at which point they reined in, frozen: On the downward side of the top of the hill ahead, perhaps thirty paces away, stood a long line of mounted Indians, nearly twenty-five horsemen quietly sitting their mounts, and staring at them. The two travelers instantly realized their peril, and Wolfgang looked at Dark Moon. Her face remained stoic and inscrutable. Their hearts were heavy as they contemplated what might lie ahead.

* * *

The fierce-looking wild horsemen sat silently, unmoving, stoically watching Wolfgang, Dark Moon, and the two wolves that kept their company. Knowing there was nothing they could do to outfight or outrun the braves, the two riders sat their mounts and stared at the warriors.

Wolfgang felt awed by the display of buffalo horn bows and feather-decorated shields attached to the Indians' saddles. Most of the braves wore their hair long and loose with little braids. Their faces had vertical black lines tattooed down their chins, a black dot on the nose, and a black circle on the forehead. Their eyelids were painted red and yellow. Some also wore full eagle skins mounted on their heads and beautifully decorated war shirts fringed with weasel skins. Many of those wearing snug fitted shirts had sleeve and shoulder bands as marks of distinction. Many also wore hip-length fringed leggings while a few wore them decorated with hair locks. And others were fringed with ermine tails, and their bare arms sported armlets.

Wolfgang stared at the nearest warrior, whose bare chest sported horizontal black paint-stripes undoubtedly representing his war exploits. He was startled at the man's pierced ears that contained small finger bones.

Others went unencumbered by clothing. The naked warriors were painted in either red and white or yellow and black. One warrior near the chief wore a headdress of two buffalo horns with weasel tails attached to the front, and another, an antelope horn headdress.

Charles A. McDonald

Chapter 37

As the two groups faced each other, Dark Moon suddenly noticed the two wolves cock their heads at one Indian in particular. The two wolves bodies quivered slightly in excitement as they turned and looked at Wolfgang and Dark Moon. Her eyes focused on one familiar-looking horse, a dull, grayish-brown dun with black extremities. As she studied the horse and rider more closely, something sparked in her eyes; suddenly, she raised her arm in greeting.

For a long moment, there was no movement whatever among the horsemen. Then the dun took several steps forward. Raising his arm, its rider lost the warrior's usual composed and dignified demeanor, and smiled.

"Ohchikaape!" he called.

Stunned momentarily, Wolfgang recognized the Crow greeting.

The warrior on horseback was Two Bulls.

* * *

As Wolfgang and Dark Moon watched and listened, Two Bulls now excitedly told the chief - his father - these were the very man and woman he had been describing since his return. The man, a great warrior whose friend was the wolf, had survived many combats thanks to the powerful medicine gained from his spirit guardian, the great bear of the east, and had left his marks on him for all to see. The scarred-faced woman was a medicine woman and a great warrior who had proven her powers during numerous adventures.

As the chief and his warriors gazed at the riders, Wolfgang's hands motioned, drawing his right hand from left to right across the front of his neck, indicating "Lakota." He balled the hand up in front of his chest and extended two fingers. With palms facing, left hand ahead, he thrust both hands forward in zigzag motion. "Two riders follow close."

The chief understood. He looked sharply down the line of watching warriors and swung his right arm out in a circling motion. Immediately four braves with full wolf skins across their shoulders peeled away from the group and rode quickly away into cover toward the west. The chief repeated the motion to the opposite side and four warriors, similarly attired, rode away to the east, and soon disappeared.

Now the chief's gaze locked onto the mysterious luminous eyes of the tall, extraordinarily beautiful woman.

"We Absaroke watching, waiting you," he signed. "Me Eagle Looks Twice. Two Bulls, my son, say you have horse power. Power come from maxpe. All people hear stories you. Stealing Pawnee horses. Count "coup" cutting horse tied tipi Sioux village. Great honor. You stay Absaroke people all time. Ah-badt-dadt-deah sent you to us. We stop winter story telling Moon of Awaking. Sign of first thunder. We come get you. "

Dark Moon turned to Two Bulls.

"What is maxpe? Who is Ah-badt-dadt-deah?" her hands gestured.

Two Bulls motioned, the sign for "medicine", followed by the sign for "Great Spirit."

"Ah-badt-dadt-deah," Two Bulls' hands said. "The Crow name for the-one-who-made-all-things, and is sacred to us."

For some moments Dark Moon sat silently. She looked deeply into the chief's eyes. Instinctively she knew she was in the presence of a great chief, and she understood how he had come to be named: the eagle was, after all, lord of the air, symbolic of the sun and wind, and blessed with superb skills. She turned over in her mind what he had said; that she had great medicine – *maxpe* – in understanding horses; that she had performed the greatest feat in the Lakota village, stealing a horse from inside the village and killing a Lakota warrior; that both acts were deserving of a feather; and that the chief believed that the Great Spirit had sent she and Wolfgang and wanted them to live with the Crow people.

Dark Moon dismounted. Reaching into her pack, she brought out a deerskin pouch. Moving to the chief, who remained astride his mount, she looked up. She again focused deeply into his eyes and gave him the pouch.

"My gift to you. There is more," her hands signed.

The chief accepted the token, opened the pouch and gazed inside. His eyes growing wide with recognition, he raised the bag to his nose. Smelling the twist of tobacco amid its seeds inside, he smiled. Looking toward his son, the chief understood how Dark Moon had known tobacco seed was sacred to the Crow tribe, who used it in so many of its rituals.

"Lakota new to this land. Lakota troublemakers. Pompous. Boastful. Steal corn while tribes hunting. No trust Lakota. Deceitful. Treacherous. You no fear Lakota. You Absaroke," his hands said.

As the Crow party rode away to the northwest, Two Bulls smiled, turned his horse and rode with his new friends.

Aware that these people – who wore the most beautiful shirts and leggings Dark Moon had ever seen – held their religion in high regard, Dark Moon thought that their offer of welcome would provide her and Wolfgang a place to live safely. She also knew, as surely as she had ever known anything that they would live happily with these people.

Epilogue

It was the ninth day in November, the time the Indians called the "Moon of Madness." The first quarter moon had risen early and was shining down on the village. Near a sharp turn in the Belle Fourche River, it was at the base of a tall bluff in the Valley of the White Wolf. Scaffolds of drying meat and stacks of firewood surrounded the village. The camp circle was a symbol of the universe. Each tall *tipi* was painted to show scenes of battle, visions, and figures symbolic of the owner's dreams and spiritual powers.

But now tribe members began to assemble near one lodge painted like no other. Images of stars, the moon in all its phases, a bear, and wolf tracks decorated its tautly stretched hides. A few old men and women sat already waiting in the light of the moon among the many fires, but most of the village was mostly swarmed with scampering feet, excited shouts, and laughter as people gathered eagerly to hear a long-awaited story.

At either side of the *tipi's* entry flap sat two large wolves, staring solemnly at those gathering. But when the animals suddenly turned their great heads toward its opening, all eyes followed to behold the white man who had arrived over one winter ago. He was the first of his kind many had ever seen. He now stood in front of them wrapped in the hide of the great, blond bear, a symbol of valor. After a moment a tall, beautiful Algonquian woman with mysterious eyes emerged and stood near him. Even strangers recognized Dark Moon by the stars she wore on the upper front and back of her dress, and the small, distinctive medicine bundle that hung around her neck. She wore two feathers in her hair, and bore the man's war shield.

Its painted edge represented bear claws, a wolf track shown was at its center, and a small black moon and a single star hovered above. The watchers knew the shield's power. The bear claws lent its owner the animal's strength and valor. The wolf track represented the magical powers from which the man's name derived, and the magical powers ascribed to his two helpers. The Moon represented the magical powers of the man's wife. The wolf track signified the magical powers ascribed to his helpers from which his name came: Wolf. Thus, the Wolf Star was a reflection of the wolf coming and going from the spirit world. The man and the woman had lived among the people now for well over one winter, but tonight, at last, the man would tell their tale.

Stories about these two newest adopted members of the tribe had swept across the eastern forest and plains. There were many legends, both French and Osage, about them and were now known well. The Iroquois far to the east had called the man *"Okwaho"* – the Wolf – and the woman "Dark Moon."

But tonight the Crow would hear the stories from the man himself. As he waited for the chiefs to sign that all were assembled and ready, those watching felt the beating of their own hearts.

At last, the old chief Eagle Looks Twice signed for the white man to begin. When the man gestured, the two huge, terrifying wolves immediately came to him at a dead run, their fluid motion like that of a long-distance plains runner. Leaping excitedly into the air, the animals whined and fawned. When the man spread both arms, they rose to stand on their back paws and lick his scarred face. His arms gathered around them, he buried his face in the neck of each and then commanded them to lie down.

Both obeyed immediately, though they kept their heads high, alertly watching their master. To the Crow, wolves were powerful and mysterious medicine animals, and the villagers accepted them as part of the man and woman's personal totems.

The white man removed the tie on his hair and shook his

head. The crowd saw that his hair was almost the same color as the great bear's fur. He allowed the hide to drop to the ground. He stood before them naked, composed and dignified, exposing his tall, well-muscled frame. A murmur swept among those assembled, everyone awestruck by the huge, lurid-looking scars that covered his body. The sight made his watchers even more eager to hear his story. His cool, penetrating eyes swept the crowd.

It was not lost upon those watching that the white man moved like a large and powerful animal as he slowly approached the line of seated chiefs and warriors, in order to let them view his body closely. They noted the jagged wounds of the great bear as well as many old knife and arrow wounds. Then, walking out just far enough for everyone to see his hands, he stood silent before the people. In the language of the Crow and the universal hand gesture language of the Plains Indians, his hands and fingers began to move rapidly, telling their story. Although some of the people were barely within hearing range, all were within sight of his hands. Since hand signing is three times faster than a man can talk, he signed slowly to keep up with his adopted language as he spoke. Now and then, he pantomimed to emphasize his story. Periodically, he would point to a wound. Everyone admired the exquisite manner in which his hands and fingers moved, rounded and sweeping movements, giving the tale added eloquence with their grace and deftness. And this was the story he told.

Charles A. McDonald

About The Author

Charles A. McDonald was born into a ranching family, the Rocking H, in Northern California. He graduated from the Erv Malnarich Outfitters and Guide School in Montana and spent four years in the Idaho wilderness working as a wrangler, fishing and hunting guide. He has a B.S. in history from Chaminade College of Honolulu. He is a life member of the Special Forces Association and Military Order of the Purple Heart. After attending the basic and advanced Vip and Executive Protection School at the North Mountain Pines Training Center at Berryville, Virginia, he worked as a Personal Protection Specialist (PPS). McDonald has contributed a dozen articles to the The Pennsylvania Outdoor Times, Bowhunting News, Instinctive Archer and The Journal of U.S. Military Special Operations.

Printed in Great Britain
by Amazon